THE BINARY CONVERSION

D. R. ROSE

Sequel to THE EXECUTION CODE

Copyright © 2017 D.R. Rose

All rights reserved.

ALSO BY D.R.ROSE

The Second Twin
The Execution Code

ACKNOWLEDGMENTS

I am immensely grateful to all those who read the earlier stories and encouraged me to continue to describe the Binaries world – and for the suggestion that Helen should speak for herself in this final story.

Cover illustration by Emily Snape, featuring Veronica Stanwell. Dress from Atelier Tammam.
..

'The warning: WATCH THOU FOR THE MUTANT! faced me as I went in, but it was much too familiar to stir a thought.'

John Wyndham, The Chrysalids.

INTRODUCTION

I dreamed of a vast mansion. It's Askeys, said my dream self knowingly, but it seemed to have been converted into a hospital. Opening one door, I saw rows of babies in cots, all connected by trails of wires while a giant face was peering in through the window, watching us. I looked for the library, but it was now a long ward, Nightingale style, with hospital beds stretching as far as I could see. These were occupied by adults, also attached by electrodes on their heads to a network of transparent wires, pulsing with coloured lights. They all seemed asleep with no one noticing as I drifted towards the end of the ward, where there was a large mirror. In my reflection, I was horrified to see that I also had electrodes attached. A nurse appeared beside me, taking my arm kindly. "Back to bed, now, Cassandra." I turned and saw the end bed was empty, with the cover neatly turned back. "No," I replied, "There's a storm coming." The nurse stood patiently, in silence, but I heard her thoughts distinctly: "It's just outsiders, making trouble as usual. Get into bed, you need more conditioning..."

1

CASSANDRA

Those who have experienced a hurricane know the eerie stillness before the storm breaks, with an unnatural calm in the air and not a leaf moving on the trees. I awoke feeling uneasy and listened. There was no wind outside, but I felt that something like a fierce tempest was brewing. For a moment I felt disorientated, then recognised the familiar bedroom in our French home. We had called it Villa Dufour, after the name we went under in France. I sat up and roused Kastor. He transmitted a quizzical thought, watching me staring into the distance.

"I sense trouble," I said.

Kastor looked around the quiet room, wondering what could have alarmed me. "I didn't hear anything outside. You've been dreaming again. We'll talk about it in the morning."

"No, it's real. Well, I have been dreaming, but I think this was a prediction. Something bad is going to happen."

Like my mythological namesake Cassandra in the Trojan wars, I had precognitive powers to add to my telepathy. Kastor, also an adept telepath, could not see future events, in common with most of the Binaries community.

"All right," he said, "but it may be weeks away, or it could be you worrying about Leo going away to school. Try to go back to sleep, we can deal with it when we're properly awake."

I sighed, knowing that it was hard to interpret my predictions, particularly those that related to me personally. My gift was an unwelcome one and I'd always found it hard to convince others of the impending dangers that I sensed. I could use precognition quite happily for the commercial work, predicting mergers or which products were most likely to succeed, a talent that the Binaries exploited to great profit. When Kastor had embarked on a dangerous mission over two years previously, neither he nor anyone else had paid sufficient attention to my warnings, until it was almost too late and he had been severely injured. Our close relationship had helped him to bring him back to health, to recover the telepathic and empathic abilities that he had lost. Such intimacy was uncommon for the Binaries, few partnerships being formalised as 'bond mates', the Binaries equivalent to marriage in the non-telepathic world outside.

I tried to focus on what dangerous event I was now sensing, wondering if Kastor was right and it related to my fears for our son Leander, Leo for short. He would be leaving us in a few months time to attend the Binaries boarding school, Lochinstoun, in Scotland. They started so early: Leo was only five years old. It was essential for the specialised training, the counsellors had advised. I had reluctantly agreed that he should not be brought up even more differently than others in the community. Kastor and I had been allowed the unprecedented concession of having both Leander and our twin girls, Tamsin and Florence, live with us in the villa next to the Binaires farm. This arrangement required a Binaries-style nursery, with a couple of nannies now that Helen's twin sons, Daniel and Zenon lived with us too.

My identical twin Helen was staying on a rare visit, having recently given birth to a girl, Grace. Helen had asked if Grace could join the nursery, as her partner Alexander was about to start a job in the USA and they would have no permanent home for a while.

"It'll be mainly hotels, not good for a baby," Helen had said airily, "and I'd be much happier knowing she's with other Binaries."

Helen's idea of being motherly was to hold the baby occasionally, before handing her back to nanny if a feed or nappy change seemed necessary. I guessed that Alexander had little idea that Grace's stay with us would be long term. I understood that Helen's upbringing from birth with the Binaries meant that separation from her baby was quite natural for her.

No, I thought, it's nothing to do with Leo, or the other children. We had passed a lovely evening, taking advantage of early summer warmth to have a barbecue on the beach. Grégoire had come over from Binaires and played songs on a guitar, with Helen uncharacteristically suggesting whimsical or other songs suitable for children. Grégoire had also held Grace with delight, commenting on her telepathic responsiveness. Almost with pride, I noted cynically, knowing my sister only too well. I thought back ten months or so, wondering if that had coincided with one of Helen's visits. Grace was only six weeks old. Along with other conditioning in growing up as a Binary, Helen had no particular inclination to fidelity. At the moment I detected, but with no wish to pry further with my thoughts, Helen was relaxing in the guest bedroom with the gardener.

"He's so sweet," she had said after her first night at the villa. "He produces images of delphiniums, gladioli and other spiked flowers. I feel like a plant that he's just digging into its bed, nice and deep. And with such powerful muscles, too."

I had smiled without comment, wondering how twins could be so different, or whether if I had not been separated from Helen while growing up on the outside, I would have a similar careless approach to partners.

Before falling asleep and experiencing the troubling dream, Kastor and I had languorously sharing happy images. I murmured, "Perhaps we should have another baby, too. Grace is adorable."

Kastor paused, staring into my eyes. It was always worrying when I made vague suggestions, which he had learned meant I was intending to do the very thing.

"Oh no, Cassandra, no more babies. We already have two beautiful girls and a son."

"Well, so few babies are born within the community. Why is that, do you think?"

He kissed me, in forlorn hope that we could just concentrate on our entwined bodies, but decided that we might as well discuss this point.

"Or is it that you don't want me to become fat – or fatter?" I said, as if there were no distraction to our conversation. He propped himself up beside me on one arm, looking appreciatively at me.

"You're not fat," he murmured, "but I wouldn't care if you were… I never liked thin women." I smiled at this correct response but Kastor knew I was still thinking about Binaries babies.

"In answer to your question, isn't what we're doing an answer? Most Binaries prefer to be satisfied by sharing minds. We're rather atypical…" His unspoken thought was that a combined mental and physical attraction had made me irresistible, apparently. Going to meet me mainly out of curiosity in Blenheim Park, some six years previously, he had soon ardently wished to enter my mind and share the combined images and sensations that only telepaths could experience. I was then living in the world of 'outsiders'.

"I'm sure they'd enjoy more sex, if they made an effort," I said "Perhaps I should offer to run classes."

"Absolutely not!" said Kastor, pleasing me by a rare flash of jealousy. "That's more in Helen's line, but they'd never permit her to enter Binaries again."

Helen could stay with us at the villa, which was a kind of annex to the French community, Binaires, but although her exploits outside had been largely forgiven when she helped to save Kastor, there was no question of her being re-admitted as a member of any of the Binary centres. By forcing me to swap places with her, she had committed a major breach of Binary rules.

"I didn't mean sex therapy," I said, knowing this was a sore point for us both, after I wanted to be the one helping him in this way, after a probe had damaged his mind abilities. It had been a bad idea, making Kastor lose any desire for me for a while.

"No," I continued, "I meant, to understand how good it is to get to know your babies, feel connected to them as they grow up. You feel that, now we have the babies with us, don't you?"

Kastor ignored the images of happy family life that I was transmitting. His face became more serious.

"Yes, but I'm very glad that we have a nursery wing, with nannies to look after them. I wasn't brought up to do that..." – he paused, watching my face carefully before continuing - "...but I knew it was the only way to make you happy." A little spark of anger from me made him even more cautious. "Of course I love sharing our lives with Leo, Florence and Tamsin. It's all part of the wonder of being with you, but the main pleasure for Binary women, when they get pregnant, is knowing they'll be contributing to the community. The babies get all the parenting they need in the nursery, while they learn about their skills. It really doesn't matter to them who their mothers and fathers are."

This put an idea into my head. "So could you be the father of other children, back in Woodstock Binaries?"

"No, I'm sure I'm not," said Kastor. "Apart from the routine genetic tests, which would identify a Binary father, our women are all on the pill or use other forms of contraception. They enjoy their lives, their equality with men. Why should they want to look after babies? Pregnancy is a conscious decision on their part, to make a donation of a baby to the rest of us. They usually go for thorough counselling before even considering it. As you should know, it's very much appreciated by the whole community..." He stopped, seeing another unwelcome idea had occurred to me.

"So you did have relationships, with lots of them, then?" I asked. I worried about this when I tried to imagine Kastor's life before we met. Sometimes, passing an attractive female of their community in the corridor of the French or British centres, I had to quash the thought that he had many liaisons prior to bonding with me. Kastor closed his eyes in frustration at this subject being raised.

"Not this, not now, Cassandra." My stare intensified, so he sighed and responded. "Well, a bit on field courses. But in the community where you grow up, the others feel more like brothers and sisters, the older ones like aunts and uncles – not potential sex partners. And most of our ventures in that area are brief, satisfying curiosity more than anything. I don't know why it bothers you so much. I wouldn't want to mind share or have… physical union with any other female, now that I have you."

He gazed at me tenderly, willing me to drop the subject and was relieved when I murmured, "Nor I," cuddling up to him at last. While he sensed I was still pondering on the strangely impersonal approach to babies, I had decided it was unfair to continue probing the topic. Kastor tried so hard to understand how different it was for me, having lived as an ordinary human from birth until, at the tender age of 18, I'd been left unconscious by Helen in a Binary tunnel, never to return to outside life.

Later, I found it impossible to return to sleep after my dream. I felt there was a doorknocker in my head, banging louder and louder to make me pay attention. Kastor had dropped off again, but sat up in alarm when I suddenly cried out.

"It's an attack! Quick, we must do something!"

He still heard nothing. I shared images with him, of people approaching the Centre Binaires and of injuries. "They're armed. They're going to attack the centre! And, oh, they're heading for the farmhouse as well…"

"Is this happening now, or in the future?" said Kastor, trying to make sense of my confused images.

"Now!" I said urgently, "Or very soon. We must warn them." I gazed into the distance, trying to pick up activity in the village beyond the Binaires estate. Anxiously, I exclaimed, "The children, they're particularly interested in the children."

Kastor had ignored my previous predictions to his peril. He telepathed to his friend and colleague Grégoire and to Dominique, the female director of the Centre Binaires. He also sent out a general mind network alert.

2

Grégoire was puzzled to receive the message: he also sensed nothing wrong. But hearing the alarm had been raised by me, he agreed at least to evacuate the nursery and toddler area and Dominique woke everyone in the Centre Binaires.

"Get them into the tunnel," signalled Kastor, "and check all the outside doors, at the farm, too if possible."

He hurriedly got up, saying he would get all the security grates closed on our windows and doors. It now seemed very wise that Gaston Ajax, head of security at the Binaries in Woodstock, had insisted on a tunnel extension to the villa where we lived. This ran a few hundred metres to the Binaires farm and connected there with a tunnel to the main centre. Access doors could be closed with a steel security gate. The one at the farm was concealed by an innocuous wooden door, which could be locked from both sides. There were also gates at intervals in the tunnel that could be securely shut if necessary. The first part of the tunnel leading from the villa was further camouflaged by a well-stocked wine cellar, with a secret door at the back. This opened into a wider area, with access to the emergency rooms. Leo used the tunnels to go to preschool at Binaires. He had explored the part near the house several times and thought it a great hiding place. So he was surprised to be got up in the night, but not particularly perturbed to be going down there. The nannies gathered up the twins into double pushchairs while one also carried Grace.

Helen was alert as soon as she sensed my alarm call. She ran to find me in the bedroom.

"I've prodded Force Musculaire awake to help with the children," she said. Force Musculaire was her nickname for the gardener.

As I did not respond, she prodded me too. "What's up, Cass?"

Then she started to pick up my images. I was aware of her presence, but lost in this vision of the turmoil approaching us.

"I can make out the village and a group of people," said Helen. "But you're more expert at remote viewing, for me it's a little blurred. How long before they get here?" She had no doubt that I was seeing something real, about to happen or already in progress.

"A few on the way now, ahead of the main group," I said in an unfamiliar, distant voice. "Others following. Some have guns." Helen relayed this to Kastor.

"What do they want, Cass?"

"Angry, very angry. There's a man with a cross…"

"A mob? Perhaps they've found out about us," said Helen in alarm. "Religious fanatics, maybe, rooting out deviants."

I came out of my semi-trance, like someone awaking from hypnosis. "Yes, I sensed fervour, in a few of them at least," I said. I knew that telepathy was not acknowledged as existing by the Catholic Church, which meant it was not so much a sin as impossible. Even so, some bigot might have worked up the villagers into a frenzy about it.

"But their main anger is about the children. Stolen babies…" I muttered, still seeing traces of the vision. Helen reinforced the relayed messages to protect the infants. Then she remembered my statement that a few had gone ahead. "Let's focus on Binaires for a moment. What can we see?"

Together, we remote viewed the centre. It seemed peaceful enough but then we both spotted movement in the field behind Binaires. Two men were creeping along, their shapes hard to distinguish in the dark. We focused on these men's thoughts, picking up their anger. Also, they expected to have help to enter the complex.

"Another traitor," hissed Helen, urgently transmitting this to Kastor and Grégoire. The evacuation was now speeding up in response to the confirmed remote sightings. The entrance to the tunnel was being guarded while a few men and women stayed in the main building, checking all the outer doors.

"Door to nursery block… they are looking for that," I murmured. This relayed, the Binaires security staff rushed to that area. It should have been impossible to penetrate, the entrance being hidden underground.

"Look around the outside area near the nursery block," said Helen, meanwhile trying to pick up thoughts in the vicinity, to locate anyone who could be helping the intruders. I focused and cried out, "A woman is holding the exterior door open, waiting for the men - they're nearly there. She's a nursery nurse!"

This was shocking. The staff trained to work with the babies and children were carefully selected. While hoping that the Binaires security officers would get there in time, we focused on the nursery nurse.

"Not a nurse, an assistant," murmured Helen, now picking her up easily. "She's in love, or something like love…"

There was a trace of distaste in the way she said this. Love that would make one betray the organization was a severe sin for Binaires. "Fabrice, she's doing this for someone called Fabrice." She added, slightly puzzled, "And for babies?" We sensed a scream and shots. The two intruders might have entered the complex. Then we felt a shared agonising pain shooting through us.

"One of the intruders has a mind probe!" I gasped, horrified. One of these weapons, illegal within our community, had been used on

Kastor in Casablanca when he was captured.

"All our network will have sensed that," said Helen grimly. "But our people must be getting control by now."

"I can't see clearly inside," I said, "but there's fighting – and shooting."

"And the mob from the village?" asked Helen, now sensing them fairly clearly herself, "They seem much nearer."

"Yes – so many, maybe 50 or 60 of them. A few are heading to the farm."

The farm buildings were not secured with the steel shutters, except for reinforced doors. Helen sent another alert, receiving the response that all the farm staff were now secure in the tunnel. She sensed fire and turned again to me.

"Yes fire," I agreed, "Torches, some of them have lit torches."

"We need a panic to scare them off," said Helen. "I can start it, but if you could help…"

I was now losing the remote view, able again to focus on the here and now. "I've never tried to induce a panic," I said uncertainly. It was a particular skill of Helen's, but worked best at close distance. Helen squirmed with impatience.

"We should try - what choice do we have?"

"All right," I said. "Warn the others, because I'm not at all sure what will happen or how we can avoid confusing our lot." Helen signalled urgently that we were going to do our best to create a panic to disrupt the mob heading for Binaires and the farm. All the telepaths would be able to sense it, but if forearmed by knowing it was a trick, they should be immune to its effects. We stood up.

"Just follow my lead, Sis. I'll home in on the bunch near Binaires first. Hard to pitch accurately, maybe we can affect those going to the farm too."

We waited until we could fairly clearly visualise the fields at the back of Binaires and the dim forms of the villagers waving torches and other weapons.

"Focus first on the one with the cross," suggested Helen. She took a deep breath and glared into the distance. At first I just felt a wave of panic, then I joined with Helen, projecting it out towards this man and the group following him. We shared shooting thought thrusts of something terrifying, as well as persuading the mob to think that dropped torches were setting them on fire.

"We need a wind illusion, something like the Sirocco or Mistral. Ready?" signalled Helen. Holding hands, it felt as though our hair was tossing around our heads as we created a powerful illusion. The men in the field turned to each other in amazement, some dropping torches, others falling to the ground. Those that could still stand started running away, others crawled on hands and feet, feeling that the wind was too strong to avoid being tossed off balance.

We turned our attention to the farm, where about ten men from the mob were trying to set fire to barns and smash windows. Helen used her ability to inject pain as well as fear into this group, illuminated in the mind images by the torches. "More wind," signalled Helen and although we were both becoming exhausted, we made another effort to widen the storm. Villagers in the fields looked up in terror as they thought they saw trees bending over and flying debris all around. We kept up the illusion until sensing that all the mob were running back towards the village, a couple of kilometres away. Then we collapsed backwards onto the bed. Helen looked anxiously towards me. "Brilliant, Cass. What a storm! It's exhilarating, isn't it, but so tiring."

"We should try to follow the villagers with it," I murmured. I felt drained by this panic creation. Wearily, we stood up again and joined hands, to increase our united electromagnetic force. I thought of the goddess Athene, whom I had embodied briefly at my bonding ceremony. I shared an image of the goddess in giant form with Helen, who nodded enthusiastically.

"Let's call on the mythological gods with our mythological skills," she signalled, fiercely. "Athene may need the Anemoi too, the gods of the winds."

Together we visualised the goddess, striding across the fields towards the villages, surrounded by swirling winds. In our minds, we tore up trees, threw farm machinery on its side, wrenched up hedgerows. While the force could not be expected to feel so strong to the villagers, it was enough to make them keep retreating, huddling together as the illusion made them believe that they were fighting against a powerful gale. This effort could not be sustained for long. When we were completely exhausted, we sank to the floor, where a couple of security officers and 'Force Musculaire' found us. Kastor was meanwhile heading to the main centre to help deal with the invasion over there.

The nursery assistant had been found standing like Joan of Arc at the door leading to the underground complex where the nursery and children's sleeping quarters were located. "This evil must end!" she was crying out. "It's God's will!" Dominique, arriving at the scene after the short skirmish, ordered that she should not be harmed because of the need to interrogate her. One of two intruders had been shooting wildly, seriously injuring a security officer. The other had wielded the mind probe causing agony to another security officer and a nanny, who had gone back to fetch feeds for the babies. The mind probe had been used on a high setting but with little skill, vaguely whirled about in the direction of the security officers, who reached the doorway just as the intruders were entering. It was enough to make the officers collapse and then the man with the probe focused his attention on the nanny, who had unluckily just run up the stairs as they entered. The intruders were quickly disarmed – Helen not being the only telepath who could inflict pain and make weapons drop – but the damage done was bad enough. Neither of the intruders was named Fabrice and if he was the man with the cross, he had also escaped with the mob.

3

When the Centre appeared to be secure again an hour later, senior members of Binaires held an emergency meeting. Kastor and I, as honorary members, were also in the group. Helen was tolerated as our guest at the Villa Dufour, but never permitted into the Binaires buildings.

Dominique addressed the gathering. "Her name is Cilisse. A disgrace to the name. Cilissa, in the Homeric tales, was the nurse who saved Orestes, sacrificing her own child."

"Her interrogation will begin shortly," said Grégoire, keeping down his anger. "Meanwhile, are all the buildings secure? The farm, villa?"

The Binaires head of security, Olivier Cerberus, nodded. "For now. There's some damage up at the farm currently being inspected by the staff there. The doors leading to the nursery block were among the first to be checked and they were fine. Cilisse must have been hiding, waiting for the chaos of evacuation to die down so she could open the outer door. We need to discover how she did that. But at least the mob was dispersed, thanks to the panic and storm."

"Yes," said Dominique, "the panic was very helpful, but I hope the villagers don't blame it on us. They already seem to think we're the spawn of the devil."

"And there's a whole village full of furious and frightened people," said Grégoire. "How could this be brought on by one deranged nursery assistant?"

"Cassandra and Helen were concentrating on remote viewing and creating the storm illusion," said Kastor, "but I managed to pick up that name, Fabrice, and something about the motive concerning babies."

He glanced for my agreement and I gave a dull nod. I was still exhausted from inducing the panic.

"Such a person should never have had contact with the outside," murmured Olivier. Security was much more lax at Binaires than at the Woodstock centre, where layers of intermediaries protected the telepaths.

"One of the nannies told me that Cilisse's work included fetching fresh milk from the farm. Clearly that was unwise," said Dominique. She was partly responsible for this disaster, because she had permitted such freedom. "But she shouldn't have had contact with outsiders through that job. She'd have been instructed to use the tunnel and wait at the door within the farmhouse for the milk to be brought to her."

"She's pretty," observed Kastor, "so possibly she sometimes dallied with the farm staff there. And that could have led to her being seen by an outsider. We'll find out."

"I would say she's not intelligent enough to have planned this herself," said Dominique. "Her abilities were fairly limited. But her assessment reports have been good. This is a complete surprise." She looked uncharacteristically humble, reproaching herself for missing this threat.

"We'll assume that she must have had an accomplice. Perhaps we'll find out more from the intruders?" asked Grégoire.

"I'd like to use the mind probe on them, at the setting designed to damage the ordinary human brain," said Olivier, head of Binaires security. He was clearly no kinder than his counterpart Gaston Ajax at Woodstock. "But I suppose we must be sensible. They'll be missed, police may come looking for them."

"We need to stage it so they seem like vandals, burglars," suggested Kastor. "But it would be very useful to find out what they know, first. We can keep them mainly sedated after interrogation and do our best to limit the memories they have of this place."

"Memory alteration is very skilled work," said Dominique. "And remember, we have a lot of village people who knew what these intruders were up to."

"Perhaps just a little work with the probe, for research?" said Olivier, a hint of vicious hope in this voice, "I mean, to dull their senses and memory?"

"Possibly it would do that," said Dominique. "But using it would make us as bad as them." We stared at the probe, lying in the centre of the table, with its vicious prongs that transmitted electromagnetic energy. Kastor looked away, remembering his torture in Casablanca, but murmured that we should get an object expert to examine it, to try to sense its origin.

"The obvious person is Cassandra," said Dominique and Kastor gazed at me anxiously, wishing there was someone less obvious to choose for this unpleasant task.

The emergency group decided that the villa did not seem to have been a concern to the mob and if the police came soon, it would be better for the occupants to be there. Security officers, as in the main centre, were rapidly stripping binary equipment in the nursery. We had to be prepared for a search of all the buildings around, if the villagers took their fears to the police. Kastor had a French name, Romain Dufour, and to the outer world he and I were a wealthy professional couple living with a large family and servants. The windows and doors remained secured, but that would be a normal precaution for a large residence. Leo and the babies were back in the nursery, tended by anxious nannies. When Kastor and I emerged from the tunnel to our house, the cook made tea for us.

"I don't understand yet how the mob got hold of one of those awful probes," said Kastor.

I looked with disgust at the box he was holding, containing the instrument. We shared a brief memory of his battle with the damage it had caused.

"I suppose our experience will be useful now," I said, gingerly lifting the lid. When I picked it up, I also felt a painful and intense rush of memories associated with it. It felt alive, as a series of rapid images fired through my mind. I shook my head to rid the recent attack on the two victims, closing my eyes to see if I could look further back. A clear picture of the man with the cross flashed up, but against a sunny white walled city, far from France.

"Fabrice!" I exclaimed. "So it was him leading the mob. He brought it to the village from Morocco." I sensed with alarm that this was the very instrument used against Kastor in the prison run by Abdul-Aziz in Casablanca. Images of that city were engraved on my mind, following our attempt to rescue him. I was too tired to conceal this from Kastor, who blanched but then shrugged.

"I can't remember my attack clearly, so don't worry."

"He's very religious, fanatically so," I murmured. "Much of this trouble is down to him, I think."

"Where is Fabrice, now, can you tell?"

"I don't know - with objects, it's usually only possible to sense their past and future, not what's happened to those in touch with them. I have an indistinct image of his appearance. Olive skinned, long nose, beard. Intense eyes."

"It seems clear that he met the nursery assistant at the farm. How their relationship developed is uncertain."

I shifted my gaze to the direction of the village. "I sense fear and confusion, but soon they'll be better organised, they may want to come to the centre again. Certainly they're thinking about police action."

"If the intruders don't return to the village, there'll be a search," said Kastor. "Grégoire is already preparing for that. We should be ready for a visit from the police."

"Someone should go to the village," I said. "Fabrice must be there. If he could be stopped, the mob may lose enthusiasm."

A voice from the doorway made us both look round. "I'll go," said Helen. "I'm not connected with Binaires and I speak fluent French. I'll ferret out this Fabrice."

"It's too dangerous," said Kastor, "They'll be suspicious of any stranger."

"Not necessarily," said Helen. "I've always wanted to dress as a nun. Perhaps a novice in this case. I'm not really up on all the behavioural niceties to pass as an experienced nun."

Kastor and I said nothing, both contemplating the mismatch between Helen and the costume of someone living a life of piety.

"If this Fabrice is a religious fanatic, what better disguise? And if possible, we need to bring him in, at least to stop him doing any more damage to us," protested Helen.

"I see the point of finding out first hand what's happening there," said Kastor. "After Casablanca, no one could doubt your abilities in the field. There may be a suitable costume in the drama department here, I'll send for one. But obviously, any expedition to the village must wait until morning."

We glanced at the grilled window: it was already dawn. Kastor replaced the probe it its box and went down to the cellar to check that everything linking us to Binaries was well hidden in the tunnel.

I eyed Helen with amusement. "A nun?"

"Why not?" said Helen, "I'll check out a recent death in the village and I'll be a visitor from a far off convent, called back to see an elderly relative but arriving too late. Fabrice will seek me out, I'm sure, when he hears of a devout visitor."

"How come they have so many costumes here?" I asked.

"Oh, you should know by now that Binaries love acting and dressing up. At Woodstock it's mainly the students, but here they all get into it. It's good practice for the field and it's not as if they can make frequent trips to the theatre outside."

"Right. I'll check the recent obituaries or funerals on the Internet," I said, pleased that my French had improved sufficiently for me to do this with ease.

"Great," said Helen, "If you have time, otherwise I can do it. I should also research a remote convent, maybe a closed order that lives in strict secrecy. As for the deceased loved one, we need someone with very few, preferably no, relatives in the village. A recluse, ideally…"

We needed to wash and get dressed for an eventful day ahead. I was already seeing disturbing visions of the future: an explosion, disruption, danger for all of us.

Breakfast was served at the villa like on any normal day. I sensed the approach of two men to the entrance. Kastor had been right about an early call from the police. I signalled to him to return.

When the doorbell sounded, the housekeeper let in two gendarmes. They introduced themselves politely as Captain Edouard Parfait and Lieutenant Yves Jourdain.

"We're sorry to disturb you so early, Madame, but we're investigating incidents at your neighbour's farm and the Villa de la Belle Mer. Is the master of the house at home?"

I explained that I was Madame Dufour and that my husband was checking the cellar for a wine order later that day. I invited them into the breakfast room, offering coffee. Leo stood up politely and said, "Bonjour messieurs." Leo gazed with interest at the police captain, who stared back as though momentarily disconcerted by this poised five year old.

"My sister and the younger children are in the nursery with their nannies," I said. I went to the cellar door and called down, hoping that Kastor had finished securing the door.

"Were you aware of an incident last night?" asked the captain, while we waited for the man of the house to join us.

"It was very windy, it woke us up," I said, "but nothing else. Our gardener will be inspecting any storm damage in the gardens this morning."

"You're not French, Madame?" asked the captain, picking up my English accent. I blushingly acknowledged that I was English, but that my husband was French. At this point, Kastor emerged from the cellar, holding a wine bottle. 'Romain Dufour' greeted the officers formally, with a slight indication of surprise. He showed suitable concern on learning that a window had been broken at the farm and an attempt made to set one of the barns on fire.

"Sometimes there are problems with young people from the village," he murmured, "but our security here is very good."

Captain Parfait said that there might be a connection with a village rumour about stolen babies. 'Monsieur Dufour' and I looked suitably alarmed.

"Two men from the village are also missing," said the captain. "We'd like to search your home, if we may, just to be on the safe side."

"Of course," said 'Monsieur Dufour', "although I hope we'd know if someone had got in."

The captain asked to come down to the cellar, while indicating to the lieutenant that he should go the nursery with 'Madame Dufour'. I took Leo's hand and led the way. We found a scene of domestic contentment. Helen was lovingly holding Grace, while the nannies gave the twins their breakfast. Helen, wearing a Buchanan tartan skirt and with her white blouse a little open, as though she had just been breast feeding, looked up enquiringly and answered their questions in fluent French.

"You have lived longer in France than your sister, Madame?" asked the lieutenant and Helen replied, "I studied French at the Sorbonne, but now I live with my husband in Scotland." She produced her passport from her bag, showing her to be Helen Buchanan.

"May I ask to see the birth certificate for your baby, Madame, and the passports for all your children?"

Helen looked surprised, until the officer explained about the story of stolen babies. Turning to one of the nannies, Helen asked her to check in the nursery cabinet. As ever, I was impressed with her organising abilities when all the documents were promptly produced. The twins surname was Davenport, which Helen shyly explained was because they were born before she married her current husband. Her passport showed her maiden name as Davenport. The birth certificates for the twins and Leo were collected from Kastor's study. The Binary Centre had provided excellent documents for our current aliases, but whether they would stand the test of forensic scrutiny was not so certain. Hopefully, the police just needed to check that all our children were legally accounted for.

While they were noting down the names and other details, I focused nervously on what was happening in the cellar. I could tell that the police captain was admiring the rows of fine wine kept by 'Romain Dufour' but also examining the racks carefully. The door to the tunnel was well concealed behind an apparently fixed wine rack, with no obvious exits from the cellar other than the stairs to the ground floor. When Captain Parfait ascended these, followed by Kastor, he ordered the lieutenant to search the rest of the house, while he interviewed the staff. They all gave the same story of hearing a fierce gale in the night, but no knowledge of a mob. Finally the police officers departed, apologising for the intrusion. We stood politely at the door, then breathed a sigh of relief as we shut it.

"Why would they be so suspicious of our children?" I asked.

"I wonder if Cilisse has been in touch with police," said Kastor with deep misgiving. "But it seems very unlikely. She was just a nursery assistant, not authorised to go anywhere except to collect milk from the farm. The police could just be being careful, given the stolen baby story being spread about in the village. Dominique is interviewing her but she's being very stubborn, like a martyr. She's saying she's answerable only to God."

"And to Fabrice…" I said. "I think we should go to the interview room. Just behind a viewing screen. If Helen is going into the village, she'll need as much information as we can gather."

"I hate you being involved with surveillance," said Kastor, while curtly nodding that of course I should help. Meanwhile, we sensed the approach of Helen, coming up from her most unaccustomed time in the nursery. The nun costume had been brought down to the tunnel area and she went down to retrieve it, while we made our way along the meandering tunnel to the Centre Binaires.

4

While Grégoire and Amélie posed as the owners of the Villa de la Belle Mer for the police, Kastor and I entered the viewing room next to the interview cell holding Cilisse, a pretty but sullen girl aged 17. Dominique was the only interviewer, with two guards standing behind Cilisse, their thoughts indicating how much they would like to beat the secrets out of her. Dominique was feeling much the same, given the girl's sulky or silent responses to questioning. Soon after taking my seat next to Kastor and another surveillance officer, I sensed that Cilisse was pregnant.

"Early stage, perhaps no more than 2 months. She knows and is very pleased about it." Dominique nodded and immediately asked Cilisse about her pregnancy. Cilisse sat up sharply, at first denying it but then shrugging, knowing that Dominique would detect the lie.

"What of it?" she asked. Dominique pressed her, asking how she became pregnant when all young women at the centre used contraception? In any case, Binaries usually sought permission before embarking on pregnancy. I was a very rare exception to this rule. Cilisse shrugged again, saying it was God's will. I focused on her intently.

"I see a barn, with Cilisse embracing Fabrice. She's leaning against the wall, protesting they should wait, but not with conviction."

I shared an image showing what happened next. My ability to dismember time, a kind of precognition in reverse, was highly unusual in the telepath community, but in my five years with them, I had learned to develop it. Kastor looked embarrassed. "Do we need this much detail?" he murmured, glancing sideways at the surveillance officer, Antoine, who was smirking.

"I suppose that Cilisse was merely satisfying curiosity," I replied, reminding Kastor with a closed thought of his reluctant confession about his liaisons before meeting me. Meanwhile, Dominique made full use of this image and Cilisse reddened, saying it was only the once. She had disobeyed orders to stay in the house, she could admit that, persuading the farm workers that she loved to see the cows.

"Hmm, and more than once," I said, transmitting an image of an equally brief encounter between the lovers, this time lying in hay at the back of the barn.

"Oh," I added, "and Fabrice brings out a bible, reading her a passage." I closed my eyes, trying to sense other meetings. "She tells Fabrice of the pregnancy, but that she will not be allowed to mother her baby. This may be when she tells him about the communal nursery…"

Dominique angrily confronted Cilisse with this story. One of the guards, a woman, stepped up to Cilisse and slapped her face hard. Nothing made Binaires women angrier than betraying their nursery of future telepaths. Dominique ordered the guard to stand back but indicated to Cilisse that she might as well tell them the rest.

"Yes, I told him how you steal other people's babies, as well as those born here. I know the story of them being orphans, the ones who come here in the night, but I keep my ears open. I've heard nannies talking about it."

"Do you think they're unhappy here, the Binaires babies? You yourself…"

Cilisse answered indignantly. "We're all conditioned to think this sin is for our own good, for telepathy, which is an affront to God. We're all living in mortal sin! I had to do something – for all of us."

"So you betrayed us, arranged with Fabrice for the villagers to be told."

"Yes!" Cilisse now had a triumphant smile. "He was horrified that our baby would be taken from me, with him having no say. He knows about telepaths too. He has a cousin in the police in Casablanca. They raided a secret prison and found a tool for interrogating telepaths."

"And Fabrice brought it here, with you agreeing he should use it?" said Dominique, very pale.

Cilisse shrugged. "Of course. He is on a mission from God."

Dominique was controlling her fury better than the guards, who looked like hunting dogs, being held back from the chance to devour a prey. "This instrument causes severe harm," said Dominique in a quiet, menacing tone. "It can kill telepaths and ordinary humans too – isn't that a sin?"

"You know nothing of sin," said Cilisse, smugly. "God knows I acted only according to his will. I hope the tool injured several of you, killed some too. Fabrice told me that was a direct order from God."

"And is that why you stopped taking the pill, because Fabrice told you it was a sin?" asked Dominique, maintaining her calm admirably, considering the milling thoughts of anger from all the Binaires present.

"It's a sin to try to stop babies," said Cilisse, smiling beatifically.

Behind the screen, Kastor looked to see how I was taking this. He knew I had deep misgivings about how some of the babies reached the Binary centres. But I was also angry with this stupid nursery assistant, who had brought harm and chaos to our world.

"There are other ways of dealing with policies one doesn't agree with," I transmitted briefly, in response to his thoughts. Meanwhile, I continued to focus on Cilisse, who had now returned to her former sullen silence. Dominique, clearly exasperated, ordered for the girl to be taken or a short comfort break, or perhaps that should be uncomfortable break, I judged, seeing the grim faces of the guards as they pulled her out of the room. Dominique came into the viewing room.

"Any ideas, before we proceed to more physical interrogation?" she demanded.

"I have an idea to break her silence," I said. During the interrogation of Abdul-Aziz in Cadiz, I had managed to project an alarming image onto the mirror in the interview room. I suggested trying this again, with Dominique ensuring that Cilisse thought that any image was for her alone.

"She's closed down her telepathy as much as she can," I observed, "but she might sense that you know what's going on, despite thinking it's a sin to detect it." Dominique nodded and went back into the interview room. She briefed the guards with a note, when they brought the prisoner back.

Kastor looked preoccupied. He had received thoughts from Grégoire that the police wanted to examine the whole site, to find the underground installation they'd heard about. They agreed that they should say it was a converted nuclear bunker, dating from the cold war era. Its use now, their story would go, was for Amélie to give art lessons to visiting students. Thanks to sliding wall gates, the underground area appeared much smaller and contained only a tunnel accessed from the ground level, leading to a set of rooms, one containing art materials. A few doors in the tunnel led to storage zones, the areas beyond camouflaged behind steel walls. Grégoire and Kastor needed urgently to get more information from the two captured villagers. Helen was waiting for the signal to start making her way to the village. She would be concealed in a farm vehicle apparently coming from another direction. Meanwhile she had researched a suitable recent death in the village and a nunnery far enough away for no one local to have heard of it, having guessed correctly that I wouldn't have time to do those Internet checks.

As Kastor left the room, the interview with Cilisse was once more under way. Cilisse stared defiantly into the distance, making the sign of the cross on her body several times. She was determined not to betray her lover any further.

"If you want to be a martyr, of course we can arrange that," Dominique was saying. "But we want to help you Cilisse. I understand, much more than you think."

The nursery assistant made no response until she suddenly screamed, staring at the mirror. She saw the Virgin Mary, gazing down at her.

"Cilisse, do not be afraid." This voice from my projected vision could be detected by all the telepaths in the room but the briefing insured that they pretended to pick up nothing. The girl looked at the guards and at Dominique, who all gave her puzzled glances.

"I can be seen only by you, my child. While I'm with you, we can only hear each other," said the Virgin Mary in the mirror. "You must protect this special baby, this gift of God."

Cilisse nodded, eyes streaming with tears, hands clasped in prayer. "Our Mary, course I shall protect the baby. Fabrice and I..."

"No, not Fabrice," said the vision. "He wants to steal this precious baby from you."

"No!" gasped Cilisse, "That can't be true. We're going to marry and live outside, in Morocco."

"And where do you think Fabrice is now, my confused one?"

"He's in the village, at his lodgings, Rue des Peupliers. I don't know the number, yet. When he isn't working, he studies the Holy Scriptures and often prays in the church. He's a good man, Holy Mother."

"He's with another woman, Cilisse. They are mocking you." The girl collapsed backwards, nearly knocking over her chair, while the guards hurried to support it. Dominique asked her what was the matter, why was she so silent but moving her lips with words they couldn't hear or read? Cilisse glared at them, turning back to the mirror where the Virgin Mary now looked very sad.

"I'm so sorry to have to tell you this. His cousin and his wife have been trying for a baby, Cilisse, and now they can take yours. You'll be taken to Casablanca, to live with his cousin's family as a servant until the baby comes. They're cruel people who think telepaths are subhuman, except for breeding and menial purposes. After the birth, you'll be sent to work as a servant in another household. You'll never see your child again."

"He wouldn't lie to me," whispered Cilisse, between sobs.

"He is a grave sinner, my child. When I bring him to you, here, you'll hear it from his lips. He only wanted to injure the telepaths, when you told him about who lived here. God needs you to make amends for allowing this great sin, Cilisse."

Cilisse now flung herself onto the floor, kneeling and holding her hands together, as she viewed the flickering vision. I was exhausted with the effort of maintaining it.

"What must I do, Holy Mother?"

"Tell Dominique everything you know, every detail. Your soul is in danger…," said the Virgin Mary, fading from view.

"Stay with me, Holy Mother!" cried Cilisse. But the mirror had returned to simply reflecting the room. She looked round at the mystified faces of Dominique and the guards, who helped her back to her chair.

"I'll tell you about the raid," she said, her voice trembling. Dominique gave her a kind, understanding smile. In the viewing room, Antoine looked at me with admiration.

"How did you know all that, about Fabrice and his cousin?" he asked.

"I didn't," I said with a smile, "I made it up. She needs to fall out of love with this dangerous man. When Fabrice is brought here, I'm sure there'll be ways of making him tell that story, for example, in an attempt to save his life."

"We could leave them in there with Fabrice knowing we're listening," said Antoine, with a grin, "and see what's left of him after mad Cilisse has got at him…"

Mad Cilisse, I thought, saying nothing. For I had a secret fear of succumbing to mental illness. My mother was bipolar, swinging from deep depression to euphoric excitement, but outside, I'd always felt I was the sane one in the family. Since entering Binaries I had learned of the risk of the enhanced telepathy making people mentally unstable. High functioning telepaths, with the ability to do remote viewing or induce visions, were particularly at risk. And I was one of those.

Dominique popped into the viewing room to thank me, during another uncomfortable break for the miserable Cilisse. She discussed the evidence. "Very empathetic," she commented. "Not a good telepath, but adequate for her work. She should have been the perfect nursery assistant, so at some point there'll have to be a full inquiry into our assessment process."

"What will happen to her now?" asked Antoine.

"This kind of religious obsession is hard to cure," said Dominique, "St. Anthony's will be the best place for her. Arrange it, would you Antoine – after she's seen Fabrice?"

Then I was taken back to Villa Dufour, the security officers shutting the cellar door behind me. As the officers retreated back to Binaires, they carefully closed each section of the tunnel.

5

HELEN

When I came back to the villa, I was just putting the finishing touches to my novice nun outfit, including an impressively large crucifix.

"Is this convincing?" I asked, twirling the grey habit and adjusting the modest grey and white veil framing my face, cleaned of all make up. "I've only got black lacey undies with me, but hopefully no one will see those."

"You look the part," Cass said, with that prim look she often has. "Perhaps glasses? I mean, supposing that police lieutenant sees you in the village?"

"When I'm in a role, no one recognises me," I assured her, "but good idea about wearing specs, just in case. Lieutenant Jourdain was giving me quite a looking over in the nursery."

When Cass told me about Cilisse's interview and 'vision', I couldn't help grinning. Cass had learned to be almost as deceitful as me. "We're such a team, who'd have thought it?" I said, but she was too worried to start talking about our troubled twin relationship. So I just informed her that I'd found the name of a suitably distant convent and also a likely candidate for the dead relative. Agnes Sanjou, a miserly recluse, had recently died. I had found no evidence that there were relatives living within the village.

I borrowed a pair of thick rimmed spectacles from the housekeeper, whose prescription was fortunately for only slight adjustment. I practised looking soulfully over the top of them, when accurate vision was needed. Grégoire transmitted what they had gleaned from the two intruders so far, such as names of others in the mob, the name of the parish priest and local church and that Fabrice had been the undoubted leader.

Then I made my way to the farmhouse, to be hidden for transport nearer the village. Small groups of Binaires were hurrying away from the centre, but Cass and Kastor had to stay in case the police came back. I thought it best not to tell Cass that I had a syringe of tranquillizer and some other drugs with me, supplied most helpfully by the Binaires head of security. It would have been a sensitive issue for Cass. I still feel bad about drugging her when I forced her into the Binary tunnels six years ago. I didn't have remorse when I swapped places with her: I'd convinced myself it was my turn to experience the outside world. I was definitely a bit unhinged at the time. Cass worries whether we are both prone to mental ill health, both through the telepathy training, our fantastic skills – well, no false modesty about those – and possibly a trait inherited from our mother, the one who sold me to the Binaries. I think she worries too much. Apart from the serious lapse of dropping Cass into the Binary centre, I reckon I've shown I can cope with both worlds, the strange environment of my upbringing and that of the boring outsiders.

The farm truck pulled up just outside the village and I slipped from under a pile of sacking and adjusted my veil. The driver and I looked at the fields, selecting a place for the pick up of Fabrice, assuming I could lure him there. We decided on a field with a large old fashioned haystack near a hedge, which would limit visibility.

Stepping down from the truck, I said, "I'll signal when it starts to look promising. We'll need two of you to bring him back."

The driver nodded eagerly. They were in deep trouble at the Binaires-run farm for having allowed the nursery assistant such freedom in visiting the farm animals alone. The farm workers shared a bitter thought that Cilisse had seemed such a sweet, guileless girl. Men, I thought, so easily duped. It would transpire later that a guard was similarly misled when he showed Cilisse how to work the locks on the outer door. She had said it was just to reassure her that the babies were safe.

I walked cautiously into the village, head bowed, every inch the devout nun. I could see the church and took a roundabout route, not keen to go through the centre. But the village was tiny and all streets either led to or passed near the village square. A crowd had gathered and I noticed Lieutenant Yves Jourdain looking on. A priest was speaking, disapprovingly, to the gathered villagers. I stopped to listen and pick up thoughts. It seemed that last night's mob had not acted with the sanction of the Church. I sensed a woman at the back of the crowd eyeing me curiously and was about to move on when the woman came to my side.

"Good morning, Sister – it's rare to see a nun, here. Have you come because of last night?"

"Last night?" I said in a quiet, puzzled voice. "No, I've been travelling for two days from our convent in the Swiss Alps. Has there been a problem?"

I guessed that the woman was the village gossip. She eagerly told me about the mob. Many of the village women had disapproved, without being able to stop their men folk going up to the Villa de la Belle Mer estate to find these stolen babies.

"I said, do it properly, through the police, but would they listen?" I gazed at her sympathetically, silently willing her to say more.

"And of course they found nothing," continued the woman, "and got caught in a windstorm for their trouble. There was an awful gale last night."

I simply shook my head, as though weighed down by the

foolishness of men. The woman looked at my nun's habit. "Which convent, did you say, Sister?"

"The Holy Order of St. Catherine and Gabriel," I murmured indistinctly, then in a clearer voice, "I'm a novice, Madame, allowed to make this visit only to visit a sick relative, Agnes Sanjou."

"Oh!" said the woman, "I'm so sorry, Sister, but Agnes Sanjou died a week or so ago. Surely your convent would have been informed?"

"We're a silent order, with no outside communications apart from letters that the Reverend Mother passes on when appropriate. I have been in retreat, but have come as soon as I could be released."

"I didn't know she had any living relatives. Certainly not a nun." I searched the woman's mind, finding she was puzzled since Agnes Sanjou had a daughter, who had died some time before.

"I'm her granddaughter," I said, softly. "But my mother bore me… out of wedlock. Grandmère Sanjou never forgave my mother and kept no evidence of me. My commitment to the Church is partly atonement for the sin which brought me into the world." I lowered my eyes, radiating great shame. The village gossip was fascinated by the tale and was looking forward to spreading it.

"But a few weeks ago," I continued to my avid listener, "Mother Superior received a letter from her, asking to see me for the first time. She felt so ill that it would also, probably, be her last chance to meet me."

"How sad," said the gossip, "that you've missed seeing her." I could tell she was also thinking about money, wondering if there had been bequests to the villagers that might be complicated by my arrival.

"I shall just go and pray at her grave and in the church. Of course I expect nothing from Grandmère's possessions. We're not allowed to accept any gifts or bequests." The gossip nodded, approvingly. I looked towards the priest, still ranting at his flock in the square.

"So it wasn't the priest who set off the angry men?" I asked.

"No, it was mainly that Fabrice Tartuffe. Fancies himself as almost a priest. He came here a few years ago, said he was persecuted as a Christian in Morocco. Last night, he led them along with a giant cross! Father Laurent is furious."

I composed a solemn expression, sending persuasive thoughts to make the woman continue.

"Yes, Fabrice, who does he think he is? Comes here and starts asking for more church services, then proposes rules about the length of women's skirts and immodest necklines. And he likes people to call him 'Father' as if he was a proper priest!" The woman grinned slyly, adding, "How's your father, more like," in French so crude and explicit that I was obliged to look deeply shocked.

"Oh, I'm so sorry, Sister. But he likes the ladies, that's for sure. Take my advice and don't go near him, a respectable woman of God like you."

Inclining my head modestly, I said that I must now go to the church and its graveyard, as I was required to return to the convent without any delay. The gossip returned to the crowd. I could be sure that this woman would announce Agnes Sanjou's shocking secret very soon. OK, that wasn't essential to our plot, but I had to explain why no one had ever heard of me. I noticed a glance from Lieutenant Jourdain but sensed no recognition. Still, it seemed wise to quickly depart. I had no wish to be questioned by him and risk detection.

Approaching the little graveyard beside the church, I easily spotted the newly dug grave for Agnes Sanjou. I sensed there was a man inside the church. Father Laurent was in the square, so this man could well be Fabrice. Taking a deep breath, as even I was nervous about this dangerous psychopath, I glided decorously into the church. A man in a black robe but no white neckband was bent in prayer in the front pew. He was a good looking Arab, if you like a lot of beard. I was convinced that he must be Fabrice. I walked quietly past, entering a side chapel from where I could easily be seen and knelt in front of the altar.

Probably, he would enter the chapel out of curiosity, but I filled his mind with the wish to speak to me. As I closed my eyes, wearing a saintly expression, I heard a little cough from the arched entrance. Slowly I stood up and faced him.

"We're honoured by your arrival here, Sister!" he said.

"I am mourning my grandmother, Agnes Sanjou." I gave him a respectful look. "But are you the one of the priests here? Your vestments are not familiar to me." I felt his excitement at being mistaken for a priest.

"I'm Fabrice, soon to be Father Fabrice. I am not yet fully ordained. " Nor ever will be, I thought, amused at his ready deceit.

"We're a closed, private order. I'm out of touch with how priests dress outside our community. But Father, does that mean you can't take confession? I should so like to do this, before making my long journey back to our convent in the mountains." I let my glasses slip down so that my large innocent eyes met his and his aroused thoughts confirmed his reputation.

"But of course, Sister!" He indicated the confessional box, moving towards it with an eager step. I had no experience of the procedure, other than what I'd gleaned from films. When he slid back the grid on his side of the box, I started off. "Forgive me Father, for I have sinned." He asked how long it had been since my last confession and prompted me to continue.

"Father, we have a tradition in our order that before we take our vows, we should experience some of the things that we must leave behind in the religious life."

"Yes?" said Fabrice, greatly interested, for he had not come across such a tradition. If he had been a genuine priest, he'd have known what I had in mind couldn't possibly exist in the Church.

"It's not an absolute requirement," I said, letting a little girlish nervousness seep into my voice, "but for example, it's felt important that we have experienced intimate union with a man, to know what we're renouncing."

"I see," said Fabrice, puzzled but equally intrigued.

"I am totally inexperienced in these matters," I lied, "but although it's not essential, I'd like to follow that tradition. Is that very wrong, Father?"

"No, my child, but it would need to be a man you could trust absolutely. Surely, for him, it would be a very serious responsibility."

"Yes, and I wondered if on this, the only trip I've been allowed to make outside the convent and the last opportunity before my vows, I'd be able to find a good man who would do this small service for me. But I haven't found one and of course I'm very timid of approaching a man. I suppose I should give up the idea of this symbolic sacrifice, this traditional task to be undertaken? It seems sinful, even to think of it."

Fabrice's mind filled with desire to assist me in this service, helped in no small part by me. "It's not a sin to follow tradition," he murmured. "I've never been asked to perform such a service myself, but if it's so important to you, perhaps I could serve…?"

"Oh Father," I gasped, with innocent enthusiasm, "it had not occurred to me to ask a priest, but if you've not yet taken full holy orders…"

"No… so I should be honoured to help you keep this tradition."

"There are a few conditions that must be fulfilled," I murmured through the grill. "The union must take place away from buildings, in countryside where we can be one with the birds and beasts of the field, in the open air."

"I understand," said Fabrice. "There are many fields near here."

"I saw an ideal spot when I walked into the village. I sensed Our Mary saying to me, that if only I could find a man, that would be the place."

"Can you take me there, my child?" He could scarcely conceal his impatience. As we both emerged from the confession box, I shyly indicated that he should follow at a discreet distance. When I appeared to hesitate, saying softly that perhaps it was a sin after all and not an absolute requirement, he took my hand, assuring me that he was the ideal man for the purpose. Just so, I thought, remembering dear old Theodora back at the Binaries, although I know she would not have approved of my methods.

"I feel bad asking you to do this penance."

"As the priest who's just heard your confession, I advise you to obey… God knows that this is right for you."

I nodded modestly and left the church, with Fabrice following about ten steps behind, as I instructed.

I took a route that avoided the main square area, where the crowd seemed to be dispersing. Reaching the field and haystack arranged with the Binaires officers, I led Fabrice to a spot out of view from the road or the rest of the field. Fabrice promptly embraced me and I drew away, with a display of prudish shock.

"No Father, this is not for my enjoyment! Another condition is that you must lie down and I must give myself to you, with the minimum of touching."

Fabrice was breathing quickly, unable to believe his luck, telling himself that this condition would be quite acceptable. He lay down on his back and I knelt beside him.

"First we shall pray," I said, "While you lie with hands outstretched, palms up to acknowledge your homage to God in doing this service. I shall lie on you in the position in which we take our vows. I'll turn away while you prepare yourself, perhaps remove any undergarments?"

"And you remove… any impediments to the union?"

"We don't wear such impediments in our order," I murmured. "Our habit is sufficient clothing."

He nodded as if this all made perfect sense and I turned away, while he hurriedly removed the pants under his robe. Then he lay back as instructed, I knelt across him, with my long black habit draped around his legs. He was very excited, grabbing me with both arms. I shrank away, sitting up and pushing his arms back into position.

"It's important for you to stay in that sacrificial pose. And your eyes must be closed. I've been instructed how to do this, but you must protect my shame by not looking."

Fabrice tried to obey, but kept opening his eyes eagerly as I positioned myself over him. So I used my talent for inflicting telepathic pain, shooting a dose of pain into his eyes, making him cry out with surprise.

"Oh Father Fabrice, God is watching us. He who knows all things will be angry if you open your eyes. Close your eyes tightly, as though your life depended on it. There'll be no pain if you observe the tradition."

He squeezed his eyes shut, finding that the pain disappeared. I started a prayer, while examining the veins in his outstretched arms. The left elbow looked easiest.

"You must clench your fists," I murmured, withdrawing my prepared syringe from a large pocket of my habit. "This will show your determination, before God, to apply the strength of your manhood within me."

His fists closed like iron, making the antecubital veins more prominent. Watching his closed eyes, I started to roll up his robe, at the same time telepathing the men on the farm truck to get ready for the collection.

"Our Father," I said reverently, "Bless this sacrifice made by your servants." His eyes flickered, requiring another pain shot to keep them closed. Bending over him, I murmured that I needed to anoint him with holy water and quickly sprayed the inner elbow area with local anaesthetic spray. Then, as I murmured breathlessly, "You may soon take me, Father," I neatly injected the small syringe of phenobarbitone into the selected vein. Fabrice felt the pressure of the needle, but the anaesthetic dulled sensation. When he tried to sneak a look, extreme pain made him close his eyes again.

"Now, Father, you must hold me and bring me in contact with your manhood." Although he must have been feeling drowsy from the drug already, he eagerly fumbled for my waist. What I do for the Binaries, I thought briefly, but it was important to concentrate on the task.

"I'm giving myself to you, Fabrice, now," I said, "…let us count together, ten, nine, eight…"

He started mumbling the numbers, but the fast acting sedative prevented him from finishing them. He fell back, deeply asleep. I looked round to see the farm workers approaching and stood up, nodding appreciatively at the sight of a couple of large sacks they had brought to wrap him in. I tucked his underpants into the package. The vehicle was parked on the other side of the hedge and the men loaded the sack containing Fabrice onto the back, covering him with more sacking.

"Heavy potatoes in this crop," said one, checking the road for any observers.

"May we give you a lift, Sister? We could take you to the next village." This was presumably for any listeners, since the farm workers knew they were taking me to the farm and its tunnel back to the villa.

"Thank you," I said, climbing into the front of the truck, then ducking my head down to be out of view through the windscreen. My task over, I did not want to be further observed.

6

Fabrice awoke in a strange room, lit only by a porthole with an electric light glowing behind it. It seemed to be underground. He realised he'd been drugged, dimly trying to remember if he had helped that sweet novice to complete her tradition. Surely she had not tricked him? Peering under the bedclothes, he saw he was still wearing his long tunic. He blearily tried to get out of bed and a nurse immediately entered the room, followed by two men.

"Monsieur Tartuffe, they're ready for you now. These men will take you." His questions about what was happening went unanswered. The guards walked him briskly to a room where two other men turned towards him, gazing at him intently.

"Fabrice," said one of the men, "do take a seat. We've been looking forward to this interview."

The interviewers were Grégoire and Kastor, who explained that they were members of the community he had attacked in the night. Fabrice, still feeling sluggish, looked around in alarm but the guards held him in his chair when he tried to get up. While frequently praying aloud for escape from these demonic telepaths, he was an easy interviewee, becoming more talkative when they intimated that this would be his ticket out of there.

"The girl, Cilisse, told me what you do here. It was my duty to rescue the babies and bring freaks of nature to God's justice."

"So making Cilisse pregnant was part of your plan?" asked Kastor.

"She gave herself willingly," said Fabrice, "and has seen the light."

"She's been sentenced to death for her part in this," said Grégoire, "but you may be able to save her. Are you ready to give your life for hers?"

"My life?" said Fabrice, "what do you mean?"

"She acted out of love for you - are you willing to save her?" asked Kastor.

"She was serving God," said Fabrice piously, "and must take the consequences in this holy war."

"So that's a no?" asked Grégoire. Fabrice shifted uneasily. "You implied I'd be able to go, if I told you everything. I merely carried the cross, to try to bring the words of God to heathen mutants. The girl opened the door to let the villagers enter. She's the one most at fault."

"Then to save your own life," said Grégoire, "you must force her to confess. She's become very disturbed since the attack – and confused, believing that she's heard from the Virgin Mary. We shall tell you what to say." Kastor outlined the story given to Cilisse.

"Give her baby to my cousin – I can't say that!" exclaimed Fabrice.

"But you had no intention of marrying her, of living with her outside this community?"

"Well, no, if every woman who gave herself to me wanted that, I'd be married several times over," said Fabrice, with a hint of pride. "And she's been contaminated by the telepathic evil. But I'd have tried to make sure she wasn't harmed, when the rest of you were taken away.

I'd have helped her to escape, possibly, to have her baby safely away from your clutches."

"Hmm," said Kastor, "but the problem is, that she's saying it was all planned by you. Unless she confirms what you say, we shall have to deal with you both in the same way."

"And… execute me?" faltered Fabrice. Grégoire and Kastor nodded solemnly. Fabrice looked nervously round the room. "She said the blame was all mine?" The interviewers nodded again. "I thought the devil had left her," said Fabrice, "but it seems she was too contaminated. If I tell her this story about the Blessed Virgin, you'll release me?"

"You'll be free of this place, but at her expense," said Grégoire, "if your conscience can take that?"

"She is nothing to me," replied Fabrice, "I have God's work to do and she's already a lost soul."

Grégoire and Kastor said that all he had to do was to confront her with the story and to ask whether the Virgin Mary had confirmed it. They took Fabrice to a cell where Cilisse was sitting miserably on a narrow bunk. "Fabrice!" she said, wiping her tears and springing up. "I knew you'd come! I had such a strange… dream, but perhaps it was because I was so afraid." Fabrice eyed her with distaste.

"You must tell them what you know, Cilisse. That you planned this attack and that you knew you'd be going to Casablanca to have the baby. It can't be mine, you know that. I only said I'd help you out of this disgrace and make sure the baby found a good family." The girl gazed at him in astonishment and burst into tears.

"But you love me, you said we'd be together…"

"I don't love you Cilisse. You use the telepathic evil, how could I love you?"

"I've given up the thought transference, you know that! We were going to be blessed by the Pope, you promised!" Kastor and

Grégoire raised their eyebrows, staring at Fabrice, filling his mind with what he'd promised to say.

"You know this is true, that Our Mary has… sent a message."

She looked aghast but flung herself at him, holding him round the waist. "No, please Fabrice… I did this for you and the baby. We'll pray for guidance."

"You confess then, that you opened that door, to let the villagers in?" said Fabrice, not responding to her embrace but not pushing her away until the required confession had been secured.

"Yes, yes, of course, I did that."

Fabrice stood back triumphantly, looking at his two interviewers. "There, you see, it was all her idea."

Cilisse stared at him in confusion, speechless under his contemptuous stare. He shrugged as he continued, "You led me into temptation. You freaks, that's what you do." He looked at his two interviewers for approval. Grégoire said coldly that quite enough had been said for their purposes. They signalled for the guard to take him out of the cell. When he was out of earshot, Kastor spoke kindly to Cilisse, "Don't worry, we won't let you be taken to Casablanca." In her distress, she communicated by thought: What will happen to me? He replied, also by thought, that she'd be taken somewhere safe.

Cilisse was put into the next transport group out of Binaires, with a guard. While the others were sent to the Woodstock Binary Centre, she found herself on a longer journey, but questions about whether it was to a special maternity unit went unanswered. On a rainy day she was marched up to the entrance of the fortified St. Anthony's treatment centre. She was put in a cell with a bible to read, which she tossed aside angrily. Why had the Virgin Mary inflicted this incarceration on her? She thought about her words about undoing the evil, weeping when she thought about how Fabrice had rejected her, while in their barn meetings, he had persuaded her of the sacred duty to submit to his desire. After a day of detention, she was relieved to be taken to see a doctor, a chubby bespectacled man who introduced himself as Dr. Asklep.

"All going well," he said cheerily after a nurse and he had examined her and confirmed the stage of pregnancy at about nine weeks. "As for your delusions, we'll ensure the best psychiatric care."

"And punishment, will I be punished?"

"Not if you volunteer for the duties we need from you here," said the doctor in a reasonable tone. She looked hopeful, thinking that possibly she would be reassigned to nursery assistant duties. "No, not with children," said the doctor, easily picking up this idea, "More along the lines of the services you gave Fabrice. I mean sex therapy, Cilisse." She stared at him in horror. The doctor gave her an oily smile.

"We sadly lack volunteers for our most severely disturbed patients. The ones who cannot stop themselves being violent, or are unpleasant to touch. Your dedication to ideals and religious conviction are just what we need to help these poor souls."

"But I'm pregnant," protested Cilisse. "You can't make me do… that, while there's a child growing inside me."

"Oh, it'll be quite safe until you're well advanced in pregnancy. We'll make sure you have an orderly present when you do your duties, to prevent any mishap."

"I won't do it!" she said angrily.

Dr. Asklep shook his head, sighing. "But you know that for us, with our mental abilities, this form of physical comfort is the only soothing remedy, when our minds are damaged and all telepathic imaging or thought transfer lost. The patients that recover will be so grateful and this simple service will help to balance the great evil you've done. You might even come to enjoy it." He glanced at her file. "I see that this Fabrice was quite rough with you, by all accounts? And he wasn't telepathic, was he? So you're really already accustomed to physically servicing those who need it…"

"I loved him. I won't do it with those disgusting patients."

"That's a very wicked way to refer to the sick, Cilisse, and such a pity."

He nodded to the nurse, who produced a large syringe with a nozzle, filled with a cloudy liquid. "In that case," continued Dr. Asklep in a forlorn tone, "other forms of punishment have been dictated for you. I had so hoped to avoid that. First, we'll need to terminate your pregnancy. It is after all, one made illegally with an outsider. Then you'll be put to hard labour. It'll be very harsh, Cilisse. It may involve helping with other types of therapy, much less pleasant than sex, I'm afraid."

"No, don't kill my baby!" Cilisse felt desperate, already in tears but now terrified. "If I… volunteer for sex therapy, my baby will be safe?"

"Yes of course. The best of care." Cilisse hung her head and nodded agreement.

"Excellent," said the doctor. "No time like the present, to start? Nurse Hart, could you take her to the special therapy room?"

She was led to a small room with a plastic covered couch standing in the middle and a sink at the side with a rubber hose, plastic gloves and towels. She looked with alarm at the leather straps hanging from the couch.

"We'll need to secure you firmly with your knees bent and ankles apart," said the female orderly. "It's then so much quicker for the patients - and for you, dearie. If you're a good girl, you won't need these restraints after a while."

Cilisse felt her resistance drain away as she was stripped naked and her wrists and ankles were placed in the leather and metal fetters, trying to console herself that this was all for her unborn son.

"I'll stay with you for the first couple," said the nurse briskly. "Lie back, relax and think how much good you're doing. You won't need to talk to them."

"Them?" whispered Cilisse, "How many?"

"Oh, just four in the first session, because we need to look after you, don't we, and the baby. Then you'll get a nice break and a meal. The orderly will wash you down and apply lubricating jelly as needed, between therapies."

Cilisse lay back, trembling, thinking of her furtive love making with Fabrice in the barn and where it had brought her.

Back in the clinic, the doctor looked up and asked Nurse Hart how Cilisse had got on.

"She struggled a lot with the first one, we had a little trouble stopping the patient hitting her to keep still. And the orderly had to use the gag when she put him off by shrieking. But she behaved a little better for the next man, even though he drooled over her rather messily. We didn't tell her about that, did we? Just as well. The hosing down helped to make her more cooperative with the third patient, but I had to leave them to it. We'll only bring in another three, after the break, as this is her first day at work. There's quite a backlog. Would it be all right to keep her volunteering daily for the first week? I'll make sure to fit in a few sessions of anti-delusional and reprogramming therapy. Then, say, one day off a week for medical checks and flexibility exercises?"

Dr. Asklep nodded. "Keep the very violent ones off her until she's got the hang of it."

"Of course," smiled the nurse. "She's so pretty and nicely formed, it'll be a real tonic for the patients."

"Give her frequent breaks at first and extra rations for the baby – and showers instead of hose downs after the first couple of days," said the doctor. "Although she's lucky not to have to work all night, after what she did."

"How long do you want full restraints?"

"Depending on compliance," said the doctor, "and progress with the re-education and anti-delusional therapy. It's better for the patients if she appears willing, without the straps. Meanwhile, check if she struggles with the others, after the break. We don't want the patients to be distressed, naturally. She'll need to learn that this therapy is a skill, to make them more contented and easier to manage. If she's obstinate, just leave her in fully tightened restraints during breaks, that should be enough. Keep me informed."

Nurse Hart checked her watch for when she needed to return, nodding with satisfaction as she focused on the treatment room and visualised their new volunteer therapist lying obediently as she was hosed down again, although they would have to do something about her miserable expression and all that whimpering. She signalled to the orderly to make sure Cilisse understood she should smile a lot more, for the patients' sake.

"What will happen to her baby?" asked Nurse Hart.

"Taken away to a nursery after birth, of course. She won't see him. She'll never be allowed near children again."

"But we won't tell her that yet?"

"No, it'd be wiser not to. After recovering from the birth, she'll soon be ready to return to therapy duties and we won't have the baby to worry about. It'll probably be quite a while before she gives up hope that her performance won't give her access to the baby – and by then…"

"…She'll understand it's a valued duty to the community," said the nurse, approvingly. "She's young. Years of service ahead."

"It's good that we're so compassionate, it isn't really a punishment at all," agreed Dr. Asklep, "It's a stroke of luck for us, getting this unexpected resource for the severely deranged or disfigured patients. If she makes progress, we may even be able to free up the volunteers and give her those who are only slightly damaged or on the way to recovery. We can use that as a kind of carrot, if she gets too discouraged in these early weeks."

"When her delusions are under control, she'll realise how fortunate she is to be allowed to live, simply lying on her back most of the day."

Nurse Hart added a thought image of the patients damaged in the attack at Binaires. Quite, agreed the doctor silently, returning to his pile of case notes. Binary members were conditioned from birth to understand that treachery against the organization, particularly their babies or to their telepathic skills, was a heinous crime for which no punishment was too severe.

7

CASSANDRA

I didn't know about Cilisse's fate until much later. Meanwhile, I heard that Fabrice was locked in a cell, instead of being released as he expected. No amount of shouting achieved any attention. The telepaths had more important matters to deal with. The emergency committee had decided that after evacuating the remaining staff that afternoon, the centre would need to be destroyed. The missing men and the tales spreading round the village of secret tunnels meant that the police would be back, despite finding nothing on their initial inspection. The plan was to make the explosion look like sabotage, with what was left of the bodies of the two intruders and Fabrice being found next to detonating equipment. When Kastor outlined this scheme to me in the villa, I was appalled.

"Isn't there another way, couldn't we just leave the centre and let those men be found there – alive?"

"So that they could inform on us? A bad idea. The centre has already been wired throughout for this purpose. A fierce fire will destroy the parts of the structure that might escape the explosion. It's important that it just looks like an old nuclear bunker, possibly larger than the police were told, but with areas that had been closed off for some time. Hopefully it'll seem plausible that the charming owners of Villa de la Belle Mer didn't know the extent of the underground buildings."

I sighed, accepting his argument.

"This attack doesn't just affect Binaires," said Kastor, "It's a threat to our whole network. We'll be the last to leave and shall have to face the police when they come. Grégoire will be the only one left at Villa de la Belle Mer, telling them that he had to send his family away because of threats from the village."

"And we'll go – where, after that?"

"Back to our apartment in England."

With the children in the communal nursery, I thought bitterly and he nodded sadly. Because of our fairly frequent return for work assignments, our apartment had remained allotted to us, but it was far too small to accommodate the five infants, six if Grace was to join us. In any case, such an arrangement would not be permitted, even if space allowed.

"You could come to the USA," said Helen, entering the room and tossing her nun's veil distastefully onto a chair. "I don't mean live with Alexander and me, but with the money from selling the villa and the rest we've all put aside, we could find a couple of houses nearby – a mini Binaires."

"Not looking forward to looking after your children on your own, then?" asked Kastor, with a cynical smile.

"Oh, I'm quite happy for them to join the Woodstock Binaries nursery for now," said Helen. "Until we're all settled."

If Captain Parfait and Lieutenant Jourdain visited the Villa Dufour after the explosion, they might link Helen to the unusual arrival of the nun in the village. So it was agreed that Helen should join the exodus of Binaires members. She was put on the last private jet to England, from where she'd catch a plane to join Alexander in the U.S.

"You'll be all right, Cass," she said as she left, "You know how to set up a panic or distraction, now."

The remaining telepaths and the children were going to have to be smuggled out without going through border controls, in case the police started checking at air or ferry ports. A Binary yacht was standing by, with new documents in case British authorities were notified of possible fugitives.

"This is such a disaster," murmured Kastor, "all because of a foolish, deluded girl. We can't afford for outsiders to find out about us. You know what that would mean."

"All these deaths and injuries… There must be another way," I said, "If we get away, I'll find one."

"When we get away," replied Kastor, "we'll have more time to talk about it."

The explosion woke us up that night. Concrete and rubble had been placed next to the exit tunnel from the cellar, to seal it off permanently, similarly at the farmhouse. After the expected visit from the police to investigate a possible terrorist act, the few remaining villa residents and staff would leave immediately. The aim was to deal with any police presence by thought work, with hopefully no further necessary violence. Kastor telephoned the police department to tell them they'd heard a loud bang. Residents on the outskirts of the village had already notified the police. Fire engines rushed to the Binaires site, where they found Grégoire desperately trying to stop the flames reaching Villa de la Belle Mer.

In a state of agitation he spoke of the threats that had driven out his family. Extinguishing the fire on the main site was hampered by a series of smaller explosions, which made the police suspect arson. The Villa de la Belle Mer was relatively unharmed and the police asked Grégoire to come back to the station to give them some more details. He agreed, saying he must first fetch his papers and some valuables from the villa. Lieutenant Jourdain asked a junior police officer to accompany him, but just as they were approaching the villa, Grégoire dashed ahead, as if in panic. The officer heard a loud scream and Grégoire disappeared down a hole that had opened up in the nearby rubble. The young officer called a fireman over and they peered into the hole. They could see only swirling dust but heard a call for help, followed by a gasp and then silence. The hole appeared to be full of unstable debris and the men looked at each other, shaking their heads at the possibility that anyone could have survived the fall into it. The portable Doppler equipment detected no life signs.

"We'll have to call in more help," said the fireman, "There may be a risk of further explosions. The whole area seems to have been wired up and the fire is spreading."

I used remote viewing to catch this from the villa, relaying it to Kastor who showed no remorse for the men that had been eliminated in this way. But I too was feeling very angry about the attack. I was going to miss France and our charmed life there. I sensed that it would be two days before charred remains of three bodies were discovered in the art room just below ground level, surrounded by detonation equipment. The two intruders and Fabrice were all were known to have been in the group that attacked the site a few nights previously. One body was that of a builder with a police record for armed burglary and use of explosives. This was a lucky coincidence for the Binaires cover-up plan.

At the Villa Dufour, we prepared to travel only with a few essentials. I picked up that the police were on their way and restlessly wandered out into our small garden. The gardener, cook and housekeeper had left. If asked, the 'Dufours' would say they had simply run off. The nannies were with the children, trying to continue a semblance of routine, while Kastor was making last minute checks to ensure that we left no evidence of links to Binaires or to Binaries. It was a warm still night, but the smell of smoke from the Binaires site was drifting over.

I looked round at our beautiful garden, full of flowers, nodding peacefully in the moonlight. I went over to the swing seat, idly pushing it and remembering happier evenings with Leo and the twins sitting with me. I stared sadly at the villa, knowing it was unlikely we would see it again after tonight. Then I felt a tingling sensation in the back of my head and spun round. In the twilight, I saw Captain Edouard Parfait walking down the path.

"Madame Dufour," he said, sitting next to me on the seat. I sensed curiosity rather than suspicion but closed my thoughts nonetheless. This was now instinctive, even in the presence of ordinary humans.

"Captain Parfait," I said, in return, noting with surprise that he was interested in me as a woman as well as a suspect in all this chaos.

"What's happening over there?" I said in a distressed voice. "Can we help?"

"Not unless you can solve the mystery of all this, Madame," he said, staring at me intently. I recaptured an image of Grégoire falling and asked if the Durantes – their name for outsiders – were all right.

"We're not sure," said Edouard Parfait. "You know them quite well, I suppose?"

"Socially, yes, And our son goes for a few art sessions with Amélie, Madame Durante. This is all such a shock. I don't understand – do you think the villagers did this? Why would they hate the Durantes so much?"

"Oh, I think you do understand," said Edouard Parfait. "Perhaps you could suggest a few reasons?"

"The baby story, that's wicked," I said. "I suppose rumours like that start up about people who keep themselves to themselves, like the Durantes."

"And like you," murmured the captain. I looked into his mind, sensing no direct menace. More than that, I realised with a start: he was at least slightly telepathic. I felt the wave of shared mental force that telepaths experience when communicating and shuttered down my thoughts with inner alarm. I had signalled to Kastor when the police captain arrived but he had indicated that I should stall him, if possible, to delay him coming into the house.

"The villagers seem to have this notion," said Edouard Parfait casually, watching my reaction, "that the Durantes, and their household, are part of a secret organization of people who can read thoughts – and that they sometimes take babies, to train them as telepathic spies."

I raised my eyebrows, shrugging. "Do you have evidence of that extraordinary idea?"

"As far as your family are concerned, no. Your documents are in order, although there may need to be further checks. This is a very serious incident. There'll be a thorough investigation."

In a closed thought, I wondered how well the false identities would stand up to a very diligent check of records. I radiated innocence and understandable dismay at the incident.

"Perhaps I should get to the point," murmured the captain. "I think you're a telepath, Madame. And your son, Leander."

"My son?' I exclaimed, realising belatedly that I should have immediately denied his statement about me.

"I too can sense thoughts. When we came to the villa yesterday and your son stood up to greet us so politely, I detected that he was asking himself why we were there and I saw an image, of a British policeman, as if in a story book."

"You wouldn't need telepathy to deduce that a five year old boy was puzzled by policemen coming to the house," I said, as dismissively as I dared.

"I'm not your enemy, Madame. I'm being honest with you. My colleagues don't know that I can occasionally detect thoughts. It's something I've known since childhood. But as you probably know, it doesn't pay to share knowledge of this ability with others."

"Some people call it intuition, others lucky guesses," I observed. I was trying to assess if my inclination to trust this man was because I was naturally trusting, or whether he was a potential ally.

"And you Madame, what do you call it?" As we sat on the seat, it moved gently and I wondered at this surreal conversation, with the captain in no apparent hurry.

"I was a very dreamy child," I said, "and I grew up to be very intuitive, although it didn't seem much help to me. I suppose it could be seen by some as a type of telepathy."

"But you didn't grow up in an organization of telepaths?" He smiled again. I shook my head, laughing and noting his fixed stare, with his expressive attractive eyes.

"No, I grew up with my mother, my parents were divorced. Just a normal English life with ordinary jobs."

"But now, you live as Sylvia Dufour – that's not your real name, I think."

I did not deny this, saying instead, "We had nothing to do with this incident." I risked sharing this with him as a thought, with an image of waking up startled in the night. He took a quick breath; I noted how he seemed to have picked up most of this.

"You can trust me," he signalled back and in astonishment, I silently asked why.

"I've always wanted to meet someone like myself, a person who could communicate like this," he said, hesitantly. I sensed genuine emotion. "There have been other rumours of a secret organization," he continued, "but if the site near Villa de la Belle Mer contained one, it was very well concealed. I suppose there was a major breach of security, leading to the villagers finding out?"

I was silent and he said, "I believe there's enough suspicion to take you and your husband away for interview. We might not be able to prove anything. I imagine you have ways of dealing with interview techniques. But then there'd be the check on your identities…"

I looked at him in silent appeal. "Her eyes touch the heart", he was thinking, for he had not learned to close off thoughts. I wished, in a well shuttered part of my mind, that Helen was sitting there in my place. Helen would probably have seduced him on the spot and put all thought of arresting us out of his thoughts. He said slowly, his hand on the bench seat very near mine, "Or alternatively, I could help you to escape, if you intend that. I feel that whatever your connection with the Villa de la Belle Mer and its strange underground buildings, you're not a criminal, a baby stealer."

"No, absolutely not that," I said.

"I suppose it's good, to be in contact with other telepaths," he said, a little wistfully. "So if such an organization existed, it would be a place for people with this… talent. They'd have to live apart, because their abilities would frighten people."

"That would make sense…" I murmured, unable to conceal my distress, knowing that the captain was playing a game with me. Perhaps he knew all about Binaires. But instead of pushing me further, he smiled sympathetically.

"I'll help you to get away, on one condition."

I looked at him questioningly.

"Well, perhaps two conditions. The first is that I'd like to meet some of these other telepaths, to see if my occasional experiences would develop into something more."

"This is all nonsense…" I stuttered. He responded with an angry image of a police interrogation. A skilled natural telepath, I thought: maybe he is genuine and not making a trap.

Edouard Parfait sensed I was giving in. "So, admit you're a telepath and that you and your companions need to escape. Then I'll help you, in return for finding out more about the organization. For myself, not for the authorities."

"It could be dangerous," I faltered, wishing that Kastor would arrive. "The others, well, they might feel a need to defend themselves against you."

"You could reassure them. My tentative plan is to use my police car to get you to some meeting point. That is presumably what you've arranged? But you have no car?"

"We have a small car, but the chauffeur left with it," I said. I felt that I had conveyed enough without explaining that the enhanced telepathy made it unsafe to drive cars.

"It'll be much safer if I take you, than if you try to call a taxi. There are officers all around, looking for people who might have come from the site of the explosion. As you know, three men are now missing from the village."

"You mentioned another condition?" I asked.

"Just a kiss, Madame."

"I only kiss my husband."

"Ah, so you're definitely English. In France, we kiss each other all the time."

"On the cheek," I said, "but I don't think you meant that."

"I would just like to know, how it feels to kiss another telepath. And you're a very attractive one, Madame. It's not such a difficult condition, for your escape from these terrible events?"

"With the children?"

"It will be a tight fit, but yes of course, all of you in the villa.

My car is just outside. I'd turn off the radio communications. My vehicle would not be apprehended." He took my hand and kissed it with a gallant flourish. "I think you trust me."

I signalled up to Kastor that he should join us, that I was having to be quite persuasive with this police captain. I felt very vulnerable, unable to suppress an attraction to him. His warm brown eyes were gazing at me with intelligence and kindness. I nodded consent to the kiss and he gently held my face. I shared thoughts of friendship and trust, which made him sigh. As our lips touched I felt a wave of emotion, not as strong as with Kastor, but sufficient to make me drop my guard. Our lips seemed to melt together as we kissed and a flow of pleasurable, tingling current raced through us. In a rush of images, I saw him sitting pensively, lonely in his life outside, while he sensed my compassion and images of laughing and playing with my children. We drew apart and Edouard Parfait closed his eyes.

"Thank you. If only we could have met, before your marriage…"

We looked up and Kastor stood before us, having approached while I was so preoccupied with Edouard Parfait. I felt him fighting down a tidal wave of jealousy.

"Monsieur Dufour, I assure you of my honourable intentions," said Edouard Parfait, as though he was addressing the angry father of a beloved daughter.

"He just wanted to kiss another telepath," I said lamely, meanwhile transmitting Edouard's plan and that I felt he could be trusted, with the alternative being probable arrest.

"My wife feels we should trust you," commented Kastor, poker faced, "but she trusts very easily. As I've just seen."

"What do you have to lose?" said Edouard Parfait. "If I show signs of betraying you, I expect you'd deal with that." He transmitted a thought that he wanted to help us and Kastor stared at him with less hostility.

"Can we trust you?" he thought back and the police captain nodded.

"I don't want to expose you," said Edouard, "because I hope that one day I shall meet others like you."

"My wife is optimistic that a day will come when everyone will accept these differences from other humans. The attack on the Durantes' home suggests that this day is far in the future."

The police captain nodded, sadly. "I shall try to put them off the scent. You're really French, Monsieur?"

"I was born in France, but lived here only for my early years."

"A French telepath," murmured Edouard. "So there must be others…"

"When we get away from here, I could contact you to arrange testing of your abilities. I know of places that do that."

The police captain shared a thought of thanks, giving Kastor his card. Considering what had just happened, I was surprised at Kastor's warm manner, but then thought coldly that recruiting telepaths was always a priority for the Binaries.

Kastor told me to fetch the others, who were already on full alert. When we came into the garden, I could tell Edouard was wondering how we would all fit into the car, possibly not knowing that the five children – and two nannies – were still in the villa. But true to his promise, Edouard led us to his car, while Kastor went back to get his briefcase and to secure the house.

8

CASSANDRA

While we waited for Kastor, I was alarmed to see the police captain take out his mobile phone. He sent an image of reassurance. He smiled with apparent surprise that this seemed to be getting easier now he was with other sentient humans. Aloud he said, "If spotted, I'll tell them I'm taking you all for interview. That would explain any possible sighting of you in the car."

The nannies and I crammed into the back with the infants, while Leo would sit in the front with Kastor.

"We're breaking several laws, as well as those on seatbelts," murmured Edouard conscientiously but I sensed his excitement at joining us on this adventure. He sent polite greetings by thought to each of the nannies, who giggled in surprise to meet a telepathic police officer.

Kastor joined us after a couple of minutes. He had signalled Olivier, suggesting a reconnoitre closer to the yacht since we now had transport. He also said that we could trust the telepathic police captain, at least for now.

"No choice, I suppose. But police are everywhere," signalled Olivier in return. He proposed meeting at a quiet junction at the docks. This had trees on three sides, with a derelict building on one corner. Edouard parked by the one of the dense clump of trees and we piled out quickly. We had passports for entering the UK, while the police captain could produce the passports for our French identities at the station, reducing suspicion that we had left France. Then Edouard paused, looking at me.

"Au revoir, Madame," he murmured bending to kiss my cheek but Kastor pulled me away.

"I don't think so," he said firmly.

"He wanted to meet other telepaths," I transmitted and Kastor thought back, "Well, he has."

If Edouard regretted this lost opportunity to meet more of the group, he also understood the need to leave the area quickly. His car was likely to be spotted by other officers.

We peered through the trees, all our senses alert to the presence of non-telepaths. But we detected only the approach of Olivier Cerberus. We had to navigate two roads before reaching where the yacht was moored. I was grateful for the strict Binary training for our obedient children, trotting along in silence. One of the nannies held Grace in a baby sling, producing a small bottle of feed to keep the baby fairly quiet as we moved towards the harbour, making small dashes to each dark area. We passed a drunk sitting in a doorway, who waved a bottle cheerfully at us. In return we filled his thoughts with pleasant amnesia so that all he would possibly remember was a couple of fellow drinkers enjoying the warm night.

At the harbour, we sensed a police officer waiting in his car, watching the boats.

"I'll deal with it," said Olivier, making his way cautiously towards the rear of the car. He produced a bottle of wine from his rucksack and opened it, spilling some on the cobbles, with obvious regret. Then he swayed nearer to the car, singing an old French drinking song at the top of his voice, "*Ma femme est morte, je suis libre…*" The officer got out of the car.

"Good evening, officer," said Olivier, "Would you like to join me?" He sang another couple of lines from the song, moving to the side of the car where the officer would not see the party boarding the yacht. The officer told him irritably to get off home.

"To my wife?" said Olivier, adding some choice swear words. The officer warned the drunk that he'd arrest him for being disorderly if he didn't move away.

"All right," slurred Olivier, putting a finger to his mouth to show that he guessed a secret reason for the officer to be there. "Always happy to help our brave gendarmes."

He lurched towards the harbour buildings. On the yacht, the crew prepared to set sail, while I watched anxiously, wondering how Olivier would be able to board unseen and how the yacht could also escape unnoticed. I signalled to Olivier that I would try to stage a small panic. If only Helen was with us! But she had said that the second time would be easier.

The yacht was moored at the end of a short narrow pier, with the harbour curving away behind the promontory. I took a deep breath, remembering how Helen and I had focused, but then I had been following her lead. Concentrating on the part of the harbour out of sight, beyond the parked police car, I projected the illusion of a crash, with shouting and sounds of heavy shoes running. The police officer leapt from his car again, hearing the loud retort and successive banging noises. After a moment's hesitation, he ran to see where the disturbance was coming from. I increased the noises and instilled a sense of panic in the policeman. He had to find out what was going on, feeling it could be connected with the explosion and fire still raging further along the coast. This gave Olivier the chance to run along the pier and board the yacht.

While I kept up the illusion of screams and other calls to keep quiet, the police officer suspected that criminals were involved. He ran behind the corner, while the yacht's engine started to take us out of the harbour. We had to work without lights, using the shipboard navigation equipment to navigate shallow areas of the coastal water. There was some distance to go before the yacht would be just a dim shape in the distance. I filled the police officer's mind with the impression of a raging fire and more cries seeming to come from one of the boathouses. He ran along the row of buildings, looking desperately for the source of the commotion. When he returned to radio the news of this possible incident, he glanced around the quiet harbour, puzzled. "Wasn't there a boat moored just there?" he thought, looking at the empty stretch of mooring.

I was exhausted from the effort of making the illusion, but Kastor came to my side, picking up the police officer's thought and transmitting the message, "No, of course not. There was no boat there," into the officer's mind.

Tired as I was, I needed to check up on Edouard Parfait and what he was going to say to his colleagues. He was remarkably easy to channel, something I would have to conceal from Kastor, as it could mean we had telepathic affinity. Binaries were intensely jealous of partners having mind contact, outside the confines of work. I could see him clearly, speaking on the phone and saying he had lost the family because he was on his own. Apparently he had been ordered to bring the family to the police station. His rapid French was a strain, but I picked up that he had interviewed us thoroughly and that I was terrified of a further attack, saying I would be going to relatives in Nice. He assured the police commander that he had taken our passports.

I couldn't pick up much of what the Commander was saying on the other end of the phone, but sensed it was about the owner of the Villa de la Belle Mer being buried in rubble. Edouard asked about life signs and I guessed he was told there were none. For I knew that Grégoire had staged this apparent tumble into death. While the observers around the hole were filled with the idea that they had seen him fall, he slipped round the other side of the villa and made his escape, reaching the yacht well before our group arrived there.

In the crowded saloon cabin, our party toasted his health and our escape so far. Olivier grinned at me, saying, "We could have just eliminated that police officer. But your distraction was impressive."

"And saved a life," I said, sensing that keeping outsider police officers alive was not a top priority for the security chief. Then we talked about whether we'd done enough to prevent the story of telepaths and a baby nursery sticking.

"Our aim," said Olivier, "is that even if they conclude there was some kind of secret organization there, they don't think of us. A labyrinth dating from the Second World War, built by the Nazis and then extended and adapted as a nuclear bunker. We're pretty sure the equipment and identifiers have all been destroyed, but of course they'll eventually find that the remnants are more recent."

Olivier contacted the British coast guards, notifying them of our yacht travelling up the Thames to London. With luck, we'd reach St. Katherine's Dock by the Tower of London by morning. I was asked if I could predict any further problems on the journey to the Binaries. Their confidence in my skills was reassuring, but I had to explain that it could never be certain when I was involved in a future event. But to put their minds at rest, I said that I'd had a brief vision of us all having a meal in a Binary restaurant. I hoped that this idea conjured up by my strange prophetic imagination would turn out to be true.

9

Our party of French tourists, with our British friends and children, passed through the UK entry checks without incident and I sent a grateful thought to Edouard, guessing he had successfully dissuaded the police authorities from asking for special surveillance on the British side of the Channel. I could not tell if he had received it, for despite a surge in his telepathic skills from meeting me and the others, he was most unlikely to be able to transmit over such a long distance. Picking up my message, Kastor shot a thought of disapproval.

"He was just satisfying curiosity," I sent back, with an image of the kiss, which appeared very brief and chaste in my version. Too bad that Kastor had seen some of this embrace. There was no opportunity to discuss this further, as our group was distributed between three cars waiting to take us to Woodstock. On the way, I kept seeing an image of the dark fort of St. Anthony's psychiatric hospital. I mentioned this to Kastor, who said that perhaps I was thinking about the two victims of the attack.

"But I keep seeing myself there," I murmured and he squeezed my hand, knowing how much I had feared going there, when I first entered the Woodstock labyrinth.

After refreshments and dispatching the children to the nursery wing, the emergency group reconvened with the addition of senior Woodstock Binaries. There was great interest in the role played by the police captain, particularly when Kastor murmured that training was a possibility. I sensed that Kastor did not want to dwell on Edouard, with the perceptive Theodora and Gaston at the table, but Gaston smiled across at me.

"Another talented natural telepath, do you think?"

"He's never met telepaths like us before. He could have betrayed us…"

"Still could," said Grégoire. "But at least we got away."

Wayland East, head of Binaries administration, said we needed to consider the strategy for managing this disaster, as well as promptly informing the international board.

"We can't reopen the French centre, even with a relocation," said Olivier Cerberus, subdued in the knowledge that lax security had contributed to the centre being discovered.

"If I may speak," I said hesitantly, ignoring a warning thought from Kastor. He was only too aware of my ideas for reform. But Wayland smiled benevolently and Gaston said, "We should always listen to our prophetess. Surely we know that, now."

"Well," I said, "I believe the strategy should involve making some major changes. For example, we need to produce more babies of our own."

"You've shown an enthusiasm for that, certainly," murmured Gaston, glancing at Kastor.

"But babies are always encouraged here," said Amélie. She stole a fond look at Manes, the surveillance administrator. Well, that's a start, I reflected, in a shuttered off thought.

"Yes, encouraged, but not enough. The birth rate is very low in our community. We perhaps need a programme of more physical contact. And also more parental interest in the babies when they arrive."

I felt the shocked thoughts of many around the table. Most of the Binary telepaths considered physical sex as an occasional weakness to be indulged only rarely. As for parenting, they had all been brought up to understand the children needed expert training, together, from birth.

"It may be wise to cut back on the baby rescuing programme, until all this dies down. So perhaps Cassandra has a point," said Olivier.

"The baby rescues need to be stopped immediately, world wide," said Gaston. "However carefully you've destroyed evidence at Binaires, the police and government security operatives may well consider monitoring pregnancies. The antenatal twin trials should also be suspended. Current ones should continue with no rescuing."

"The outsiders would call our rescues 'abductions', would they not?" said Theodora, who rarely spoke at meetings so all heads turned. "Gaston is right. All rescues must be halted."

I brimmed with enthusiasm. "I'd be happy to run some classes, to get Binary members more interested in making babies."

Kastor stared down at the table, trying to conceal his great disapproval from everyone but me.

"You mean, turn us all into sex therapists?" said Gaston, enjoying Kastor's discomfort.

"No. I mean teaching them about loving relationships," I said, indignantly. I would like to have banned sex therapy altogether. "They wouldn't just be volunteers, doing a duty for the organization. They'd be taking a personal interest." I paused, seeing a sudden vision of Binary family groups playing in the Askeys grounds, at least those well shielded from prying eyes, drones or planes overhead. Theodora was watching me closely. "We should run parenting classes too," I ran on, "so they'd see the point of having more contact with their children."

"But the communal nurseries are essential," said Grégoire.

"We can keep those. I'd only envisage more frequent contact by parents. My children's development hasn't suffered from my seeing them often."

Kastor thought about how much he'd enjoyed getting to know Leo, Tamsin and Florence.

"What Cassandra means," he said, "is that our life at Villa Dufour has shown that a compromise is possible. The current crisis makes a change in policy essential. I believe we all understand that."

"Good," murmured Theodora, as she noted a nod from Wayland. "An early decision."

The next practical matter was accommodation for the new arrivals. Some would occupy the guest wing, others would need to share with Binary residents temporarily. Olivier took Gaston's spare room, while Amélie accepted Manes' kind offer to stay in his. Remembering seeing Amélie's photograph on Manes' office desk, I smiled. Kastor and I were not asked to put up any of the refugees, since it would be unthinkable for telepaths not to have a bedroom to themselves and we only had two. Also, we were insisting on daily visits to our apartment by our children and Helen's twin boys. Even with a nanny in attendance, this would be too much noise and disruption for guest telepaths to put up with.

For the next two weeks or so, apart from the ban on baby rescues, Binary life seemed to be returning to normal. With the discovery of the remains of the three men at Binaires and evidence of setting up an explosion, the French police seemed to be going along with the idea of sabotage, inspired by the Moroccan zealot in the nearby village. Kastor and I felt that Captain Edouard Parfait was still helping us, possibly by downplaying the tales of telepathy and babies.

Meetings to discuss strategy and developments continued and I attended one about two weeks after escaping from Villa Dufour. The pregnancy and parenting classes remained a contentious issue, despite some support for my idea from Theodora, Kastor and even Gaston. During this particular meeting, Wayland was outlining plans to expand the Binary centre in Devon, so that the French Binaires could restart work there until it was deemed safe enough to rebuild one in their home country. The French were arguing that possibly Quebec would be preferable, when the meeting was interrupted by a silent knock at the door. Dr. Hagen Philips came in, looking very agitated.

"We're in conference," said Wayland sternly, but Dr. Philips waved a hand, transmitting the thought that there was an emergency.

"I've just heard from St. Anthony's. One of the mind explorers is trapped inside the mind-damaged guard from Binaires. The guard fell asleep and the mind repairer is now unrousable."

I went pale and glanced at Kastor, sharing the memory of how I had been nearly sucked into his subconscious when he started to fall asleep during one of my mind repair explorations.

"When did this happen?" I asked anxiously.

"A few minutes ago. Dr. Foucoe wants to speak with you urgently."

I left the room with Dr. Philips to over to the medical unit.

"Has Dr. Foucoe tried to go in to rescue the mind explorer?" I asked.

"No," said Hagen Philips, sharing a significant thought of why Dr. Foucoe was reluctant. "She wants you to try." My heart raced with alarm.

Dr. Clytemnestra Foucoe's reluctance was based on her lack of experience at mind repair, despite having received accolades at a Binary medical conference for developing the technique. The method had been completely my inspiration, initially opposed by Clytemnestra, but Kastor's rapid and complete recovery had vindicated this approach. With my help, the clinical staff had initiated a training programme in mind repair. This had already revolutionised the treatment of mind damaged Binaries. I wasn't angry at Dr. Foucoe taking the credit. I was not a doctor and had no wish to appear at medical conferences.

With Theodora's assistance I had devised out ways of identifying the telepaths most suited to work as mind repairers. As head of assessment at Binaries, Theodora was adept at developing suitable tests and training regimes. When Dr. Philips and I reached the medical unit, I was put straight through to Dr. Foucoe on the medical hotline. We both could send thoughts at long distance, but accuracy was essential in this case, hence the need for telephone backup. I knew the psychiatrist well enough to use her shortened name, Clea, but avoided Kastor's nickname of 'Clyppie', which would certainly irritate the proud woman. On this occasion, I had no opportunity to use either name as the psychiatrist spoke abruptly into the phone.

"Cassandra, can you come up straight away? We'll lose the guard unless someone can go in, someone with expert skills."

I sensed how humiliating this was for Clea. But entering a damaged mind was dangerous. The guard would not be able to assist the explorer to escape, even when awake. Even with the techniques I had developed, they were not tested on delving to the deep, subconscious layers of the mind. I thought of the shadowy beings from Kastor's subconscious, who had wanted to draw me in, to absorb me into their depths.

"It may be too late, Clea."

"We've woken up the guard and we're keeping him alert with drugs. All I'm asking is for you to take a quick look, to assess if there's any hope of recovery."

I was silent, thinking of the dangers and how Kastor would not want me to go.

"A helicopter is waiting to bring you directly here. Normally it lands at Lochinstoun, with the rest of the journey by car and ferry, as you know."

I understood that they kept helicopter landings to a minimum, to avoid attracting attention to the activities at St. Anthony's, located on a small island off the north west coast of Scotland.

"Please come, Cassandra. I'd be so grateful - and we really need you…"

I sighed. "All right, but I won't go in alone. Select the best mind repairer from your team and prepare them."

When I put the phone down, Hagen Philips expressed his gratitude. He was the first doctor that I'd met when I literally fell into Binaries and he had looked after my injuries. Now he and his bond mate, Nurse Phyllis Williams, were friends.

"If you're really grateful, there's something I'd like you to do," I said, with a persuasive wave of thought. He sent a questioning thought in reply.

"The baby rescue programme is suspended because of the crisis. So you and Phyllis need to work on increasing the Binary birth rate. Starting tonight, preferably."

The images made my meaning clear and he smiled. "Phyllis has been thinking about going for pregnancy counselling. I wasn't sure…"

"Forget the counselling," I said. "This is an emergency."

"If you make that a condition for going to St. Anthony's, we'll do our best," said Dr. Philips with a grin. A silent knock at the clinic door alerted us that an officer had arrived to escort me to the helicopter port.

"I'll need to go back to Askeys, first, to collect a few things," I said firmly.

10

I signalled for Kastor to meet me at the apartment. He agreed immediately to leave the meeting.

"You can refuse to go," he said, as I hurriedly packed a case. The urgency was too great to wait for the household staff to assist.

"Clyppie can't do it, you know that," I replied, "I've said I'll only go in with another mind repairer. I won't take unnecessary risks."

"You always take risks," he murmured, "but I need to know if you can see a good outcome."

"It's a forlorn hope for the mind explorer," I said sadly, "but I'd never forgive myself if I didn't attempt to save him, or her – they haven't given me details."

"I didn't mean the explorer, or the patient," said Kastor, "I meant a good outcome for you, that you'll be safe. Can you see into the future about that?"

I stopped packing and sat on the bed, trying to focus on the next few days. It was so much harder to see accurately into my own future. Theodora had explained that, although they did not understand the rules, there appeared to be a natural barrier to making predictions about oneself. While I sat in thought, I received images of a ward at St.

Anthony's and other mind pictures of the area featuring cars, trains and stormy weather. But as for what would happen there, it was just a confused melée of possibilities.

"I honestly don't know," I said finally, knowing that Kastor was sitting by me, nervously waiting to hear good news. "I think the mind repair will go OK - for me at least – but I saw a storm, a lot of anger, and a train, for some reason."

"So long as you come back safely, I don't care how many storms you cause," said Kastor, smiling.

"Who, me, make a storm? I could only do that at the villa with Helen's help."

"Well, if someone else makes a storm or enrages you, I feel sorry for them," said Kastor. "When you're angry, there's really no stopping you."

I got up to complete the packing. When Kastor saw me slip a bundle of money notes into my shoulder bag, he was surprised.

"You won't need money at St. Anthony's."

"This is my secret stash. Helen advised I should always have some, if I had to go out on a mission."

"You could always sell the earrings," said Kastor, looking at the flash of diamonds and green crystal, his parting gift to me before the disastrous mission to Cadiz.

"Never, nor our bonding rings." I held up my hand to look at the hand made gold ring, with its filigree pattern of ones and zeros, to represent the Binaries.

"I'd get you some new jewellery. Promise me you'll sell it if you need to. Anything to get back here."

Kastor was now standing close, emanating thoughts of love and safety. I brought my hands up to nearly touch his, feeling our combined electromagnetic force and we took a little plunge into each other's minds, emerging with regret. We looked out towards the site of the helicopter pad in the grounds. It was time to go.

I had never flown in a helicopter and despite my worries, gazed down in excitement at the countryside beneath. I filed memories of the landscape for use in mental flying and making visions for group meditations. As we flew over the Moray Firth, I thought of plane and helicopter crashes that I'd seen in dreams, always unhappy to find that these were predictions. But I felt no danger from a crash on this flight. The pilot pointed to a small island in the distance: St. Anthony's Isle. There was a mist surrounding the island and the fortified building that I called the dark fort. There was a landing stage for boats and a small rocky area around the fort, sloping down to the sea. The locals knew it was a private mental institution of some kind, but it never caused them any trouble and they were grateful that the management of its inmates did not include care in the community. The helicopter landed in a large courtyard in the centre of the granite buildings. As I stepped out, Dr. Foucoe approached, dispensing with greetings in her impatience to get me up to the mind repair unit.

"He's still awake, come with me."

"I need the loo, a wash and some food," I said. "I'm in no state to do mind entry until we've sorted that. But get the mind repair team along to the dining room – I guess you've selected someone to go in with me?"

"Yes, Ariadne Tartaros, she's our best deep explorer."

"Tartaros," I murmured. I knew much more about mythology now I was living with Binaries, "A place in the underworld – and a deity too?"

"We can discuss gods later, Cassandra. This is an emergency, yes?"

I let a thought escape, "You should have been able to deal with this, taking such pride in your techniques – and receiving a lot of praise," and noted that Dr. Foucoe had the grace to blush. But then I said more kindly, "I won't waste time. Let's get inside." An officer took my case to deliver it to the visitors' wing. I liked what I sensed about Ariadne Tartaros: competent, brave and organised. We discussed the difficulties already experienced in the mind of the guard, Marc, who had suffered a quick but deep invasion by the mind probe.

"His mind structure is straightforward, nothing too imaginative," said Ariadne, "but in addition to the puncture wounds there's a large cavity going through about four layers. Ingrid was working on the second layer when he went to sleep and we're assuming she was so confident that she hadn't yet secured her ladder for the ascent."

I shook my head in despair at this carelessness. The training included strong emphasis on safety procedures. "But she'd made one, surely?"

"There was one already there, I left it on my last entry. But I had to leave quickly. It wasn't very stable, but even if it had fallen from its upper grips, all she had to do was attach it to a column."

"We can prepare more mind ladders, before we consider going to that layer, but the question is, will Ingrid still be there?"

"She'd have been using a harness," replied Ariadne. "I hope she attached that to one of the structures when she sensed Marc losing consciousness."

"Or she may have just rushed for the ladder, to get up to a safer level," I said, frowning. "We'll have to see." I wondered what Marc's subconscious beings were like and whether they would have already absorbed the lost explorer.

St. Anthony's interior was not as forbidding as might have been expected from its grim outer appearance. In many ways it was just like a hospital in normal human world, with wards, treatment centres and communal rooms. The architecture was mainly Victorian gothic, but the decoration and fittings were modern. Dr. Foucoe led me down a series of corridors. At a point transected by another corridor, I sensed screaming and anguish coming from a gloomy passageway leading off one of the corridors.

"That's one of the closed wards, for very disturbed patients," said Dr. Foucoe. "Such wards have to be kept locked, as many of them are violent."

"Are they patients with traumatic mind damage?"

"No, mostly the damage is from medical conditions, or severe mental illness. Some are paranoid schizophrenics. Schizophrenia is a particular risk for telepaths, often diagnosed late because having voices in our heads telling us to do things is perfectly normal for us."

In my mind's eye I glimpsed cushioned walls and patients in strait jackets. Psychiatric treatment in Binary world was a long way behind the times, in comparison with the outside world. One of the Binary strengths was their love of tradition, of not seeking to change what worked for them. But this was also a weakness. I wondered how discussion of my pregnancy reform was going back in the Woodstock labyrinth.

The corridor to the mind repair unit was bright and well lit. The mind-damaged patients received the best care that St. Anthony's could deliver, nursed in comfortably furnished single rooms and soothing decorations. Marc had been moved to a larger room, with couches on each side of his bed for the mind explorers. We had found that the explorer should ideally be lying next to the patient to be fully relaxed before entry, but this was also a safety measure. If the exit from the patient's mind was difficult, the explorer could easily lose consciousness. I had nearly succumbed to this when I started to try to repair Kastor's mind.

Ariadne and I took the couches on either side of Marc, who was awake and anxious. "I'm sorry I can't help her get out," he said, frustrated at his impotence.

Escape could only be aided by the healthy functioning mind and his was only in the very early stages of healing. When Dr. Foucoe introduced me, he exclaimed, "Cassandra! I'll be OK if you're involved."

"Just don't go to sleep on us," said Ariadne, "or let your subconscious think they should keep us. Your mind is still there, you know. It's just a bit disconnected. So we'll be relying on you too."

"I so want to recover my abilities," he said.

Clea gave him a professionally optimistic smile. "And you will, Marc. Soon you'll be fit enough to have more physical therapy, to help with the mental pain."

"Including sex therapy?" he asked hopefully.

"Any therapy you need," said the psychiatrist, pressing his hand. Injured telepaths needed much more physical contact than the normal level between Binaries. Turning to me, she said, "We don't have much of a problem with volunteers for this type of patient. With our more disturbed psychiatric patients, it's not so easy." I was silent, aware that Clea knew all about my opinion of this particular therapy.

Dr. Foucoe drew back, to allow Ariadne and I to focus on our task. We had to envision ourselves as becoming miniature, like little walking instruments, to effect the repairs. We also needed to visualise appropriate equipment, such as torches on a band round their heads and non-slip footwear. This would not be possible to do once we had entered Marc's mind.

"I'll go first, if that's OK with you," said Ariadne. "I've been in a few times so I'll wait for you on the surface. We've put binding strips across the crater, so you won't fall in."

She took a deep breath and then appeared to be in a trance. I waited a few seconds before plunging in as well.

11

The surface of Marc's mind only slightly resembled the crisp snowy surface of Kastor's. The damage had resulted in dull, greyish areas with green slime and jagged points from the columns below, but the remaining normal structure was more like concrete, with neat dividing lines that resembled spaces in a multistorey car park. Where this concrete was undamaged, it sparkled slightly. Ariadne was standing near the crater, adjusting her lamp and checking her harness. I felt a glimmer of pride at the result of the mental training techniques. Mind repairers now had the ability to construct these aids for safer entry. But there was no time for self-congratulation. I cautiously traversed the edges of the crater, seeing that the dividing lines were sagging. This would mean that the normal overlapping nature of the surface had been compromised, with the risk of tumbling down a crack. I was impressed with the intricate binding that had been put across the crater, leaving a gap at the edge for mind repairers to move to the next layer.

"Did you do this?" I asked Ariadne, who smiled proudly.

"Yes, webbing repair is one of my specialties. I was inspired by the myths of Ariadne and Arachne to work especially hard on this type of bandaging."

"I hope you're as good at ladders."

We looked down the access hole. As we had suspected, the

ladder had fallen down to the next layer. We scanned the area for suitable construction materials. The frosty concrete was not as utilisable as the lumps of snow I had found in Kastor's damaged mind, nor were there any handy jagged points near to the gap in the crater. I pointed to a sharp piece, covered with healing foam, on the other side of the crater.

"Our access hole should be over there, so we can attach the ladder more securely."

First we constructed the ladder from transparent Band-Aids, imaginary mental constructs that I had found could be conjured up in this surreal landscape. It seemed to take far too long, although we both knew that time stood still while we were inside a mind. I completed the ladder, whilst Ariadne cautiously loosened some of the webbing near the crag formed by the jutting up column. She deftly rewove it to make a gap big enough for two of us to ascend together. I sensed that the efficient young woman was thinking of the possibility of somehow carrying Ingrid up, if we found her. In this surreal environment, thoughts sounded like voices in a cave, with a distinct echo. I had done explorations with a companion back in the Woodstock Binaries, but that was mainly on normal volunteers. This felt more urgent and the echoing thoughts were more alarming than reassuring.

Before descending, we both tried calling to Ingrid. There was no response. We clambered down the ladder to the next layer. The floor near our new ladder was slippery, slanting towards the smaller crater on that level. We edged towards one of the columns. This had not been repaired, apart from the healing foam, so we were able to cling to loose filaments while we looked about. The chamber was more like an open plan office than the curving Norman architecture of Kastor's upper levels. Instead of his ornate chests and bookcases, Marc's mind was organised into metallic grey filing cabinets and a few open shelves for frequently retrieved thoughts. But there was no sign of Ingrid. We shone our torches through the hole at the side of the webbed crater.

"It's a mess down there," I commented, looking at the tumbled filing cabinets, loose filaments waving about and mind tissue clustering like tangled cobwebs, preventing any clear view of the chamber.

"We've repaired several of the columns," said Ariadne, feeling that they had not reached my standards.

"I'm sorry, I didn't mean to seem to criticise. The repairs are going well, it's just so worrying that we can't find Ingrid. Either the subconscious beings took her down to their level when Marc fell asleep, or she managed to tether herself to a structure, but still lost consciousness."

"So do you think they could now both be in a type of coma?"

"Yes," I said, slowly. "I don't know how this operates, but if the subconscious doesn't want to absorb you, maybe they just wall you off, something like that?" We both thought of the consequences of a wall that could permanently conceal Ingrid from our searches.

"We shouldn't stay too long," I said, looking around and sensing Marc's great fatigue. The drug induced waking state could not be maintained indefinitely and it might damage the young guard. Reluctantly we made our way up to the mind surface again.

"Let's try and exit together," I said and we held hands and concentrated on impelling ourselves upwards. We overshot slightly, soaring for a moment over St. Anthony's, but landed safely in our own minds. Our bodies, lying by Marc, stirred slightly and the ward staff rushed to aid us.

"Well?" said Dr. Foucoe eagerly, when we drowsily opened our eyes.

"We couldn't find her," I said. Marc, who had found the mind entrance painful, sighed with frustration. Dr. Foucoe crossed her arms.

"You must go in again," she said, "This is all your fault, this dangerous type of mind repair…"

She stopped, remembering that the Board had given her an award for services to medicine, on the basis of her acclaimed research. She noticed that a couple of the staff looked curiously at her, including that ambitious upstart, Dr. Asklep.

"I mean," she added hurriedly, "if my instructions had been properly followed, this wouldn't have occurred."

I did not want to expose the psychiatrist as a fraud, knowing that Clea genuinely wanted to help these patients and was adept at helping their telepathy to improve, once the repairs had helped to unblock the connections.

I sat up and looked at Marc. "You must be very tired," I said.

He nodded, but said plaintively, "But you must find Ingrid. I can't sense her within my mind but just knowing she is trapped there – it seems it could be stopping my recovery too."

"You must stay awake, Marc," said Dr. Foucoe. "They'll go in again."

"No," I said. "Not today. We're tired now and I need to sleep on the problem. Let Marc get some sleep. But first, may I see Ingrid?"

I went with Ariadne to another room on the ward, where Ingrid's body lay under one of the igloo tents used to protect damaged telepaths. It prevented exposure to outside noise and thoughts, while the telepath recovered. Ingrid seemed to be sleeping peacefully. A drip and tubes peeping from below the bedcovers were attending to her physical needs, while monitoring equipment recorded a steady heart trace.

"She looks like *Sleeping Beauty*," I said, thinking the St. Anthony's fort could be a castle in a dark fairy tale, with Ingrid trapped within it.

"But I don't think a kiss would wake her, even if we could find a prince," said Ariadne, sadly.

"With Kastor, the secret was a key, to unlock the processes governing the mind," I murmured. "This problem is different. Both

Ingrid and her mind exploring persona are detached from conscious thought. I'm feeling drained after the exploration of Marc, but let's see if I can contact her."

I sat quietly inside the igloo tent, holding the sleeping girl's hand. Closing my eyes, I saw a long tunnel, stretching as far as I could see. It was empty. I tried to project into this tunnel. Its walls appeared to consist of many densely circling lines, as if drawn by a soft graphite pencil. Standing in the circular structure, I heard faint echoes, like trains moving in the distance.

"Ingrid, where are you?" I called softly, in my mind. There was no immediate response but the echoes became louder. They sounded more like the rushing of water through narrow channels, with a rhythm resembling heart sounds heard through a stethoscope.

I called again and glimpsed a figure in the distance. Approaching, I saw an older woman, sitting like a concierge in the hallway of a French apartment block.

"She's not here," said the woman, who was bent over a tapestry frame. I guessed she was a figure from Ingrid's subconscious.

"I know," I said, "but do you know if she's safe, still alive?" The woman reached down for a skein of silk from a bag at her side. "I wouldn't be here if she'd perished," she said, in a resigned tone. "But I can't work on this scene forever, we need her back."

The tapestry picture appeared to represent the inner structure of a mind. It was about two thirds complete.

"How do we get her back?" I asked desperately, sensing that when the tapestry was finished, the subconscious parts of her mind would fade away and take Ingrid's life with them.

"If I knew that, I'd tell you," said the old woman, stitching little pink highlights into a filament.

I pulled myself out of the tunnel image, sitting up with a start. Ariadne came into the tent. I said quietly, "She's alive in Marc's mind, but there isn't a lot of time. We both need to sleep and see what dreams bring us."

"I don't have your powers, Cassandra, I mean, to get visions, prophecies and secrets from dreams."

"We all have dreams," I said. "If you just try to focus on finding Ingrid, while you're asleep, it may help."

To the disappointment of Dr. Foucoe and the other clinical staff, I then insisted that we should leave the ward. Considering that Clea had written a few papers on mind exploration techniques and training, she seemed remarkably cavalier about the essential need to rest after attempting mind repair.

12

The guest wing was luxuriously equipped and as at other Binary establishments, food and other needs were well catered for. Through the arched window I viewed the bleak rocky scene and misty sea beyond. I had asked for a meal in my room, not feeling like facing Dr. Foucoe and the others over dinner in the staff dining hall. I communicated telepathically with Kastor, who was pleased to know I had survived the mind exploration.

"You mustn't risk yourself, you're not immortal," he signalled. "Everyone will be grateful you even tried. Come back, perhaps the answer will emerge when you're relaxing here. It can't be pleasant for you, at St. Anthony's."

"Perhaps I should return," I replied. "I'll see how I feel about it in the morning. It's not too bad here, the guest wing is like a hotel."

I caught a worried thought from Kastor, about a hotel that was difficult to check out from. He also asked about storms.

"No storms yet," said my smiling face in his mind. I put the meal tray aside and ran a bath, tipping in generous quantities of the expensive bath oils laid out for guests. Then, very sleepy, I got into the bed and turned on the music channel of the radio. It was playing a Mendelssohn extract from the opera '*A Midsummer's Night Dream*'. I loved the way music in the Binaries always seemed appropriate for the moment. In this case, the melody made me think of an army of mind repairers, scrambling up and down flimsy, fairytale ladders. Eventually the music and soft sounds of the summer night outside lulled me to sleep.

I dreamed that I was in a busy city street, looking up at an office block. A sign over the entrance showed it to be '*Surveillants S.p.A, Proprietor: Marc Lesange*'. A few steps led to a small foyer. A man sitting at a reception desk glanced up.

"Do you have an appointment?" he asked, in a forbidding manner.

"Well, no, but I'm part of the repair team."

"Name?" he said, consulting a ledger.

"Cassandra." He looked me up and down, in the manner of a doctor's receptionist who wanted to get off work, irritated that more patients kept arriving.

"You're on the list. Take the lift."

"Which floor?" I asked, but he was writing something on a clipboard, with no further interest in me. I entered the lift and examined the buttons. They were all unnumbered, so I pressed one in the middle and the lift started to ascend. When the doors opened, I stepped into a hallway with open plan offices leading off on each side. I went towards the one on the left, peeping through the glass doors. There were several desks, unoccupied, with a row of filing cabinets around the walls. The windows had vertical venetian blinds, through which only a dark night sky was visible. I cautiously opened one of the glass doors, looking to see if anyone was in the office. It seemed that the workers had long departed for their homes. I checked the office on the other side, finding it to be similarly deserted. Sighing, I pressed the open button for the lift and tried another floor, lower down.

The offices on this floor showed more activity. Entering the one on the right, I found a classroom, with some kind of adult evening class in progress. The students were oddly dressed, some as Roman centurions, others as modern soldiers or police officers. There were posters on the walls, one showing a couple of men wearing sailor hats and little else, another a smiling waiter, wearing a bow tie and leather shorts, proffering a tray of drinks. At the end of the room, someone was mixing drinks at a bar and a couple of men were sitting on stools, having an inaudible conversation.

"Is this a gay bar?" I asked, for I was the only woman in the room, apart from the clue of the posters.

"It used to be," said one of the centurions sullenly. "But now strange women seem to be taking it over." He looked towards the instructor for the class, standing by a white board at the front.

"You may as well take a seat," said a friendlier soldier, "He doesn't like interruptions."

The instructor noticed my entry, but did not stop talking. He was pointing to a map on the screen. It was unlike any map of countries that I had ever seen, with coloured shapes and what might be seas, but covered with little arrows and labels.

"The foreign body, as I said, is about here." He used a pointer to indicate a grey mass at the edge of one of the coloured shapes. "We've contained it, but it's holding up the liberation manoeuvres, obviously. Now it's covered up, we can't find it again. Has anyone a suggestion about what should be done next?"

"Absorb it?" asked a keen soldier at the front. The others gave him a withering glance.

"In some situations that is the correct approach," said the instructor. "But then we'd have to deal with her being with us down below. In this case, the proprietor wants her out of the building."

"We could dissolve the foreign body, so only a trace remained –

as a fragmented substance that wouldn't bother him too much?" suggested a man in a smart white uniform. Despite several nods of agreement from the class, the instructor shook his head.

"The proprietor would like this intrusion removed safely, without damage. There's no contact from his conscious mind, sadly, to give us further guidance. But attempts to remove the foreign body to lower levels have been unsuccessful. He's blocking us, for some reason."

"He's exhausted, poor love," called one of the men at the bar. "He hasn't been allowed to sleep for a couple of days – we're all going mad, waiting."

I put up my hand nervously. The instructor raised his eyebrows but indicated that I could speak. "I was wondering if I could help?"

A couple of students sniggered, then I found I was standing by the white board. I peered at the grey mass that represented the foreign body. It was like a cocoon fashioned from many layers of cobwebs.

"But this is Ingrid," I said, "look, there's her face." At one end of the cocoon there was the indistinct shape of a young woman's head, turned towards us, eyes shut.

"Well, this Ingrid is a great nuisance," said the instructor, which was received with ripples of "Hear, hear" throughout the class.

"I could try to remove her," I murmured, "if you could tell me how."

"If we knew that, the foreign body wouldn't still be here."

"Take me to her," I said and the instructor shrugged. "We're busy, if you hadn't noticed. Take the lift."

"But there are no numbers…"

"Well, of course not. His mind is all over the place! You'll just have to try one of the upper floors, that's where we think she is."

In my sleep, I turned restlessly. The dream faded but I woke with a start, hearing someone singing. *"He doesn't say the things he should..."* It was Judy Garland, singing '*As long as he needs me*' on the radio, left on when I dropped off to sleep. I drowsily moved to turn the switch. But the words caught my attention, "*I miss him so much when he's gone...*" I thought about Judy Garland singing in the *Wizard of Oz* and smiled to think how easy it would be if the answer lay at the end of a rainbow. My dream vision had been more like a story from *Alice in Wonderland*, full of grumpy fantastical characters.

Falling asleep again, I was back in the lift of that strange office block. One of the lift buttons had a rainbow on it, so I gave it a try. The lift opened on a level apparently being redecorated. Sheets of cloth were draped on the floor and a ladder with a can of paint was lying against the other lifts. The only light was from dirty windows, but it was a clear night with the moon nearly full, so I cautiously stepped into the area. There were cavities in the pillars supporting the ceiling, with wires hanging from them. Filing cabinets lay on their sides, with papers spewing out. I edged round a hole in the floor, noticing a concentrated pile of debris at the end of the office. Coming closer, I saw the grey cobwebbed cocoon from the instructor's diagram and, in the way of dreams, found myself right next to it. I gently touched the cobwebs, starting to pull them away.

"What do you think you're doing?" shouted a centurion, suddenly stepping from behind the cocoon.

"I need to free her, to take her away," I explained.

"We can't allow that," said the man, "There's been no decision."

"But this will solve it, your problem," I said desperately. "Go and tell the others, I'm going to take the foreign body away tomorrow."

"I'd do that, if I knew how to get back to them," he said sourly, incongruously starting to sing,

"The night is bitter, the stars have lost their glitter…"

Another Judy Garland song. I guessed that Marc was a fan.

"What's the name of that song?" I asked and he replied, with a gloomy face, " *'The man who got away'* of course."

I pointed to the lift area. "Try the button above the one in the middle. I'll stay here and guard the foreign body."

He looked at me suspiciously. "And who are you?"

"I am Cassandra," I said, since this had worked at reception.

"Ah!" he exclaimed, "Well I suppose that's all right then."

Picking up his sword, he marched towards the lifts. Left with the cocoon, I pulled away the cobwebs covering Ingrid's face. I stroked it: there was no response. "Wake up Ingrid," I murmured. "We're coming for you tomorrow, you must leave Marc's mind."

The cocooned body did not move but I heard a voice, somewhere, saying, "You'll need to smoke her out. Smoke, get some smoke." I started to smell smoke, fearing a fire had started in the debris. I woke up in alarm, but the bedroom was quiet and peaceful.

"What an odd dream," I thought, "and probably mainly confused thoughts, because of our mind exploration today." While I found it hard to interpret my dreams or understand what part of the future they might be revealing, I nevertheless thought over the details of this one, thinking I would remember it in the morning.

13

I contacted Dr. Foucoe early and said we would try another exploration, but only if Marc was allowed to get further sleep. He had been woken up ready for us.

"Are you mad?" asked Clea. "You can't go in while he's asleep."

"I can't explain," I said, "but I think his subconscious wants Ingrid out and doesn't want to harm her. But even the subconscious needs rest, if we're going to receive any help from it."

"Marc is exhausted," agreed the psychiatrist. "But what evidence do you have that this'll be better than keeping him awake for a few more hours, to let you and Ariadne enter again?"

"Only a dream, but it's what I feel to be right."

Clea gave an exasperated sigh. Then she reflected that the mind repairs had only started because of my intuitive feeling that I could work on Kastor's injuries. "I shall put the full responsibility of this on you," she said and I signalled, 'Fine', adding in a closed off thought, "and you'll take all the credit if it works out."

"One more thing," I said into the phone. "Try playing Judy Garland songs while he sleeps. *'Smoke gets in your eyes'* would be good, I'm sure she sang that one. I think it may soothe him." Dr. Foucoe was still spluttering her irritation at this suggestion when I ended the call.

I breakfasted with Ariadne and asked her to show me round St. Anthony's, at least the parts not occupied by patients. The area around the main entrance hall was like a baronial castle. I was surprised not to see suits of armour and shields on the walls. The main staircase had a wide start with magnificent carved wooden stair rails. It curved up to divide into two smaller staircases with a gallery overlooking the hall.

"This entrance is just for visitors and staff," explained Ariadne. "Patients come in at the back, near the helicopter pad."

"Can you leave, to visit the mainland?"

"No, only a few security and intermediary staff can do that, the ones who bring in supplies and so on. It wouldn't be safe if we were to wander about near the houses by the shore. There's a small ferry, though the ferryman is very grumpy. I've heard the delivery staff complain that he always says they must wait until his schedule shows it's time to collect them. The ferry returns to this side after each trip, of course, never staying by the shore for outsiders to think of using it."

Ariadne showed me the library and some sitting rooms. A few recovering patients looked up.

"The man over there is a mind repair," she whispered. "You'd think he'd be so grateful. If he continues to make progress, Dr. Foucoe is going to let him out soon. But she's assessed him as unsuitable for his previous work, so he's not too happy at the moment."

"It's good to think of patients leaving here," I said, thinking of how Kastor was so nearly condemned to this place of exile and incurable disorders.

"Yes, it really makes the work worthwhile. But of course the prisoners in St. Anthony's are a different matter."

"Prison, what, for ordinary criminals?"

"Oh, they're all officially mentally disturbed. As you know, crime definitely doesn't pay in our world. The sane ones are executed, if the crime is serious enough – then there are the labour camps. But the ones that come here almost never leave."

"Can we visit that area?"

"The detention block? No, not at all," said Ariadne, a little shocked. "They're highly dangerous and disturbed. And I understand the punishments can be upsetting to watch."

"Quite a deterrent," I murmured. Ariadne shrugged. Binaries were not encouraged to show sympathy for transgressors. She had never visited the dungeons or upper levels of the detention zone and, like other staff at St. Anthony's, had learned to ignore the occasional scream or image of misery emanating from that part of the institution.

After a walk outside on the limited land of St. Anthony's Isle, we went to the staff dining room for an early lunch sitting. Dr. Foucoe was there and glared at me.

"He's fast asleep, with Ingrid possibly disappearing as we speak," said Clea, in a bad temper at this delay.

"Let me know the moment he wakes up," I replied. "We'll go in straight away – oh, and make sure Ingrid is brought here to lie on a couch nearby."

While Dr. Foucoe was speaking authoritatively to the others, I asked Ariadne if she had dreamed in the night.

"Yes, it was very peculiar," said Ariadne. "It was like a maze and you were calling to me. Funny thing though, you kept asking about smoke, and when I looked, I was carrying a huge canister of something, like a gas cylinder. I suppose it was the after effect of our unsuccessful trip, but I hope I wasn't thinking of making an explosion as the answer!"

"No," I said thoughtfully. "But you know those machines for

making mists, the ones used at parties and theatres?" Ariadne nodded. "Well, I think we should meditate on how to construct a mist or smoke making apparatus, to take in with us." The young woman looked surprised, but I was the expert. "Oh," I added, "and I think he's gay. I'll try to check with the Binaires members. It may help – it may even be the reason why Ingrid wasn't absorbed by his subconscious as soon as he fell asleep."

"You mean, he wouldn't want a pretty young woman cluttering up the deepest part of his psyche?"

"Something like that," I said with a smile.

It was a couple of hours later that we received a call from the mind repair unit, saying that Marc was stirring. We shared a tense look, but we had been practising the visualisation of mist generators and had also discussed ways of shifting the grey cocoon that I expected to find. Marc looked up warily when we arrived at either side of his bed.

"I shouldn't have slept," he muttered. "And now I've got a headache."

"It's the drugs," I said. "You'll feel better as they wear off, but we've got to go in again, Marc. Your subconscious seems to be telling me that time is running out."

"It was so brave of Ingrid, but if she… dies inside me, what'll that mean for me?"

He looked nervously at Ingrid's immobile form on the couch. Dr. Foucoe came over and took his hand.

"It's not going to happen, Marc. I've given them full instructions." She raised her voice for the benefit of any clinical staff listening. "I've had a new idea, about how to fix this. Just trust me. And of course I've every confidence in these two efficient mind repairers." Ariadne and I exchanged a knowing smile. Everything depended on us and if it failed, Dr. Foucoe would say we had not followed her guidance. Marc could not communicate telepathically, but his eyes showed his concern. "I promise to stay awake," he said. "Despite the headache, I feel so much better for some rest."

We landed neatly on the mind surface, quickly traversing down to the first level and preparing a safe ladder for the second. There was no time for repairs on this trip. As Ariadne had claimed, several columns near the hole had been repaired, but the edges of this cavern were dark and cluttered, with damaged parts of columns and filaments making the terrain hazardous. I recalled the building site from my dream. Encumbered by the mist machine and cylinder, shared between us, we moved cautiously round, looking for the cocoon that I had shared as an image with Ariadne. Eventually, behind a filing cabinet, we found a grey mound.

"Ingrid surely can't be under all that – or alive if she is," murmured Ariadne, trying not to think that it was hopeless.

We approached and started to try to peel off the layers of grey, dusty threads. "It's like unravelling a ball of wool that's been rolled up untidily," said Ariadne. We focused on carefully rolling each complete strand up into a new smaller ball.

"It may be part of mind structure," I agreed, as we painstakingly reduced the covering. "We can't just tear if off."

We had left the mist machine to one side, so that we could work faster and as we toiled, we hoped that Marc was still alert.

"I wouldn't put it past Clea to just leave us to it, not keep checking on him," muttered Ariadne. "She hardly ever does mind entry beyond the upper surfaces, I suppose you know that."

"We'll be OK," I said, feeling that we would, although it was a long way up if Marc dozed off.

When we had uncovered most of Ingrid's body, we could see that Ingrid had attached her harness to the handle of a filing cabinet drawer, but marks in the delicate floor suggested that this had been dragged, with her sleeping form along with it. The subconscious instructor, as I now assumed him to be, had talked about trying to move the 'foreign body' in my dream.

"We must wake her up," I said. We both yelled, but neither this nor squeezing her hands, shaking her, or as a last resort, tickling her feet, made any apparent effect. "OK," I said, "Now we have to try the smoke. Ariadne, check the ladder, we may have to reinforce it."

I attached the cylinder to the mist machine and started it off. A grey vapour started to fill the chamber. I signalled to Ariadne to concentrate on the illusion of the smell of fire, starting it off and hoping that Ariadne had the skills to expand it.

"Fire!" I shouted at Ingrid. "You have to get out! Wake up Ingrid, it's a fire!"

The chamber became so smoky that we could scarcely see her. At last Ingrid stirred and then opened her eyes, looking round in alarm. Ariadne and I repeated the alarm calls, urging her to follow us up. She stood up slowly and stiffly and we helped her to ascend the ladders to the mind surface.

Here, Ingrid looked around puzzled and it was clear that she had neither the energy nor willpower to make the leap out of Marc's mind. Ariadne and I looked at each other.

"A three-person jump?" Ariadne asked nervously. I hadn't ever tried this either, but nodded confidently. Standing on either side of Ingrid and holding hands, we counted to make sure that we made the effort synchronously. With a deep breath we focused on leaving his mind and surged upwards, Ingrid dangling between us like a miniature rag doll. For a moment it seemed that her weight would drag us back, but Ariadne and I held on desperately. We knew we were emerging close to our bodies, hoping that this would be enough to ensure Ingrid reached hers. But we lost consciousness as we re-entered our own minds, so had no way of knowing.

I woke up first, looking at Marc. He was alert and grinning. "You did it," he murmured. "Ingrid's still unconscious, but she stirred and they believe she's back in her own self."

Ariadne now awoke. "We left the mist machine," she said, ignoring Marc's disconcerted expression.

"Oh, don't worry about that, just an imaginary construct. I'm sure Dr. Foucoe will nip in and collect it later, if she's concerned," I said.

We couldn't resist giggling at this unlikely thought and Marc, happy at least to be free of the 'foreign body', grinned with us.

"We'll do some more mind repair later, Marc," added Ariadne, "but perhaps you need some quiet relaxation now."

"Yes, catch up on some sleep," I said, sitting up. I sensed the approach of Clea Foucoe.

"It's too early to be certain," said Clea, "but it seems you had some success. Perhaps you should leave the ward now, so we can attend to the patients."

"I feel wonderful," said Ariadne. "Normally it's so tiring, but that was exhilarating. The triple leap!"

"Me too," I agreed. Dr. Foucoe glanced at Ingrid, who was moving in her sleep. She said loudly, "I'm delighted my idea worked. Splendid."

Ariadne and I exchanged a thought of letting Clea know later, much later, about the mist machine. Not until after she had regaled colleagues with her clever plan, but inexplicably missing out the key detail.

14

Ariadne went to check on the other mind damaged patient before getting some rest, while I left the ward with a spring in my step, swinging my shoulder bag and looking forward to returning to speak to Ingrid. I knew it would be wise to relax back in my room. A mind exploration would normally be followed by hours of quiet recovery. My high spirits at the moment were probably due more to adrenaline rush from our success and dramatic departure from Marc's mind. As I pushed the exit door, I sensed one of the other doctors coming up to speak to me. Turning, I saw the portly Dr. Asklep, who attended to general medical assessments and also had charge of behavioural therapy at St. Anthony's.

He had to run to catch up with me, adding breathlessness to his normally obsequious manner. "Such an honour to have you here – the pioneer of this new treatment for mind damage." He lowered his voice. "A few of us guessed it wasn't all Dr. Foucoe's own work. She should have given you a lot more credit."

"Oh, I've no ambitions in this field, I just wanted to help."

"Glad to not have to write up research all the time, I expect," said Dr. Asklep chattily. "I'm working on a paper myself at the moment, as a matter of fact."

I nodded polite interest. I found it more than a little creepy, the way the professional staff regarded many of their patients as fodder for research projects. But Dr. Asklep guided me eagerly to a corridor that I had not been down before.

"If you've got a few minutes, I can show you the subject. I think you'll be particularly intrigued."

I thought briefly, oh, not Ryden. I didn't think I could stand to be that close to the man who caused such harm to Kastor. Picking this up, Dr. Asklep shook his head. "Not our big baby, no – that's Clea's special project. But I won't say any more until we get there."

We reached a side ward, where a shambling queue of male patients, attended by orderlies, were waiting with mumbling impatience to enter. Sweeping past the patients without a glance, Dr. Asklep opened the door. It was a fairly small room with a sink and side trolley. The couch had adjustable metal rings with leather straps hanging down from it. A female orderly was wiping down the plastic covering of the couch and looked up inquiringly.

"Where is she, Martha?" asked Dr. Asklep, dismayed that his surprise revelation of the special subject had been spoiled.

"On a break, she's had a re-education session, then a shower and snack," said the orderly with disinterest, "She'll be back soon, she won't want to keep the patients waiting."

Dr. Asklep looked down the corridor, then signalled excitedly to me. A nurse was guiding a teenager towards us. Her charge was walking awkwardly, staring ahead as if not seeing her surroundings. She wore a simple hospital gown done up in front with a row of Velcro fastening. Her legs were bare and her feet shuffled slowly in hospital clogs. The girl's hair was clean but hung straight around her head, with a simple parting to one side. Her face was garishly made up with bright red lipstick and heavy mascara and rouge. Despite her much changed appearance, I recognised the errant nursery assistant, Cilisse.

"We're not late are we?" asked the nurse, "She needed more

make up."

"Bless her," said Martha. "She needs it to cheer the patients up, even if she now knows to smile at them – don't you pet?" Cilisse smiled meekly as the female orderly ushered her into the side ward off the short corridor, with a larger ward beyond.

"We've got a nice long list for you this afternoon," Martha said to the girl, who stood uncertainly in the presence of the doctor and visitor. "Look a bit more grateful, dearie. We don't want more of that sulky look, do we, the one you used to have?"

Cilisse immediately produced a small upturn to her mouth. Dr. Asklep approached the girl, eyeing her severely. "Come, come, Cilisse, that's not a very encouraging smile is it? Show our visitor how you can smile for the patients."

She turned obediently to me, with a wide, leering grin that made me recoil inwardly, hoping I had not made this repulsion too obvious.

"Do you see?" said Dr. Asklep excitedly, not bothering to introduce me to the girl, "All down to expert training. But wait until you see what else she can do, without any need for discipline."

The doctor closed the side room door behind us, to moans of disappointment from the queue of waiting patients. "She's made remarkable progress. I never met someone so responsive to re-education programming. Not over bright and very impressionable, I suppose that was part of the trouble, with what she did?"

"I suppose," I uttered softly, embarrassed that he was talking about Cilisse in this way while she stood silently in the room, gazing into the distance.

"Now, watch this," said the doctor enthusiastically. "Cilisse, Dr. Asklep says, get into position – using the restraints." The girl smiled dutifully and flicked open the front of her hospital gown, removing it and handing it to Martha. Cilisse clearly found it painful to bend, lifting her legs stiffly to remove her underpants, her only other garment. Then she heaved herself up onto the couch. She pushed her ankles into the circular buckles with leather straps at the end of the couch, putting her wrists into those near its head. The orderly pulled the buckles tight, forcing the girl to bend her legs while the ankle fetters were ratcheted up from wires attached to a bar on the ceiling, with an ominous clicking sound that increasingly widened the gap between her legs and raised them. Cilisse looked up for approval when in position.

Dr. Asklep nodded without smiling, saying, "Now demonstrate how you do your work."

Cilisse pushed her body to and fro within the limits of the fetters, concentrating with a pathetic wish to please the doctor. "I'm ready to do my duty," she said, looking around the room, slightly puzzled at the delay.

I watched with shocked fascination as Dr. Asklep explained cheerfully, "She now performs well without compulsory restraints, we just use them for patients she might find… difficult, or for occasional discipline reinforcement of course. Do please note the now complete, submissive obedience. It's remarkable considering she only started this work, unwillingly, little more than a fortnight ago. We keep her in solitary confinement, naturally, as this speeds up the behavioural adjustment." He signalled for Martha to remove the ankle restraints. "A busy list today, you said?"

"Yes, doctor, but an easy one to start this session." She donned a pair of plastic gloves, picked up a large jar of cream and turned to Cilisse. "The first patient's a regular and he's asked specially for you."

"Does he love me?" asked the girl and I felt deeply for her. Mind damaged telepaths usually lost all ordinary feeling, as well as their enhanced empathy, so love didn't come into it.

"Yes of course he does, dear," replied Martha, starting to lather her body with cream.

"And he doesn't mind my duties with the others?" asked Cilisse.

Dr. Asklep stepped up to her. "No, he understands you've been very bad and loves that you do this service for others. He wants you to do as many therapies as you possibly can." Cilisse nodded, as though this made sense.

I gazed at the girl, who seemed unconcerned at her vulnerable nudity.

"Couldn't you at least cover her with a sheet?"

"Oh no," said the orderly, "It's better for the patients this way. Some need a bit of help with arousal. They need to look at you, don't they pet?" Cilisse's docile smile was heart rending. I stepped nearer, noticing several bruises and other marks on her body.

"What are all those? Have you been beating her?" I said, aghast.

"The very idea!" sniffed Martha, dabbing the cream on. "It's just a few bites and knocks, some of the patients can't control themselves very well. We keep it to a minimum, don't we dearie? Stay still while I wipe off the excess."

Dr. Asklep said, "Do the bites and scratches bother you, Cilisse?"

"No, I deserve them," she murmured, "I've been a wicked, evil girl."

Dr. Asklep nodded proudly at this demonstration of the behaviour training, glancing at me to receive a look of praise. But he sensed instead that I very much wanted to leave this scene. Wait, he signalled, as though I would miss the key part of the demonstration. Martha took a large glob of lubricant and generously smoothed it between Cilisse's legs. "All over the important bit," she said to Cilisse.

"Thank you," said the girl.

"And you like this work, don't you?" asked Martha.

When Cilisse replied obediently, "Yes, I'm so very blessed to have found my vocation," the orderly looked at me with a triumphant air, as if to say, how dare you imply this isn't the luckiest girl in the world? Martha patted Cilisse's perineum with a last smear of gel and to me it seemed she was being treated like a prize fowl being prepared for the oven. I was fuming with anger. Yes, this girl had been very foolish, but in the outside world, her punishment would have been no more than a fairly light prison sentence.

"How long are you going to make her do this?" I asked. The orderly raised her eyes heavenward and Dr. Asklep looked baffled.

"Why, indefinitely, of course. This is her life now. She understands the need to atone for her great sins and disobedience."

I knelt down to the level of the girl's pale face under the grotesque make-up, noting the expression devoid of personality.

"You don't want to be abused like this, do you Cilisse?"

The girl gave a bewildered smile and anxious look at the orderly and doctor.

"I'm a volunteer. It's my sacred obligation, because I've been so very bad." Then she looked into my face, bewilderment turning to joy, thinking that she once more saw an image of the Virgin Mary. I guessed that when I projected this during the interrogation, the face remained my own.

I quickly transmitted a thought, "They can hear us here, Cilisse, speak to me only in your mind."

"I'm being very good now, Holy Mother," the girl sent back.

"I can see that," I thought in return, wanting to cry.

Dr. Asklep sensed we were communicating and came closer to catch the content, but I stood up and just touched the girl's hand briefly, transmitting some strength and courage.

"We do need to get on, doctor," said Martha, losing patience. "She's got about six special needs patients for this session, on top of the usual list, and then we're going to take her round the closed wards this evening. First time, but you're not worried, are you dearie?"

I saw a momentary flicker of alarm in Cilisse's eyes, quickly replaced by the subservient smile she had been taught to produce when spoken to. Dr. Asklep, annoyed at my interference, turned to the girl and ordered, "Cilisse, Dr. Asklep says, get ready for the therapy. Normal position."

The girl, now all creamed and buttered, resumed the correct bent and open legs posture, leering vacantly as she started to mechanically move her pelvis. "Can we get on now?" said the orderly to the doctor and the first patient was led in, grunting his anticipated pleasure when he spied Cilisse's robotic smile and well formed body. Dr. Asklep looked on, beaming. "We can watch if you like, she knows we're monitoring her performance."

"No thanks," I said, walking out of the room and shutting the door behind me. Standing outside, raging at the cruelty of the Binary culture, I wished I had the courage to put a stop to this 'therapy' altogether, this instant. I tried to calm myself, feeling vulnerable deep in the fort of St. Anthony's.

Dr. Asklep followed me out, perturbed that I had been less impressed than he had hoped, but his fawning manner was increased by his need to win my approval.

"I don't think you fully appreciate the psychological transformation that we've achieved here. An absolute find for sex therapy. She'd work round the clock if we let her!"

"For the rest of her life...," I said, "And how long will that be? Or is the punishment intended to literally grind her to death?" I pictured Cilisse as an elderly woman, still gyrating her hips painfully on the couch and dripping lubrication gel. But surely, she would not survive long enough to experience even middle age.

Dr. Asklep clasped his hands, speaking in the tones of a vicar needing to address one his flock. "I must explain. You see, we've been able to completely convert her religious tendency into a calling for this work. We thought that her obsession with the baby would be a problem, but no! She now accepts the pregnancy is a nuisance, which will disrupt her vocation. I honestly don't think she'll be bothered about not seeing the baby when it comes, she's already showing little interest in it."

The side room door opened and an orderly brought the male patient out, now smiling as vacantly as Cilisse. I heard Martha fussing over her creamed victim. "I'll just wipe you if you don't mind, dear. No time for a shower. You won't mind, will you pet?"

"I don't mind," murmured the girl. "It's my duty to make them happy."

The next man was shown in. The doctor glanced with more than professional interest as the door was left open, with the patient getting down to business straight away, grabbing at Cilisse as though she was a bag of packaged food that needed to be torn open. The orderly just stood by nodding approvingly, despite the girl flinching with pain and suppressing a scream. I guessed that she had been taught that such outbursts would be punished. I lurched forward, instinctively wanting to end this, but Cilisse responded by turning her face towards the open door, smiling beatifically like a martyr who knows that suffering will be followed by great spiritual rewards.

Dr. Asklep closed the door tactfully, still wishing to justify their use of Cilisse, which seemed to worry me so much.

"There were plenty who'd have liked her to have a painful execution, but this is better. She knows she's atoning for her sins. We'll be training her in various techniques and so on. She's still got a lot to learn, but such a devout student."

He took me aside, confidingly. "Actually, her devotion to the work has proved to be a bit of a problem this week. A couple of the male warders found that just by saying, 'Cilisse, get into position,' she'd lie down immediately on any horizontal surface and invite them to have therapy. Well, obviously we had to apply some discipline."

"I should think so!" I exclaimed, "The warders should know better."

"Oh, not the warders, I mean we had to discipline her. She's not here to enjoy herself."

I did not like to think what discipline meant in this regard, but the doctor nodded in response to this thought.

"Nothing too severe, icy cold hose downs mainly. She's really very compliant. Did you notice how I've now altered the command, so she'll only obey when the order is 'Dr. Asklep says…?' " I didn't respond, but this did not deter him.

"I fully expect my research into this case to be a highlight at the next Binary medical conference." He tried to look persuasive. "You possibly don't understand the importance of sex treatment for damaged Binary members."

This was a particularly thorny topic for me, given the upset it had caused for me and Kastor.

"Oh, but I think I do!" I retorted, "and I don't believe that any physical appetite needs a girl to be sacrificed. She's not really a volunteer at all – just brain washed and tortured!"

Dr. Asklep rubbed his hands in frustration at not getting his point across.

"She was happy to have the babies stolen and our members maimed – but now she only wants to serve. That's an improvement, you surely must agree? And she's quite content, as you heard yourself."

"She was deranged, mentally unstable – this is no treatment for that. I could understand if you put her on… laundry or washing up duties along with appropriate psychiatric therapy, but this, this cruelty is unacceptable."

At this point, Dr. Asklep made a grave error in his efforts to appease me. "Washing up duties, dear me! As an outsider, I suppose it was too much to expect you to understand the different management needed for Binaries. We're brought up to accept both discipline and obedience."

"Outsider," I repeated, feeling a surge of anger, as I remembered all I'd endured to become a respected member of their community. "Yes, I was brought up to respect fellow beings, not abuse them. I'll give you outsider!"

A powerful force field caused Dr. Asklep to flatten himself against the wall as I developed this into a tornado of emotion, like a harsh gale blowing around us and spreading down the ward. Resembling characters in a cartoon, staff and patients alike leaned back against the wind, some losing their balance and toppling backwards. An orderly dispensing tea from a trolley tried desperately to hold onto a couple of cups of tea, before they span away from him, flying into the air and spilling, the tea forming large droplets and cascading in apparent slow motion, adding to the chaos.

I flung open the door of the side room, where the patient was just being helped off the submissive body beneath him. "Get him out of here," I roared and the male orderly grabbed the confused man's arm, dragging him away.

Martha, although looking considerably less smug, pressed a buzzer on the wall, presumably summoning security staff.

"That won't help you," I said, my hair now blowing about my face and it seemed to Martha that I glided towards her, staring fiercely into her eyes. "Fetch a wheelchair – and find a nurse who isn't a sadist. Now!"

Martha hurried out, bending against the gale in the corridor. From the corner of my left eye, I saw security guards approaching. I hurled an illusion of a wall of fire in front of them and, borrowing Helen's skill with telepathic pain, made them drop their batons and cower back. Dr. Asklep was still pinned against the wall, his hands gripping it for safety, gaping at this transformation. I turned to the double doors at the other end of the ward, sensing the nurse and Martha were hovering there, scared, with the wheelchair.

"Come in!" I ordered and allowed the gale to part to allow them to scurry up to the side room door.

"Get into the chair, Cilisse," I said and the girl obeyed, as though unaware of the whirlwind terrifying everyone else.

To the nurse I asked fiercely, "Do you know how to be kind?" The nurse nodded, trembling.

"Right," I said, "take this exhausted, tormented girl and give her a warm bath, then tuck her up in bed. I'll know if you don't do it!"

The nurse started to push the chair back towards the double doors, away from the wall of fire at the side room end. Sensing the arrival of security guards just outside the double doors, I marched through the ward towards them, my force propelling back anyone in my way. "Keep back!" I yelled at the guards, bathing them in panic and pain when they made a halting effort to disobey.

I whirled round at all the terrified faces in the ward and corridor. Taking a deep breath, I threw out a mental vision of ice and snow, so cold that the staff and patients froze, unable to move. For the patients I relented, giving them the illusion of warm coats and scarves.

"There'll be no more sex therapy today," I announced. Then I turned on my heel and strode out of the ward, past the astonished guards. My fury subsided only slowly, sparks seeming to come from me as I rushed to the entrance area of the dark fort, rattling down the large curving stairway so that its old timbers quaked. I knew I had to restore my energy, beginning to feel that I was now in serious trouble. I signalled urgently to Kastor and Theodora that I was in danger and needed to leave St. Anthony's without delay. I marched out of the gothic doors, where the single guard on duty felt it wiser not to try to apprehend me, having heard about the tornado upstairs. I approached the landing stage for the ferry.

I was now sensing angry and confused thoughts coming from the fort, but stepped onto the ferry and demanded to be taken to the mainland. The ferryman looked at his watch, muttering it was not due to leave for another hour. I filled his mind with the will to obey my command and the consequences of not complying.

"I am Cassandra," I said, "and I urgently need to make this journey." He released the mooring rope, but still hesitated.

"They're ordering me to keep you here."

"Oh, just work the ferry or I'll do it myself," I said in a voice so sinister that he hurried to the controls. He ferried me across in silence, nervously aware of dark, foreboding images that would become real if he did not take this famous telepath to the other shore. I sat breathing rapidly, recovering my strength and reflecting that Helen couldn't have done better.

15

When I disembarked, I looked back at St. Anthony's, with its perpetual mist and dark profile merging with the sky. It occurred to me that asking for a Binary car to collect me might not be the best plan. I did not want to be taken into custody, or worse, back to the fort. I felt in the shoulder bag for the wad of money I had tucked in when leaving Woodstock. Helen had left it with me 'for a rainy day' – and this was such an occasion in both meanings, with rain clouds swelling, ready to burst, and the need to get as far away as possible from St. Anthony's Isle. I walked into the small seaside village near the ferry landing, thinking possibly to get a taxi from there. But I decided against this plan, since it was too near to St. Anthony's for field officers not to be working there, perhaps even running the taxi company. An image of Kastor's face came into my mind, looking very concerned.

I briefly signalled that I had caused a 'bit of a panic' and was relieved to see his face smile at this likely understatement. News of my disgraceful behaviour would probably have reached the Binary Centre by now.

"I was severely provoked," I signalled, wishing he was by my side and we could communicate more easily. He rolled his eyes, but signalled, "Stay safe. We're in touch with the St. Anthony's authorities. Catch a train to Edinburgh. I'll meet you if I can, let me know."

I wished I knew where the nearest railway station was located. The normal Binary transport to St. Anthony's was by taxi from a private airport. It was starting to rain and my smart shoes were hardly suitable for a gravelly country road. I had no coat or umbrella. Also, it was a long time since I had walked any distance on the roads outside Binary centres. I decided to keep to the coastal roads, trying to work out if I was heading south. The grey sky, with no sign of the sun, gave little clue. After half an hour I was drenched and exhausted, all the energy surge from that leap out of Marc's mind having evaporated. If the St. Anthony's security officers were coming after me, it would not be hard for them to catch up. No traffic had passed on the narrow road and I was wondering if would be safe or wise to move further inland, when a battered car approached. Sensing that it was slowing down, I bent my head and walked on, as if I hadn't noticed. If it was a car sent by St. Anthony's, there was no chance of escape, but I didn't want to make it easy for them.

The car came to a stop. "Hey there," said a friendly voice with a strong Scottish accent. "Want a lift?" The driver was a man of about my age with short, curly ginger hair. I detected no menace or sinister motive in his offer, but shook my head. Undeterred the driver got out.

"You're soaked – you must need a lift. It's not a problem, hop in!"

"It's all right," I said, "Really. I just forgot to bring an umbrella."

"And now you want me to be soaked too?"

I sensed he was thinking that I was wary of getting into a car with a strange man.

"Look," he shouted, "If you were from these parts, you'd know we always help each other out. Go on, get in, it's absolutely safe."

I contemplated my wet clothes and weary feet. I thought of how

Helen would handle it: martial arts and pain illusions, if she felt threatened. Now that I knew I could at least manage the pain bit, I gave the driver a forlorn nod of thanks, getting into the passenger seat.

"I'm sorry, I'll be dripping all over your car," I murmured.

"Not a problem – you'll notice it isn't the tidiest of interiors." I glanced at the floor covered with old drinks cartons and the back seat was littered with folders. They contained photographs, I sensed, unable to avoid remote viewing these days. But nothing prurient or shocking, to suggest I'd stepped into a pervert's vehicle. I leaned back in the seat, so grateful to be resting my legs. Then I noticed he was looking at me expectantly.

"Where can I take you?"

"The nearest railway station?" I hazarded, having no idea which that might be.

"Well, that could be Forres. Where are you heading?"

"Oh it's a bit complicated," I said. I needed little acting to appear a damsel in distress. "My husband and I were driving to Edinburgh, but we had a row – I got out and thought he'd just come straight back and pick me up, but I seem to have taken a wrong turning. So now I don't know if he's looking for me or has gone straight on to Edinburgh."

"Must have been some row," said the Scotsman.

"It wasn't raining then. I'm sure he's looking – but he's got my mobile phone."

"Use mine," said the driver. "By the way, I'm Toby MacDonald."

"Helen Buchanan," I said. This was on impulse, but after all, Helen had been living in Scotland, just north of Glasgow, so it was a logical alias. I took the phone and fumbled as I put in some random numbers. There was an emergency number for the Binaries, but this was not the time to use it.

"Oh dear," I said, "I keep Alexander's number on speed dial and now I can't remember it." Tears sprang up. I could tell that Toby MacDonald was chivalrous, feeling protective towards his drenched passenger.

"Not to worry. We MacDonalds like to help our Buchanan kinsfolk. Would you be staying at a hotel in Edinburgh?"

"Yes, it's supposed to be an anniversary break…" I faltered. "He said he'd booked a luxury hotel, it was to be a surprise."

"Well, let's get you to the station – it shouldn't be hard to track down your hubbie at the luxury hotels in Edinburgh."

Toby MacDonald started the car and outside, the rain was now pouring down.

"Thank you for rescuing me from that," I murmured and he glanced across, smiling.

"It could take half an hour to get to Forres. But the trains run quite frequently. You'll probably need to change at Aberdeen, mind, the rail journey will be some five hours."

"I'm sure I'll find him in Edinburgh."

"Perhaps we should stop at a police station? He might have called in, knowing you haven't got your phone."

"No, he wouldn't do that. It was a silly row, but he was furious. He knows I've got enough money on me for a rail ticket. In fact he said, 'OK, see you in Edinburgh, or not, just as you like…' "

"Some row, what was it about? I don't think I'd let my wife get out in the middle of nowhere, if I had a wife, that is."

"It's a bit embarrassing," I faltered. "About an ex-girlfriend of Alexander's – oh, do you mind if we don't talk about it?"

"Not at all," said Toby, although his expression remained curious. I decided to reverse the interrogation.

"This is probably miles out of your way - and you've probably got work to do," I said.

"Work, oh, I've done my bit for today. Though whether it'll bear fruit is less certain. I'm a photographer – I've just been to the post office to send off some shots to agents in London."

"A photographer, how interesting! Do you have any pictures with you?"

Toby nodded to indicate the back seat. "Plenty. I couldn't decide which to send, also brought along some duplicates. Help yourself."

I leaned back and took one of the folders. They were a mix of scenery, people in the street, fashion models, sport and some close ups of flowers and animals. "These are really good," I said, sincerely. "Do you work for a paper, or..?"

"I'm freelance. Sometimes I sell a picture to one of the Scottish papers, but I'm trying to branch out. There really isn't enough work up here, paid work that is, and it's hard to compete with the city boys."

"I think you're more than up to it," I murmured, getting a sudden vision of Toby doing very well, with an expensively equipped studio. Then I was surprised to see a mind image of Marcie Brown, the fashion journalist who had helped with Kastor's escape from Casablanca, although Helen had led Marcie to believe they were just tricking a man who had let them both down badly. This man, Ryden Asgard, was now the 'big baby' with a mental age of a toddler, incarcerated in St. Anthony's. I had a feeling that Marcie would like Toby, and perhaps a phone call from 'Jasmina' – Helen's cover name - would help to put them in touch.

"I know someone in London who hires fashion photographers – or perhaps others," I said casually. "Would you like me to put a word in?"

"I certainly would," said Toby. "I've a few contacts in London, but you can never have enough." He reached into a pocket, taking out a card.

"I'll telephone her from Edinburgh," I promised. If I get there, I thought gloomily. I was glancing out of the windows frequently, expecting a Binary white van to appear.

It was strange that they were making no attempt to capture me. Perhaps they intended to do this more easily when I reached Edinburgh. By the end of our journey we were chatting about life in Scotland, the problem with the English and other topics far from Binary life. I didn't attempt a Scottish accent, something that Helen would have done with ease. After all, not all Scots speak with a strong accent, I reasoned. As we drew into the Forres station car park, a train was departing.

"Well, it means they're running," said Toby. "I was going to get out and check." I sensed that he was sorry to lose me. "I could come in with you and see if the snack bar is open."

"I don't want to keep you…" I murmured, feeling quite safe with this amiable photographer.

He grinned and said, "You're probably a bit peckish – the snack bar isn't up to much. Let's check the trains and see if you've time to sample one of the local hostelries."

We found it would be a 45 minute wait, so after I'd bought a ticket, we went to a café. My clothes were still damp, clinging to me, but I felt warm and a long way from St. Anthony's. I insisted on paying for the meal, as Toby refused any cash for the petrol, and waved goodbye fondly as I went into the station. I fingered his card in my shoulder bag. I would need to explain to Marcie why I'd called myself Helen on this car trip, but that was an easily manageable detail.

Once on the train, I signalled to Kastor that I was en route to Edinburgh and was surprised to receive the response that he'd meet me there. I told him the train would arrive late, about 11 p.m. and sent a clock showing the exact time of arrival, with 'Waverley' written round the clock face. The thought image of Kastor nodded, smiling. He didn't seem angry at all, but was probably mostly relieved that I had completed the mind repair emergency.

I asked if Ingrid was OK and received another nod. But he was rushing, he signalled. I guessed he would be taking a plane, probably a scheduled flight, too tired to check his thoughts for that detail. I felt guilty for brewing up such trouble, but settled into my first class seat and prepared to enjoy the unusual experience of travelling by rail. Sipping the complimentary coffee, I allowed my mind to focus on what was happening at St. Anthony's. Not wanting Dr. Foucoe to pick up my thoughts, I used my inner device of a roving camera to sweep around the interior of the institution.

The ward at the centre of the storm no longer seemed in disarray, but the sex therapy room was empty. I focused on Cilisse and was pleased to detect that she seemed to be in bed, in her detention cell. Perhaps that meant they had followed my barked instructions. Probably it would be only a temporary reprieve, unless I could apply more pressure. And my influence on advising about Binary behaviour would at a low ebb after the upheaval I'd caused. The difficult outsider, I mused, but with some satisfaction. I turned my attention to the free magazines in the rack. An article about France made me wonder what the helpful Edouard Parfait was doing. I focused for a moment on him, seeing an image of the police captain sitting at a desk looking pensive. Perhaps his telepathic abilities have increased, as mine did after meeting Kastor, I thought. To my alarm, he turned slightly as if looking straight into my distance viewer. I shut down the channel immediately. Hopefully it would only seem that a thought of 'Madame Dufour' had come into his mind. But this made me feel little less guilty, knowing that if his thoughts strayed to me it would include the kiss and wanting to touch me again.

16

I climbed down the step onto the platform at Waverley Station and looked around. I sensed no field officers, but Kastor was definitely near. I turned to see him running towards me. I ran to meet him too, thinking, this is like a film, two people finding each other again during a dangerous war. Kastor lifted me off his feet as he hugged me. You're safe, his thoughts said and mine were a wave of happiness at seeing him again. My clothes were almost dry, but dishevelled and crumpled. He guided me through the station, not transmitting much as he shuttered off the noise and bustle.

"The hotel's just here," he said, after a short walk by Waverley Bridge. He explained that he too had come by train, as it was faster than my journey of several stops and a connection in Aberdeen. I radiated apology for dragging him up to Edinburgh, but he simply hugged me again. I sensed that there would be no reprimands until we were safely in the hotel room, perhaps not even then, as he seemed so delighted to have me back.

We ordered room service and meanwhile, I took off my clothes and had a warm shower. Kastor sent them off for laundry and pressing, despite my worry that I might have nothing to wear in the morning, if the service was slow.

"I quite like you wearing this," he said, wrapping a hotel

dressing gown round me. "I've missed you," he added, unnecessarily, as his thoughts and caressing hands said it all.

I told him about Toby Macdonald's good Samaritan act and Kastor was in such a good mood, there was not a flicker of jealousy. "I guessed you wouldn't walk all the way to the station," he murmured. "You'd still be on those roads, in the dark. And I knew you'd be able to sense danger and deal with it." A quick image of my storm at St. Anthony's told me that he knew a lot about it.

"The storm wasn't such a big deal," I said, when we pushed away the trays of food and settled down onto the bed with large whiskies.

"Just enough to terrify the entire population of St. Anthony's. Quite modest by your standards, I'll agree."

I checked that his eyes were smiling, then said, "I suppose I'm in a storm of trouble, though, but I had to do something. They're using that nursery assistant as a sex slave, round the clock, chained up too."

"Dr. Asklep was most misguided to show that to you. He thought you'd be filled with admiration. Chained up, you say?"

"Fettered, beaten, trussed up like a turkey – and they've conditioned her to believe it's her religious duty. Oh, she could hardly walk and it's only been a couple of weeks – imagine. She's not very intelligent, well, she's very dim. Also so young – a child really, and impressionable."

"And deranged?" added Kastor.

"Well, they've just swapped her obsession with Fabrice and his bigotry for another type of religious obedience. They're just keeping her mad, if you like, for their purposes."

Kastor lay back on the pillows, inviting me to join him. He held me close, with my head lying on his chest.

"That isn't the story Dr. Asklep tells, of course," he said. "He says they had to fight to have Cilisse given pleasant duties and that she's been willing, happy and very keen. He was flabbergasted, his word, when you appeared to fly off into a rage for no reason at all."

I lifted my head to sip the whisky. "It wasn't just the extreme cruelty – and my feelings about sex therapy – but, Kastor, he said I couldn't be expected to understand, because I'm…. an outsider."

Kastor sat up, angry, nearly spilling his tumbler of single malt. "What? He called you that? How dare he." He expelled a breath noisily.

"Well, I am an outsider – or was. I know that can never be forgotten in Binary world."

Kastor gazed at me, sharing his furious thoughts about Dr. Asklep. "You're not an outsider. You were living on the outside, but were always one of us, a natural, exceptional telepath. That's completely different! And with all your skills and what you've done for the organization…"

"It tipped me over the edge," I admitted. "I was trying to control myself but when he said that, I just blew up."

"Understandable," said Kastor. "Wait until I tell the others. Theodora will be incandescent."

"So you're not too… annoyed with me?"

Kastor appeared to have to think about this. Finally he said, "No. Of course not. Lately you've had to rapidly expand your powers to meet emergencies – it takes time to learn how to control that kind of talent. You shouldn't have had to go to that awful place at all, if Clyppie was all she claims to be in the mind repair business. You saved one of us from certain death – or at best, living death - in another's mind, and then they drag you off to see a girl being abused. You should've been resting! I'd like to have both those doctors struck off, Clyppie and the sadist pervert Asklep. And your compassion does you so much credit. The Binary conditioning makes us forget how cruel our punishments can be."

"I suppose Clyppie and Asklep said I was insane," I commented, "and needing psychiatric treatment…"

He knew my fears of mental illness. "Well, in the heat of the moment they said a lot of things. What you did was perhaps ill advised, but I understand. You're not mad."

I turned to face him. "Except madly in love with you," I said, curling up against his body. "Body mingling first, mind later?" I whispered seductively, letting the towelling dressing gown slip from my shoulders, and leaning close to rub his nose with mine.

"Hmm," he said, "just this once – or whenever you wish, in fact." He touched my ears, the earrings still safely in place. "And I'm so glad you didn't have to sell the earrings that match your beautiful eyes."

But I was moving over him so sensuously that he soon had no words, only shared images and desire.

Usually it was me who woke in the night, but when Kastor found himself unable to get back to sleep at 3 a.m., I seemed to be lying peacefully in a deep slumber, curled up in the bed. I didn't let him know that his gaze upon me woke me up. I kept my eyes shut, enjoying his thoughts. He was thinking, and not disapprovingly, of the havoc I'd caused at St. Anthony's. The staff must have been terrified, he reflected, as this tornado with the ability to create three dimensional, frightening illusions had charged through the ward and corridors. Possibly, without the forbidding messages from Woodstock Binaries, they would have been able to detain me until I calmed down, but they would not have dared to harm me. A quick image of Gaston made me alarmed, until I sensed that Gaston had vetoed any idea of following me or using brute force to stop my trail of anger through the dark fort.

When I stirred, Kastor made me some tea from the tray in the room. He told me that Theodora had ordered an immediate stop to behavioural re-education until the methods used at St. Anthony's could be re-assessed. Kastor would have been her first choice to do this, but because of his personal involvement, she had selected Joel Grigora instead. Joel, the brilliant Ethiopian telepath who had the unusual gift of precognition, like me. Kastor was angry with all the senior staff at St. Anthony's, but particularly Dr. Clytemnestra Foucoe. She was clever and capable of kindness, but her unjustified fame as a mind repairer had gone to her head.

"She didn't take care to look after you on this dangerous mission. From what I've picked up, Clyppie was graceless and consumed by needing to minimise any praise of your abilities," he said heatedly.

I had dropped off to sleep again when the room service breakfast arrived. Kastor used gentle thoughts to rouse me, although when I understood that breakfast was available, I sat up eagerly, declaring that I was ravenous. I went over to the window, enjoying being within a city. Binary establishments were always so cut off from outsider life. Munching a piece of toast covered with Marmite, I looked out onto the streets below.

"Shops," I murmured. "Will there be time to do some shopping – just to brush up my commercial skills?"

He took his coffee to the window, looking down with me. The noisy streets did not attract him and the idea of being in a crowded shop was painful. With my long experience of the outside, I was much more able to shutter off the barrage of talking and thoughts.

I picked up his uneasiness, saying immediately, "I could go on my own, just a short trip."

"A car will be coming to collect us for the airport very soon," he said, regretfully, "The Binary centre crisis is still a major problem."

"But we could delay the journey, just briefly?" I pleaded.

"What about the inquiry into St. Anthony's..." he started to say, before I interrupted.

"You said you weren't bothered about that."

"Well, I'm not bothered, or angry, but Clyppie wants you exiled to the South Pole, further if possible – and Dr. Asklep is calling for a disciplinary tribunal. You'll be completely exonerated, I'm sure, but we need to sort it out."

"Are my clothes back?" I asked, making Kastor think that I would just go to the shops anyway. I really was a very disobedient Binary. He checked outside the door and shook his head.

"But they promised them for 8:30, and it's only half past seven. Just in case, I'll go down and get the manager to open the hotel shop – they sell a few clothes."

"All right," I agreed, "It would be good to buy a new outfit in an outside shop though. Those clothes will have been ruined by the rain – and my shoes might have shrunk."

"Hmm," said Kastor. "Well, if this is a shopping emergency, I'll get the field officer from the car to go with you. As it happens, he's very experienced on shopping trips, one of Simon Arbalest's team."

Simon Arbalest was a senior telepath in the commercial centre where I worked. I smiled, guessing that Kastor had laid on a suitable officer with just this thought in mind. I went to shower while Kastor signalled to the driver and field officer that we would delay going to the airport for at least an hour.

The hotel shop stocked mainly leisure clothes, so I had to go out in a tracksuit, but was not dismayed. I was hobbling a little in the rain-damaged shoes, as footwear was not sold in the hotel boutique. So I announced that our first stop would be a shoe shop. I had intended to spend from my stash of banknotes, but Kastor said the field officer would pay for everything on a Binary credit card.

"It's a trip to hone up your product placement skills after all," he said, smiling, as I rushed out of the hotel with the officer, promising to be back within the hour. He checked his watch and informed the driver of a likely two-hour delay, while changing our flight to a later time. Binaries always travelled first class, which helped in altering such arrangements. He had bought me some sunglasses with pink shades from the boutique. It was unlikely that anyone who knew me would be shopping in Princes Street that morning, but the Cassandra who had lived on the outside was officially dead, so it was best to be careful. Helen had told me that she always wore a wig and large glasses on her rare outings while living there, but even so, recognition was a risk.

When I returned, the field officer struggling to balance an enormous number of bags, Kastor's time estimate was shown to be correct. I was thrilled with my shopping treat and I wanted to show him everything, but Kastor had already checked 'Mr. and Mrs. Hardy' – one of our aliases - out of the hotel and ushered me into the waiting car. I insisted on bringing the bag with toys into the car, while the rest were stashed in the boot. It contained a robot and six teddy bears in different tartan outfits. In case Leo thought he was too grown up to have the same toy as his younger siblings and cousins, the robot was especially for him. It could be programmed to speak short sentences.

We amused ourselves on the journey by customising the robot's commands to say things like "Binaries obey!", "I love flying," and "Let's share thoughts." It was important to use phrases that Leo could show off to his friends in the nursery wing, where the difference in his upbringing was still controversial. Leo was showing promise as a mental flyer and he had inherited my gift for imagery. He also seemed well adjusted to having infrequent contact with Kastor and me, now that he was back in the children's dormitory.

I reflected that there were many good things about Binary life and resolved to draw up a list of aspects to conserve and those to try to change, in my zeal for reform. Kastor was simply happy that I'd been distracted from my grim experiences at St. Anthony's and the disruption to our life since leaving our lovely French home.

17

While we were returning to the Binary Centre, Joel Grigora was arriving at St. Anthony's. I heard all about it later from Joel, who kindly supplied good images too. How much outsiders miss, I reflected, not being able to run through events together. But only remote viewers like Joel and I could do this so fluently. He had brought some surveillance footage along, in case the remote viewing drained us too much. Usually half an hour or so was the limit, even for us.

We switched on the viewing screen. The small, indignant delegation that met Joel included Dr. Foucoe and Dr. Asklep, fuming at the idea of an inspection of their methods. They had repaired to an elegant meeting room and the first film showed them sitting around an oval mahogany table.

"I suppose Cassandra has been detained," said Dr. Foucoe.

"She's returning to Binaries as we speak," said Joel gravely. "But my visit is purely concerned with a review of re-educating and re-programming methods."

"Of course we want to cooperate with the inquiry," said Dr. Asklep, rubbing his hands and wearing a false smile, "but surely the first priority should be to discipline Cassandra and devise appropriate treatment."

"And why has Theodora not come herself, if it's so important?

Or has she been influenced by this little witch like so many others?" demanded Dr. Foucoe.

Pausing the surveillance film, Joel shared a quick thought with me, as I started at the description of me as a witch. An unpardonable insult in our community and not the first offensive remark from Clea Foucoe.

"Sorry, perhaps I should have had that edited out," Joel said apologetically. "Some of the staff there have a deep antipathy to you as a favourite of the most senior telepaths at Binaries. They were irritated that you even seemed to have won round Gaston. As you know, he vetoed their proposal to use stun guns on you."

I smiled. "Hard but fair, that's Gaston."

Joel nodded, glad to take a rest from enriching the transmission with captured thoughts from the group.

"Gaston also appeared unconcerned with the disruption of what Dr. Asklep had called 'essential therapy'."

I did not confide that Gaston had experience of therapy at St. Antony's, something I had learned in secret during our adventure in Cadiz. But Joel would have picked that up from me, no doubt. I was confident that he was very discreet. We took some tea and sat quietly before pressing the play button on the screen again. Joel was looking sternly at the staff group assembled around the table.

"I should advise you that everything you say will be reported to Theodora," said Joel. "Perhaps you'd like to withdraw the description 'little witch.' It's a forbidden insult in our community, as you are well aware."

Dr. Foucoe bit her lip, silently apologising for her use of language. "It was only natural," she murmured, "that I should be so angry about her behaviour." Joel merely gazed at her until she looked distinctly uncomfortable.

"It seems that behavioural readjustment may need to be considered for some of the staff here," he said. "Sometimes in remote parts of the organization, staff diverge from agreed policies and procedures. As for whether Theodora should come, she's conducting essential assessments at present, but I can assure you that it'll be easier for you if I'm in charge of the early part of this investigation."

He turned to Dr. Asklep, who had been enjoying the critical focus on Dr. Foucoe. "Speaking of the use of language," Joel intoned, "you apparently called Cassandra an outsider."

Several in the group in the meeting room turned their heads in shocked astonishment. Knowing little of my history, people assumed that I had spent time outside for some reason, perhaps to train my extraordinary talents. But even if this included being born outside, it was a grave insult. Dr. Asklep had omitted this detail from his account of the incident. Clea Foucoe, smarting from the angry thought that Joel had shot over at her use of 'witch', raised her eyebrows with both disapproval and relief to be released from Joel's searching gaze.

Dr. Asklep took off his spectacles and made a show of cleaning them before he responded.

"I don't think I used that word. As I recall, I merely mentioned her experience outside, which might make it hard for her to understand our methods."

Joel smiled as he pressed the pause button. "At this point," he confided, "I closed my eyes to try to capture this conversation." Like me, he could sometimes retrieve the images of an event in the past.

"The others around the table could sense only an apparent rapid relay of sounds and jerky images, like an old silent movie film running backwards in slow motion."

"But you were seeing it more clearly?" I asked unnecessarily, for I had no doubt that Joel could do that.

"Yes. They were disconcerted when I seemed distressed at a

couple of points. But they were even more put out when I came out of that past retrieval." He resumed the surveillance film transmission.

Joel was smiling broadly at the group. He gazed particularly at Dr. Asklep.

"No, you definitely said 'outsider'. Apparently that was the igniting point for Cassandra, who was understandably exhausted by her excellent work in the mind repair unit."

Joel turned to an administrator in the group. "Perhaps you could fetch Ariadne Tartaros, who may help in telling us what happened just before the incident."

Dr. Foucoe stared down at her notes. Ariadne had not yet described Ingrid's rescue in detail to her colleagues, but meanwhile Clea had been taking all the credit for Ingrid's welcome recovery.

"She provoked me, in extremis," blustered Dr. Asklep. "Everyone knows that the treacherous girl Cilisse has been treated most leniently, most graciously. And yet Cassandra was talking as though we were monsters."

"Using Cilisse as a sex slave," said Joel. "Training her with fear and torture. Allowing deranged patients to attack her while she's chained up. Is that your definition of lenience and grace, Dr. Asklep?"

"She deserved every bit of it," said the rotund doctor, now sweating, but looking around the table for support. "Two of us were mind damaged, another shot, because of her. She should have been executed. It was only the pregnancy that stopped that being done before she got here."

"But it's not your job to mete out punishment, is it?" asked Joel. "I find no documents which sentenced her to your distasteful regime. Only a diagnosis of mental illness, a delusion that contributed to the tragic events at Binaires. Even Binaries don't hold the mentally sick responsible for crimes."

Ariadne entered the room and confirmed that Dr. Asklep had taken me from the mind repair unit, while she had gone back to her quarters to rest. She described how we had worked on a strategy to free Marc's mind of the 'foreign body'. While she did not mention Dr. Foucoe's obstructive manner and behaviour, it was evident that the self-styled heroine of mind repair had played little part in Ingrid's rescue.

"So Marc is gay," murmured the administrator with interest, but the others silently admonished him that this was scarcely the time to discuss sexual preference. After covering all the main points, Joel indicated that he would reconvene after refreshments.

"We have work to do," said Dr. Foucoe. "I think, all things considered, that we'd like to draw a veil over this incident and move on."

"Move on," murmured Joel. He explained to me that at this point, he shared an image of Clea working in a mosquito infested jungle in one of their experimental units, where conditions were extremely harsh. Dr. Foucoe paled and said nothing more.

"I shall be interviewing Cilisse on her own after the break," continued Joel authoritatively. "Kindly bring her to an appropriate room. Just one escort, a nurse not involved in this disgraceful episode."

"I must insist on attending," said Dr. Asklep, "since her behavioural conditioning is at a very delicate stage."

"If you insist," said Joel, "you may watch through a two way mirror. It'll be most interesting to film your reactions to her interview. In fact, thank you for suggesting it, I shall make that a requirement. But once you enter the viewing chamber, it'll be locked. I don't wish my collection of evidence to be disturbed." Dr. Asklep looked round for others to veto the suggestion, but they were all nodding.

"I'm being made a scapegoat, I can see that," he said. "But what about the nurses and orderlies who looked after Cilisse?"

"They'll all be interviewed and sent for re-education as required," said Joel, nodding to the administrator that the meeting should be concluded.

We took another break while Joel searched for the file containing the film of the interview with Cilisse. This showed her being brought into the interview room, with a solicitous nurse. She was still wearing the front opening hospital gown and clogs.

"Fetch her some more suitable clothes," said Joel, disapprovingly. "I see at least that you've bandaged the sores on her wrists and ankles." The nurse scurried out. Cilisse had sat down as indicated in a chair in front of his desk.

"Have I come here to do my duty?" she asked, looking around the room for a couch and fetters.

"And what is that, Cilisse?"

She promptly stood up and started stripping. Before Joel could stop her, she was lying naked on the floor and leering at him.

"But you can't have therapy unless you say the right words," she wheedled. Joel signalled for the female warder waiting outside to come in, who promptly wrapped Cilisse in a blanket.

"No therapy here, Cilisse," she murmured.

"I can tell you the words if you like," said Cilisse with a cunning smile.

I was sitting tensely, viewing this evidence of the success of Cilisse's reconditioning as a sex slave. Joel paused the film, nodding gravely.

"I glimpsed an image of her being... intimate with the warders, who laughed at her stupidity. She gave them the latest rewording of her conditioning. Paradoxically, these were her most gentle physical experiences at St. Anthony's."

"They seem very into physical experience there," I muttered.

"It's a stressful environment for the staff – and the warders," Joel acknowledged. "But as you may imagine, I have recommended re-education," – he tactfully avoided the word 'discipline' – "for the warders. The female warders all turned a blind eye to the abuse of Cilisse. It was humbling for me to see the cruel side of our Binary enthusiasm for punishment."

He pressed the play button again, as I had nothing to say in response. In the surveillance film the girl, sitting back on the chair with the warder holding the blanket round her, was looking very bewildered.

"Did the Holy Mother send you?" she asked. "But I've been good, I'm serving patients and making them happy." Her disturbed mind was now even more confused following Dr. Asklep's so-called re-programming.

"I'm here to help you get better, Cilisse," said Joel. "I need to know what you'd really like to do while you serve your sentence."

Cilisse tried to remove the blanket. She could think only of the 'work' that she had been conditioned to provide.

"I want to do my duty," she said stubbornly, adding a smile and looking up to her warder for approval.

Cilisse was taken behind a screen to be dressed in a detention centre tracksuit. Then, Joel went through various psychological and intelligence tests with her. He fast forwarded this, as I didn't need such detail.

"She has very little aptitude for skilled work, but scored highly on cleanliness and tidiness," he explained to me, pausing the film again. "So I ordered that she should be re-assigned to light laundry duties while a more appropriate psychiatric treatment could be devised."

"Good," I muttered.

"An improvement, yes," agreed Joel. "Apart from the staff being mainly female, which would limit exploitation of this pregnant girl, she is not physically strong enough at present to do more arduous work. It will take some time to reverse the conditioned responses, relentlessly instilled by Dr. Asklep and reinforced by the nurses."

"What about Dr. Asklep, was he watching this interview?"

"Yes, as per his request. There was the usual two-way mirror in the room, for us to film and for him to sit without her being embarrassed by his presence, or influenced."

"What was his response?"

"A trusted staff member was sitting with him. At one point he stood up, protesting that this conditioning was quite routine. But then he remembered the recording. He started wondering if he could blame all this on the eager help of his nursing colleagues."

"Slimey toad," I commented, which made Joel raise his eyebrows.

"Your metaphors from the outside are so interesting," he commented. "I myself have never seen a toad. Does Dr. Asklep look like one?"

"It's just an expression. Probably very unfair on toads," I said with a smile, "although now you come to mention it, he did make me think of a toad. They have rather self satisfied faces, but that's us putting human emotions onto them."

"Just so," said Joel, trying to see the humour in this.

The next interview film was with Chief Nurse Hart, in charge of sex therapy and assisting with conditioning techniques. She arrived indignantly, demanding to know why sex therapy had been suspended, before he had a chance to speak.

"Such therapy was never intended to be forced," said Joel. "This girl was mentally disturbed, easily manipulated. The case means that the whole policy must be re-evaluated."

"Nonsense," said the nurse. "Her low intelligence makes her ideal for this work – and her crime means we needn't be overly concerned with whether she volunteered to escape something worse, or didn't volunteer at all."

"Do you treat the other volunteers like that?"

"No, not exactly. Well, all right, previously only condemned prisoners have been offered this option. But this girl has been a godsend to patients for whom volunteers are very rare."

"The patients will have to get by without this therapy. Perhaps the policy has been wrong all these years." The nurse just glared at him in astonishment. Joel continued, "We have a statement from a mind damaged Binary who made a complete and rapid recovery without needing volunteer sex therapists. The Binary Council has made a decision. From now on, the policy will be consensual relations between adults only. There's never been a Binaries bar on that."

"One evil girl, and you change a whole policy."

In the film, Joel was looking at her with a stern, unwavering gaze. He paused the transmission to explain. "I could see images of her encouraging the orderly to tighten the fetters and add ever more cases to Cilisse's list of customers."

"I'm thrilled the Board has agreed," I said eagerly. "I guess the Council reports to the Board?" The higher levels of controlling our organization were still a mystery to me. But Joel merely shrugged, letting me know that he could not discuss that. He pressed the play button again.

After he had shared the images of the chained up Cilisse with the nurse, he said, "The organization is in crisis, as you're aware. A wind of change is blowing through. Many aspects of our culture and way of life may alter. We've already suspended all baby and child rescues."

"The world has gone mad!" exclaimed the nurse. "And if you mean encouraging dangerous telepaths who can create wind illusions, that should be stopped forthwith. Several patients are still very disturbed…"

"The Binary Council regrets the disturbance, of course, but the timing is ideal for this period of great upheaval. Meanwhile, you and Dr. Asklep will attend immediate re-education sessions, along with all the other staff involved. A small team will be arriving. Also they will start the de-programming of Cilisse so that she can serve our community in less unsavoury ways. That'll be all for the moment, Nurse Hart."

There were no more interviews to show me, or at least that he thought appropriate to share with me.

"I left St. Anthony's after a couple of days," he said, "once the re-programming team had arrived. When I reported back to Theodora in the Binary assessment centre, I said it would be difficult to completely reverse the girl's conditioning."

I sighed, but he went on, "Ironically, Cilisse was only looking for affection and security. Theodora believes that she'll always be quite… free with her favours, even when she understands she need only do that voluntarily, when there's a mutual attraction."

"So she'll become a sex therapist after all?" I asked, disappointed.

"We've stopped that," Joel reminded me. "She'll probably be a hard working member of the St. Anthony's community, in time. Theodora has recommended her transfer to a two bed cell, with a sensible young woman who's recovering from her psychiatric problems."

"And how are the clinical staff adapting?" I asked, thinking of Dr. Foucoe and Dr. Asklep, as well as the nurses.

"The clinical staff are proving a little resistant to their re-education," said Joel. With no willingness to add more, he said that he had to get back to work.

18

Pleased with how my reforms for St. Anthony's seemed to be going, I returned to play with my children at the apartment. It was a sunny afternoon in June. When the nanny announced it was time to return for tea, Leo asked if he could stay longer. To my surprise, the nanny said she'd send someone over later to collect him. It seemed that I was being allowed great leeway these days.

I had returned to work in the commercial centre, since maintaining income was a priority for the organization, with the relocation of the French Binaires group to arrange. Some would go the Canadian centre and a few to the Virginia Centre in the US, as the extension of the Devon unit was going to take some time.

Leo performed a new song for me. He'd learned it at pre-school. It was all about how much they loved being Binaries. More conditioning, I noted, tartly. Leo would be leaving in early September for the junior part of the Lochinstoun boarding school. He seemed to be looking forward to it. Finley and Astra, his particular friends, would be going at the same time. I suggested reading a book together but he asked about a paper on my desk. He'd seen me working on when he arrived. With his telepathic powers daily increasing, he had sensed my pre-occupation with it.

"It's a list of good and not so good things about the Binaries," I said.

"But it's all good, Mummy," he said, puzzled.

"Well, when we had to leave the Villa Dufour, which was not so good, I thought I should make a list, to help us plan."

Leo had enjoyed the escape from the villa and now often asked when he could visit the Tower of London, glimpsed tantalisingly from the boat when we'd arrived in London. And he liked school better at the Woodstock Binaries. So he couldn't think why I needed to plan anything. "It's hard to explain, Leo," I murmured, thinking that his list of possibly not so good things might include cabbage, having to go to bed when told and not being able to visit some of the places he was learning about. Whereas my list of negative factors included:

Rigid conditioning

Unwillingness to change

Sex therapy (but progress made on that)

Abducting babies and children

Harsh punishments and 'eliminations'

Very limited freedom

Constant threat of discovery or kidnapping

People knowing your thoughts (also included on the plus side)

Earning money rather shadily, on occasion

Shopping from catalogues, not going to outside shops

Never being able to go to an outside restaurant for dinner

No theatre visits

Limited contact with our own children

Socially restricted to friends within Binaries

Cut off from family outside

No independent money

Leo looked over my shoulder. He could read quite well, since education started at an early age for Binary children. "You haven't put much under 'Good', Mummy," he observed. The good list of Binary things read:

Kastor and the children

Good friends

Sharing thoughts & images

People knowing when you're upset or in trouble

Developing skills/ respect for abilities

Servants and no need to cook

I hastily screwed up the paper, making a mental note to destroy it later. "I hadn't put all the good things down yet. Just silly Mummy playing, of course everything is perfect here." Leo, however loyal to me, might let slip about the list and put me into further bad books at the nursery. I said cautiously, "Our secret, Leo?" and he nodded gravely. Even at five, he knew that his mother was both an exceptional telepath, revered within the organization, but also in need of protection. He sensed this often from his father. When the nanny came to collect him, he said "Goodbye" in his formal, approved way, but also gave me a quick mental wink.

19

Kastor and I went for dinner in Manes' apartment that night, with Amélie arranging a French menu. We had settled down to play a quiz game – with mutual promises not to cheat by reading the mind of the questioner, although this was hard to do in practice – when I received a thought message from Dr. Philips.

"Oh no," I exclaimed to the others. "Another mind repairer's been lost, this time within the mind of the nanny."

"Clyppie's getting very careless," observed Kastor.

"They want me to go to St. Anthony's again, immediately," I said, sharing my dislike of the idea with our friends.

"No, not there," said Kastor, "Definitely not."

Manes nodded. "After that incident, it'll be very difficult for you to return to St. Anthony's." He glanced at Kastor. "Are you suggesting that Clea has possibly engineered this, to make Cassandra do another dangerous mind entry?"

"I'd hope not," murmured Kastor, "but with all the talk, now, about her having exaggerated her mind repair expertise – and the re-education – it's possible she wouldn't mind seeing Cassandra fail."

I was quiet, receiving more information from Dr. Philips. When

I turned back to the others, I said, "They're keeping her awake, just as with the guard. And it's Ariadne Tartaros who's lost this time. I can't understand it, she's so organised and careful."

"Don't even think of saying you'll go," said Kastor, firmly.

"But surely it's an emergency," said Amélie in distress, who knew the mind injured nanny, Althaea, well. "And if anyone can do the rescue, it's Cassandra."

"I'd better go to the medical unit, at least to discuss it," I said.

"I'm coming with you," said Kastor, "to make sure they don't whisk you into a helicopter."

We travelled on the underground railway to the medical unit, with the tunnel eerily dark and quiet at this time of night. Dr. Hagen Philips was waiting anxiously. "The helicopter's ready…" he began, but Kastor stopped him short.

"Hagen – I understand your concern, but I'm more worried about Cassandra making another trip to St. Anthony's." He ignored my thought that I would go if it was the only way to save the mind repairer. Dr. Philips looked at us both in despair.

"But what other option is there? If someone else from the mind repair team up there goes in, we might lose them as well."

"That could happen to Cassandra," said Kastor, "and surely she's done enough for Clyppie – who should be dealing with this herself."

I sat down, picturing the distraught team up at St. Anthony's and the silent body of Ariadne, lying on a couch next to the nanny. "There is another option," I said slowly. "Althaea and Ariadne could be brought here, with another member of the mind repair team."

"But the journey could be dangerous for both of them," protested Hagen.

"It's dangerous either way," I said. "But Kastor's right. I

shouldn't go to St. Anthony's again. I caused a storm last time and they won't have forgotten that. The place has a bad effect on me."

"If a mind repairer came here with the two women, perhaps you could just supervise them, not go in yourself," said Kastor, tentatively.

"We'd have to see," I replied, sharing a thought that we both knew I'd be expected to embark on the difficult mind entry. While Clea had been glad enough to assume credit for the mind work, she was right in one element at least: it was dangerous. I felt responsible for having introduced it to the community.

"Meanwhile, tell them to let the nanny sleep," I advised. "Either the subconscious will have absorbed her already, or she could be walled up like Ariadne. I don't think further slumber will make much of a difference. This is unknown territory for all of us."

Dr. Philips sighed and reached for the medical hotline. "Clea is not going to like this." We all shared a thought that this was a low priority.

After a tense conversation over the phone, Dr. Philips turned to Kastor and me. "She's agreed, but says the responsibility is all yours."

He couldn't resist a slight smile. Clea Foucoe would be humiliated by this second failure of her repair team, with further evidence that she was not able to use her highly publicised skills to put it right. "They can't travel until tomorrow morning," he said.

Kastor narrowed his eyes, still suspicious of Clea's motives. "Cassandra should choose the mind repairer who comes with them. Perhaps there should be two?"

"Good idea," I said. "If Ingrid Vesta feels up to it, she should come - she has first hand experience of being almost absorbed by the subconscious. And Dylan Comus. I remember he showed a lot of promise and originality."

"I'll help too," said Hagen, "I'll go in with you Cassandra, if necessary."

Hagen Philips had no experience of mind repair, but sensed the worry about how this difficult procedure might go.

"I appreciate that offer," I said, "but you'll be needed to keep a close watch while they or I go in - and to keep the nanny awake during the exploration." Dr. Philips signalled to Clea that they should have another phone conversation and Kastor and I left him to deal with the irate psychiatrist.

On the return journey to Askeys, I gazed at the curving walls of the underground railway, which reminded me of the spiralling lines of the tunnel I had seen when trying to communicate with Ingrid's subconscious. Kastor sat tensely, picking up this strange image and wishing I was not always so happy to plunge into things, except when I dived into his mind.

"I'm going to investigate how this happened," he said, as we approached the stop for the Askeys staircase. "It's almost as if Clyppie has laid on a test for you, to see the limits of your abilities. I can't bear the thought of you going into danger again."

I pressed his hand. "If the worst comes to the worst, you'll have to come in as well and we'll make a colony in the nanny's subconscious. If we brought the children in too, perhaps the subconscious would give up the battle and eject us all, just to get some peace!"

He laughed, picturing a miniature Binaries nursery deep in a nanny's subconscious. "That might actually be quite appealing to Althaea," he said, "otherwise it's not a bad idea."

In the apartment, he suggested we listen to some music before getting some rest. While he hesitated between a Mozart sonata and something modern, I remembered the screwed up paper containing my list on the desk and went over to make sure it was safely destroyed. But the ever perceptive Kastor turned to me curiously.

"What's that?"

"Just a list, of pros and cons about living here," I said, deciding that honesty was the only course. I uncrumpled the piece of paper so that he could look at it. I knew he would not approve.

"You've put '*Kastor and the children*' as the first reason on the 'plus' side," he murmured. "Whereas if it were my list, the first ten good things would just say '*Cassandra.*' Then possibly the children…"

"I'd only just started on the plus side," I said hastily, taking the paper from him and tearing it into tiny pieces. "It was just a thought aid, a foolish idea. I was feeling rather negative, not wanting to put lots of pros down on the list. Now you mention it, the first hundred of mine would say '*Kastor*'." I looked at him cajolingly. "You're the first and last reason for my being here. It'll always overpower any negative feelings I have about the organization."

I looked so regretful about the list that he drew me towards him. "You shouldn't make lists that people could find," he murmured, "How am I to protect you, if you're always courting danger?"

"You're always in my thoughts. I hope we give each other strength – and I promise to be very careful with this latest emergency."

"Even though sharing thoughts was on your list of negative points," said Kastor, smiling.

"And on the positive side," I protested, "but speaking of sharing minds, I'd like to plunge into yours, right now." Forgetting the idea of listening to music, we went to the main bedroom.

Kastor emerged from a brief exploration of my mind with an expression of delight. "There's more structure these days, but still the wonderful endless oceans," he murmured.

"And mermaids?" I asked, as this had become a private joke. "No mermaids yet, I'm rather glad to say," he replied, "for I'd probably never want to leave."

I smiled happily, wondering if we had the energy for some body mingling after the mental efforts of exploration. But just as I sensed that Kastor would rather just fall asleep, I had another idea concerning my list.

"Why are there no old people in the Binaries, I mean really old people?"

He sighed. A peaceful slumber seemed some way off. "We have old people's homes, just as on the outside."

"So they're not just put to sleep, the old people who're too frail, or unable to think clearly?"

"You want to add euthanasia to your list of negatives?"

"It never occurred to me before. I feel bad not to have wondered about it."

"The ones that need special care have to be protected. Their thoughts wander and they can be unpredictable in behaviour, so they could be detected by outsiders."

"Have you ever seen one of these homes?" I asked suspiciously. It seemed that the Binaries were just as dislocated from their old folk as from their children. Kastor put his arms around me, willing me to drop the subject.

"Please don't try to reform everything about the Binaries, all at once. When we're old, we'll find a home where we can be safe, that's all you need to know."

When he sensed that I was still pondering about the plight of ancient Binaries, he held me closer. "I thought you were too tired..." I murmured, as he started kissing my shoulder.

"Yes, but we'd better make the most of our bodies, before we're shipped off to a care home," he replied, laughing.

"Quite right," she said, "we should take every opportunity..."

He stopped further speech with a passionate kiss.

In the early hours of the morning, I awoke from a disturbing dream and sat up, trying to dispel the images. The bedroom seemed to have transformed into a dungeon with chains hanging from its walls. This after image vanished, but I could still remember the dream. At first it had seemed pleasant enough. There was a medieval castle with fairy tale turrets and stone passages filled with children and adults, laughing and running up and down the spiral staircases. But then I had discovered a dark stairway. It led downwards to a labyrinth of dungeons. A man wearing a black leather eye mask strolled past, giving me an ominous glance. A uniformed nanny stopped me.

"We've got one in here already, we don't need you."

I looked into the dungeon from which the nanny had emerged. To my horror, Althaea was hanging from two wrist fetters on the wall. A woman was standing beside her, holding a short multi-tailed whip that I recognised as the type used to punish sailors on ships in former times: a cat o'nine tails.

"I must be in St. Anthony's," my dream-self murmured, as I dashed into the dungeon to rescue Althaea. But the chained up nanny gave me a sly smile, reminding me of the unfortunate Cilisse.

"Go away," said Althaea, "I'm enjoying my punishment."

The female warder waved her whip menacingly. "We're busy, don't interfere." I gasped when I recognised the warder as Ariadne, who turned and struck the nanny. Althaea let out a scream and I found myself screaming too, until I woke up.

Kastor put on the bedside light. "A bad nightmare?" he asked.

I nodded. "It must be jumbled memories of my visit to St. Anthony's. But Althaea was in a dungeon, being whipped – by Ariadne."

"Your dreams are never a simple hashing of memories. It could just be a reflection of your worries about another mind exploration – but on the other hand...." He paused and shifted awkwardly.

"What?" I demanded.

"Well, Binary nannies can be quite enthusiastic about physical exercise, punishing routines...."

My eyes widened, prompting him silently to continue. Kastor looked at the clock: it was 4 a.m. "I'll make some tea," he said, resignedly. While he was in the kitchen, I sensed him contacting the medical unit. When he returned with two mugs of tea, he picked up the phone. "I need to spell this out," he explained, "in case the night staff didn't catch my full message. I'm asking them to send Clyppie down with the mind repairers and patients." I was now wide awake, waiting for an explanation about the punishing routines he had mentioned, after he had made the call.

"You've never seen the nannies working out, I suppose," Kastor began and I shook my head. "Well, you have to consider what it must be like looking after all those babies and children, day after day. They have to be patient, kind, controlled..."

"And strict..." I added.

"But not hitting the children, of course, so they have to let off steam somehow. Some of them take to what you might call a dominatrix lifestyle, out of hours."

"Like Helen?" I asked, unable to picture Helen as a nanny.

"OK, not just the nannies," said Kastor, smiling at this idea. "It's part of the way we adapt to using our minds so much. When we were kids, we'd sometimes sneak into the school gym to watch them."

"That must have been forbidden."

"Yes, strictly off limits, but there was a storage cupboard with louvred doors for equipment, which they rarely opened during the session, so we'd take it turns to hide in there and peek out through the cracks in the wooden slats. They'd use whips, canes, bats – that kind of stuff – on each other. In addition to judo and so on, which was encouraged."

"How old were you?"

"Oh, thirteen, fourteen - they'd catch us occasionally, but luckily I never got nabbed. I wasn't particularly interested, in fact, it was just the illicit thrill."

I narrowed my eyes. "Not particularly interested, eh? But I guess most of them were women, dressed in tight little shorts and sports bras."

"Tracksuits mainly, but yes…," Kastor smiled dreamily at the memory. "We only saw them usually in their prim uniforms."

"Where does Clyppie come into this?"

"Your dream made me think that there could be a mutual interest in a bit of punishment, deep in the subconscious. Ariadne's quite a sporty girl, isn't she?"

"A dominant personality, you think," I said cautiously, wondering how many of the Binaries women – or men – were into sadomasochistic leisure pursuits.

"Exactly. And Clyppie's an excellent psychiatrist, even if mind repair isn't her forte. This could be a chance for her to redeem her damaged reputation."

I sipped the tea, my thoughts full of whether Kastor was more than casually interested in punishments. My boyfriend on the outside, Roderick, had this taste, exploited by Helen when she took over my identity. Picking this up, Kastor stroked my arm.

"I've never wanted to do any of that with you, Cassandra."

"Are you sure? You've had to make so many compromises with

me. Now I'm worrying."

"We don't all yearn to spank and whip each other. It's just a bit more common than on the outside. I prefer a normal work out in the gym. And in any case, even if I did have that… predilection, it'd be a very brave man who took you on."

"So long as you don't feel deprived."

He laughed. "I get plenty of physical release of tension with you already. You want me to wear myself out even more thinking up bondage and discipline routines as well?"

"Physical release…" I murmured, snuggling closer.

"But right now," he replied, "We should get some sleep. It should be an interesting day."

20

The group from St. Anthony's arrived mid morning. The nanny, Althaea, had been sedated for the journey but Dr. Clytemnestra Foucoe was wide awake and enthusiastic, repairing to a side room with Kastor and Dr. Hagen Philips to discuss the possibility that Ariadne had been lured into Althaea's subconscious. Seeing them all chatting together, remembering their formative years and discussing yet more aspects of Binary culture of which I knew little, I felt a pang of exclusion. I wished that Helen was around as she would have been sure to give me the low down on who had been fond of "a bit of discipline." Meanwhile, I talked to the two mind repairers, Ingrid Vesta and Dylan Comus. I was surprised to learn that Althaea had been awake when Ariadne had been lost in her mind.

"We only realised something was wrong when Ariadne didn't wake up," said Dylan Comus. "Althaea had deep damage through several mind layers and we think she must have tumbled down through an unseen crater."

"But we know you can't really be injured when inside another's mind," I said pensively, "At least, so I thought."

"We've both explored Althaea's mind," said Ingrid Vesta. "The repairs were going really well but we hadn't been further down than the fourth layer."

"Let's see if we can contact Ariadne's subconscious," I suggested. "I don't know any other way of determining how she's faring down there."

We went to the side room where Ariadne was lying in a silent sleep. "I'll focus on entering her mind," I said. "Don't try to go in with me. Just wake me up if I seem troubled."

A couch was put next to Ariadne's bed so that I could lie face to face with her. I closed my eyes and concentrated, as I had done with Marc.

At first, I could only see a black, starlit sky. It was soft underfoot. I seemed to be standing on a transparent, flexible walkway under the arching firmament. I edged forwards cautiously, not looking down into the fathomless dark below. In my mind I called out to Ariadne. A section of the sky ahead seemed to condense into a grey shadowy mass. I called again, gliding towards this shape. I felt feathery strands touching my face and arms and looking around, saw a structure like a gossamer web. I thought of the myth of Arachne, the 'spider goddess' often linked to Ariadne. In that myth, she was the princess who provided a ball of thread so that Theseus would find his way through the labyrinth and escape the Minotaur.

I felt a frisson of fear at the idea that Ariadne might have identified so closely with these myths that both a monster and a giant spider could be lurking in her subconscious. But this would surely be too whimsical for the practical Ariadne. Another feature of the myth came to mind, where Arachne was so proud of her weaving that she refused to show respect to the goddess Athene. She was turned into a spider as punishment. Ariadne was possibly over-confident of her skills, but what did her subconscious make of all this? The threads were becoming thicker and harder to move through as I stepped over low swinging parts of the web. I spotted a part that looked like an overgrown tunnel and stooped to enter it. Now I could hear sounds like rushing water or an underground train sweeping by, reminding me of exploring Ingrid's subconscious. In the dim light of the tunnel, I saw a figure about half way along.

Initially I thought the figure was a man, wearing a backpack and apparently dressed for a hiking expedition. Coming nearer, I saw an athletic woman, older than Ariadne, standing and staring into the distance. She showed no sign of noticing my approach.

"Ariadne?" I said, uncertainly. The hiker turned very slowly and fixed sad, deep eyes on me.

"Over confident," murmured the hiker, "yes, but we didn't expect her to be so drawn in. Now, we can't reach her at all."

It seemed quite logical that the hiker would have picked up my thoughts.

"Do you know where she is?" I asked and the hiker shook her head mournfully.

"It's going to take more than a ball of thread," she murmured. She pointed to a hole in the tunnel and I stepped back, alarmed at its depth and darkness.

"Look down," said the hiker. I peered cautiously, holding onto the woven threads of the tunnel walls. The hole was like an old well with rings of aged bricks and green algal slime clinging to the sides. Far below, I glimpsed a flashing light, like a torch being switched on and off. "It's getting fainter," sighed the hiker.

"Is that Ariadne?" I asked and the hiker shrugged. I pictured a trapped Ariadne, weakly trying to signal. Perhaps she had tired of engaging in discipline activities, I thought darkly, but then found she could not ascend through the layers. I looked again at the flashing light and it seemed that it was silently keeping beat with a tune. I wished I were more musical. The despondent hiker started to hum in an absent minded way and turned away, looking again into the distance.

"What's that tune?" I asked but the hiker made no reply. "But music may be the clue?" I persisted. The hiker reached into her backpack, taking out a small mirror, holding it up to me. There was a dim reflection of Ariadne. "This is fading, too," said the hiker. "I'll do what I can," I said, wondering how these enigmatic images and tunes could possibly help. The hiker walked away and there was no alternative than to leave this depressing scene.

When I emerged from the trance, Dylan and Ingrid were watching anxiously.

"You were muttering something," said Ingrid, "but we couldn't make it out."

"Music and mirrors," I said. "It doesn't make sense, but it seems clear that Ariadne is trapped and... fading."

"Can we start to meditate on anything we could take in with us?" asked Ingrid.

"A ball of thread, possibly. Mirrors – I wish I could come up with more. I dreamed of dungeons and Althaea in chains, but that didn't make a lot of sense either."

Dr. Clea Foucoe came out of the side room. "A fascinating case," she said, looking happier than I had ever seen her. No doubt she was already planning a conference paper on the subject. "I shall lead the expedition. It seems that we need to delve into the subconscious desires of both these women."

Kastor took me aside. "I think you can leave them to do this one without your aid." He looked tremendously relieved. But I was pondering on the tune I had picked up on my quick dip into Althaea's subconscious.

"I'd like to get Theodora's help on that, it may be a way of contacting Ariadne."

"If you insist," said Kastor, "but take Clyppie with you to see Theodora, so that she feels in charge."

Theodora took the psychiatrist and me into her private study.

"You are considering that there's a musical key to this?" asked Theodora, picking up my confused images and thoughts. "Perhaps we should all focus on the lost Ariadne for a moment, something else may come."

In the quiet of Theodora's book-lined study, we closed our eyes. I recaptured the image of the deep well and the faintly flashing light and shared it with Theodora and Clea, hoping that they were accurately receiving the rhythm of the light coming off and on.

"Interesting," murmured Theodora, "it could be '*The Lost Chord*'. When you first thought of a musical link, I wondered about the Strauss opera, *Ariadne auf Naxos*, but that doesn't seem appropriate for our Ariadne. Then there's the music from a Charlie Chaplin film, where he's lost in a maze of mirrors, but I'd doubt that Ariadne is familiar with that."

" '*The Lost Chord*'," I said. "Can you hum it for me?"

"It's a very old song, a poem put to music by Arthur Sullivan."

"Of Gilbert and Sullivan? That sounds more like Ariadne."

"Yes, she sang in a Gilbert and Sullivan production when she was a student here," said Theodora. Music was an important part of Binary culture, although I was very much a beginner at either appreciation or playing.

Theodora continued, "She has a tuneful voice. Now let me see, it starts '*Seated one day at the organ, I was weary and ill at ease...*' " Theodora started to hum the tune, then added words, "*I knew not what I was playing or what I was dreaming then, but I struck one chord of music - and it was like the sound of a great Amen.*' Sullivan was inspired at the deathbed of his brother. It's been sung at many sad occasions, for example in a concert for the Titanic disaster."

" '*The great Amen*'," I said, "sounds way out of my league – a lament for someone who's already lost, beyond help?"

"She was over confident," pronounced Clea, "possibly simply curious about the subconscious currents – but now finds she cannot leave."

"If she was able to transmit the tune, there's hope," said Theodora. "But you need to be well prepared. Are you confident, Clea, that you could penetrate the subconscious mind? Usually that's only possible in dreams or mental visions, such as Cassandra has demonstrated. Music could help to draw her to the surface, but not on its own."

"I shall also make a preliminary examination of the nanny's subconscious," said Clea authoritatively. "You've done well, as usual, Cassandra, but this case would benefit from those more familiar with Binary culture, such as exercise routines used by nannies – and what might have attracted Ariadne to travel too deep."

"Yes, of course," I said quickly, ignoring the slight about my lack of familiarity with Binary world. At least she had learned not to call me an 'outsider'. Or refer to me as a witch, I added, in a closed part of my mind. A thin smile from the perceptive Dr. Theodora Sage told me that she had picked this up, but Clea was too busy thinking about the mind exploration and was obviously impatient to get started. Theodora plucked a disc from a shelf and gave it to the psychiatrist. "A recording of the *The Lost Chord*, it may help."

At the medical unit, the team was assembled in Althaea's room, with three couches ready for Dr. Foucoe and the two mind repairers. Althaea looked very nervous at the party about to invade her mind.

"I wish I could help you," she said plaintively. "I can feel that something's not quite right. It's horrible to think that someone is lost inside me."

"Is it so horrible?" asked Dr. Foucoe, gazing at her. "We need you to be totally honest, Althaea. If the others could wait outside for a moment, I'd like to assess how your subconscious is feeling about all this."

Althaea nodded uncertainly and the others left the room. The mind repairers were concerned to hear that I would not be entering Althaea's mind with them.

"Just follow Dr. Foucoe's instructions," I said. "Mention those items we discussed, but make sure she agrees. This is more about communing with the subconscious than mind repair."

Kastor was still hovering, wanting me to leave. "Clyppie will be more confident if you're not around," he whispered. "And I'd really be happier with you not getting any ideas about discipline."

I smiled mischievously, passing a silent message about whether we needed to get back to normal work.

"I think we deserve some more rest back at the apartment," he sent back, with a winking face image.

21

I leant against Kastor as we travelled in the underground train back to Askeys. "I'd like to do an exploration of someone else's mind with you," I murmured.

"So that we'd be lost together?" asked Kastor. "I'm not an adept mind explorer."

"We wouldn't be lost, I'm sure of it."

He put his arm around me as we neared the staircase stop. "You'll be suggesting next that one of the children should come in with us."

I sat up, with the eagerness of a meerkat. "That's a great idea – Leo would understand a nanny's mind and Althaea's subconscious wouldn't want to harm him, or keep him."

"A five year old mind explorer? I don't think so. And what makes you think a nanny wouldn't want to hang on to a child? Or... do things that aren't possible in the real world outside the mind. It's unthinkable."

Our son had a double dose of adventurous spirit from the pair of us and Kastor had secret pride that Leander would one day demonstrate a combination of our talents. But even our gifted son was not ready to deal with the darker layers of the subconscious.

"I wonder what Althaea's mind looks like," I persisted. "Pink and blue, do you think, with rows of prams and push chairs?"

"I'm sure Dylan and Ingrid will give you a full report," said Kastor. "Right now, I'm only interested in your mind. Your lovely mind that only I can fully enter. If all goes well, I'm looking forward to an end to your career as a mind repairer – it's terrifying to think of you doing that."

I felt guilty at my enthusiasm and looked up at him gratefully. "I should've realised what it meant for you. I love your mind too, it's more than enough excitement."

Within a couple of minutes of arriving back in our apartment, we were lying together, touching with just with fingertips. We swooped into each other's mind, feeling the elation of being able to plunge so easily and relax. We swam in a sea of thoughts before reluctantly emerging and lying quietly, sharing after-images of star lit skies where we could travel with no sense of space or time.

We reluctantly returned to the Binary underground centres to do some work while waiting for any report from the medical unit. Kastor was preoccupied with surveillance matters but I had little to do in the commercial centre offices. So I visited the medical wing and found Hagen Philips in his office.

"It went well," he said, smiling, in response to my anxious, silent enquiry. "Ingrid and Dylan are sleeping, but Clea can't stop talking. We think that Ariadne's back, but still asleep."

"Did *The Lost Chord* help?"

"Yes, they played it on the mind surface, but the main thing was unblocking Althaea's resistance to letting Ariadne go. Clea was in her element, delving into their subconscious wishes."

"I didn't know about all this discipline, this physical need…" I murmured, cautiously.

"Nannies liking to be chained up and beaten? And the pent up anger from some of us, growing up under their firm control? Well, it's an eye opener for me too, but perhaps I understand it better than you'd be expected to. The dark side of Binary upbringing – more fuel for your reforms, I suppose?"

"I won't ask them about all that," I said. "It's rather embarrassing. I don't intend to change what works for Binaries."

Hagen smiled, saying nothing and I hoped that a closed thought about whether he and his bond mate enjoyed spanking was far too deep to be detected.

"Clea is over the moon, she's already planning an extensive counselling programme. Apparently she had to go down several layers to help Ariadne back."

"Another paper for the next medical conference, then," I said. Hagen nodded but before we could exchange some knowing thoughts about that, Clea entered the room. I offered her warm congratulations and the psychiatrist beamed.

"There's so much more to consider, other than these structural repairs, yes?" said Clea, smugly. I took the wisest option of nodding demurely and muttering about attending to a product analysis in the commercial centre. This was not the time to remind the psychiatrist that my dream of dungeons had provided the vital clue.

I went over to the assessment centre to let Theodora know that the rescue had been successful, although guessing that this news would already have reached her. Theodora was examining an assessment report, but when I signalled that I didn't wish to disturb her, Theodora looked up and beckoned me to a seat by her desk.

"This report may be of interest to you," she said. "A police officer in France…"

"Edouard Parfait?" I said immediately, blushing. Theodora looked at me keenly.

"Kastor arranged for him to be tested at one of our university connections. He promised this police captain that he'd do so, did he not?"

"Yes, but it's only been a few weeks – I thought he'd wait until the investigation was complete."

"The police captain was impatient to have his telepathy assessed. One of Kastor's duties is to assess those on the outside who may have unusually good natural abilities."

"Like me," I said, thinking of the meetings with Kastor in Blenheim Park.

"In your case, Kastor had a personal interest. He didn't report that he was doing an assessment and, as an assessment, it was most irregular." I blushed again, recalling our telepathic intimate encounters, the mental flying, the exciting feel of his touch. Theodora smiled kindly.

"While you were being detained, he told me in confidence that he'd met with you. He didn't want you to enter Binaries, as you must be aware, at least, not in the way that your twin arranged."

"I'm not at all sure he'd want Edouard Parfait in the Binaries, either," I said. "He caught us kissing, but it was very innocent. I was gaining his trust."

Theodora raised her eyebrows and pursed her lips cynically. "No doubt," she observed.

"Is the police captain exceptional?" I said, avoiding meeting Dr. Sage's penetrating gaze.

"Not at your level, Cassandra, but yes, he has strong natural ability. At present, he's not been given any indication of this. The university tests are ostensibly part of a project and he'll have been told that he couldn't ask questions about joining our organization. He knows he must wait to be contacted. Grégoire has been in touch with him and it seems he wants very much to join the organization, since the tests prove his potential."

I looked down at my hands, knowing that Kastor would not want me to meet with Edouard again, while I was afraid that the police captain might have another reason to want to join the organization, rather too closely related to me.

"You're nervous of seeing him again, are you not?"

"There was a connection," I admitted. "Not overwhelming, like my link to Kastor, but…"

"You'd like to kiss him again?" asked Theodora.

"No, of course not!" Feeling Theodora's knowing eyes on me, I knew my denial was unconvincing.

"Dealing with mental and physical attraction is part of Binary life," said Theodora. "Some choose to investigate and enjoy those feelings - permanent relationships are very rare, as you know. You should talk to Kastor about it."

"I don't want a relationship with Edouard Parfait," I said. "And I wouldn't want Kastor to explore his feelings for other women. But in any case, he isn't going to come here, is he?"

"With the French centre closed, this would be the obvious place. Many of the Binaires community are here."

"How soon?" I asked.

"Normally, someone from the French centre would meet with him outside, to explain the implications. It would be an irreversible decision. But it isn't safe for any of the Binaires members to go back to France at the moment. Possibly, a meeting in London will be arranged, in connection with a police conference, something of that sort."

"Kastor could have just waited a lot longer, before these university tests were arranged." I felt he should have mentioned all this to me, but knew full well why he had not.

Theodora tapped the file containing Edouard's test results. "It's his duty to promptly assess anyone who may be… one of us."

I sat silently, remembering Edouard's face when we parted near the docks in France. I knew he was strongly attracted to me and felt guilty that I had enjoyed the kiss. Theodora closed the file on her desk and gazed across at me.

"These tests don't tell me if the police captain is a gentleman, someone who'd respect a strong relationship such as yours with Kastor. It was scarcely gentlemanly, was it not, for him to demand a kiss of you? Anyway, you'll be the best judge of that, if he comes here in the next few weeks or months."

"Does he have good ability at remote viewing – or precognition?"

"I can't discuss his results with you, Cassandra. But he doesn't match your unique range of telepathic skills. However, you should consider that he may be able to pick up your thoughts or transmit messages to you."

I nodded, worrying about Kastor's reaction to the possible imminent arrival of Edouard. I also felt tense at my own reaction. Since arriving at Binaries, I had felt no serious attraction to any other telepath. I was relieved that whatever Theodora sensed would be confidential. I just hoped that I'd be able to deal with it.

22

A celebratory party was held on the evening before the mind repair team returned to St. Anthony's. I had steered clear of the medical unit following Ariadne's rescue, worried that my embarrassment about the punishment revelations would be easily detected. When I saw Ariadne's joyful face, I realised this would not be a concern.

"They don't see it as cruel or unnatural," I thought, recalling Dr. Asklep's perplexed face when I argued about Cilisse's 'duties'. I wondered if I'd ever truly understand the Binaries who were now my constant companions.

Ariadne talked excitedly of a new programme of subconscious contact to assist with mind repair. "Althaea had to admit that she rather wanted me to stay. I only intended to explore a bit more deeply, then started to forget about the world outside the mind, until I realised I was lost within those dungeons."

None of them seemed embarrassed at all and Dr. Foucoe was jubilant, with unusual friendliness towards me. Althaea was laughing about a chest of drawers containing whips in one of the upper levels, which had sparked Ariadne's interest.

"The programme will include more focused gym routines," said Clea, joining in the laughter and I picked up her thoughts about equipping a new gymnasium at St. Anthony's. Kastor whispered in my ear that this would help in re-assessing the role of sex therapy, which remained banned.

"They can't all have a Cassandra to get them better," he murmured.

"I hope our children don't get this taste for discipline."

"If they take after you, it will be giving it rather than being on the receiving end. Your storms are quite punishing, don't you think?"

I frowned and passed a thought that I hadn't seen them in this way, but the idea that I was not after all so very different from the other telepaths was strangely cheering.

"I don't create storms and panics for fun," I said, while also blushing at the thought that they were also exhilarating, stimulating and hard to control. I understood how Helen had developed her pain skills with obvious enjoyment. Kastor was gazing at me, drinking in these thoughts.

"I'm so very glad you grew up on the outside," he said eventually, leading me back to the buffet table and the happy shared images of the mind repair team.

Over the next couple of months, Binary life settled to its usual routines and I almost forgot about Edouard Parfait. I saw occasional flashes of his face but took care to close any possible thought channel between us. So it was a surprise when I saw him walking towards me in a corridor near the training centre.

"Madame Dufour," he said, smiling. "What a great pleasure to see you again."

"Captain Parfait," I replied with studied formality. "But perhaps you have a different name now?"

"Like you, I shall probably keep my own name within the organization. If I need to go outside, I'll have a cover name. But my training has only just begun - it'll be a long time before I can go outside."

"It seems so soon for that big decision. Your disappearance from your post must have caused concern?"

"I applied for a post in Guadeloupe, but went missing there soon after arrival. It appears I unwisely swam out too far, unused to the strong currents…"

"I see," I said, feeling uncomfortable at his intense gaze. "Well, the best of luck with the training. It takes a lot of getting used to."

"I hardly know anyone here," said Edouard. "So it's been a little lonely. Perhaps we could meet for coffee, or lunch?"

"Yes, possibly," I said, "but not…" I failed to suppress the image of our kiss. Alarmingly, he took my hand and kissed it softly. I looked around to see if anyone was observing us in the corridor, remembering that there were surveillance cameras everywhere. I pulled my hand away sharply and glared at him.

"Don't do that again!"

He smiled with mock remorse. "Why ever not?"

"Physical contact in public is not customary here," I said, "and as I told you in France, I'm happily married."

"But marriage is very different here, isn't it? Men and women are much more free to explore their feelings."

"I'm sure you'll meet someone soon… to explore your feelings with," I said angrily, furious at myself for the undeniable attraction to this good looking ex-police officer. Before he could reply, I turned and marched back along the corridor, uncomfortably aware of his gaze following me.

That evening in the apartment, I wondered whether to mention

Edouard's arrival to Kastor, guessing that he knew already, since he had been involved with the assessment and possibly also the training and aptitude tests. Kastor was relaxed and happy, having secured permission for us to accompany Leo when he went up to Scotland to enroll at Lochinstoun School.

"We could perhaps take a tour in the area before returning," he said, knowing how much I missed trips to the outside. "And do some shopping, to help with your commercial skills."

"Great," I said, trying to smile, but he raised his eyebrows at my lack of enthusiasm. He sat down on the sofa, beckoning me to sit next to him.

"So what's the matter – other than worrying about Leander leaving us? He'll be coming back in the holidays."

I noted he was guarding his thoughts. He knows I've seen Edouard, I thought quickly.

"Edouard Parfait… I've just found out he's here."

Kastor's eyes grew cold, watchful. "He's training. What of it?"

"He's looking for friends…" I said lamely.

"And he wants to be friends with you, I suppose?"

"Yes, but he makes me feel uncomfortable. He doesn't seem to understand that I… that we…"

"Do you want to get to know him better? We could ask him for dinner…"

"No!" I said, alarmed at the idea. "Oh, Kastor, you know very well that he seems to be attracted to me."

"Of course he is," said Kastor, "like several of the men here. But perhaps you're worried because you feel something for him?" His casual tone was not matched by the intense expression in his eyes.

"You're all I want," I murmured, squirming under his scrutiny.

"But this is the first time you've met a telepath who's grown up on the outside, like you. It's something that's always worried me, that you'd feel a strong affinity for someone who shares that experience. If it was just a physical thing, I'd say have an affair with him…"

"I think he'd want more than that," I said very quietly, "but in any case, I don't want a physical relationship with anyone but you."

"I couldn't bear it if you shared minds, as we do," said Kastor after a long pause and I felt a jolt of pain at his anguish. "If you were more like Helen, I'd at least try to understand. She would just get it out of her system and forget about it. But you couldn't, could you?"

"I'll try not to see him. He'll surely meet another female telepath who'd be willing to… be friends, because after all…"

"He's handsome and attractive," said Kastor, completing my thought with a bitter smile.

"Do you ever want to get closer to another woman?"

"Never. I told you, it's now and forever, the way I feel about you. But I got all that out of my system, if we can put it that way, a long time ago. Whereas your longest relationship was with Roderick, hardly a very fulfilling one. Now you're tempted, aren't you, by the idea of another telepath who wants to seduce you?"

I shook my head, tears springing up. "He just makes me feel confused, that's all. I really don't want an affair with him."

"Well, that's all right then," said Kastor, wiping away my tears. "I'll speak to him, if you like."

"No, that might make it more of a challenge for him," I said. "Theodora said, well implied, that he wasn't very gentlemanly…"

"You've discussed it with Theodora?" Kastor's eyes grew angry again.

"She told me that he might be coming here, and sensed..."

"I see. So it looks as though I'll have to kill him. Pity, as he has potential to be a good surveillance officer."

"Couldn't the organization relocate him, a long way off?"

Kastor sighed. "Yes, he'll probably be relocated to the Virginia Centre after the initial training. But in our world, distance doesn't stop transmission of feelings, as you know. You're just going to have to deal with this yourself."

I leant into his arms, wishing that I had not brought up the subject at all. "Now you're angry," I murmured.

"I'm never really angry with you," he said, "but perhaps a little terrified. He doesn't know the extent of your powers, while I do. If he hurts you, or upsets you, I guess I'd have to eliminate him, before you did..."

I laughed and looked up at him mischievously. "I wonder if this could be a Norwich moment. You know, 'Nickers Off Ready...'"

"I hope you're wearing knickers," he said darkly. "Or I really shall start to worry about this Frenchman's effect on you..."

"Yes, I'm wearing them for the moment," I giggled, jumping up. The tension between us was, for the moment, dispelled.

23

Another week passed in which I successfully avoiding Edouard, despite knowing that he was trying to contact me by thought. In a couple of weeks we would be travelling up to Scotland with Leo, in the private plane that would transport the other children starting their main education. On a sunny afternoon, after Leo had been taken back to the nursery from a visit to their apartment, I walked in the grounds of Askeys, pleased to see a couple in the distance embracing fondly.

"My programme for more physical enjoyment is going well," I thought, wondering if I should ask Dr. Artemis Chiron if the pregnancy rate was beginning to reflect the relationship classes. I wandered over to the pagoda and found the seat where I had talked to Phoebe about the rescue mission to Cadiz and Casablanca. Trees, some showing early autumn colour, surrounded this spot. I leant back and relaxed, breathing in the soft air and noting another positive point to add to my list of the advantages of living in this beautiful place. I closed my eyes, thinking of how well I had adapted, despite the continuing challenges.

In my calm, meditative state I did not notice that someone had approached the seat and jumped up in alarm when my arm was stroked. Edouard Parfait was sitting next to me, smiling warmly.

"I didn't mean to startle you. You looked so beautiful."

"How did you find me?" I said, springing up and away from his encircling arms.

"Just by luck. A very fortunate chance - you've been avoiding me."

"Very little happens here by chance," I said. I guessed that he had been actively trying to sense my whereabouts, which meant that his telepathy was improving by leaps and bounds if he had penetrated my defences.

"I can't get you out of my mind," he said, following me as I walked towards the trees. "It's torture. You must know that I fell in love with you, that evening in your garden at the villa."

"Please stop this." I wondered if I should make a run for the Pagoda train station entrance. He was standing close, willing me to turn and face him.

"It was why I helped you and your family escape. Surely you know this and feel for me too? Please, cherie…" He held my shoulders, turning me towards him. "Just a kiss, that's all I ask. You want that too, don't you?"

"I'm grateful for your help, we're all grateful, but I don't want this, not at all!"

He folded me in a tight embrace and looked down at my face, radiating desire. I was about to pull myself away when he kissed me hard, pushing me back against a tree. I felt a wave of excitement and pleasure and found myself responding, returning the kiss. He sighed and pulled me closer. I felt his strong arousal and longing.

"I knew you wanted me," he murmured, his hands grabbing the top of my jeans and slipping in to stroke my skin. My resolve started to weaken, as he kissed me more passionately, pulling me down towards the grass.

"No!" I whimpered, despite the contrary evidence of my compliant body. "Please, stop…"

I would liked to have thought that loyalty to Kastor would have won the day, but it was in fact the arrival of someone else on the scene that helped to strengthen my resistance.

"Well, well," said a familiar voice. "An unexpected thrill, Cassandra, to see your programme of relationship education going so… effectively."

Edouard released his grip, turning to face Gaston Ajax. "Monsieur Ajax," he said respectfully.

"I was looking for you, Monsieur Parfait, to go over some security details," said Gaston. "And sensed that you were here, enjoying the fine weather. To find you with my favourite prophetess is an additional bonus."

I took the opportunity to adjust my clothing, blushing under Gaston's amused gaze. Edouard did not look guilty at all, feeling only irritation at being disturbed, but he knew enough about Binaries to try to mask this from the powerful head of security.

"I am at your disposal," he said to Gaston, "although if it could wait a few minutes…"

I was desperately transmitting thoughts to Gaston in a closed channel. I sensed that he'd known full well that I was here with Edouard. Could he possibly be trying to protect me? While Gaston would find an affair between us entertaining, his relationship with Aunt V might have made him more concerned for my wellbeing. "I'm attracted to him, that's all – I don't want an affair", I signalled, seeing him nod imperceptibly at this silent communication.

"Regrettably, security must come first," said Gaston smoothly. "If you wouldn't mind making your way to the security centre, I'll meet you there. First I have a matter to discuss with the delightful Cassandra, in private."

Edouard seemed reluctant to go, but seeing a shift in Gaston's calm demeanour and a menacing glint in his eyes, he shrugged.

"I shall contact you later," Edouard said softly to me, turning and walking away.

I stood awkwardly, trying to tidy my hair.

"Thank you, Gaston," I said. "I can't imagine what came over me."

"Can't you?" He grinned unexpectedly. "I must say, it is a tad disappointing to find that you don't wish to follow your own advice. A child between you and this new telepath would be a most welcome addition to our community."

"A child!" I recoiled in shock. "Gaston, he's just adjusting to this new life – I can't imagine he wants a child with me - and I'd never consider that."

"He's rather excited about the opportunities here," said Gaston, "including increasing our numbers. So of course he'd want to help, especially with you."

I looked down, in deep embarrassment. "Will you tell Kastor? I was just taken unawares, I really didn't mean…"

"Our secret," murmured Gaston, suppressing the lascivious smile that this idea would normally have evoked. His fondness for Aunt V seemed indeed to have extended to me. "But this new arrival has – how to put it? - predatory tendencies. I suppose he's told you he's in love with you?" I blushed as he continued, "Quite. I'd advise much more caution, knowing you as I do. Our charming little risk taker. We wouldn't want Kastor to take dramatic action, would we?" He shared an image of Edouard being assassinated in brutal fashion, making me flinch.

"It'll be all right," continued Gaston reassuringly, as if the image had arisen quite by chance without him noticing. "Stay away from him, but watch and observe. Edouard will adjust, as you say. His feelings are not that deep."

I felt a little offended and Gaston, picking up this thought, murmured, "It's flattering to have admirers, but you're not alone in responding to Monsieur Parfait's charms."

He indicated that he had to get back to the centre, knowing I wanted to ask him more. Silently he signalled goodbye and walked towards the Pagoda station. I stood for a few moments, hoping that Kastor had picked up none of this. He rarely tried to contact me by thought when at work. Suppressing the guilty pleasure of my latest encounter with Edouard, I walked back to the Askeys mansion.

24

If Kastor noticed that I was unusually subdued when he returned to the apartment, he said nothing. But when I suggested we could watch a film while eating supper, he muttered that he had work to catch up with and would eat sandwiches in his study. I watched a film on my own and went to bed early, hoping that Kastor would join me. But when I heard the study door close and sounds of water running in the bathroom, then silence, I guessed he was using the bedroom by his study. I listlessly tried to read a book, but could not concentrate. I looked across at the cheval mirror, wondering whether to try to contact Helen and ask her advice. But it was the middle of the night in the American hotel where Helen was staying. In any case, I reflected, Helen might scoff at my dilemma with the attractive ex-police officer. She'd probably say something like, "Give it a go, sis. You can't be a boring married woman for ever."

Turning restlessly in bed, I wondered if Kastor was leaving me alone so that I could choose between him and Edouard. An image of Edouard appeared in my thoughts, looking yearningly sweet and apparently pleading for me to meet him.

"No," I shot back with the image of my face mouthing the word and shaking my head firmly.

"I just need to talk to you," persisted the thought image of Edouard.

But Gaston's warning rang in my head and I was starting to reappraise Captain Parfait's enthusiasm for the free sexual culture of the Binaries. I shut off thoughts from him and tried to pick up Kastor's. He appeared to be blocking me in the same way and I had a sudden fear that he knew all about the kiss by the pagoda – and that it had been more than just a quick kiss. I had shown lamentably little control at the first real temptation since our union as bond mates. Guilty tears started to flow and I buried my head in the pillow, which soon became uncomfortably wet. My confused thoughts and things that I should say to both Kastor and Edouard prevented any real rest.

Rising at 6 a.m. I went into the kitchen, deciding to cook my own breakfast rather than disturb the catering department at this hour. While stirring the scrambled eggs, I left the toast in too long and by the time I had retrieved the burnt pieces of bread, the eggs had turned into a leathery mass. I sighed and poured a cup of coffee, but had placed the cup too near the edge of the counter and it tumbled off, showering me with splashes of hot brown liquid before it smashed on the tiles. Uncharacteristically, I swore and slammed the pan of eggs against the cooker, looking around for a cloth to wipe up the mess. I turned to see Kastor staring, sleepy eyed at this early hour.

"You look almost as awful as the breakfast you're ruining," he observed drily. I burst into tears and started to run out of the kitchen, but he caught my arm. "I really shall have to eliminate Monsieur Parfait, if he has this effect on you," he said in a kinder tone, although without a smile. I stood still in his grip, but communicated such a deep sense of misery that he relented, folding his arms around me.

"If making a storm would make it better," he murmured, "go ahead, it's only kitchen crockery."

"I'm so sorry Kastor," I mumbled into his dressing gown, not able to look him in the eye.

"Why, what've you done? Apart from wrecking our kitchen…"

"Nothing, well almost nothing. I really don't want an affair with Edouard, please believe me."

"Almost nothing," he repeated carefully. "Does that mean you haven't... indulged in mind sharing?"

"No, of course not," I gasped. "I think he's just after my body and I don't want to share that, either. And now you seem to hate me, I can't bear it..."

Kastor looked around the kitchen. "Go back to bed and I'll bring you some tea, if you've left any cups intact." I hesitated, but noticing his faint smile, I nodded and left the room.

When Kastor brought the tea, I was curled up with my head submerged in the pillow. He put the cups down. "Hey," he said, "I don't hate you, I could never hate you." I turned cautiously as he touched the pillow, feeling its wetness from my tears.

"Have you been crying all night? Oh, Cassandra, I just wanted you to have a chance to think things through." He pulled the pillow from under me and tossed it onto the floor.

"Why did you arrange for him to come here?" I asked desperately.

"It's part of my job. You know that – and you of all people should want us to bring in sentient adults from the outside."

"So in Blenheim Park, you were assessing me? Did you seek me out, to do that?"

"That first lovely encounter," he sighed, sharing images of walking towards me in the park and later enjoying the picnic. "At least, our first proper meeting after I'd mistaken you for Helen in Woodstock. But I didn't arrange that. It was a surprise, finding that you were coming there with Roderick."

We sat on the bed so that we could drink the tea, before I hesitantly continued, "So you were just in the park to meet those mysterious investors, the ones that Roderick was so keen to connect with?"

Roderick had pretended it was a pleasure trip for us, but with the real aim of tracking down another contract. I'd since learned that the investors were Binary contacts.

"Yes. We wanted a meeting away from offices and left clues that your unpleasant boyfriend so eagerly picked up. I was there to make sure it all ran smoothly – and met with them after we parted. I should've been shadowing them more closely, but then there was this fascinating distraction."

"Me?" I asked. He nodded, smiling. "Yes, darling Cassandra, you. When I realised how telepathic you were, so innocent of your abilities, I almost forgot my reason for being there."

"And I was angry with you, for being able to put images into my mind and make me feel so helpless. And when you touched me, I didn't want you to take your hand away and that made me wonder if you were using thoughts to ensnare me…"

"As if," he laughed, holding my arm and kissing me lightly, just as he had in the park. I relived the electric charge of instant attraction.

"But you didn't fall in love with me straight away," I murmured.

"I did," he protested, "although I didn't want to admit it. I couldn't believe my luck, finding this sexy telepath on the outside, with the courage to pursue such a dangerous search for her twin. I'd never imagined I'd find the answer to my dreams outside our Binary world."

"So you dreamt of me, before you met me?" My eyes were now shining happily.

"Not exactly – because it never occurred to me that Helen's twin would be my dream woman. I dreamed of finding someone with mysterious powers who could fill my emptiness. Funny, beautiful, adventurous, affectionate and with a mind like a thousand seas…. " I shook my head at this description, but he nodded gravely. "Yes, it was you all along."

"While I was just obsessed with finding Helen. If she hadn't tricked me into going down into the Binaries labyrinth, would you have tried to see me again?"

"Oh yes," he murmured, "and if you recall, I was trying to meet you but you said no. I suppose I would've just had to keep contacting you until you gave in. It was agonising, trying to win your trust. I'd never wanted anything, anyone, so much."

"You have my trust now," I said. "But with this... episode with Edouard, I feel I've lost yours."

He gazed with such intensity that I breathed sharply, as though a needle had pricked me. "Sooner or later I knew you'd find another man who seriously attracted you. You hadn't gained a lot of experience of men on the outside, had you? And your relationship with Roderick was rather... unrewarding. So now you've met Edouard, we'll have to deal with it. I wouldn't hold you to your bond oaths."

"It's just a foolish attraction. It's nothing to what we have. Please don't say things like that, as though you want me to go off with him."

"I don't want that at all – how many times do I have to tell you?"

I returned his intense gaze, sharing the wish that I had never met the police officer, even if he had helped us to escape.

"How can I make it right again?" I pleaded. "Would you like to beat me? You know, pretend I'm one of those nannies needing lots of punishment and discipline..." His eyes gleamed as though he was considering this, noting my slightly wistful smile. Then he laughed, although with more of a snort than sign of merriment. "I don't think I'm a coward, but I'd really hesitate to beat the powerful Cassandra, even if I wanted to. And I don't. But if you were thinking of some other kind of morning exercise, I might be up for that."

I stretched my arms submissively above my head and drawled, "Show no mercy," with an enticing smile. My smile faded when I saw Kastor's disappointingly severe expression.

"Is this how…" he began, stopping himself from continuing although I sensed he was thinking of my encounter with Edouard Parfait.

"No, of course not," I said, realising too late that this was not at all the moment to be playful. Kastor was staring angrily, with a smouldering expression that did not look like desire. He closed his eyes, as if to shake off an unwanted image. When he opened them, his eyes bore into me with a furious intensity and I felt my skin start to tingle. Without any physical contact, he was mentally stimulating my skin, starting with my face and working slowly down. Each part that his darting thoughts touched rippled and ached. I glanced down to see if my skin was coming up in goose bumps but there was no visible response to the onslaught, except for my body trying to move back, away from this invisible touching.

I couldn't speak to say that the sensation of small electric shocks were becoming painful. When he reached the soles of my feet, I had the sensation of an unbearable cramp, but he had not moved. It was all illusion, but agonisingly real. He seemed lost in this torture of my nerve endings, until I managed to send a wave of remorse and helplessness. He looked shocked, breathed in quickly and went out of the room. I lay in a state of high arousal with nerve cells sparking in confusion, unable to move. I tried to call out but found even my voice was affected, coming out like a squeak, while all I could hear was the shower running in the bathroom.

After a few minutes he returned fully dressed and said he was going to work.

"Kastor," I said weakly, trying to lift my arms, "Please don't leave me like this."

"Perhaps I got a bit carried away," he said, awkwardly. "I guess

I was angrier than I realised – anyway, now you may understand how I feel, when you torment me with the idea of wanting to kiss another man, to share his mind…"

I made an inaudible protest and tried to sit up but it was as if all my nerve endings were sticking out like pins, making any movement unbearable. I pulled a sheet up over me, wincing at its touch, but Kastor had already left the room, muttering "See you later," as if this was just an ordinary morning and nothing had happened. Seconds later I heard the door of the apartment slam. So much for him being frightened of my powers, I thought bitterly, as I writhed under the sheet, finding no relief from the waves of throbbing sensation that were wracking my body.

The hour for leaving to go to work came and went, but I was still scarcely able to move. I could not even cry and tried in vain to calm my body and thoughts. He had been speaking so lovingly of how we met, then this. I curled up, closing my eyes and trying to meditate on soothing scenes, but saw only dungeons and dark tunnels and felt only pain, so intense that death would have been a welcome relief.

"Perhaps I'm dying!" I thought, trying to cope with the waves of sensation that continually built up to an excruciating crescendo, subsiding only to resurge with greater intensity each time. When Evadne, one of the housekeepers, arrived, I heard her exclaim at the mess in the kitchen; then she came into the bedroom.

"What's happened?" she asked, concerned at my distressed appearance. "Are you ill?"

I shook my head, then nodded, confused. I felt dreadful. My mind and body were drained, but still reeling from the continuing torture from the stimulated nerves.

"I'll call a doctor," said Evadne.

"No!" I gasped, forcing myself to speak. The humiliating thought of Dr. Philips, or any doctor, seeing me like this was as unbearable as the searing sensations ripping through me.

"I have to call someone," said Evadne firmly, "Kastor, then."

I closed my eyes and whispered, "No. Perhaps call Theodora, … Dr. Sage."

The housekeeper picked up the phone. Her telepathy was not strong enough to communicate except at close distance. I arched my back, groaning at the pain, dreading anyone seeing me in this condition. But of all people, Theodora would be most likely to be able to help. Within a few minutes, Theodora entered the bedroom and gasped at my pale face and tormented eyes. She sat on the bed and projected a wave of emotional balm, which lessened the pain a little. She said nothing, but picked up enough from my confused thoughts.

"You've been hyper-stimulated," she uttered, in a deep tone of disapproval. She continued to transmit waves of calm that felt like soft cotton wool, protecting the nerve endings and gradually soothing the unremitting waves of aching pain. When I was breathing more evenly, although still obviously distressed, I saw Theodora looking intently towards the Binary labyrinth. I sensed dimly that she was contacting Kastor, wanting to ask her not to do this. I dreaded seeing him again and feeling his cold eyes on me.

Theodora left the bedroom and I heard her talking to Evadne, who was tidying up the kitchen. Then she returned to my side, radiating calm and sympathy. The nerve endings that had seemed about to snap in the agonising tension started slowly to relax. The housekeeper came in with a cup of chamomile tea. In my heightened state, the aroma seemed overwhelming. Evadne touched my hand, pointing to the tea and I nearly jumped off the bed at this contact, which set all my nerves flaring again.

"Don't touch her," said Theodora. "She needs absolute rest."

The housekeeper apologised, confused. I was usually so cheerful and polite that she found it hard to recognise me in this helpless, writhing state. Theodora waited for the drink to cool, then indicated that I should try to sit up. She gently held the cup against my lips, letting me take little sips. "I'll fetch one of my herbal remedies when you've finished this," she said. Evadne was moving around the apartment, vacuuming and tidying and Theodora said nothing more until she had left. Then she turned to me, with a serious, concerned expression.

"I'm most displeased with Kastor. I suppose this is all to do with that police officer. But Kastor should know that to hyper-stimulate someone with your extreme receptiveness is dangerous. With your level of trust, there would be insufficient resistance to prevent damage."

"He'd never want to harm me," I protested. "I suggested punishment, in fun mainly, but I didn't mean this… I suppose he was really jealous, much more than I knew." I lay back, exhausted at the effort of speaking.

"I shall be dealing with him later," said Theodora. "He obviously needs an update in control classes. It's not as if you deserved punishment. I'm sure his rational side acknowledged that, did he not?"

I nodded. "Yesterday, Edouard tried to seduce me…" I flushed guiltily at the memory of beginning to respond, as he held me against the tree by the pagoda.

Theodora smiled knowingly, sending another wave of balm that felt like water on my parched, tingling skin. "I'll also deal with Monsieur Parfait," she murmured. "He seems to think we live in some kind of erotic pleasure dome."

When I had finished the tea, Theodora indicated that she'd fetch the promised herbal remedy. "Kastor will be here soon," she said. "He'll be most contrite, so don't worry." When she left, I thought I should get up and dress, but my body ached and the idea of putting on clothes was painful. It was distressing enough just to have the sheet draped over me. I sank back against the pillow, wondering if my body would ever feel normal again. I closed my eyes, feeling a welcome sleepiness. My thoughts were too jangled to be aware that Kastor had entered the room until he was standing close by the bed. I looked up at him drowsily, but his expression startled me into a more alert state. He looked aghast, horror struck.

"What is it?" I asked, frightened. I glanced down at my sheet-covered body, wondering if I had grown an extra limb or turned green. He looked as though he had seen a ghost, or possibly an alien monster.

"Cassandra," he whispered, staring with deep anguish. "I'm so sorry, I… don't know what to say. How can you ever forgive me?"

He looked at the bed, wondering whether to sit down next to me and then decided on bringing a chair up to the side. He rested his elbows on his knees, his hands covering his mouth, while he could not take his eyes off me. "You're so pale," he said miserably. "I've never seen you look so ill."

My face was pinched with pain. He sat up, clenching his hands, and I felt a growing sense of alarm when I saw tears springing from his eyes.

"Do I look that bad?" I whispered.

"Yes," he gasped, making me draw in my breath and writhe as a wave of electric shock scorched my nerves. "I mean, no," he added quickly. "You're beautiful, as always, but I can't believe I did this to you." I sensed his overwhelming remorse and love, feeling reassured that at least I had not grown an extra head, even if it felt that my body had expanded into a sphere of pain.

"Next time, couldn't you just spank me, or something?" I wondered if my eyes showed a hint of humour. Nothing seemed funny at present.

"There'll never be a next time," he said, with desperate firmness. "After this, you'll probably never want me to touch you again, anyway. I suddenly felt so angry and jealous, with you seeming to take it all so lightly…"

"Like crying all night?" I asked, puzzled.

"I thought you might be crying because you wanted to be with him. And then you were so sunny and playful... But it doesn't excuse me. I thought you'd just feel aroused and wanting me, then we'd make up later. I should've known better…"

"Yes indeed, Kastor," said a chilling voice as Theodora entered the room.

Theodora was carrying a tray with a teapot and a cup. She placed it carefully on the bedside table and gave Kastor an icy glance, so that he jumped up to allow Theodora to sit down on the bed.

"I suggest you cancel all your work for the day," she said. "She must not be left alone. Unless you're too busy, in which case I'll recommend transfer to the medical unit."

"No, of course I'll stay," he muttered. Watching them both, I imagined Kastor as much younger, being chastised for appalling performance in a test. Theodora turned kindly to me, sending a soothing thought and pouring out a cup of amber liquid.

"Try to drink some of this, it will help. I need to speak to Kastor in the sitting room."

She marched off, with Kastor following meekly, giving an anxious backward glance at me. I was too exhausted to try to pick up their conversation, finding that the effort of picking up the cup extended me completely. When Kastor returned, he looked ashen. Theodora bustled in behind him, addressing me with a reassuring tone.

"How are you feeling, Cassandra?"

"A little better," she said, "but I can still hardly move."

"Would you like me to stay?" asked Theodora. "I know you'll be safe with Kastor, but it's up to you. At the moment I'd like to banish him to the dungeons of St. Anthony's."

My eyes widened at this unpleasant thought, but shook my head. "No, I'll be all right with Kastor. Please don't be too severe with him, it was all my fault really."

Theodora arched her eyebrows. "I think not. You are fortunate,

Kastor, that Cassandra was brought up to have a good deal more compassion than you."

He squirmed, closing his eyes briefly and then glancing quickly at me, sending waves of misery – and compassion.

"Better late than never," said Theodora crisply. "Well, I'll leave you for now and I'll expect a report in a couple of hours. Contact me if…" Kastor nodded quickly and I tried to pick up the thought exchange. To what was Theodora referring?

"Am I in danger?" I croaked. "No," said Theodora soothingly. "It may take a couple of days but you'll be fine." With a final sweep of calming thought, she left the apartment.

Left alone, Kastor stood uncertainly, shifting from one foot to the other and then gingerly settling at the end of the bed.

"I'm sorry you've had to come back from work," I said, to break the uneasy silence.

"Please don't say you're sorry, for anything," he mumbled. I stretched painfully to pick up the cup of herbal tea and he quickly took it, sitting more closely and helping me to drink it. When his hand brushed against mine, supporting the cup, I recoiled and he immediately drew back, gazing down at his fingers as though they had seriously misbehaved.

"Oh God, what have I done? Theodora will never forgive me either."

"I've almost forgiven you already," I said, noticing that he had tears in his eyes again. "What you did, is that something you learned, as a weapon? It's very effective…"

"No, not a weapon, oh, I feel so bad. When we grow up, we learn how to control our effect on others, the way we can stimulate by thought. And just as we learn to block out thoughts, we practise closing off our bodies too, so that we can defend ourselves. That's one reason why it's so wonderful when we make love, with someone we truly trust - all defences down, all sensations allowed. But I wasn't thinking when I stimulated you, forgetting that you don't have any of that training... and forgetting how much you trust me not to harm you."

"You didn't mean to hurt me."

He closed his eyes, clenching his fists. "No, of course not, but I hadn't accepted how furious I was. That damn police officer. I was mad to arrange the assessment."

"It's you I love," I said quietly, wondering how I could ever have felt the faintest attraction to Edouard. In my current state, I was starting to blame him for everything, including my shattered nervous system. Kastor edged closer.

"Theodora suggested that if you could bear it, I should lie next to you, but not touch you. I could try to soothe those nerves, like she did."

"I'd like that," I said. "But first I think I need the bathroom, only I'm not sure I can walk."

He sprang up, taking my dressing gown from the hook behind the door. He tenderly wrapped it round me, taking care not to touch me otherwise. Then holding only the parts covered by the dressing gown, he helped me up from the bed. I lowered my legs to the floor and felt searing pain in soles of my feet as I tried to stand on them. It was as if I had stepped into scalding water. I winced and he mirrored my expression, knowing that if he tried to pick me up and carry me to the bathroom, it could be even more painful. With small shuffling steps and his support, I slowly crossed the floor. At the bathroom door, I said I'd like to try to use the toilet on my own. He stood outside with the door ajar.

I was alarmed to find that passing urine was no less painful than the other sensations surging through me. "What has he done to me?" I thought, as I slowly stood up afterwards. Meaning to go to wash my hands, I felt faint and tumbled to the floor and Kastor burst into the bathroom, gathering me up in his arms and carrying me back to the bedroom. He placed me carefully on the bed, draping the sheet over me. Then he projected an envelope of calm around my body. It was not quite as effective as Theodora's balm thoughts, but it was touched with his love and that made up for his lesser ability in the soothing department. He stretched out next to me, close but not touching. My eyes closed gratefully as sleep overtook me.

25

I woke up to find Kastor was no longer beside me. I glanced at the clock: 2 p.m. I heaved myself up, pleased to find a little strength returning. Kastor came into the room, carrying a cup of tea.

"I noticed you were coming round," he said huskily. "So I wondered if you'd like a drink. Or are you hungry?"

I shook my head, not at all sure that I could hold a knife and fork. He produced a small bottle containing pills. "Hagen Philips sent these over. They're one of our formulations, they dull the senses but not the mind. He thinks they may help."

Kastor looked at me, asking for permission to give me a couple of the pills and I nodded. He looked tired, miserable and guilty. "I suppose Theodora spoke to Hagen," he muttered. I smiled, hating to see him so depressed, even if he had gone too far.

"I'm sure I'll be OK," I said, swallowing the pills with some of the tea. "I'll be better by the time we go up to Scotland."

"Sunday week – but it's Thursday already. We may have to cancel that."

"Oh no, I've been looking forward to it. Fresh air, highland walks and shops - just thinking about it makes me feel better already."

Kastor looked away, murmuring, "We'll see," and I wondered if he was fighting back more of his uncharacteristic tears. He glanced warily into my eyes. "Right now, I couldn't refuse you anything in the world."

I pulled myself up, pulling the sheet modestly around my chest. My body still felt very weak. "I don't understand why it had such a huge effect on me," I said, "because telepathic pain shots usually wear off quickly."

He stared at the floor bleakly, worrying whether the after shocks of the hyperstimulation would ever fade completely. "It's unforgiveable. Theodora spelled it out. With your extreme sensitivity, everything I did expanded and intensified – creating a kind of repeating echo, only one that became stronger with each circuit of the electric impulses in your nervous system. And you let me do it, so trustingly. For some reason that made me angrier, more jealous. Your sweet nature, always wanting to please and thinking of how the other person is feeling."

I was silent, thinking of how my gratitude to Edouard had been a factor in making me respond to him. That, and the novelty of a man seeming to want me so much, who did not behave with the usual Binary courtesy or avoidance of touching in public. But I had never intended to upset my relationship with Kastor and I now felt only resentment towards Edouard for putting us in this sorry state.

"If you feel like it," I said timidly, "I think it would help if you tried a little dip into my mind, just to see how it is. I'm not really up to plunging into yours."

He climbed onto the bed. "Of course I feel like it," he said, with a surge of relief spreading over his face. "I was afraid you'd never want me to do that, or anything else, again. I am so very sorry – you're the world to me and the first problem we have, I abuse and persecute you."

"I'll think of it as shock therapy." This was painfully accurate as I still felt that electrified rods were needling me. "After all, consider what I might have done to you if the situation were reversed." I conjured an image of blowing him into outer space, becoming a faint twin star like his mythological namesake.

"Don't try to make any images," he said, unable to resist a smile, "You're supposed to be resting. Let me see if I can take that little mind dip. If there's any pain, you'll tell me?"

I nodded, gazing into his eyes and taking a deep breath as I felt him slide into my mind. In my hypersensitive state, I felt a rush of emotion as though a waterfall had started to cascade within my head. There was no pain but a series of tingling sensations as he seemed to move deeper. I concentrated on breathing evenly, willing my body to relax and lose the sensation that someone was continually hitting my joints with a hammer to elicit reflexes. Gradually the focus was only in the mind, with my limbs becoming lax. After a minute or two I felt as though there was a calm beach on the surface of my mind, with the sea gently moving with the tide. When the tide receded further, leaving the beach shining and covered with shells, I felt Kastor leave and breathed deeply at the pleasure of my mind seemingly bathed by a warm sea.

"Your mind is lovely, as always," he said, "just a few more rocks than usual and a very angry mermaid in the distance."

"Did you really see a mermaid?"

"Not exactly, I just knew she was there. Was it, you know, comfortable?"

I nodded. "Yes, very – it took away the pain. Perhaps you could look again in an hour or so?"

"But now you should rest. I'll be right here, reading a book. Or would you like me to read to you?" I opted for the latter, delighting in a distant memory of being read to in childhood and was asleep before Kastor had finished the first chapter.

Later that evening, he got into bed next to me, wrapped in a duvet, as Theodora had been so stern about limiting physical contact. I moved constantly, occasionally making little moans and whimpering sounds that prevented him getting much sleep at all and in the early hours he gave up. I sensed him lying there, feeling deep remorse. Once or twice I murmured "Kastor" and I could tell he longed to stroke my face and hair. When I opened my eyes at around 6 a.m. he was still gazing at me. He looked very weary and anxious.

"I'm getting better," I said reassuringly. "I'll get up and make some tea." But I moved so slowly and painfully that he insisted on my lying down again. So Kastor made the tea and then took me to the shower, standing outside the glass partition in case I fell.

"Water feels good," I said. "Why don't you come in with me?"

He stepped in cautiously, feeling it would be safer for him to be there, in case I slipped. Normally we enjoyed showering together but it was much harder trying to avoid touching. When I toppled slightly and leant against him, he felt me shudder. Wrapped in towels afterwards and drinking the tea, I looked up at him cautiously.

"I've turned into the incredible untouchable woman," I said, "How long do you think this will last?"

He shook his head miserably and mumbled something about a couple of days, although he could not avoid my picking up his fears. "At least you have something else to add to your negative list about the Binaries," he said glumly.

"I think you're supposed to be cheering me up. Yes, I guess 'being tortured by your lover' doesn't sound very positive, but on the other side, I could put, 'endless amazing experiences'. I'm sure I'll see the funny side of this, eventually."

Kastor produced a thin smile. "I'll never see what happened as remotely amusing. I honestly didn't realise how jealous and furious I was – and it was your sense of humour that tipped me over, made me want to show you I cared about... Edouard." He said the name with contempt.

"Well, I don't care about him at all," I said firmly. "He took advantage of me and obviously, I wasn't thinking clearly either. But today I'm going to focus on self-healing – and take some more of Hagen's pills, so that you can go to work."

"I'm staying here," he announced, "until you can walk without falling over." But he agreed at least to reassessing how I was in the afternoon. After a huge breakfast, where I demonstrated a return of appetite, he suggested we try another mind swoop.

"OK," I said, looking with concern at his drooping eyelids and sensing the waves of despair emanating from him, "but let's start by just resting."

When we lay on the bed, Kastor looked even more exhausted. I tried to conjure up the Brahms lullaby that Theodora had once used to calm her. My musical talents being limited, the notes came out wrong, with different melodies interfering with the flow. When I tried to sing along to catch the tune more accurately, he burst out laughing and visibly relaxed.

"You really must be getting better," he murmured, "I think you're almost in tune."

I raised my eyebrows in mock offence and sent soothing, sleepy thoughts instead. He closed his eyes, muttering that he'd get on with the mind plunge shortly, but within seconds was deeply asleep. I got up and gingerly dressed in a tracksuit, still finding my skin tender to the touch. I went into the sitting room and tried to read. Kastor found me peacefully dozing with the book draped over me when he got up a few hours later. He ordered a sandwich lunch and had just signalled to Manes that it was unlikely that he'd be coming back to work, when I sat up.

"I'd like to see the children," I said, looking with surprise at the time. Kastor began to say that might not be wise, stopping when he saw my determined expression.

"You could go to work Kastor, I'll be fine. Perhaps I could take them for a walk in the grounds."

"I'm staying with you," he said firmly. "You shouldn't be

walking anywhere yet."

I stood up and stretched. "I feel a surge of energy."

"That's an after effect. Look in the mirror, you're still very pale."

"You don't look so good yourself. We need fresh air." I looked up at his drawn face. "You could try kissing me, to give me some colour back."

He shook his head but I sent such a longing thought that he bent forwards and kissed me lightly on the lips, immediately withdrawing with a loud "Ow!" A sharp tingling sensation swept through his body.

"Does that hurt?" I said innocently, clasping his face in my hands and planting another kiss.

"Ouch, yes," he said, trying to pull away.

My eyes narrowed. "Do you know, I think this is good for me, giving you back a little of your... therapy." Holding his head, I ran a finger over his upper, then lower, lip and kissed him again. "The incredible, untouchable, *electrified* woman," I murmured, "It must make you feel like Dr. Frankenstein."

He stood rigidly still, absorbing the shock waves and gazing with alarmed eyes. "I'd take all the pain from you if I could, but I don't think it works like that. You shouldn't get excited..."

In reply, I suddenly pushed him off his balance so that he tumbled backwards onto the sofa. I leapt onto his lap and stroked his face. "I think I need to discharge some of this electricity."

I kissed him again and he groaned. It was like having a bandage whipped off an unhealed wound. I sighed and kissed his neck and pushed his shirt aside to kiss his shoulder. He flinched, stiffening with the effort of not crying out.

"My senses are dulled by those pills," I whispered, "so it feels great to me. I can feel some of that highly charged nervous activity seeping away. But how is it for you?"

"Please stop," he moaned, as I started to plant firm kisses down his chest.

"Stop?" I murmured, "Where have I heard that before? Oh yes, it was when I was begging you to stop. I'd no idea you could be so cruel."

I looked into his eyes with a burning intensity that he experienced like a knife, adding to the painful shocks from the kisses. He shut his eyes and I kissed the lids, forcing them to spring open. But just as he was resigning himself to more of this justified revenge, I drew back and watched as his rapid breathing slowed and his body started to relax. Tears replaced my brief ferocity and I convulsed beside him, sobbing.

"You see, you really have made me into a monster. You don't even find me attractive any more. And nor will anyone else – is that what you wanted?"

He stared, sharing the thought that he had never been so unhappy. Why had Theodora not warned him of this stage in the after effects?

"You're still irresistible, even if it means pain," he said.

But I was in no state for compliments. I curled up, crying inconsolably. He cautiously wrapped an arm round me.

"I just want you, Cassandra, only you – electrified for ever if necessary. Although it won't be forever."

What was the right thing to say in these circumstances? Give me all your pain? Or pretend it didn't hurt? Or just make love and hope to survive? He held me tighter, making me flinch slightly, but my sobbing became less violent. My tears fell on his chest and it was his turn to shudder at their painful landings. Gradually we both relaxed.

"You're the love of my life," he confessed. "I'm terrified you won't forgive me. And you're the most attractive woman I've ever met."

"Even now?" I whispered into his chest so that the words were scarcely audible.

"Especially now," he sighed.

"So you think you could get used to the pain?"

"Definitely. The places where you kissed me now feel unbearably aroused. I guess there are men who'd pay a fortune for having that kind of pain inflicted on them."

"Unbearably aroused," I said, with a little smile. "I know that feeling. What would you like to do about that arousal, Mr. Bondmate?"

"I'd like to make mad, electric love with you," he said quickly, kissing me and quivering with the exquisite agony of feeling the pain shoot through him. I sat up and pulled him from the sofa.

"Come with me," I said seductively, "let's try it before I've managed to control these strange effects."

In the bedroom, he sat nervously on the bed. "Perhaps we should wait," he said tentatively, while I stripped slowly, watching his reaction.

"You're not afraid, are you?" I said, unbuttoning his shirt and gently removing it.

"Scared stiff," he admitted, as I continued to undress him.

"Would you like a couple of Hagen's pills?" I murmured, stroking his chest and then moving light fingers down his stomach.

"No, I think I should have the full experience," he said, leaning back on the bed. He gasped and squirmed at each electric touch. I stroked his neck and chest where I had kissed him before. "Do these areas feel unbearably aroused?" I asked, brushing my lips over the same points.

"Yes," he groaned, as I turned to kissing more obviously erogenous zones.

"Is it painful?" I murmured, seeing how he seemed to steel himself before every contact from her lips.

"Excruciating, exquisite pain," he gasped.

"Now try kissing me," I breathed and he kissed the curve of my neck, then traced soft kisses down my gently writhing body. I curved towards him, moaning with pain and pleasure.

"I'm not hurting you?" he asked and I laughed. "Yes, of course it hurts." He stopped, gazing intensely.

I sighed. "It's a good type of pain, Kastor, for a change."

We both yelped at the searing shock of the intimate contact. We were locked in a tender, tingling embrace, moving away only to seek more of this tender torture.

Afterwards we had to wait for the impression of electric sparks to subside. I looked up at him shyly. He grinned, no longer afraid of holding me tightly, wondering at the sensation of having seemingly made love with an electric pylon.

"Oh my," he murmured, "what would Theodora say if she could see us now?"

"What makes you think she can't?" I said, giggling, "Although I'm sure she'd be too polite to linger on it."

He shared a thought of concern about having ignored advice not to touch me, let alone go this far.

"I knew it would help," I said, still shivering at the tingling. "My nerve endings feel quite happy and sated. It was like quenching a thirst after trekking through a hot, dry desert. But perhaps a bit too hot for you?"

"Well, it was certainly hot. It was like being consumed by pain," he said. "And then, soaring pleasure. I think that puts paid to any idea of working for the rest of today."

"So we'll take the children for a walk?"

"We may have established that you've good energy while lying down, but I'll insist on you sitting outside and just watching us walk."

We signalled for the nanny to bring Leo, Tamsin and Florence to the apartment. Kastor advised keeping to the area at the side of the Askeys mansion, where there was a tall hedge maze rather like the one at Hampton Court Palace. A rarely used sun terrace had seats where I could sit while they explored the maze. This was a cunning suggestion of Kastor's, who knew that I would not be keen on trying to find my way through the maze. Once, I'd ventured there alone, becoming so lost that I had to call for help. I had tried to follow the instruction of following the hedge to my left, but was soon frustratingly wandering up and down the narrow paths. I had eventually found the centre, where there was a small love seat and bower of roses, only to find that every subsequent path brought me back to this area again. When rescued, I had vowed never to re-enter the maze. So I agreed to sit and wave as Kastor and Leo marched up to the entrance. The nanny took Tamsin and Florence on a walk through the adjacent rose garden. I sat back, relaxing in the warm September air and feeling so much better, after my pain and passion session with Kastor.

When it seemed only a few minutes before Kastor and Leo returned to the terrace, I wondered if I had dozed off. Leo was running towards me and Kastor wore a thunderous expression. I looked towards the maze, sensing that there was someone else within in its paths. I detected two people, one of them being Edouard Parfait.

"We found people kissing!" said Leo excitedly, jumping up next to me on the garden seat.

Kastor nodded grimly. "He ran ahead to the centre, no problem with his sense of direction." I silently acknowledged the benefit of this particular gene having come from Kastor. "They weren't kissing when I got there," he added. Leo was beaming. The children rarely saw any expression of affection between couples, "It was the nice French policeman," he confided. Kastor raised his eyebrows at the word 'nice' and sat down on the bench.

"Yes, the French ex-policeman, with Lamella, one of the assessment officers." Kastor's ironic expression spoke volumes. My heart sank but he seemed rather amused. "They scurried off," he added with a faint sneer. The exit to the maze was on the other side, not visible from the terrace. I sent a thought that Theodora had promised to speak to Edouard, but Kastor glanced anxiously at our perceptive son. He shot back the thought that she may have simply specified one person whom the amorous policeman should avoid. I blushed, knowing he meant me. I thought of Gaston's reference to other women succumbing to Edouard's charms.

"Fancy him liking Lamella," I thought, thinking of the rather plain but undeniably buxom girl who normally bustled about her duties efficiently, in her white, close fitting uniform. I wondered how many other conquests Edouard had managed in his short time at the Binaries. How vain of me to imagine I was the only target of his affections, I reflected. I noticed a sidelong glance from Kastor despite having tried to close off this thought.

The nanny approached with the twins, unaware of the excitement in the maze. Kastor indicated silently to Leo that he should not mention the kiss. This would not be an approved experience for Binary children of his age. Then he said that I needed to return to the apartment to rest and I didn't argue. I wanted to leave this scene as soon as possible. The nanny took the children into the gardens, towards the Pagoda stop, while Kastor and I returned to the house. In the apartment, I stood quietly, hoping that this new evidence of Edouard's wanton behaviour would not have destroyed our previous good mood. But Kastor smiled, taking my arm and squeezing it, noting happily that this time I did not flinch.

"I'm sure he was particularly interested in you," he said softly, "It's hard to blame him completely, even if I'd like to kill him."

"That won't be necessary, will it?" I asked, never surprised at how far Binaries would go to protect what was dear to them.

"Probably not," he said, with a tinge of regret.

26

After a much better night, I woke up, delighted to find that my body was only slightly aching and my head far clearer. Kastor was still sleeping, with a contented smile on his face. I lay back on the pillow and thought about the last couple of days, which seemed of far greater duration. I wondered briefly whether Edouard knew anything about what I had been going through, noticing that there was no thought channel between us. Perhaps he's been confined in one of those thought protective tents, I mused, imagining one of the nannies standing sternly over him with a tennis racquet, threatening to whack him if he let out a stray idea of flirting with any woman ever again. The thought made me giggle and Kastor opened his eyes.

"What's amusing you so much?"

I hesitated, deciding on the truth. "I was just imagining a nanny punishing Monsieur Parfait." I carefully avoided saying his first name, not wanting to darken Kastor's mood.

"Please don't think about him," said Kastor, in a quiet, serious tone. "He's being taken care of." Seeing my flicker of alarm, imagining him being dragged away by security guards to a painful fate, he smiled. "I meant, he's having a rapid education in control techniques, to improve his behaviour." I wondered if that would involve tennis racquets and could not help giggling again. He picked up the image and smiled more grimly.

"And don't think about punishments, either. It reminds me of my bad behaviour towards you."

"You Binaries and your punishments," I sighed. "I think I've been quite punishing to you."

"I'm just grateful you're too kind to really punish me," he murmured, remembering my painful kisses but now rather missing them because of the exquisite pleasure that followed in their wake.

"That's right," I said, leaning my head on his shoulders and feeling so relieved that touch was not an agony of disordered sensation. "Because you wouldn't survive, if I was as angry with you."

I started giggling again, picturing myself in tight black leather with Kastor chained up, begging for mercy.

"Resistance would be futile, Mr. Bondmate," I said in a mock menacing tone that came out as more sinister than I'd intended. I rippled with laughter again. "I can't stop laughing," I said apologetically through the giggles. "Is this an after-effect, do you think?"

"Hopefully a pleasant one," he said cautiously as my laughing grew louder and I drew my legs up to try to control it. "I love to hear you laugh – I wish I could laugh so freely."

"Try it!" I gasped between paroxysms of giggles, shaking with mirth. He was looking with such concern that I forced myself to calm down. "Perhaps I should tickle you," I said, my fingers seeking possible vulnerable spots.

"I'm not ticklish." His eyes were smiling but I caught a sad thought.

"Didn't you get tickled, when you were a child?" He shook his head. I was still giggling occasionally, although able to form a serious face. "But you did laugh, have fun?"

"Yes of course. You've seen the children in the nursery, enjoying playing. It was just like that."

"You've tickled Leo, Tamsin and Florence…"

"I've just tried to follow your lead – into unfamiliar territory."

"You need to laugh more, I'll try to think of some jokes. I know you <u>can</u> laugh…"

"The last two days haven't been very funny for either of us," he muttered, but then chuckled softly.

"Does that mean you're beginning to see the funny side?" I asked tentatively.

"No, I was just thinking about your awful jokes…"

I grinned. "OK, try this one. Two very clever and philosophical binaries went camping. One was called Kastor and the other… Pollux."

He gazed warily but my chuckle was infectious. He said, "Is that the joke? Well, I suppose Pollux is quite an amusing name," laughing despite not getting it.

I shook my head, sniggering at the idea of a twin called Bollocks. "No, listen, they pitched their tent in a field, just near one of the Binary manholes into the labyrinth. When night fell, they went to sleep happily, but after a few hours, Kastor woke Pollux up while it was still very dark. He said, 'Look up at the stars, Pollux and tell me what you sense.' So Pollux stared into the sky and said, 'I see trillions of stars and even if only a few of them have planets, it's possible that some of those planets are like Earth and may have telepathic beings like ourselves.' He gazed up dreamily, but then Kastor said, 'Pollux, you idiot – somebody stole our tent'."

I could scarcely get the punch line out as I rolled with laughter.

"Someone stole their tent, I see," said Kastor. "Yes that's quite funny."

"Perhaps I didn't tell it right," I said, my smile fading. "A joke along those lines was voted one of the funniest ever."

Kastor laughed at last. "You don't need jokes to make me laugh, I find you funny just in yourself."

"Funny peculiar…"

"Funny amazing." He gazed into my eyes and I chortled again. "I think I'm going to laugh all day," I murmured. "It feels so good to be something like myself again."

Kastor beamed. Then he got out of bed abruptly. "While you're in such a good mood, I have something for you."

"A present?" I asked, wondering how he would have had the opportunity to get one, having been by my side for two days.

"Wait and see," he said, leaving the room. When he returned, he had a gift-wrapped box, about the size of a mantel clock. I sat up in bed, eyes shining with anticipation.

"I ordered this for your birthday, but it only arrived a few days ago. And it didn't seem the right moment to give it to you then."

I nodded a little anxiously, sharing a thought of the distracting business with Edouard.

"But you gave me a lovely birthday present – that necklace to match the earrings."

"When the special order couldn't be completed in time, I had to find something else."

I held the box, trying to determine what was inside. "A kind of clock but not a clock, something musical." As I focused more strongly, he took the box away.

"Don't try to see it, just open it." He handed it back and I took off the wrapping. Inside was a beautifully made small cabinet shaped like a Georgian building, with a clock face set into the top and delicately veneered wooded recesses representing windows. "It looks like Woodstock Town Hall," I gasped. Beneath the clock sat a pair of doors with little brass handles. I opened the doors carefully and could hardly believe what I saw. Within the compartment there was an intricate garden scene. At the back stood the Askeys pagoda, gleaming white. Little figures began moving in the garden along a labyrinth of paths as a tune started to play. It was the recurring melody from the first stanza of Mozart's Sonata in C major no.16, the tune I had played constantly while pregnant with Leo.

"It's wonderful," I said, entranced. "How ever did you manage to get this made? It looks like something crafted a long time ago."

"It wasn't easy," he said proudly. "The case and Askeys scene were made by craftsmen in England but the music box movement is Swiss."

"And you managed to keep it a secret from me."

"I know you don't pry into my thoughts – or search my study. You trust me." A shadow fell cross his face as he recalled me inviting him to punish me.

I looked up, beaming, reassuring him. "Of course I trust you, Kastor. I needed a jolt to bring me to my senses. Perhaps you overdid it – well you definitely overdid it, but don't let's think about it any more."

"If you insist," he said, a frown turning rapidly to a broad smile. He took the musical box and showed me three knobs on the side. "You can wind this one to keep playing the tune – or rotate the one above to set it as an alarm clock."

"It's more likely to send me to sleep. But what about the third knob?"

"If you wind it up, it plays the whole first movement."

"Wow," I said, winding it. "Leo will love this."

"At a distance," said Kastor reprovingly. "It's not a toy."

"And I guess it cost a fortune." I examined the workmanship and watching the tiny marionettes moving in time with the tune.

"Another good point about Binary life, our almost limitless budget?" he asked, looking into my eyes.

I nodded. "Yet another point for the list. In addition to 'Kastor's presents' – I can never match them."

He closed his eyes, taking in my excitement and happiness. "I thought it would be a reminder of when we met and that I'll always love you. You loving me back – that's the best present I'll ever get from you."

"We'll have to see about that," I said, holding the musical box and starting to think of what I could possibly plan for his birthday in November.

Over the next few days, I recovered completely and we were both fit for work by the end of the weekend. Manes and Amélie invited us to a party on Wednesday evening.

"It'll mainly be the Binaires crowd," said Kastor on Tuesday, when Manes sent a thought message with a clock time to remind us. He saw a trace of anxiety in my eyes, so added, "But not him."

"Where is he?" I asked, realising I had not seen or heard of Edouard since he had been caught in the love seat in the maze.

"I told you," said Kastor, "he's having a rapid induction into controlling his behaviour. He'd be far too busy to come – but Manes wouldn't invite him, anyway."

"You've spoken to Manes about it?" I asked, embarrassed.

"No, but he doesn't approve of Monsieur Parfait's over eager embrace of Binary females, any more than I do." I wondered if Edouard had tried it on with Amélie, but did not dare to ask. My thoughts turned instead to what I could wear, as Manes had said to dress up.

"You've a wardrobe full of clothes," muttered Kastor.

"But no party dress, not one I haven't worn a dozen times," she complained.

"You'll look great, whatever you wear," he said, getting up and going to the study. Later he found me in the bedroom, sifting through dresses disconsolately.

"The Binaires women always look so chic," I moaned. While they had escaped from the French centre with only what they were wearing, they had made up for it since. I heard a rustling of paper and turned. Kastor was holding a large parcel.

"It came today," he said shyly. "I ordered it on Saturday. Arthur had strict instructions to hide it in the study."

I tore open the parcel. It contained a low cut black evening dress, close fitting with diagonal swirls of satin around the middle and a gossamer light over-skirt that would float as I moved. It looked a lot shorter than the usual clothes Kastor liked me to wear, although he had tried to train me out of jeans and leggings.

"I thought it would go well with the necklace," he said nonchalantly, as I posed in front of the mirror, holding the dress around me.

"Another present, you're really spoiling me," I laughed. I stripped off the work clothes and put it on, with Kastor watching admiringly.

"You look gorgeous. I couldn't have you feeling those French women have an iota of your charm and style. You'll be the sexiest woman in the room."

"I don't think so," I said, thinking of Amélie and Dominique – I judged the latter to be in her forties, but Dominique was the epitome of a mature beauty, with a knowing spark in her dark eyes that reduced most men to muttering submissiveness.

"I'll wear Lily's shoes," I said, going to the section of the wardrobe reserved for my alias as Lily West, the entrepreneur. To date I had gone to very few business meetings on the outside with this alias, but I used the clothes on other rare trips outside, with a platinum blonde wig and much heavier make up. I donned a pair of Manolo Blahnik high-heeled shoes and pranced in front of him.

"I'm beginning to wonder if I should have ordered something less revealing," he murmured. "None of the men will be able to take their eyes off you." I laughed and shook my head. I had never felt much admired by men on the outside, still amazed that Kastor constantly called me beautiful.

"Meanwhile," he said, gazing at me, "take it off. I want to see the parts they won't be able to ogle."

"Nothing you haven't seen before," I said dismissively, running my hands down the dress and watching my reflection. Helen would approve, I thought. Kastor stepped behind me and pulled down the zip. "Resistance is futile, Mrs. Bondmate," he said seductively, as the dress dropped to my feet and he took me in his arms.

27

On the Wednesday evening, we were half an hour later than the allotted time for arrival at the party. We could hear merriment while waiting for our silent knock to be answered and in the end, we looked at each other knowingly and walked in. We were surprised by the transformation in the normally rather austere furnishings. Fairy lights were strung all around the walls, with the chairs pushed to the side and a large table covered with food to one side. An Edith Piaf song was playing: '*Je ne regrette rien*.' Manes greeted us warmly, sweeping his eyes over me and whistling softly.

"You're obviously better," he said. "I was so sorry to hear you'd been ill."

I nodded, embarrassed at the idea that Manes knew or suspected the cause. He had probably been with Kastor when Theodora summoned him back to the flat. But if he knew, he disguised it well, drawing us towards the group of people already drinking cocktails and talking loudly. "You know everyone, I think," he said.

There were waiters on hand to give out drinks and a catering assistant standing by the buffet table to replace dishes and help guests to plates and cutlery. Kastor was reluctant to leave my side, but I had no wish to circulate on my own. I kept looking around anxiously to see if Edouard would arrive after all. I imagined that he would love this party and was cheeky enough to turn up.

I caught a snatch of conversation between Grégoire and one of the French assessment officers, with two attractively attired Binaires nannies drinking rather too much of the punch. They were speaking in French, but I was fluent enough to understand most of it, after our residence in France.

"And that's what I can't fathom, her sending that old song, *'The Lost Chord'*."

"You mean, it should have been *'Hit me, baby, one more time'*?" asked the assessment officer and they laughed, with the nannies convulsing in giggles. I looked around for Ariadne, thinking she would not want to be discussed in this way, then remembered that of course Ariadne had returned to work at St. Anthony's.

"I suppose she was feeling sorry for herself," said the assessment officer.

"Or hadn't wanted to shock Cassandra!" chuckled Grégoire, who hadn't noticed that I was so near them. A thought dart from me made him turn round and he grinned sheepishly. There was no need for him to ask or wonder if I'd heard him.

"You look divine, Cassandra," he said, transmitting a thought that he had not meant to offend me.

I smiled, accepting a glass of punch from one of the waiters. "I think I need to catch up with all of you, in many ways," I said, allowing just sufficient flashing warning from my eyes to get him to change the subject of the trapped mind repairer. Observing this exchange, Kastor took me over to another group. Dominique was in sparkling form, chattering about the progress in the Devon extension to the Binaires, where Grégoire and a few others from their group would be living temporarily, before transfer to French Canada.

"But where is Edouard?" asked Antoine, the surveillance officer from Binaires. His question was innocent, with no apparent knowledge of recent events. Dominique glanced at Kastor and muttered something about him working late. She smiled at me and complimented me on my dress and jewellery.

"I left so much behind," said Dominique. "I just brought a few pieces of jewellery with me." She was wearing a stunning double rope of pearls and matching earrings. The necklace dipped into her cleavage. She smiled modestly when I complimented her on the ensemble, a severe azure dress that clung to her well preserved figure. "Oh this," she said, "just something from the drama department."

Antoine took another glass of punch, returning to his question. "No, seriously, where is he? He helped us to escape, so I expected him to be here – particularly since you, Dominique…"

Dominique's smile tightened, making him pause. Antoine was being particularly dense, possibly connected with the intoxicating punch and cocktails on offer.

"Since I've been helping with his training, you mean?" she said casually. Another Binaires surveillance officer joined the group, one of Dominique's admirers, although he stole a covetous glance at me too. Kastor put his hand around my waist, uncharacteristically showing a public physical display of affection. Dominique downed a large glass of punch, trying to conceal that she was ill at ease. I had sensed something in her thoughts, an image of Edouard, sitting in what looked like one of the detention cells. Picking this up as well, Kastor tried unsuccessfully to steer me away. For I was now fascinated. Edouard seemed to be wearing only black leather shorts and a matching jerkin, which did little to cover his muscular torso. I sensed that Dominique was rapidly working on blocking this image, but she had consumed too much of the punch. Focusing more closely, I noticed that Edouard appeared also to be wearing a leather collar. I tried to suppress shock when I realised the collar was attached to a chain in the wall. Kastor gripped me more tightly, saying, "I think we should sample the excellent food."

I remained rooted to the spot, now seeing other images of Dominique standing sternly over Edouard, holding a whip. Dominique flushed and I immediately blocked the series of images, embarrassed to be caught prying. I let Kastor take me towards the buffet table.

"Why do you think her nickname is 'Dom the dom?' " murmured Kastor.

"Oh," I said, "so it's just in her imagination, then, but it seemed so real." I held a plate for the catering assistant to fill it with food. Checking that we were well out of earshot, Kastor coughed nervously and said softly, "It is real." Speaking was much safer than sending thoughts when surrounded by telepaths.

I widened my eyes. "So that's what you meant by behavioural training?" He nodded, shame-faced, watching warily for a blaze of anger about Binary punishment routines. We heard Dominique's voice across the room, loud with the amplifying effect of alcohol.

"He's been such a naughty boy," she was saying in French, with a wicked laugh. "He needed taking in hand."

I kept my voice low, deciding to go easy on any further sampling of the punch, in case I started to be similarly indiscreet.

"But Kastor, he's chained up... with a collar?"

"Until he learns to behave. Dominique is really rather fond of him. Like a lot of the women around here," he added, with a bitter edge to his words.

"She's old enough to be his mother, well, nearly," I said, rejecting an image of Edouard making love to Dominique with an abrupt shuttering of my thoughts.

"Only if she was a mother at about 12 years old," he replied.

I paused, reckoning the years. Edouard was 35 or so. It meant that Dominique was looking good at 47. We were distracted by a guffaw from Grégoire, who had joined the group surrounding the vivacious – and loquacious – Dominique.

"It's a shame for Edouard to miss all these lovely ladies," he shouted, unaware he was speaking above normal conversational level. "And the food, of course – Manes and Amélie have done us proud."

"Oh, he'll get some of the food, I'm sure," laughed Dominique. "I'll take a doggy bag." The group dissolved into laughter. I recalled seeing a metal bowl on the floor from my inadvertent glimpse into Dominique's images of Edouard.

"She's treating him like a dog?" I whispered to Kastor.

"Well, he's behaved like one," he said, with no sign of compassion. Perhaps remembering Theodora's admonishment, he softened his expression. "I don't know all the details - it's personal, between them. But trust me, he'll be enjoying most of it."

I thought briefly of the police officer's wistful face, dreaming of what it would be like to be within a community of telepaths. Be careful what you wish for, I thought, reflecting how my destiny had taken such a dramatically different course after meeting Kastor and my twin.

The subject closed. I knew it would spoil Kastor's mood and he only too willing to distract me from Edouard's retraining. The buffet meal was followed by dance music and he led me onto the central section of the parquet floor that had been cleared for the party.

"I'm not sure I can dance in these shoes," I said cautiously. "I'll hold you," he whispered and whirled me round so that my feet left the floor. Some of the guests clapped enthusiastically. This kind of physical contact in public was much better tolerated. I was feeling happier than for weeks and soon most of us were reeling around the room. Edouard was forgotten as I created an image of dancing in the sky, with the fairy lights transforming into a glorious star-lit night.

28

Kastor dropped off to sleep soon after we returned to our apartment, but I lay awake, thinking about Edouard's behavioural training. I was morbidly fascinated in the great contrast between the starry heights of mental communication amongst Binaries – literally, while we were dancing under shared images of stars – and the physical cruelty of some of their other habits. Keeping Edouard chained up in a cell seemed very harsh treatment for a man whose only crime was to be very fond of women. I didn't mean to try remote viewing into the detention centre, but drowsiness and the effects of the punch made it hard to resist.

After a few moments, I could see Dominique in the cell with Edouard. It seemed she had just entered. He jumped up to greet her, delighted. "Dominique!" he said, "I didn't expect…" She took a small whip down from a high shelf, well beyond the range of Edouard's chain.

"Kneel!" she commanded, wielding the whip across his chest. He knelt immediately, looking up with fear and respect.

"I'm sorry mistress, I forgot, it was so good to see you."

"You forgot your manners. What does that mean, dog?"

"It means I must be punished."

She slashed the whip cross his chest, angrily. "It means what?" she said, glaring.

"It means I must be punished, <u>mistress,</u>" he mumbled. He looked up her, submissively. "Sorry, mistress. Please punish me."

"Get over in the corner," she ordered, kicking his feeding bowl to one side. He shuffled quickly to where she pointed, stretching the chain so that it pulled on his collar. He looked up at her appealingly.

I tried unsuccessfully to shut out these images, but because of my mental affinity with Edouard, I couldn't stop prying. I was amazed to find he was thinking that she was overwhelmingly attractive, relishing her transmitted brutal images with fear and arousal. Was this how Helen had made my ex-boyfriend Roderick do anything she wanted?

They were too involved in this savage encounter, I hoped, to notice that I had tuned in to them. Also I had become so much more adept at one way communication, shutting off the other end from knowing it was me. And if Dominique, a much more experienced telepath than Edouard, sensed me, would she really care?

Dominique, still wearing the tight azure dress, took a chair from the small reading desk in the cell, placing it near the door, out of his reach. "How dare you look at me like that," she said. "Look down while I'm speaking to you." He obeyed, staring at his ludicrously tight shorts. "That girl, Lamella. She came to see me today," said Dominique, playing with the whip as she spoke. He stared at the floor fearfully.

"Yes, the one you've been playing with, telling her that you loved her. Well, she's pregnant."

He could not resist looking up in surprise, but there was also a faint smile. She sprang up and slapped his face, making him whimper. "Sorry mistress," he mumbled incoherently.

"So you persuaded her to dispense with contraception?"

demanded Dominique.

"Mistress, she needed no persuasion. She knows about the programme to make more babies and she offered to try…"

"We haven't dispensed with permission for pregnancy," snarled Dominique. "We can't have you going around fathering babies, *willy nilly*." She used the English words, rolling her tongue around them for emphasis.

"I'm sorry mistress, but she was so very eager. I wanted to do something for the community."

"So you're prepared to be her bond mate?" asked Dominique, imperiously.

Watching this, I suspected that the idea was deeply unwelcome to him. Lamella was willing and nubile, but scarcely an amusing companion and not nearly pretty enough for his tastes. I shuttered a thought that he would have much preferred to bond with me.

Dominique narrowed her eyes and strode behind him. She took a pair of handcuffs and grabbed his arms, pulling them back to secure them in the cuffs. "I'm waiting for your answer," she whispered into his ear.

"Yes mistress, if you order it."

"Good, perhaps we'll arrange it. In due course, when your training is complete. If that's what Lamella wants, or I decide. But meanwhile, how dare you even think of Cassandra."

Oh, I thought, I didn't pick that up while I was busy shuttering my connection with this dark scene. I no longer fancied Edouard at all, after the damage done to my relationship with Kastor, but I couldn't help feeling sorry for him.

In the cell, Dominique leaned over him menacingly. "You cur, you're not fit to lick her shoes. Answer me!"

"Mistress, I'm not fit to lick her shoes. Forgive me, please."

"Bend over," she ordered and he nervously stretched forward, waiting for more lashes of the whip. But she crossed the cell and kicked the bowl towards him. She emptied a bag of party food into it. "Eat, petit chien," she said. He leant forward, picking up a piece of chicken with his teeth. He chewed nervously. "Mistress, I'm not hungry," he said plaintively and she pushed his head into the bowl.

I was dangerously near to opening the channels and ordering this torture to end. But now Dominique switched to apparent tenderness, feeding him from the bowl and then wiping his face, since his hands were still cuffed. Then she released his hands. "I'll leave you now, to think about your behaviour."

"Mistress, I am yours to command."

She stroked his chest, running her finger down to his shorts. "You're such a dog," she said affectionately. "Work on the exercises I gave you and I'll reward you tomorrow."

She left the cell, leaving him smiling gratefully and with excitement at this possible reward. I shut off the remote viewing and thought of the conversation back at our villa. Edouard had dreamed of this, having a relationship with a French telepath. Bonding with Lamella would be a small price to pay.

In our apartment, Kastor stirred happily in his sleep. Cassandra, Cassandra, he murmured. He had told me that he was the luckiest man in all the world of telepaths to have won me back. I knew that he would not consider Edouard's training to be too cruel, considering he had tried to steal his beloved. I gazed at his face, grateful that our relationship did not involve any dominatrix games. I nuzzled against him and sighed at the pleasure of feeling him close, made sweeter by the recent inability to touch or be touched.

29

A couple of days later I was sitting on my own in the labyrinth restaurant when Lamella timidly approached. I looked up politely: we scarcely knew each other.

"May I join you?" asked Lamella and I nodded.

"So how are you, Lamella?" I guessed that the young assessment officer knew that I would have been told about the tryst with Edouard in the maze. The young woman beamed, suffusing her plain face with happiness.

"I'm fine, well, more than fine." She lowered her voice. "I've just heard that I'm pregnant. I wanted you to be one of the first to know, considering your relationship programme."

"Congratulations," I said warily, realising immediately that Edouard could be the father. Picking this up, Lamella smiled shyly.

"Yes it's wonderful – we're so in love. I can't wait for us to attend the parenting classes."

"Hmm, yes." I forced an insincere smile. But Lamella was oblivious to such nuances of expression. I sensed that her thoughts were full of bonding with Edouard – and their child. "I don't suppose you've seen him?" asked Lamella, failing to sound casual. I shook my head.

"Not since last week," I replied carefully. Lamella looked around the restaurant disconsolately. "I know he's been going to the training centre, but I seem to keep missing him."

I closed my thoughts, realising that Lamella knew nothing about Dominique's training sessions or the detention cell. "Can't you sense where he is?" I asked.

"No, I'm not that good. If he were here somewhere in the restaurant, I'd know, but I'm not an expert like you." She looked as though about to plead for me to do a mental search for him. I had no intention of trying to locate Edouard, in case he was now able to sense such things.

"Let me see," I said, as though focusing on his whereabouts. "Have you tried the coffee lounge?" Lamella got up eagerly, saying she would look for him there. As she dashed towards the restaurant exit and I sighed for her. Pregnant, I thought: that's partly my fault for encouraging more births. Then I stiffened to see the departing Lamella nearly colliding with Dominique. Following behind Dominique, his head bent, was a very subdued Edouard. I was relieved that he was dressed more normally than in the images sensed at the party and by remote viewing. He was wearing a Binary tracksuit. I suppressed an amused thought of Edouard striding into the restaurant in black leather hot pants, a collar and little else. The tracksuit was zipped up high with the collar turned up. I wondered grimly if this was to conceal the mark made by the leather restraint.

"Edouard! Where have you been?" said the delighted Lamella. He looked nervously at Dominique, who nodded briskly, transmitting that he should greet the eager young woman with charm and courtesy. I watched as Edouard, still looking down, mumbled a greeting and forced a smile.

"You must forgive him," said Dominique. "He's very tired. We're keeping him hard at his training." Edouard nodded gratefully, standing meekly at Dominique's side.

"I need to see you," whispered Lamella. "When can we meet?"

Edouard waited for an instruction from Dominique. She gave the rosy cheeked future mother of his baby a patronising smile. In an off-hand tone, she said, "I'm afraid he is in intensive training at the moment, Lamella. Isn't that right, Edouard?" He nodded, looking apologetically at Lamella. Dominique smiled with more intensity at the confused young woman. "Perhaps in a few days," she said briskly. "I'll make sure he doesn't forget."

Lamella hesitated, looking yearningly at Edouard, but knew she had been dismissed. Dominique stared after her, before indicating to Edouard that he could go up to the serving counter. She went with him, leaning over the dishes and pointing to what he would be allowed to eat. I rapidly finished my meal, alarmed at the thought that Dominique would further test Edouard's behaviour by bringing him to my table. But Dominique turned and nodded in greeting, transmitting that I was the last person whom Edouard would be allowed to sit with. Dominique loaded the tray with both their meals, indicated that Edouard should carry it and pointed to the far side of the restaurant, where there were two or three empty tables.

"Go and sit down," she ordered, although in a kinder voice than the one I had picked up in the cell. He nodded immediately, keeping his eyes on the tray and the floor as he obeyed. He did not seem to have noticed my presence, or did not dare to reveal it. As Dominique passed my table she murmured, "He's coming on very well. This is the first time he's been here since we started on the training." She swept on to the far table, where I saw that Edouard was sitting quietly, staring at the food and waiting for permission to eat it. So now he had one of his deepest wishes, a telepathic mistress. Well, a mistress in at least two ways, I reflected, closing my mind to what Dominique might have in store for him as his training progressed.

Later, back in the apartment, I asked Kastor if he knew about Lamella's pregnancy. He frowned, admitting that he had heard something about it. "There's a chance the baby will be quite good looking, as well as telepathic," he said casually.

"Lamella wants to bond with him," I replied.

"That will be more than he deserves," he replied, switching the subject immediately to our trip to Scotland at the weekend. I sighed, regretting that there would be no opportunity to gossip about Lamella with a female friend, or with my twin. I could only discuss this with Kastor, and then only when he seemed very calm and receptive. For the first time in years, I thought of my school friend Anne. Helen had told me that she had married soon after my entry into Binaries, but nothing else. It was impossible to think of meeting Anne again, who believed that the Cassandra she knew had died on a remote Caribbean island. Even if I could explain the strange life I now led, Anne was a lawyer and might report the existence of the Binary community.

That night, I dreamed that I was walking with Aunt V in the grounds of Blenheim Park, pointing out where I had met Kastor.

My aunt laughed and said "None of this really happened you know!"

I looked around, wondering where Kastor was, Aunt V said crisply, "No one can see you, you don't exist here."

I started to protest, but an orchestra incongruously started to play, drowning our voices. In a panic, I started to run, feeling everyone looking at me and thinking, they can see me, they know who I am. When I woke up, I pinched myself as if to test that my life in the Binaries was real. The familiar Askeys bedroom came into focus with Kastor looking at me curiously.

"Just a dream," I murmured, as there was no point in discussing my old life. But I added, "It would be good to see Aunt V again, do you think it could be arranged?"

"Were you dreaming about her?" asked Kastor, noticing that I had closed off my thoughts. I nodded and he smiled, saying that of course a visit could be arranged, when we returned from Scotland.

30

It was the Saturday before the trip to Scotland. I spent the morning at the nursery, playing with my children but taking care to show attention to the others. I consoled myself with the thought that Leo's departure for Lochinstoun would give me more time for the twins. Leo tended to monopolise conversation with me. He chattered happily about the school and how he would send me drawings as well as his thoughts. They are trained to do this, I reflected, to do without parents and just be together with schoolmates. Even on the journey to Scotland, Kastor and I would not be sitting with Leo, nor would emotional partings be allowed. Almost pointless to go, I thought sadly. When I returned to the apartment, Kastor emerged from his study with a delighted smile.

"It looks as though you'll have a chance to see Aunt V sooner than we imagined."

He explained that Gaston and Aunt V had planned to go to a concert at Blenheim Palace but that two friends of Aunt V could no longer attend. So if we wanted, we could take their tickets.

"It's an outdoor concert, celebrating something or other – they've booked a picnic."

He paused, seeing I did not seem entirely happy with the idea. To his questioning thought, I replied, "Well, that would be lovely – it's just that I dreamed of Blenheim last night."

"Ah, so that's it. I sensed your dream had troubled you. Are you worried that something may happen?"

"I dreamed I met with Aunt V at Blenheim, that's all. My dreams are never straightforward, perhaps it was just a prediction that we'd have the opportunity to go to Blenheim."

"We don't have to go, it was just an idea." Kastor was disappointed.

"I'd love to go," I said, knowing how hard Kastor was trying to make me happy, after the hyperstimulation episode.

"You'll be quite safe with Gaston and me," said Kastor, encouragingly. "Even if someone thought they recognised the old Cassandra, or Helen, we could handle that easily. It's been several years, after all."

I thought how wonderful it would be to escape the Binaries, just for a short time.

Kastor was watching carefully. "So shall I say yes? I know your aunt would be thrilled to see you – and a chance for me to meet her at last. And we could witness the transformation she's worked on Gaston."

I glanced at the sunny scene in the gardens. It was good weather for an outdoor event and there would probably be some kind of cover if it rained. I remembered the picnic Kastor and I had shared, six summers previously.

"Yes – let's go," I said and he grinned. Outside visits for pleasure were extremely rare for Binaries and I sensed his excitement. I dismissed further worries, as prediction of my own life was rarely accurate, still less giving definite warnings.

We set off in the early evening, making the short journey in a car with Gaston, who was in good humour despite sharing a quick thought that there was a small risk involved. He was pleased to note my dark wig with a fringe, heavy make up and glasses. "Well done," he murmured.

"Probably only Kastor would recognise you under all that."

The concert seating was in the courtyard by the staterooms, with the orchestra shielded from possible rain and many of the audience had come prepared, with umbrellas. But looking up at the cloudless sky, there seemed little risk of a downpour. It also boded well for the long interval when we could take the picnic into the grounds to enjoy the twilight. Aunt V appeared nervous at first with Kastor, perhaps wondering what I had said about her to him and also recalling the time when he was just the strange man I'd met at Blenheim. Kastor was similarly ill at ease, perhaps worrying about an interrogation about how well he was treating me. Aunt V did not know about the hyperstimulation and her manner warmed when she saw how much we were in love.

We took our seats amidst a large crowd, with two field officers sitting discreetly nearby. I started to relax. I sat next to Aunt V so that we could talk in between the musical pieces, all familiar classics. By the time the interval arrived, I had almost dismissed worries of being recognised by anyone from my past, or that of Helen's. One of the field officers collected our large picnic hamper and carried it to a seat in the grounds. We spread it out. It was a much grander affair than the picnic coolbag I had shared with Kastor all those years before.

I was laughing politely at a rare joke from Gaston, an allusion to 18th century culture that had Aunt V chortling with mirth, when I felt a prickling at the back of my head.

"Who is looking at us, Aunt V?" I asked and she turned, cautiously. Aunt V understood that it was important for no one to recognise me. She turned back quickly.

"I think it's Anne Duncan, or Anne Dean, as she is now. I haven't seen her since... Cassandra's funeral."

Gaston's pleasant demeanour changed immediately, picking up from Kastor that this very old friend of mine was a potential threat.

"Say nothing, or as little as possible," he said quickly. To Aunt

V he murmured, "Just follow our lead, Veronica."

I froze, staring at my plate and wishing I could run from the scene. Kastor put his arm round me, alarmed at my extreme nervousness. He poured a glass of wine and steadied my hand.

"Don't worry," he murmured, "it'll be fine."

I tried to calm myself, sipping the wine as I sensed Anne coming nearer. My friend was not alone, I realised, guessing that her companion could be the boyfriend to whom Anne became engaged to just before I disappeared into the Binaries. I stole a glance at Gaston and Kastor, who looked perfectly relaxed, helping themselves to the picnic and making uncharacteristic small talk. All that acting while they were growing up, I thought, this is what it was for. They could slip into other personae as easily as I could try on clothes.

A familiar voice rang out. "Veronica, is that you? Aunt V?" Not daring to look, I sensed Aunt V turning to greet Anne with credible surprise.

"Goodness, Anne – how lovely to see you!"

"It's been years, but you haven't changed at all," said Anne. "You've met my husband Peter, although it was ages ago."

"How extraordinary to see you again, I thought you'd left Oxford," said Aunt V.

"Yes, we live in London now, but we're staying overnight – Peter wanted to see one of my old haunts."

I sensed that Anne was looking curiously at our group, possibly waiting to be introduced. Aunt V tried to conceal her fluster with a casual wave of her hand.

"We didn't want to miss this last concert of the season," she murmured. I realised she had no idea how to introduce us all and Gaston stepped in.

"Colin Winstanley," he said, using the academic name that Aunt V had first known him by, before she met him as Gaston Ajax. "Do introduce us, Veronica."

"Anne and Peter Dean," murmured Aunt V, with admirable poise. "Anne used to live in Oxford."

Aunt V hesitated when it came to introducing Kastor and me, perhaps trying to remember our assumed names for this outing. Gaston smiled warmly. "And this is Leonard Hardy and Sylvie, his wife."

"Delighted," said Kastor. I looked at the couple for the first time, forcing a smile. Anne was as slim and elegant as ever. Peter was thicker set, with penetrating eyes. I'd met him a few times as her boyfriend, serious even then and now looking far older than the five or so years difference with Anne and me. He was without doubt a trained professional. I remembered that he was already in the police when Anne met him, hoping that he had changed his career direction but feeling anxiously that this had not occurred.

"We didn't order a picnic," said Peter, "so we've had to make do with the other refreshments on offer."

They seemed to be hoping to be invited to join us. I transmitted an anxious thought to Kastor that this should be avoided. But he quickly signalled that we would not get rid of them without letting Anne talk to my aunt.

"May we join you for a moment?" asked Anne, ignoring the other guests, "It would be good to catch up with you, Veronica."

"I'm afraid we've rather demolished our picnic," said Gaston casually, "or you could have some. There may be a sandwich left, if you're hungry?"

"No, thank you, wouldn't dream of it," said Anne, sitting down on the grass next to Aunt V. Peter joined her, gazing at the rest of us with interest. I sensed he was wondering if we too knew Cassandra, the tragic widow whom he could scarcely remember. When Helen was posing as me, she had staged an apparent suicide, shortly before a planned visit to Antigua by Anne and Peter.

Anne smiled brightly at Aunt V. "When you last met Peter, he was just a sergeant. Now he's a chief inspector." Police, I thought in alarm, so I was right. Of all the outsiders, the Binaries were most nervous of police officers – and this one seemed rather too perceptive.

"Congratulations!" said Aunt V. "In the Thames Valley?"

"No, the Met," said Alex.

"And what do you do in the Metropolitan Police?" asked Gaston.

"Oh, it's mainly desk work," said Peter, but Anne said proudly, "He's very senior – in charge of fraud investigations. We met during a legal case when I was a student."

"Almost as boring as legal contract work," said Peter modestly. I tensed, hoping my trembling was invisible. Kastor was holding my arm, transmitting calm.

"But how are you Veronica?" asked Anne. "I feel terrible for not coming to see you again. It was just so sad, losing Cassandra, I wasn't sure if you'd want…"

"Yes it was a very miserable time," said Aunt V. "But I've enjoyed your Christmas cards. It was kind of you to remember me."

"She called herself Sandra then. She talked about you a lot," said Anne. "I often think of her. It was so astonishing when she married Roderick – and then the double tragedy."

"Yes," murmured Aunt V, adding in a quiet tone to her companions, "Anne was a school friend of Cassandra, you know, my niece, who died."

Gaston and Kastor nodded sympathetically. I assumed a serious expression, as though I had just heard this sad news. Anne looked at me curiously, studying me for the first time.

"So are you still working on contracts?" asked Aunt V and I thought, ah, Anne became a contract lawyer.

"Yes, and wondering if I'll ever be a partner in the firm, or whether we should just have a baby."

"Although that seems a bit unlikely," said Peter and I detected that they had been trying for a baby for some time. Perhaps they had been receiving infertility treatment, I wondered, picking up Anne's anxiety and regret for raising the subject. So possibly it was just as well that I could not tell Anne about my children. Anne was now staring at me and I cautiously met her gaze, mustering an innocent smile.

"You know," said Anne, "Sylvie looks a bit like Cassandra, don't you think, Veronica?" Aunt V raised her eyebrows, as though the idea was preposterous.

"We never met her, unfortunately," said Kastor. "Veronica has told me of the tragedy, but I was working in France at that time. It was where I met Sylvie."

"So you're French?" asked Peter, joining his wife in staring intently at me.

"Oui, I mean yes," I muttered, in a just passable French accent. "Please excuse my poor English," I added, huskily. I was terrified that Anne would recognise my voice.

"You should hear my French," laughed Anne. "But honestly, you're very like Cassandra. That's a compliment, by the way. She had lovely eyes, like you."

I smiled politely, giving a Gallic shrug and glancing at Kastor, begging for help.

"Was that the bell for the second half of the concert?" Kastor asked casually. "We need to get back."

Gaston took the cue, glancing towards the concert area. "I think you're right, Leonard." He drained his glass and stood up. Anne was reluctant to leave. "It's been great to see you again, Veronica. Perhaps we could move to sit near you – I expect some people won't go back."

"There were very few free seats," murmured Aunt V, but Gaston said airily, "Well, it's worth a try. Veronica and I'll go with you to see if we can find seats – if you two wouldn't mind packing up the picnic and taking the empties back?"

He smiled encouragingly at Kastor and me, while we nodded agreement.

"I'll help you with that," said Anne, bending to put plates back in the box. Gaston waved her away. "I wouldn't hear of it, my dear, you might miss the beginning."

Anne bristled at being called 'my dear', which Gaston also picked up, smiling apologetically. He stood in front of the picnic debris, saying, "No, Anne, you and Peter go along with Veronica and continue catching up."

I sensed the persuasive thoughts emanating towards Anne and the police inspector, who hesitated only briefly before joining Aunt V, now standing and smiling at them expectantly.

"How fortunate to have met like this. We can perhaps have a proper chat afterwards," she said.

Gaston took Aunt V's arm and ushered Peter and Anne away. Anne gave a quick backward glance at me. I smiled in response: a small, tight smile that I hoped would not remind Anne of my enthusiastic grins.

"See you shortly," said Peter. I wondered if Anne had told him about my search for a twin. I had told Anne that I had abandoned the search and was sure Helen would have confirmed this, when she assumed my identity. But Anne had an excellent memory and had helped in the initial search for Helen. It would surely not be long before she suggested that 'Sylvie' could almost be Cassandra's twin.

When we were safely at a distance, I collapsed into Kastor's arms, trembling and fighting back tears of terror.

"Please take me away, now!" I whispered after a few moments.

"It's all right, she didn't recognise you," he said, reassuringly. I sensed he was signalling to Gaston, telling him to return to us when they'd found some seats.

"She's known me since I was five," I said. "A wig and glasses wouldn't fool her if we were sitting close and talking. At the very least she'd start thinking of twins, then Peter would get interested and then…" We shared thoughts of a police investigation, while Kastor tried to dismiss these as unlikely.

"It will look odd for us to leave suddenly," said Kastor.

"I don't care, it will be safer for us to go. Please – I can't control this trembling, they'll be certain to wonder why I'm so nervous."

Kastor closed his eyes briefly, thinking miserably that I had not fully recovered from my recent physical and mental tortures. I had seemed fine, but my reaction to meeting Anne was evidence of my still heightened responses. He signalled to the field officers to have the car ready for us. They had been picnicking nearby and one had remained there, waiting for Kastor and I to join the others.

"It'll be all right," he said. "We'll go home now – just wait for Gaston, he'll need to make a plausible excuse." He finished putting the remains of the picnic in the box. I was now very pale and visibly trembling. He held me tightly, signalling our intention to Gaston. Dismally, I focused on what was happening in the concert area.

Anne was right about there being more seats available. Many of the concertgoers were lingering over the picnic, perhaps thinking that they could hear the music from where they were sitting on the grass, an attractive setting with the palace silhouetted against the evening sky. Peter efficiently located a row of seats that would accommodate us all. The orchestra performers were in place, tuning up while a pianist walked onto the platform for the first piece, Liszt's *La Campenella*. Ironically, this was the etude that I had listened to while contemplating the fate of Ryden Asgard's twin, Patrick. Patrick had been eliminated to make way for the ill-fated swap of identity with Ryden. Glancing at the programme as we waited in the park, Kastor knew that this would only worsen my state.

In the concert area, Gaston smiled at his companions. "Whatever is keeping them?" he said. "I'll just go and check if they've got lost." Peter offered to come with him but he said confidingly, "No need, Peter. They're only recently married, I expect they wanted a couple of moments to themselves. They're probably on their way – they wouldn't want you to miss *La Campenella*."

Most people were now seated and the pianist was striking the first tinkling chords. Gaston marched purposefully away before Peter could protest further. Kastor and I picked up that Gaston was telling us to move to another part of the park, in case Peter decided to follow. He found us standing behind a large tree and was shocked to see my state, now breathing rapidly and shaking.

"She's not well," said Kastor, avoiding Gaston's gaze. The observant head of security would easily deduce that I was still recovering from his angry treatment due to jealousy of Edouard. Gaston looked at him coolly. He might not know all the details but was very protective towards me as Veronica's niece. He understood, even better than Kastor, that my exceptional telepathic sensitivity made me extremely vulnerable.

"Get Cassandra away from here. Police officers seem to have a remarkably bad effect on her. I'll make sure to minimise suspicion."

Kastor led me towards the car park, while Gaston quickly returned to the concert area. *La Campenella* had finished and the orchestra was about to play the Hungarian Rhapsody.

"Such a shame," he muttered anxiously to Aunt V, "Sylvie's feeling very ill. Apparently she's been off work and this concert was her first outing. Leonard is looking after her and if she feels better, they'll join us later."

I sensed that he was warning Aunt V to stay with the concert group and not come to look for me. Aunt V's telepathy had blossomed with her friendship with Gaston. She couldn't pick up conversations but was good at sensing warnings. She smiled understandingly. "I thought she looked a bit pale, and she scarcely ate a thing," she murmured, "I suppose they may just go home."

The orchestra had started to play and people sitting near them were glaring and hissing them to keep quiet. Gaston nodded at them apologetically and took his seat. I couldn't pick up any more, as I hurried from the park, but Gaston told me afterwards that Peter appeared to have no thoughts of the twin story in his mind. Even if Anne had talked about it at the time of my twin's marriage and accident, that was a long time ago. Gaston had focused on filling Anne's mind with forgetting any idea that Sylvie resembled Cassandra, while the stirring music raced along and helped to dispel interest in their new acquaintance. When the notes reached the loud finale, Gaston assured me, Anne and Peter were no longer thinking about Sylvie at all.

31

Accompanied by one of the field officers, the car bearing Kastor and me raced back to Askeys. I leant against Kastor, controlling my tears but not the shivering. I knew I could not speak of the meeting. While the drivers we used were loyal and trusted, they had no idea of the true nature of Binary life. They knew it was a secret organization, possibly linked to government security, but nothing of the telepathy, the babies, or other Binary dark secrets. The car entered the grounds by a discreet side gate and stopped near the house.

By this point, I was scarcely able to walk, having to be helped out of the car by Kastor and the field officer. They supported me on each side, propelling me into the entrance hall. Kastor pressed the lift button and signalled to the field officer that he could manage. The car would need to return to Blenheim to pick up Gaston and Aunt V at the end of the concert. When the lift reached the second floor, I seemed a little calmer, relieved to be home. Kastor guided me to the sofa and we sat down. I was now crying openly, my tears a mixture of shock and fear.

"I'm sorry," I said. "It was such a lovely evening and now I've ruined it."

"Your friend ruined it," he replied. "Nothing to be sorry about. You must have been terrified to meet Anne again. You're safe now."

"Safe? Kastor, we can never be safe. I've longed to see Anne again, to talk to her, like in the old days. She was my best friend…"

"Yes, I know." Kastor put his arm round me and stroked my hair. Then he remembered it was just a wig and carefully detached it. I took it from him and glowered at it, as if chastising it for the evening's events.

"This horrid wig – I'll never wear it again. But it doesn't make any difference – nothing can protect us from outside threats. We can never go anywhere without escorts, never have an ordinary evening, doing what other humans do."

"It's not so very different from being very rich or famous," said Kastor quietly. "Those people can hardly go out either, except very privately."

"But at least they can see friends occasionally!" I blurted.

"Well, so can we. Some friends, anyway. Ones that can be truly trusted. Like your aunt."

I curled up on the sofa, tossing the wig to the floor where it fell in a little heap, resembling a much abused cat. I watched it subside, fascinated and smiled at the idea of it having a life of its own, free from having to serve as a partial disguise. Detecting this slight alteration of my dismal mood, Kastor suggested some tea and I nodded gratefully. When he returned a few minutes later, the wig was nowhere to be seen and a familiar tune was playing: *La Campenella.* He tried to ignore this, questioning me silently about the wig. I nodded towards a corner of the room, where we kept a few toys for the children to play with on their visits. A teddy bear was no longer wearing his Tam-o-Shanter tartan cap. The bear now stared out indignantly under a black fringe, the rest of the wig draped around his ears. To add to the bear's humiliation, my spectacles were perched precariously on his nose.

"That bear certainly couldn't go out," he murmured. "Spitting image of you."

I laughed, taking the mug of tea and sipping it. When *La Campenella* finished, I got up to replay the haunting tune. I conjured an image of two teddy bears, gingerly hopping through a mysterious woodland, looking from side to side at possible watchers in the trees. They edged forward when the notes were trilling, only to pause anxiously when the main melody returned. Then one bear scrambled up into a tree, leaving the other looking around, finally climbing up into the tree too, where they hugged each other for comfort as the piece reached its crescendo and a stampede of black dogs raced through the trees, searching for them. Kastor responded to this image by hugging me tightly. "This bear will never let you go – or be caught."

I smiled wistfully. "But as we're not able to disguise ourselves so well, or climb up trees. We can't go to Scotland."

He looked stricken. "You mean tomorrow, you want to cancel?"

"Yes. Can't you see, Kastor, I couldn't handle any more… excitement of that kind. There are so many people up there who could recognise me, or Helen."

"But you only saw that photographer on the outside, when you were escaping from St. Anthony's?"

"Only him close up, but who knows if I was spotted by others, in the village, on the train, in Edinburgh? Think of all the people Helen must have met, while living on the outside up there."

"I'm sure Helen was always very careful." Even as he said this, we shared a thought of Helen's risk taking and that she would have enjoyed making trips outside when Alexander was away.

"I don't mean that I never want to go up to Scotland, to see Leo at school," I said, forcing myself to think rationally. Even if the photographer, Toby MacDonald, happened to meet with us, I could easily slip into the identity of Helen Buchanan again. "It's just that I couldn't cope with it at the moment."

"The field officers will be disappointed," said Kastor. He'd selected two from the commercial centre, so that I could enjoy some shopping. "And I was looking forward to our being... almost alone."

"I know," I sighed. "But cancel it anyway – it's for the best. I'll be happier staying here with you."

He finished his tea and picked up the phone to call off the arrangements. Relieved, I said, "We can see the children off in the morning."

I was now consoling myself with missing the trip to the school, with the idea that it was hardly a family occasion.

"With all the other adults who attend such occasions. Leo will scarcely notice," I argued. "It's not as if we could spend time with him on the journey, or when we get there."

Kastor nodded sadly. I could tell he was feeling deeply guilty that I was still experiencing after effects of his harsh treatment.

I touched his arm. "It's OK, it would've been fine if I hadn't met Anne at the concert. I'm much better, Kastor, and I know you didn't expect me to react so severely."

"But I should have expected it," he said bitterly. "I'll never forgive myself."

"Good, I wouldn't want to go through that again. And you and Gaston were great tonight, so calm and collected. Aunt V was very smooth, too."

"Yes – pity we couldn't bring your entire family in here. They'd all fit in, I'm sure."

"Only, that wild unpredictable gene would cause havoc, with more of us to disturb you Binaries."

We both laughed at the idea of Aunt V let loose within their community, with even Gaston quailing at reforms that she would suggest. I curved into his arms, thinking about my family, what was left of it. I reflected that I had been an ideal Binary entrant, with no cousins, a father an ocean away who scarcely ever contacted me and a mother with ailing health, who had preferred to spend her last days on a world cruise rather than with her daughter. In many ways, I had more sense of family here in the Binaries.

"I'm so very glad I met you," I murmured sleepily. He grinned and took my hand, stroking the binary ring.

"And you've made my life worthwhile. But I'd really like to see you without that make up – you look more like a panda than a bear, right now."

The tears had made the mascara run and I jumped up, examining my panda eyes in the mirror. "Time for a wash and bed," I said, laughing at the reflection.

32

I slept soundly for a change and awoke to find Kastor gazing at me. It was early, with the dawn only just transforming into a sunny morning.

"Have I still got panda eyes?" I asked, remembering the quick cleansing of the heavy make up before tumbling into bed.

"Not at all. I was just watching you sleeping. It's so good to see you at rest, with no apparent worries."

"I feel better, now we've cancelled that trip. But I'm ready for a different kind of journey, if you fancy some mind mingling."

"Always." He plunged into my mind and I breathed in sharply, recovering from the wave of pleasure after a few moments, so that I could dive into his. We seemed to be travelling within a warm waterfall, sliding within its flowing torrent but in control, so that we could occasionally slither back up and ride on the surface of the cascading columns of water. When we both emerged, we lay happily, our heads close but not touching.

"Is my mind still the same?" I asked, thinking of its recent disturbance and Kastor mentioning that he had detected 'a few rocks' peeping up through the water.

"It's lovelier, if anything. Your mind is so adaptable - it helps you to overcome things in a way that our rigidly disciplined minds can't. I sometimes think we'd all be better growing up just with innate natural telepathy, if we have that. Then, learning to control it later, as you've had to do."

"I feel the same," I murmured. "You Binaries and your discipline – and punishments. But I wouldn't have developed, out there. Few people would ever realize their potential without the training you get here. If only we could be accepted and encouraged by the outsiders, it would be better."

But that's an impossible dream, he thought silently and I nodded reluctantly. The absurd idea of school tests in telepathy subsided as soon as it had flashed through my mind.

"We have to change more, to adapt to them," I said. "Then perhaps we could live outside. We could get jobs, live as they do."

"You want to leave?"

"Only if you'd come with me. I could get a job, commercial work like here. And you…"

"…would have to work as a spy? What else am I qualified to do, out there?"

I rolled my eyes. "Dozens of things. Teaching, for example."

"With no recognised qualifications? I suppose we could have falsified certificates, to match the degrees we've taken at our colleges. And our forged identities, always vulnerable to a thorough check. It would be a difficult life – and we'd be much poorer. We'd have to give up the servants and you'd have to do all your own cooking."

"While you could become a chef – you've more of a gift for it than I – plus there wouldn't be as many checks on your qualifications."

He grimaced. "I can cook eggs, admittedly – and make tea. Not exactly cordon bleu. As for looking after children, neither of us have much experience."

"You're right, of course," I said sadly. "I've hardly ever changed a nappy, or put them to bed, or made them a meal. Not much of a mother, really."

"You're a wonderful mother, the best one here. You just have servants to do the chores, that's all. Only the very rich, outside, have our lifestyle and we have so much more – don't you think?"

"You mean all the dangers and fears, the rocky moments and near death experiences?"

"I was thinking of our many ways of communicating," he replied, with a trace of admonishment. He wondered how our blissful mind dips had moved on to this discussion. I now had the pensive expression that meant I was going to ask a difficult question. Propping myself up on my elbows, I gave him a steady, disconcerting look. "Rocky moments," I said. "It made me think of those rocks you said you saw in my mind, when I was getting better. Are they still there – or even bigger?"

I was afraid that he had not wanted to tell me if my mind structure had altered.

He gave me a reassuring hug. "I wasn't looking. It was a plunge, not an exploration. What I said then, well it was a metaphor. There was the illusion of rocks, not surprising given what you'd been through."

"Could you take a good look?" I asked timidly. "I really want to know. I think to get fully better, I need to know what I'm dealing with."

"So you think you could shift rocks? Even illusory ones?"

I smiled diffidently. "Well, yes. I'm pretty sure I could do something about them, if they're really there. Can you doubt it?"

"With you, anything is possible," he murmured, stroking me and wondering if he could turn my mind towards body mingling, while the morning was still so fresh and the events of the coming day not near enough to worry either of us.

"So go on, take a look." I shifted away from his touch, gazing deeply into his eyes. He sighed. My expression became pleading, impossible to resist. I was drawing him in, my eyes becoming deep and enticing: twin sirens, beckoning him across an ocean.

"I can hear faint singing, but can't catch the words," he whispered. Slowly, at first with reluctance and then with growing passion, he slipped into my mind. I had to force myself to stay awake, it was so pleasurable to feel him exploring in there. I was sure my subconscious was delighted, after all we'd suffered lately, to have a chance to draw Kastor in.

Time having no meaning on a mind exploration, it was only a few seconds later that I saw with alarm that he was losing consciousness. I felt him going deeper into my mind. Calling his name had no effect so eventually I had to slap his cheek, screaming into his ear to come back. I punched his chest, trying to replace the delights of the mind with physical sensation. At last he drowsily opened his eyes, which seemed unfocused.

"I so wanted to stay," he said, when able to speak.

"I shouldn't have let you hear the sirens," I guiltily replied. When he had recovered, I insisted on all the details.

"At first, I was floating on the surface of a warm, moving pool and looked around, seeing a stretch of endless sea. Then I discerned distant shapes, some like waterspouts in tropical oceans, others seeming to be moss covered rocks. On one of the largest formations, an island with beaches, there was a castle with many turrets and extensions."

"My thought house," I said, thinking how grand this little thought structure had grown, since I'd become a Binary.

"When I entered your mind, the singing became louder but its source was source invisible. I thought it might be behind the island, so I floated towards it. As I approached the island, I saw some rocks."

"Rocks," I said nervously. "Oh dear, I'm sure they're new."

"All islands have rocks," he muttered. "A few were dark, granite-like in appearance, but most resembled many coloured crystals. When I touched one that appeared to be rose quartz, it was pleasingly soft. So you see, not really a rock at all."

"I could sense you moving around my mind, longing to see what you were experiencing," I said happily, reassured.

"So," continued Kastor. "I floated towards the singing, at last seeing the source. Sirens on a glittering rock that reflected the sea and swirling mists. The melody was hard to place, as it seemed to shift from one song to another."

"I can never keep to a tune," I acknowledged.

"The sound was alluring, drawing me closer. The currents carried me along. I wanted to be absorbed by them so that I would never have to leave. I drifted away from the thought island and into a warmer, deeper part of your ocean."

"That felt wonderful, I also wanted to absorb you," I admitted.

"The seas became more turbulent, tossing me from side to side. I grabbed at one of the small rocky projections, only to find it dissolving in a froth of foam. I could no longer float easily on the surface, feeling an undercurrent pulling me down."

We were still lying down, as I listened with widened eyes to this account of his journey, that I could now visualise through his thoughts.

"Tidal waves swept over me," he said. "I sensed that I could drown. Then I heard shouting in a far distant place."

"I was trying to rouse you," I said.

"A raft appeared from nowhere, so I clambered onto it, although this felt scarcely safer, as it soared up with the crest of a wave, like a slippery and unstable surfboard. I tried to cling tightly. The board started to shake."

I shook my head, alarmed at what I could also now see.

"You were trying to control the board and steer it through the waves," I murmured.

"Yes, it took enormous effort. The waves were high, with torrents of foam so I couldn't see."

He closed his eyes, then opened them with a smile.

"And then I heard my name, being called repeatedly. Somehow I managed to propel upwards. So here we are again," he concluded contentedly. "But I really wanted to stay inside your mind."

"Kastor – I could feel you going deeper, far too deep."

"The sirens were holding me, with that enticing singing" he replied. His breathing was unnaturally loud, as if he had been running very fast.

"I thought I'd lost you – well, lost you inside me," I said, haltingly. "At first I almost wanted that too, it was so good feeling you slide within my mind. Then I realised you were being absorbed. I'd rather have you out here, for now."

He touched me, as if to check if I were real. "I saw her – saw your mermaid."

"Really?" I was pleased, then concerned. "I don't think it's good to see the mermaid when you're in there. She was pulling you towards her, wasn't she?"

"Yes, it felt amazing." He closed his eyes at the memory but he was not allowed to dwell on it as I thumped his chest in alarm. "Stay with me Kastor. You can't be with that mermaid – she'd never let you go."

He put his hand where I had thumped him, with a rueful smile.

"That's quite a punch you've got, Mrs. Bondmate. While the mermaid just has gentle, caressing hands, a face like a goddess and hair that blows in the sea breeze."

"Just like me then," I said smugly, but then pinched him hard so that he jumped. "You said caressing hands – you got that close? Oh Kastor, didn't you realize what was happening? You were being pulled in to my subconscious."

"I didn't actually feel her hands, just knew what they'd be like when they touched me." He grabbed my hands, half to stop me pinching or thumping him again, half to determine that I was truly there.

"And she had such a beautiful, tuneful voice," he murmured. This time I didn't say "Just like me," as he normally laughed, albeit kindly, at my singing.

"What was she singing?" I asked.

"Many entrancing songs." I freed his hands and sat further back, looking down at him, questioningly.

He sighed. "I can't remember, I was succumbing to the siren call at the time."

"Try to remember at least one. Please..."

He closed his eyes, recalling the warm seas and the mermaid, although the image was already blurry, fading away. He hummed a tune and I smiled.

"It sounds like '*Early one morning*'."

"Yes, a bit like that. But far lovelier."

I sang, tentatively, "*Oh don't deceive me, oh never leave me – how could you use a poor maiden so?*"

"I didn't catch all the words, she sang many different melodies. But yes, that was one of them."

"*Oh never leave me,*" I repeated. "We sang that song in primary school and had to learn the words. I remember not really understanding them, but finding them sad. '*Remember the vows that you made to me truly, remember how tenderly you nestled close to me.*' And then she has to wander alone, talking pitifully to the roses in the meadow, because he's left her to find a new love."

I looked at Kastor rather accusingly and he protested, "I hope you're not identifying me as the lover in that song. I've never deceived you, nor would ever leave you."

"That's not the mermaid's story, I feel." I looked stern. "You've blocked your thoughts when you didn't want me to find things out, like what happened to Roderick and my mother, or what you get up to in surveillance work. A kind of deception, don't you think?"

"But not in the spirit of that song. It was your mermaid, not mine. Frankly, I think she was rather irresponsible, luring me along with that love ballad. Of course I'd want to prove her wrong, by fusing with her forever."

"You think I have irresponsible mermaids in my mind?"

"Several, probably." He tugged me towards him so quickly that I fell forwards and could not avoid his kiss.

"Do I look just a little like the mermaid?" I said, emerging for air.

"Yes, very much," he murmured, kissing me again. It was one of the few ways he knew to stop me talking.

Later that morning, as we walked hand in hand towards the nursery centre, I squeezed his hand affectionately. "About that mermaid," I said. He looked wary as I continued, "I think we'll keep her outside, in future. I concede that she was rather irresponsible and I couldn't control her, in there."

"I'll bear that in mind," he said, smiling at the double meaning. Then he suddenly cupped my face in his and kissed me passionately. "I can hardly control her outside, either," he murmured, delighted at my shock at this expression of affection in the open air where someone might see us.

I caught a thought, before he rapidly tried to hide it, that it wasn't just natural telepaths reared on the outside - like Edouard - who could behave amorously in public. "I'd like to make love in a bed of roses, like the maiden in the valley," I murmured, drawing Kastor towards a clump of trees where we could not be spied upon.

He laughed, resisting reluctantly. We were far too near the nursery and he sensed other adults approaching to see the children on this important day.

"Perhaps later," he murmured. "I'll order a few rose garlands – and have them shed into petals for you to lie on." Another advantage of being a privileged Binary, he transmitted. We could have whatever they wanted, within reason. I conjured up an image of the petals, like a deep mattress. Such an easy image for me to create without needing to wait for a florist, but he shook his head.

"Really, Mrs. Bondmate – our son is waiting for us."

I drew back, sighing. Not much of a mother, I thought guiltily and he put his arm round me. His concession to the moment was to keep his arm firmly around my waist as we entered the nursery wing, earning several startled glances from the people already there in the entrance hall. "They're just jealous of your advanced relationship skills," he whispered into my ear, not releasing me until he sensed I was very embarrassed by all the stares and somewhat scandalised thoughts of those surrounding us.

33

When all the adults were assembled, we followed the senior housemother into the school hall.

"Do all these Binaries have children?" I asked, in a whisper.

Kastor replied, "I don't know. Some, of course, but the annual departure for boarding school is an important event for all of us. We can remember when we left to go there."

Artemis Chiron, the obstetrician, approached us with a smile. "Your parenting programme is going to keep me very busy, Cassandra. Three pregnancies already since it started!" I noticed Hagen Philip and Phyllis Williams sitting a few rows ahead of, hoping that one of the pregnancies was theirs. Lamella was sitting nearby, with no sign of Edouard. Too busy training with Dominique, I deduced. But there was no opportunity to ponder this further as the six children due to leave were brought onto the stage, proudly wearing their new school uniforms. Leander, taller than most in the group, stole a glance at us and sent an image of a kiss. This was followed by an image of Kastor kissing me on the way to the nursery wing and we both looked up, startled, hoping that none of the nannies had picked this up.

"He's unusually good at remote viewing for his age," murmured Kastor with a disapproving tone. "We know where he gets that from."

"I'll try to speak to him before they set off," I said, equally embarrassed, wondering if Leander now thought that kissing was a suitable greeting for social contact in the Binaries. The nursery rhyme about Georgie Porgie kissing the girls and making them cry came to mind and Kastor produced a thin smile in response.

"Well, we know where he gets all the kissing from," I whispered, "so you should probably have a word with him about it too."

A nursery teacher called for silence. A group meditation was about to commence. These were important shared experiences for Binaries at any ceremony. The children stepped forward and nervously started to create a group image of the school, based on pictures they had been shown. The adults quickly joined in, converting the flat images into more complicated scenes. They knew every inch of the school buildings and its grounds. At first I absorbed these images with fascinated interest, picturing Kastor at Leo's age, running through the corridors and talking in the dormitories. I had only seen photographs of the Binary school, but was soon able to explore the rooms with the adults, expanding the images with my gift for creating three-dimensional illusions.

I gazed briefly around the audience, taking in all the entranced adults and with a deft surge of thought, drew them into the scenes as well, so that we found ourselves standing in a ring around the main school building, then holding hands in the large assembly hall. I pictured them at various ages as they completed their education, sitting in classrooms, playing games, having midnight feasts and sliding down the grand staircase. Several people glanced in astonishment as I developed the images, making them travel through time. The children on the stage were delighted and Leo smiled proudly, knowing I was responsible. Suddenly abashed that I might be thought to be showing off, I faded the additional images so that the others could finish the group meditation. Kastor nodded approvingly as the nursery teachers took over with scenes of dedicated study and rolls of school certificates floating by.

When the meditation ended, the children came down from the stage to be congratulated by the grown ups and to share the buffet laid out at the side. Kastor and I were pleased to see Leander politely greeting many of the adults before shyly approaching us. Kastor took him to one side for a short talk about kissing being inappropriate and I saw him nodding earnestly, glancing only briefly to send me a quick winking image.

"No, really," I shot back. "Leo, the others wouldn't understand. Our secret." He nodded, thinking, another one?

When Kastor rejoined me, letting Leo go with his friends to the buffet, he murmured, "Just wait until our twins and Helen's reach his age. So many Binaries with disobedient genes being raised here." I smiled, replying, "I do hope so."

When we walked back across the grounds to the nursery station, my eyes strayed towards the copse of trees and I smiled. I didn't think that Kastor had noticed, but he abruptly left from the path and then ran towards the trees, beckoning me to follow. I obeyed cautiously. Several other Binaries were making their way to the station. They could all have used the tunnel route but today was special and the weather fine. There was a small glade within the trees, covered with a layer of early autumn leaves.

"Roses aren't in season yet," said Kastor, "I'll get some as soon as I can, but meanwhile..." He pulled me down into the leaves and started to kiss me ardently, running his hands down my loose top and moving them round my back to release my bra.

"Kastor!" I exclaimed, looking out from the glade where the path from the nursery wing could just be glimpsed. "We'll be seen..."

"I know," he murmured. "It just occurred to me that we should spice up our relationship. Maybe we need to give the others some ideas too."

I laughed; a happy carefree gust of mirth that made him laugh as well. I had started to help him undo my belt when he stopped, lifting himself up on his arms and gazing at me.

"Was it like this with him?" he asked, "I mean, doing it

outside?"

My eyes clouded. "We didn't '*do*' it, Kastor and no, nothing like this."

"Well, what did you do? I want to know, how he touched you."

I sat up, drawing away. "I've told you, it was just a kiss. He came and sat next to me while I was dozing and when I realised he was coming on to me, I tried to get away. Then he pinned me against a tree – and I couldn't stop him kissing me."

"You could have stopped him, with your powers. So you wanted it. Did he touch you here?" He stroked the bare skin of my midriff. I flinched and glared at him.

"Please stop this. Haven't you punished me enough for a foolish lapse? He caught me by surprise. And you know I care nothing for him, don't you?"

He closed his eyes, angry with himself for spoiling the moment. "Yes, but I'd no idea I'd feel so jealous. I just can't get rid of the idea, that you might have mind shared with him."

"We didn't… I wouldn't ever do that… Look, we know he's been amorous with half a dozen women since he got here. He must have seduced Lamella within days of arriving. I'd closed my thoughts to him completely, didn't even know he was here."

"I'm sorry," he muttered. "You mean, he didn't even try to get into your mind?"

"No – I think he's been far too excited about the possibilities of physical union in our community. I expect Dominique is teaching him all about sharing minds, right now probably."

He stroked my face gently, full of apologetic thought, but I turned away. I was now furious. I sprang up and gazed down at him and he caught the unwelcome image of a tennis racquet swinging menacingly in my hand, all the more disturbing as I did not play tennis, or any other sport of which he was aware.

"If you can't let this go, we're going to need counselling – or a separation."

"I'll try to forget about it, I promise."

But I picked up a fleeting thought that Edouard might have stroked my earrings. My hand darted up to one of the earrings, to show him that he hadn't managed to block this idea. Then I took the earrings off and held them out to him.

"So these are tainted too? Well, take them back. Better still…" I threw them into the leaves on the ground, where they disappeared from sight. "…there, all gone. Or perhaps you'd like to chop my ears off, in case he touched them?"

He was looking anxiously at the ground, trying to see where the precious earrings had fallen. They had been his gift when leaving for Cadiz, that I said I'd wear constantly until he returned. Recovering in his hospital bed in the Binario centre at Cadiz, he told me that he had often imagined me wearing them, smiling up at him with trust and love. While he searched for them now, I strode away, adjusting my clothing and brushing the leaves from my hair.

"Don't follow me," I signalled, "I don't want to see you or hear any more about this."

I took a train back to Askeys, ignoring curious glances from other Binaries at the station, but generated thoughts of missing the children so that they would not suspect the real reason for my ill ease. Back in the apartment, I played loud, fierce music and stared out at the park. Before this business with Edouard, it had always been me feeling jealous of his past entanglements with women, which he had laughed off and made me feel petty for wondering whether any of these women lived alongside us at the Binaries. And I knew he secretly liked the idea that colleagues, such as Simon Arbalest in the commercial centre, found me attractive. Yet this newly recruited police officer had driven him to wild, jealous, torturing behaviour. *"Fear of the outside,"* said a small voice from my subconscious and I relented slightly. *"Fear of natural unconditioned telepaths, with minds perhaps like yours."*

I sighed, wondering how we could recover from this, or from others coming in from the outside, which I had hoped so much would help the Binaries to reform. I had been blocking my thoughts to Kastor but now tried to visualise him, wondering if he had gone to the gym to work out some of his Binary need for physical exertion. It was a surprise to sense that he was still in that copse, sitting miserably in the cool shade. I focused and saw he was holding one of the earrings, staring at it and I felt a pang of regret at tossing them away. I sensed he had been desperately looking for the other, but seemed to have given up the search. I switched off the music and went to the Askeys staircase station of the underground railway.

When I approached the copse, sensing that Kastor was still there, I caught a feeling of hope from him. He looked up anxiously when I entered the glade.

"I couldn't leave here until I'd found them," he mumbled. "Even if you don't want them, or me." His eyes were full of pain. I sat down next to him and took his hand, the one holding the sole earring. The green Lalique crystal had been carefully chosen to match the colour of my eyes.

"Of course I want you - and them."

Our eyes met and we fell into each other's arms. I transmitted thoughts of forgiveness. His hand was tightly gripped around the earring and I gently opened it, then put the earring back in my left ear.

"I'll just wear the one, to remind us never to quarrel about this again."

He was sitting against one of the trees and I rested my head, with its earring, on his chest. I remembered the images I had generated about him as a small boy at Lochinstoun, a boy without parents, living with the other 'orphans'.

Picking this up, he smiled. "Your images were breathtaking as usual," he murmured. "Those unaware of your story would never have guessed you didn't spend time at the school. Although I was a bit worried when you showed those children sliding down a banister."

"That main staircase looked rather inviting, but I guess that sliding down it was strictly forbidden."

"We did it all the same," he admitted, laughing. "Only you showed me leading them on. I was never caught, so now they'll suspect I was a ringleader in such wayward behaviour. And giving ideas to the children about to go up there."

"As if children needed to be told how to misbehave! Especially Leo. I suppose they'll teach him it's not appropriate to pry and try to see parents or anyone else in private moments."

"His remote viewing is way in advance of his years," murmured Kastor proudly. "But yes, the teachers will take care of all that. They'll assess his abilities and adjust training accordingly."

"I wish I could have grown up there with you," I said. "We could have known each other all these years."

"I'm so glad you didn't. I'm constantly learning from you. And you might have turned out like Helen…"

"She saved your life, in Casablanca – and your mind."

He nodded. "Yes, she's shown loyalty to the organization and to us. And she's taught you a thing or two about your skills – perhaps a bit too much. Perhaps in time we'd have been better friends, but I'd never have fallen in love with her. And you together, you'd have been the terrible twins, always taking risks."

I looked thoughtfully at the leaves and Kastor, who was now looking happy and relaxed.

"Let's live a little dangerously now," I said, leaning back and giving him a wicked, seductive smile, which would have met with

Helen's full approval.

We rolled and tumbled around the leaves like truant teenagers exploring our bodies for the first time. Then we brushed off the leaves, laughing. He took my hand to lead me out of the copse, but I hesitated, looking down. Then I stooped, pushed some leaves apart and held up the other earring.

"You knew where it was all the time?" he exclaimed, taking it and putting it his pocket, as I shook my head at the idea of wearing it in my other ear lobe.

"I'm just good at finding things," I said airily.

"I don't deserve you," he said. "It's not just your skills. Your capacity for forgiveness seems to have been mostly absent from my education."

"That's right, Mr. Bondmate, you don't. Please don't forget it again."

I looked at him with mock severity and he held my hand tightly, like a young boy about to cross a terrifyingly busy road. Another difficult crossing, I thought, as I sensed jealousy of Edouard slipping out of his mind.

34

Perhaps it was because I was thinking of children that an unexpected image came into my mind later, when the school flight would be arriving in Scotland. Leo and his particular friends Finley and Astra would be meeting children from other Binary centres, making the difficult transition from being the oldest children in their world to being the lowest members of the school community, with older children bossing them about.

I pictured him finding his bed in the dormitory and going to eat his first meal in the dining hall. This image was suddenly replaced by a schoolroom somewhere else. With a start, I recognised it as the room in which I had visualised the son of an American commercial client. Three years previously, just before the adventures in Casablanca and Cadiz, Jeannette Summers had insisted on a personal meeting with 'Lily West' as a condition to signing up my marketing consultancy. On the outside, I was only known as Lily West. When we had met briefly alone, I had sensed that the real reason was Jeannette's search for her lost son, because she assumed Lily West's astounding accuracy in predicting success or failure of products was linked to psychic gifts. I had admitted that I could sense the presence of her son as an older boy and still alive somewhere, but I had been careful to say this had nothing to do with the way I worked commercially. I told her that I was not ready to explore this 'gift' and help Jeannette to find her son. This was partly because I had realised that the children in the schoolroom vision were communicating telepathically, suggesting that a Binary community had abducted the son. The exciting and dangerous events of that day had buried this memory until this moment. I had not even mentioned it to Kastor.

Now, viewing the image of the schoolroom, the boy had aged to about 13 years. He seemed happy enough, sharing a joke with schoolmates and then applying himself to the work in front of him on his desk. I wondered why I had channelled this. I put it down initially to my efforts in conjuring up the interior of the Binary school. I focused more closely and sensed strongly that the boy's schoolroom was at Lochinstoun.

Back in the apartment, I glanced at a photograph of the school hanging over the desk in the corner of our living room. I pondered whether I would be detected if I tried to slip mentally into this image and explore, to see if I could locate the present position of Jeannette Summer's son. I decided against it. Lochinstoun would be full of skilled telepaths, always alert to intruders, mental or otherwise. Thinking that Kastor might be able to help, I signalled to him and he emerged after a few moments from his study. He came up to the desk and rested his hands on my shoulders, stooping to kiss the earlobe without an earring.

"What can I do for you?" he asked, picking up my images of the school and thinking at first that I was simply missing Leo. I told him briefly about the meeting with Jeannette Summers and the current vision. He was puzzled at the idea of the abduction of a five year old.

"I don't see that as likely. I know you think we're child stealing monsters, but I'm only aware of the twin rescues – and the occasional teenager or young adult who come here voluntarily."

I got up from the desk and paced about the large room. "I don't think I'm mistaken. Perhaps sometimes children are 'rescued'…" – I paused to let him know I used this as a euphemism – "…if they are orphaned or found abandoned, something like that?"

Kastor caught up with me in my worried pacing. He guided me over to the sofa so that we could talk face to face.

"It would still be most unusual. And in this case, he had a mother who obviously cared about him very much. We just wouldn't do that, even if he had fantastic telepathic powers. The most that would happen, if one of our field teachers spotted his abilities, would be to monitor him and hope to recruit him when he was old enough to make such a decision."

Kastor offered to make some tea and, checking the time, ordered a supper as well. I sat pensively, thinking of the lost boy and wishing I had at least asked for his name. I knew it would be unwise to contact Jeannette, even though Simon Arbalest would know how to do this through official business channels. He would definitely not approve of contact that involved revealing Lily West's unusual skills; and I had not told Simon about the conversation with Mrs. Summers. I had detected no telepathic ability in the distraught woman, thankfully, but knew that she had been visiting psychics in her search for her son. Obviously, if the boy was at the Binary boarding school, such 'psychic' help had been unsuccessful. I was so deep in thought that I scarcely noticed that Kastor sitting beside me again, holding out a mug of tea.

"Can't you think of any reason why this boy would have been… rescued?" I said eventually, sipping the tea.

"Well, there is one possibility," muttered Kastor. "What did she say about her husband in all this?"

"I can't remember exactly – I know she was married and she referred to the boy as "our son", I think. I assumed her husband had been seeking their son, as keenly as her."

"Supposing he was not the husband's son," said Kastor.

"You mean, an affair on the outside, with one of us?" I sat up, immediately seeing the possibilities. "But most Binary parents, particularly men I'd say, would not be so concerned as to take that enormous risk."

"Perhaps he got to know the child somehow, bonded with him, wanted to bring him into our community…"

"I wish now that we'd taken the trip to Scotland," I said, "We could have investigated first hand."

"I'm very glad that fate intervened – however unsettling that was for you," said Kastor, with a brief shared image of Anne staring intently. "Parents simply never visit the school. The most we'd have been allowed would be a brief entry into the hall, perhaps a formal chance to say goodbye to our son."

"But we could go up at half term?"

He shook his head, then caught my imploring expression. "I'd do my best to arrange it, if it was just a visit to see Leo. But you've got another quest in mind. If this story about Jeannette's son is true, it's a well buried secret – and you should know by now not to disturb Binary secrets."

"You could at least investigate a little?" I asked, thinking of all the surveillance facilities that Kastor had at his disposal.

"I don't know if that would be at all wise. Let's say the father is one of our community here, but has never revealed himself. It wouldn't be good to drag that up and expose him – and it could be dangerous."

I did not want Kastor in danger again. But I sighed, knowing that these visions always had a meaning, possibly predicting my future involvement. Picking this up, Kastor grimaced. "Don't do or say anything for the moment. Let's see if you receive any more images and go from there." I nodded, smiling. He put his arm around me protectively and murmured, "Never a dull moment with you. Here was I thinking we'd settled briefly into peaceful existence again."

I laughed impishly, making a mental note to at least ask how the business connection with Jeannette Summers and her colleague was going when I went to the commercial centre. Surely, I thought, there could be little harm in just checking all was well with our contract. If Kastor detected this idea, he said nothing. He was very happy we seemed to have moved on from the Edouard threat to our relationship and had no wish to upset me by reminders of the restrictions of our world, where even asking questions could be hazardous.

In the commercial centre that afternoon, Simon Arbalest looked up with surprise when I asked about Jeannette Summers and the contract of three years ago.

"Why the interest? Have you sensed something about her or Leo Garston? It's all going swimmingly, as far as I'm aware."

Leo Garston, that was the name. I had been trying to recall Jeannette's business partner. "Oh, it's probably nothing," I said carefully, shuttering my thoughts, "I just had a sense of Mrs. Summers having second thoughts about the deal."

Simon always paid keen attention to any intuitions that I mentioned. "She was very hesitant at first, as you know, but your predictions since then have been spot on, Cassandra. Perhaps you picked up that there's an annual review due soon – I'll give it careful consideration, but I'm anticipating that they'll renew the contract."

"Are they coming over to London?" I asked, casually.

"Doubtful," said Simon. "They have business interests in New York, Washington, Los Angeles – probably several other places. The London trip when you met them was a one off. A few underlings have visited the London centre since then – well, you know that, because it was when there were new products for you to examine."

I nodded and murmured, "Hmm. I could have been picking her worrying about something else. I wasn't tuning in – and wouldn't do that without checking with you."

"Tune in by all means," said Simon, smiling. "If she's thinking of leaving the company or a merger, we'd want to know."

Our attention returned to studying reports on a possible financial problem in one of the companies in their stock portfolio. Binary investments had phenomenal success due to the ability of some of us being able to detect or predict problems, mooted mergers or changes in direction, long before market analysts were aware of them. Simon had to reassure me from time to time that this was all perfectly legal.

"But if they knew we could do this, they'd legislate against it," I had once protested.

"And how would they do that, do you think? An anti-telepathy law? Laughable, even if it got anywhere near a parliamentary debate. More to the point, how would they detect our investigations? There'd be no evidence of memos, tweets, conversations, any signs that we'd been snooping or sharing insider information."

"All the same," I said, "it seems like unfair competition."

Simon had smiled kindly, attributing these qualms to my upbringing on the outside.

"Is it unfair that some actors are better than others and get well paid parts? Or that some artists are particularly gifted or lucky, with work that brings huge commercial success?" he asked. "Or even that others use their connections to get jobs and then prove annoyingly good at them? Outsiders do their best to exploit their abilities and networks. As for us, it's just using our talents. If we lived alongside them, with full knowledge of how we worked, it would still be legal – only we'd have a lot of enemies, some of whom would want to… eliminate us from the competition. Particularly if they knew about your wide range of skills. It's why we have to live separately and work through intermediaries."

"Just as well most of the telepaths are inside, working with us," I murmured, thinking briefly of Edouard and wondering how many there were like him. But on the outside, his skills had been of little use, except to detect that Leo and I were telepaths. His ability had never developed to the extent of being able to use it reliably in police investigation.

"Yes, I'm very glad we found you and persuaded you in," said Simon, who was unaware of my forced entry into their community. "And of course, we're always on the alert to anyone who might be picking up how we do this. You'd no idea, had you, while you were outside?"

I shook my head, thinking of my innocent life working for a charity before meeting Kastor and my twin. I felt a slight chill at a thought, rapidly suppressed, of what happened to people who threatened to expose the Binaries. They were unhesitatingly ruthless about threats. The longer I lived with them, the more I understood our vulnerability. When I had assisted with interrogations, I had helped them to uncover secrets and probably condemn enemies of the organization to a rapid disappearance, so I was no longer an innocent in all this.

Later that day, I asked one of the nannies to bring over my twins and Helen's twin boys, all now lively three year olds. I felt a need to reconnect with the children in Leo's absence. The nanny was one of my favourites, a cheerful and playful young woman called Megan. Megan was always up for a bit of fun and we re-arranged the furniture in the living room to make an imaginary boat, using dining chairs for the children to sit and pretend to row. After we had rowed it *'merrily up the stream'* a few times, I suggested an old sailing song.

"They sang this in the old days, when they were off on another great sailing adventure on the ocean," I said, when the song was playing on our music centre. I brought in the globe from Kastor's study so that they could see how much of our planet was covered by sea. Soon they did not need the recording of *'Heart of Oak'* to be able to sing the words heartily, the children joining in enthusiastically despite not understanding half the words. Shared images of rocking on the waves and mermaids waving at us in the distance completed the illusion of steering our old ship past pirates and looking ahoy for land. When Kastor returned early from work, since his desk had been cleared of all but urgent files in anticipation of the trip to Scotland, he heard the noise from the apartment as he climbed the stairs to the second floor. It was a combination of laughing, singing and shouts from Megan for us to row harder.

Entering the living room he found a chaotic scene. The sofa had been turned on its side to make the prow of the boat and a good perch for Megan, who was guiding the efforts of the crew, waving her hand imperiously to increase our rowing efforts, while the singing was led by me at the top of my voice. It was a few moments before he recognised the tune as *'Heart of Oak'*, mainly from the words.

"Heart of oak are our ships, Heart of oak are our men..." - "and women" chimed in Megan – *"We always are ready. Steady, boys, steady! We'll fight and we'll conquer again and again!"*

We fell silent when we sensed Kastor standing at the entrance to the room. The children were caught in mid cry, their mouths open, as they immediately stopped singing. Respect for adults was an early part of their disciplined training.

"I reckon you could be heard all over the house," he said sternly and the nanny blushed, perhaps fearing she would be reported for encouraging unruly behaviour. Then he grinned and we relaxed. Kastor fetched another chair and placed it at the aft of our ship.

"Tamsin, Florence, Daniel and Zenon – you'll now sing just in your minds, OK?"

"Thought sounds and pictures only," explained Megan softly.

"Excellent practice," I added approvingly. Kastor signalled for the grown ups to begin on his count and started to sing.

"Come cheer up my lads, tis to glory we steer, To add something more to this wonderful year..."

Faltering on the words in contrast to this rousing performance by my bond-mate, I realised I had never heard Kastor singing except through the water in the shower. He had an attractive, deep voice and, unlike me, could faithfully reproduce a tune. Megan and I joined in the chorus with more confidence while the children sang silently, sharing images of our ship at sea. It was one of those moments that outsiders would have deeply envied, an ability to transport ourselves to another scene, sharing thoughts to support the illusion. The adults could see the sails billowing on the masts and the uniforms of the 18th century English navy, celebrating victories, remembering too that the American revolutionaries had adopted the tune across the Atlantic. I was in my element, conjuring up the smell of tar and the sound of the waves. After we had sung the chorus twice, Kastor got up and signalled that probably we had disturbed Askeys enough, the children only faintly protesting as

Nanny Megan returned to her more accustomed role of keeping them in order.

When the living room furniture had been restored to its usual state and the children had departed with Megan, I looked anxiously at Kastor to see if he was going to reprimand me for encouraging the rowdy mob in our home. But he hugged me and laughed.

"What will you do next, the battle of Waterloo?" he asked, touching my bare earlobe and wondering briefly if I'd ever wear both earrings again. My eyes sparkled with mischief at the thought of staging a battle, although I shook my head to reassure him about that, if not yet about the earrings.

"Did you notice how good they all are at imaging?" I said. "And I think they have the musical gene, too."

"I love your voice," he said, "It's just a bit untrained, that's all. We do a lot of singing, growing up here. And yes, of course our daughters and nephews are superbly talented."

"Do you think Helen will want Daniel and Zenon, or Grace, to join her in America?"

"It wouldn't be allowed, even if she wanted it. Possibly Grace could go. She's too young to remember her time here. Anyway, Helen is more than happy for them to be brought up as Binaries."

"Alexander may be missing his daughter, at least," I mused, shuttering the thought that Grace's true father might be Grégoire. I had not contacted my sister in months and wondered if they had found a permanent home.

"I'm sure Helen will deal with that," said Kastor, a little too dismissively. I caught a sinister thought about Helen relating Grace's tragic death to her husband, if Alexander started to press too insistently for their child to join them. I started to think about a staged funeral with a compliant funeral director showing them the little plot in a cemetery.

Kastor murmured, "Yes, something like that – but don't worry, Grace will always be safe here. Or if Helen undergoes an amazing transformation to being more motherly, we'd arrange for Grace to join her, so long as it's before the age of, say, a year. Some months away."

I tried to focus on Helen, to pick up her thoughts. Helen was probably in closed-down mode most of the time while living on the outside and she would not be expecting me to contact her. I could obtain only a fleeting image of Helen's face and then a blurred impression of her laughing and talking somewhere.

"Perhaps you could try your mirror method, some time?" suggested Kastor. "Seeing all the twins together made me think of you and Helen, and your unlikely alliance after everything that had happened."

"Do you ever think of your twin?" I asked and Kastor shrugged.

"Never. The children I grew up with are my family. You know we aren't even aware that we have twins, most of us. And as the organization tried unsuccessfully to impress upon Helen, seeking out the other twin is unwise and dangerous."

"Yet it brought us together," I murmured, shyly locking hands with his. Yes, he said silently, taking a brief plunge into my mind so that I gasped with pleasurable shock.

"We're the exception that proves the rule," he said, emerging quickly and gripping my hands tightly as I swayed with the experience of the mind dip. "My heart of oak," he whispered, "which you conquer again and again." Mind mingling, but no mermaids, I signalled, as we ran to the bedroom, laughing and with the tune and words ringing in our heads.

35

A few days later, with no further images of the lost boy in the classroom coming to mind, I had tried to put any idea of a search for him aside. Perhaps, I thought, it was just a memory brought up by our son going off to school. An announcement from Kastor was a further distraction. He needed to make a quick trip to Madrid to assess the work of a couple of surveillance officers. He reassured me that this was not a hazardous assignment, like the one to Cadiz that Ryden Asgard had tricked him into.

"They've been doing so well that they've come up for promotion, possibly transfer here or to the Virginia centre," he explained.

"If you say so," I replied doubtfully. "But I wish I could come with you, just to make sure."

"What makes you think I'd be safer with you, my darling risk taker?" he said, amused.

"I hope I've proved that," I said, with thought images of our adventures three years previously. He contemplated the idea of my coming and then surprised me by nodding.

"I don't see why not. It's only for a couple of days, but perhaps you could go on a shopping expedition with Simon's field officers – the ones who were disappointed to miss out on the trip to Scotland."

"So long as Anne and her policeman aren't planning a weekend break in Spain," I murmured, recalling the Saturday evening concert.

"We'll check," said Kastor. "Gaston's team has already ascertained that there haven't been any unusual enquiries within the police. I must admit, it would be great to have you there with me. We've hardly tried out many different beds, have we?"

"Hardly any," I agreed, thinking, just France, mostly separately in Cadiz and our one night in Edinburgh.

Simon Arbalest was delighted, saying we needed more research on the Spanish market. With no evidence that Anne would be in Madrid, I eagerly looked forward to the trip and travelling as my alter ego, Lily West. I was thrilled that we would be staying in a luxury hotel in the centre, rather than in the small Madrid Binary branch on the outskirts. Kastor would be booked in as Charles West, an identity already devised. There was a busy department within the Binaries with the sole purpose of checking and maintaining the various aliases needed for outside trips.

In blonde wig and sunglasses I stood confidently in the foyer when we registered with the field officers, travelling with them as part of a business team. I looked round approvingly at the marble and chandeliers of this grand hotel. It was well located for the Salamanca shopping area and Simon had also arranged a short interview with one of our major clients, very excited to be meeting with the enigmatic Lily West. I had studied files on their Spanish commercial interests and attended a couple of sessions in the language lab, just to polish a few phrases. On the Saturday, Kastor left me after breakfast in the hotel suite, leaving me to arrange the meeting and the shopping visits with the field officers.

The meeting with the client went well and I was bubbling with confidence as I strolled with the field officers through a branch of *El Corte Inglés*. I saw a dress that would be perfect for dinner that evening and went to try it on, with the female officer, Nicole, hovering outside. As I emerged from the cubicle to view myself in the full length mirror, I was startled to hear a voice say, "Jasmina, is that you?" I whirled to see a woman I recognised as Marcie Brown. We had never met, but Marcie had met Helen in Casablanca. Helen had been travelling as Jasmina. Marcie was the ex-girlfriend of Patrick, the reporter who had been replaced by his twin, the devious Ryden Asgard. I quickly signalled to Nicole that we had a situation, but probably containable.

"Call me Helen," I transmitted, "And give me a shout that we've run out of time in a few moments."

Marcie Brown was wearing a long jacket with a brightly coloured top and leggings. She had a clever, gamine face and was smiling at me now with more confident recognition. I cursed myself for removing my sunglasses while trying on the dress.

"Or should I call you Helen?" she said, having heard Nicole call out to me.

I picked up that she had met with the photographer, Toby MacDonald. He only knew me as Helen Buchanan. How complicated these Binary aliases were to get right! I guessed that there must be courses to train them in these, if the young Binaries were selected for surveillance training. I should have known better than to put Toby and Marcie in contact, after he had helped to get me to Edinburgh. I had only told Kastor about it after making the call. He had been so pleased to recover me safely after the storm at St. Anthony's that he had merely said, "When will you learn - that all outside contacts are dangerous for us?" Painfully true, I thought. This present dilemma only served me right.

Smiling brightly at Marcie, I rolled my eyes at being called Helen. "Yes, 'Jasmina' was just my name in Casablanca – and while I knew Patrick. So you've met up with Toby? I hope you didn't mind my putting you both in touch."

"Mind? Not a bit, we're an item now. He's moved in with me. How discerning of you, Jasmina, to find me a decent man at last. But he told me you're married now, did you ever sort out that tiff? I heard about how Toby rescued you from a downpour in the middle of nowhere."

"Yes, all sorted out. I guess you're covering a fashion show here?" I asked. I had already detected this from Marcie's thoughts. Marcie was intuitive, but not nearly enough to realise she was communicating so clearly with me.

"Yes. I just popped in here to buy a few things. I've time for coffee…"

A voice called me from outside the changing booths. "Helen, so sorry to rush you, it's time for the next appointment."

I looked round, with a quickly formed regretful expression, although this was sincere. I would have enjoyed chatting more with Marcie. "Sorry, it'd be great, but I'm here on business."

Marcie looked disappointed. I had never felt more grateful for the lack of any photographs of Lily West appearing in the media. Explaining a third identity would be a challenge with this perceptive reporter.

"Shame," said Marcie. She produced a card and handed it to me. "Well, you could always look Toby and me up, when you're next in London."

"Definitely," I said, thinking sadly that this would never happen.

"That dress is so you," said Marcie, as I went back into the cubicle. I sensed that she was remembering the steamy night with Ryden in Casablanca while he posed as Patrick, although neither she nor Helen had fulfilled Ryden's hopes from the encounter. I braced myself for an inevitable question, which came promptly.

"Hey, did you ever find out what happened to Patrick? I tried to follow the story, but couldn't get further than some rumour he'd died in a prison riot."

Nicole entered the changing area, smiling apologetically. "Helen, we really have to go. Give me the dress, I'll settle up while you change."

"Of course," I said, slipping off the dress and passing it out of the cubicle. To Marcie, still standing outside, I said nonchalantly, "Patrick? Never heard another peep from him."

Marcie's thoughts were still straying to that night, with Ryden-Patrick tied helplessly by the pair of them on the bed and later arrested by the secret police. When I emerged from the cubicle, Marcie was standing there, holding a knitted top that she planned to buy and looking pensive.

"He was a rat, but I don't like to think of him coming to a violent end," said Marcie, who had been Patrick's mistress for some time, before being dumped by the usurping twin.

"Yes," I said simply, gazing into her eyes, "but our joke had nothing to do with it, if he did. And I wouldn't like Alexander to know about it. Our secret?" Marcie had no idea that she was being subjected to powerful persuasive thoughts.

"Toby wouldn't approve either," she said with a rueful smile. "Quite the Scottish puritan, on those matters. Yes, …Helen, our secret. I do hope we can meet again."

"So do I," I said, with genuine feeling. I hoped that the supposed urgency of my next appointment would be sufficient explanation for not handing Marcie my card in exchange, or mentioning where I worked. I was already thinking up a story of being employed mainly in Glasgow, near where Helen and Alexander had lived, but Marcie did not press me, just giving me a stylish wave. The fashion journalist was accustomed to meeting and getting to know people briefly, then moving on to her next circle of contacts.

At the hotel that evening, Kastor was naturally alarmed to hear I had been spotted in the department store. "I warned you to be careful," he said simply, but with relief that the encounter appeared to have required no security measures. We were both only too aware of what such measures meant in Binary world.

"Even if I'd not linked her up with Toby, she'd have recognised me as Jasmina," I said. "It's good that Helen gave me a blow by blow account of their adventure." Blow by blow, repeated Kastor silently, sharing a thought that Helen could simply have knocked Ryden out and left him in his room to be discovered by the police, without the need for a bit of fun involving an outsider. But possibly, she would have found that harder to do with Ryden on his own, with his telepathic abilities and physical strength both in full working order.

"So now you're a fully fledged field operative," he murmured, cupping my face. "I'm so glad to have found Helen's twin – and not the scheming dominatrix that Helen turned into, growing up in the Binaries."

I gave him a knowing smile. "I could be like that, if you ever wanted me to be stricter with you," I said mischievously.

"I know - I'm just grateful that we cruel Binaries haven't corrupted you too much, yet."

He admired the tight fitting evening dress that I had selected for our evening out in Madrid, thinking that my taste in clothing, at least, had benefitted from coming into his world. But because of the risk of meeting up with Marcie again, he transmitted sadly that I would be wearing it just for him, with a meal from room service.

"I don't mind," I said, hoping he would not pick up my regret at the rare treat of eating in a restaurant outside. I indicated the TV and the card showing the various films on offer. "We could watch a dirty film, unless you think that would be too corrupting?"

"I'd rather be the one doing any corrupting of you," he said, his eyes darkening. He indicated one of the less 'adult' movies on the list. "I believe this one features telepathy, so that could be a laugh. If we have any time to watch it, once I've got you out of that sexy dress…"

"What ever you want, senor," I replied, looking forward to a good evening.

36

Kastor had to work on assessments on the Sunday so I and the field officers, Nicole and Noah, set off for the El Rastro market area, travelling by the Madrid metro. This was a particular thrill for me; I had not been on an underground train on the outside for six years. I lingered over the antique stalls, with Nicole tutting that this could scarcely be called work for the commercial centre.

"It's all ideas and images," I murmured, "you just don't know when they're going to come in useful."

But in fact I was looking for a present for Kastor and finally spotted a large china mermaid at the back of one of the stalls, as well as a small item that I bought and secreted in my shoulder bag. About one foot tall, the mermaid was languorously combing her long dark hair and her other arm supported a small lyre. Perhaps it had been an ornament for a fish restaurant, with bright colours and gilding on the fins. I thought it was too well made to be just a vulgar shop adornment, stroking the fins and wondering if the mermaid's face resembled mine, just a little. The field officers glanced at each other, bemused, when I said it was simply perfect and told Noah to hand over the cash.

"Mermaids are so in, or are going to be," I said softly. While most of the items would be stored in the commercial centre, I had other plans for this one and told them not to mention it to Kastor. Noah joked he was going to need an ark to get all the purchases back to the hotel. He set off by taxi while Nicole and I found a pavement café to have a quick lunch in the autumn sunshine. The plan was for Noah to return and for us travel back together by metro. Noah had detected that Marcie Brown was busy elsewhere, so we relaxed over the meal.

I liked Nicole, guessing she was much the same age as me. I asked her about her time at Lochinstoun.

"It was great," she said, "I suppose you know I was in a class group just a couple of years behind Kastor, Artemis and Simon." I smiled as though I did know this. Kastor hardly ever spoke of his school days and my eyes sparkled at the prospect of finding more about them. I wondered why we did not spend more time socially with his school friends, suspecting that it was not just because he did not want me to feel excluded from his past experience. Also, he probably didn't want me to hear their anecdotes about him. He was always very careful in responding to questions about his past, saying that his life had really started after meeting me.

"So what was Kastor like at school?" I asked.

"Oh, clever, cool – like now really," said Nicole diplomatically. I sensed with disappointment that Nicole was too well trained to gossip with a work colleague. I tried a different tack, refilling Nicole's glass with the good Rioja wine.

"So, did you know at school that you would do this kind of work?"

"I always knew it would be something to do with commerce – but my aptitude for field work was assessed later, during college. You know, good shutting down skills and being able to mix with them all out here. Relatively few of us can do that easily." Nicole smiled proudly.

"Have you ever been tempted to have a relationship with one of them outside?" I asked, knowing this was dangerous ground. Nicole promptly closed off her thoughts and looked at me quizzically.

"Not really, no – I mean, it isn't allowed for one thing. If I were lucky enough to meet a natural telepath, I'd have to report it anyway. And I wouldn't want a relationship with an <u>outsider</u>."

Her voice had such a dismissive tone that I looked upset, thinking of how Helen had called non-telepathic humans 'talking potatoes' – but I had been one of these, until my telepathy had developed.

Nicole immediately apologised. "I'm sorry, I didn't mean people like you. You're one of us, it's easy to forget you grew up on the outside."

"I often think of it," I admitted, "of how my life and relationships would have developed, if I'd stayed outside."

"But you found Kastor. I can't imagine you living happily out here – and he was such a catch." She blushed slightly, feeling she had said too much.

"So he was popular with girls?"

"Yes, of course," said Nicole, falling silent as she focused on the food on her plate and drank some wine.

I wanted to know more, suppressing an unwelcome idea that Nicole might have been one of Kastor's early girlfriends. "So what about you?" I asked confidingly. "Are you seeing someone?"

"I've been attending relationship classes and I've been for pregnancy counselling – but I'm not sure yet. I've seen Antoine a few times, you know, the French surveillance officer. He's quite keen on this baby project, so I might consider it."

"Oh, and bond with him?"

"I wouldn't say I'd go that far, such a big step." She smiled shyly at me, fingering her wine glass. The bottle was more than half empty, with Nicole's much greater share of it making her more talkative. "You know that Binary relationships are different to those on the outside.

We're quite happy living separately – and linking up with a new partner from time to time. Of course it's different for you and Kastor, I didn't mean to appear to criticise."

I sensed that my domestic arrangements and close bond with Kastor was a possible frequent topic of conversation, hoping that very few knew of the ups and downs we had been through lately.

"I suppose we are a bit… different," I responded, "but don't you get jealous, sometimes, when someone you like decides to go with someone else? That's how it is on the outside, anyway."

I noticed a quick sharp glance from Nicole and added hastily, "Well, it doesn't apply to me and Kastor, of course, but sometimes I worry."

"Binaries don't get jealous," said Nicole and I caught a sudden idea that this was a frequent phrase transmitted to them in their early conditioning. "We're encouraged to explore feelings, mental and physical. I guess we all secretly hope to meet 'the one', the one we'd want to stay with forever – but we know how rare and unlikely that is. You're so lucky, you've found 'the one', haven't you?"

I nodded, but was thinking in a closed part of my mind of Kastor's recent jealousy. He certainly seemed to have overcome his early conditioning on that score.

"I mean," said Nicole, taking another gulp of wine, "there are several other men I'd quite like to know better. Simon for instance, but that wouldn't work, with seeing him professionally in the commercial centre."

"Does Simon have someone special in his life?" I reflected that I'd never heard a hint of anyone, nor seen a photograph or other giveaway sign, unlike Manes who had a picture of Amélie tucked away on desk.

Nicole leaned across, now in a much more indiscreet mood. "I think he carries a torch for Artemis and she for him. But classmates at

Lochinstoun, they're more like brothers and sisters, especially those in the same set. We live together for years, sharing dormitories and study bedrooms. It feels ... naughty, even slightly incestuous, to have a relationship with one of them."

"I expect Simon had lots of girlfriends outside that close group," I murmured.

"You bet! I went out with him briefly, but so did lots of others."

"I suppose it was the same with Kastor?" I was conscious that I was using my powerful persuasive gifts to make Nicole to say more.

"Oh, Kastor was very picky. Several girls had a thing for him, but he was one of the high fliers, always studying. Then, if he was at all interested, he would give one of his looks..."

"What, a come hither kind of look?" We both laughed and Nicole tilted her head, looking at me sideways through her lashes.

"It was a slanting look, like this, but not smiling. And he'd just gaze at them for a few moments and..."

"...they'd fall into his arms?" I refilled Nicole's wine glass to disguise my discomfort. I wasn't sure I was familiar with this 'look', trying to remember how he'd gazed at me during our first meetings.

"Hmm, something like that. But as I said, he was very choosy. These were rare occasions and the relationship never lasted long. Like he was just trying them out. Not that they minded."

I nodded, but an unspoken thought that Nicole was one of these fortunate schoolgirls made the field officer jump back into a more careful mode of speaking.

"I wasn't one of them, I never got the look. I think the wine's made me say too much. It was all a long time ago..."

I was about to say I wished I'd been at school with them, before remembering that Helen had been one of the girls there, perhaps in

Nicole's year or at most, one below. I knew that Helen had proposed a relationship with Kastor. He'd told me that he said no. I smiled to think of brazen Helen not waiting for 'the look', just plunging in with her sexual confidence. Nicole picked up a thought about Helen and smiled at me kindly, while downing the last of the wine.

"You're very different from Helen. I expect you wonder if you'd have grown up like her. She was absolutely wild at Lochinstoun – if it was an ordinary school that expelled pupils, she'd have been on the list."

I grinned, feeling we should move away from this subject, but it reminded me of my plan to contact Helen by mirror, perhaps tonight when we arrived back at Askeys. "So anyway, you're thinking about pregnancy. I've heard that there've been three already?"

"Yes, great isn't it!" Nicole was also relieved to leave the topic of her schooldays. "Phoebe Star was the biggest surprise for me. I didn't know she was that keen on Gregory Bonmot."

She realised from my widened eyes that this was news to me. Phoebe Star, who had lived outside until the age of 16 as Sophie. Then, the death of the real Binary, Phoebe, had meant that she would have to take her twin's place. The 'new' Phoebe was now working in the commercial unit, so of course Nicole would know her quite well.

"I'm being very indiscreet," mumbled Nicole, embarrassed. "We've been in the same relationship classes. Did you meet Phoebe when she made that tragic trip outside?"

I shook my head. "No, but I met her mother. It's sad that she'll never know she may be having a grandchild."

I thought of Melanie Campbell, staring at the photograph of her lost daughter, crying at the guilty memory of having taken part in a twin trial. I looked around anxiously, as though Melanie was going to approach us with a puzzled smile and recognise me. It seemed to be my time for these chance meetings. But in the blonde wig and sunglasses, wearing designer clothes, Melanie would surely not recognise me, even in the unlikely event of her being in Madrid. Nicole glanced round too, picking up my concern.

"That would be one coincidence too many, don't worry. Yes it's a shame, but at least Phoebe knows she had a mother. With the new programme, that'll apply to more of us at Binaries. You've done so much for the community."

"I try to keep my natural enthusiasm for reform in check," I murmured, smiling. "Anyway, it's good news about Phoebe. I was with her when she met Gregory and I guess that's how it started."

"Cassandra the matchmaker," said Nicole. "Well, I hope you can fix it for me too."

"Antoine's quite hot," I said. "You could do a lot worse." We giggled, but it was time to return to the hotel and we sensed the approach of Noah to escort us both back. We silently agreed to keep our conversational topics to ourselves.

A late check out had been arranged for the group and I found Kastor finishing our packing. He looked tired and I felt guilty that I had been enjoying a trip to El Rastro, also gossiping about him. I flung myself into his arms as if we had not seen each other for days and he immediately asked if something had happened. He gazed at me with concern, while I wondered about 'the look' and whether I had ever been on the receiving end of it, such as when I was so strongly attracted to him in Blenheim Park. I tilted my head to one side, as Nicole had done, and gave him my best 'come hither' shot to distract him from any idea that we'd been talking about him. Although he probably guessed.

"Hmm," he murmured, "I'd love to mingle with you right now, but it's a scheduled flight. We can't miss the plane."

"I've missed you," I said, since this was the simple truth. "All those ordinary humans out there, it made me long to be back with you."

"Good," he said, his manner uncertain. "I'd hate to lose you to one of them."

"Never!" My eyes glowed with the message that he wouldn't lose me to anyone on the inside either. I could tell he was starting to think, perhaps we had a few minutes for a quick mind dip or some physical mingling. I sighed with pleasure at the idea of him melting into my arms, having found 'the one'. He was holding me so tenderly.

"Oh, I bought you something in the market," I said as he reluctantly released me, "but you'll have to give me a coin, or something in exchange."

"Really." He smiled. "So you want me to pay for your gift?"

I produced a scruffily wrapped slim item from my bag in explanation. It was a silver paper knife with an ornate pattern on its handle. "I know you don't get many envelopes to open," I said apologetically, "but you can use it to cut up pieces of paper."

"It's beautiful," he said, examining the pattern and seeing it was an embossed city scene, somewhere in Spain, with little medieval figures busy trading.

"I don't know if you're aware of the tradition, that the gift of a knife must always be paid for with a coin or similar, or it might cut the friendship. It's the same with gloves, you know, throwing down the gauntlet."

He stroked the knife thoughtfully. "I see. But we don't carry cash, so what am I to do, give it back?"

"I'll take a kiss," I said cautiously, wishing now I had chosen something else.

"I don't think kisses count as fair exchange, but perhaps these would do." He reached into a trouser pocket and pulled out a small box. Inside nestled a pair of ruby and pearl earrings. Each ruby was cut in a heart shape, with the pearls set around it.

"How did you get these? I thought you were working?" I let him attach them carefully to each ear, then rushed to a mirror to admire them.

"I noticed them in the jewellery shop within the hotel. I thought they might be a reminder that you have my heart – and the pearls could remind me to never make you cry or suffer again."

He stood a little awkwardly behind me, gazing at our joint reflection in the mirror. My eyes filled with tears as I took in his wave of emotion, remembering all the anguish of recent weeks.

"Well, that didn't work," he said with mock solemnity, wiping away my tears.

"I'm just so happy," I said, "happy to have found you." He signalled to the field officers that we were still packing and would see them in the foyer in half an hour. Nicole smiled knowingly when she received this transmission, too polite to pry, but feeling a pang of envy. Lucky Cassandra, she mused, with a brief wistful memory of hoping for 'the look' from Kastor during their schooldays.

37

When we arrived back in our department in the early evening I was happy to be within the secure environment of the Binaries once more. It seemed that my past identity – and that of Helen - would always haunt me on the outside. Binaries like Gaston or Nicole could roam fairly freely, but I would always run the risk of meeting an Anne or a Marcie to challenge me.

"It will get easier in time," said Kastor, sensing these thoughts and I replied, "What, when I'm old and fat and no one could see the resemblance?"

Kastor paused before saying, "Long before that." He did not want to get into discussion about whether my increasing curves meant I was fat already, a perennial concern.

"I'll love you whatever you look like," he said tentatively and when I shot him a glance he added, "When you're old, I'll be old too."

I thought, yes, and we'll be in one of those secret nursing homes for old telepaths, lying under a protective thought tent so that no one can sense our disturbed minds. He decided it would be best not to respond to this, instead looking through his suitcase for the paper knife.

"I'm going to try this out, folding pieces of paper and cutting them in the study," he murmured and left me to finish unpacking my case. I looked at the bedroom mirror and checked the time. Washington was five hours behind, so it would be mid afternoon there – perhaps a good time to contact Helen? I strolled across to it, first admiring the new earrings again, then focusing on trying to reach my twin.

I thought of the first time that Helen and I had discovered our ability to send thoughts via mirrors, when I stood in Mum's bedroom and felt my reflection had moved. Perhaps we had found this route of communication much earlier, in childhood, without knowing what it meant, both having dreams about a sister and occasionally seeing a puzzling image. Theodora had explained it was a very rare phenomenon, unavailable to most telepaths. During the Casablanca and Cadiz crisis, Helen and I had been able to create the illusion of slipping through the glass and speaking in a strange, blurred narrow space behind the mirror.

Helen thought the mirror mind construction mainly existed at times when we needed help from each other, particularly to give her a chance to make amends for trapping me within the Binaries. As I concentrated on calling to Helen through the glass, I wondered if unravelling the mystery of Jeannette Summer's son was sufficient reason for the mirror to work for us. Her reflection remained the same, just myself looking out with a serious, troubled stare, as if to confirm that it was simply a mirror in a bedroom. I turned away, disappointed, then heard a low voice.

"Sis? Is that you?" I spun back to the reflection. It had shifted slightly. The image shimmered and I saw myself, but with very short hair. "Helen?" I whispered and the mirror image nodded.

"Who were you expecting?" said Helen, with slight exasperation. "No one else can do this, Sis, just us. I sensed you trying to contact me and rushed in here. We've got guests, I've only got a few minutes. Try and step through, so we can have a quick chat." I focused on being Alice through the looking glass, pushing my arm through the now pliant surface of the mirror. It had been a long time since I had done this and I had forgotten the bizarre sensation of slipping through into the tight space in which both of us seemed two dimensional, surrounded by formless shadows.

"You look so different with that hair cut," I murmured.

"Like it? I thought I was getting too old for long hair. Not that it doesn't still look good on you, Cass. But I'm a sleek Washington wife these days and couldn't be bothered to keep putting my hair up to look as sophisticated as the others."

"Suits you," I said, wondering if I should try a new style.

"Enough on hair, what's up?"

I quickly explained about the missing boy and my vision of him being possibly at the Binary boarding school. Helen was as puzzled as Kastor had been about the idea of a five year old being abducted.

"And his mother, this Summers woman, do you know her address in the States?"

I shook my head, explaining the difficulty of not making obvious enquiries. Helen glanced sideways, possibly sensing her guests in their house "We're having a house warming, got to go. Try reaching me early in the morning – say about noon your time."

I replied, "I'll take an early lunch and come back here," as my sister disappeared from the space and I slipped back into the bedroom.

I told Kastor that I had contacted Helen and he looked wary. "You haven't asked her to help with this missing boy idea?"

"Not exactly," I said, "I may have just mentioned it."

"Which means that Helen will already be trying to track down Jeannette Summers. You must put her off. Haven't you had enough excitement, lately? This secret sounds very dangerous. It obviously isn't something official that the surveillance squad would know about, but whoever knows will want to protect the story."

"She won't be doing anything now – they're in a new house, giving a house warming party."

"Good, well next time you're in contact, tell her you don't want to pursue it."

I looked down demurely and he sighed. "I'm guessing that's a no. But please be very careful and keep me informed. You know what Helen's like, she's probably already looking forward to getting into disguise and having a new adventure."

"I'll tell her she mustn't do anything rash," I said and was relieved when Kastor laughed and replied, "We both know how cautious and timid she is – not at all. But if you insist on involving her, involve me too?"

Standing very close to him, I felt surrounded by a powerful electromagnetic force, protective, trying to shield my from harm.

"You don't need to do this," he said, "You could let sleeping dogs lie, as Wayland would say. Whatever his real origins, the boy is growing up as one of us. His mother could never safely meet him."

"I know," I said. "It's this terrible, cursed gift that I have. But just like Helen knew she had to help me when you were in trouble, I don't seem to be able to dismiss a plea for help. It may be my destiny to be involved."

He sighed and took my hands, so that an electric charge passed through both of us. "You're always looking for the truth, however dangerous. But that kind of quest led you to me, so I'm grateful it's part of you. You're my destiny, which means I have to help you – and try to keep you safe. See if you have any dreams tonight and we'll talk about what to do."

I gazed at him with such gratitude and trust that for a moment he was lost in my eyes, hearing the soft song of the sirens within my mind.

"Cassandra," he murmured slowly, pronouncing every syllable, as he reluctantly drew back. "Who would have imagined that you were out there, waiting to swirl us all into questioning so much of our world. Storms, reform, change – how it will it end?"

I cast my eyes sideways, possibly looking into the future. "A binary conversion?" I suggested.

He replied, "Into what?" and I shrugged, smiling but sending a thought, "Something better?" Then I announced abruptly, "Meanwhile, I'm starving, shall we go to the Askeys restaurant and enjoy one of the things about life here that I'd hate to change?"

He laughed. "You are looking a bit thin, so great idea."

For a few hours at least, we talked of other things, including Kastor's memories of his first couple of years at Lochinstoun School, although he demanded to hear my memories of school outside in return.

The next day, I looked at the file concerning the contract between Jeannette Summers' company and Lily West. Simon nodded approvingly, asking me to let him know if I sensed anything about possible changes in their arrangement. I focused purely on the business, finding no major concerns, as Simon had thought. Examining the information we had on the wide interests of the company, I sensed that they possibly wanted to narrow their range of products, and also a worry that the toy business was suffering from imported, cheaper playthings.

I pictured their range, wondering if it was time to suggest more home made products to take advantage of consumer wishes to support businesses at home, but what could they make that would also not come in at a high price? I thought of the simple toys in the Binary nursery, all designed to stretch the imagination. These would seem quaint and old fashioned to children outside. But older people liked to buy such toys for children, so that was a commercial possibility – the aunt, uncle and grandparent market. I discussed it with Simon, mentioning boats, ships, some update on the traditional game of Battleships, perhaps. Binary children only played that type of game to test their ability to detect the other players' choices, a pastime that they soon grew out of. Simon nodded thoughtfully, saying he would bring it up at the review, just as a modest suggestion. We preferred to work with clients' ideas, predicting what would work or not, but there was no reason why we should not seem interested in increasing clients' profits in other ways. "Home products, cottage industry, yes, worth bringing up," he murmured, handing me a file about a different company that had just come in. He loved it when I was in full working mode, sparking ideas.

Meanwhile, I had noted that Jeannette Summers had an apartment in Washington for when they were checking on corporate legal matters. The file did not tell me whether Jeannette shared the apartment with her husband. Where was he in all this and what did he do for a living? Perhaps they were separated. I made my mind reach out to Washington, to try to picture Jeannette there. I caught a glimpse of Jeannette sitting moodily in a smartly decorated room. Modern furnishings, very little ornaments: but I could detect a photograph on a sideboard, a smiling boy. Nearby there was something round and glass, sitting on a stand. A crystal ball, placed to make a stylish feature, but with a deeper meaning for Jeannette. She would never cease trying to find her son. I imagined her occasionally picking up the ball and staring listlessly into it, hoping for a magic vision. Preoccupied with the other file, I didn't notice the time passing and was alarmed to see it was nearly 12: time to rush back to the apartment as promised and to contact Helen.

The Askeys mansion was a couple of miles away from the main underground complex and the underground train was busy with others moving around at lunchtime. I tapped my foot impatiently as it stopped at nearly every station on the route. When I reached the house and dashed up to the apartment, it was nearly 12:15 and I found Helen waiting for me impatiently.

38

HELEN

I was pleased when Cass seemed to need my help again. I was getting bored of playing the good outsider, even though Washington had its attractions. All those Senators and interns, with their secrets. Alexander didn't seem to mind if I flirted at the cocktail evenings and benefit events, so long as it was to increase his circle of useful contacts. But I never tried to contact Cass. Apart from this being strictly forbidden by Gaston, I didn't want to get her into trouble. In my mature years, well now that I've reached the ancient age of 24, I've often thought about my stupid and dangerous switch into her life.

If only I had been more patient, arranging more meetings until the adventure of a swap could have appealed to her. If I had planned it, fixing a better fake wrist tattoo, no one would have guessed, maybe for days. Especially as I was having all that dreary rehab, where telepathy was less important than responding to all the counselling. I detected that she had enough telepathy to pass muster for that. We could have arranged a signal, or a regular meeting to decide when the game was over. And then we could have switched back again. But this would have meant that I was a kind, thoughtful twin, worrying about her well being. At that time, nothing of the sort was in my mind. Once I had discovered that she was living outside, within reach of the Binary complex, my only thoughts were jealousy. She had parents, friends, holidays and the freedom to go wherever she wanted outside. While I was a conditioned freak, designed to serve Binary purposes and within their strict rules.

I don't think Cass realises how different my upbringing made me, even now. Or whether she understands what all this enhanced telepathy is for. Yes, she knows about spying and commercial secrets. And she seems to have settled obediently into earning money for the organization. Because that is all the organization cares about, making money. The Binary Council, the International Board: that's all they discuss, except when there are dire emergencies such as the attack on the French centre. The conditioning is relentless as we grow up, so that very few question the need for absolute loyalty. We were told how lucky we were, to be living in this best of all possible worlds. Those of us who became good telepaths knew it was our duty to serve the organization, just as the less talented felt lucky not to have to take the risks involved. I was thrilled when I was picked out for fast tracking. I graduated two years ahead of others of my age and I was sent on advanced courses. By the time I was 17, I had already started to do outside missions, although always escorted or with field officer surveillance to keep me safe.

When they recognised my talents with men, I was pleased to serve them in that too. It was fun at first, extracting secrets and reporting back. After all, the men were only outsiders, so they deserved to be strung along. At least, that's what my supervisors convinced me, the word prostitution not being used by Binaries. I was trained in computer hacking and electronics, but this is when it started to unravel. I found the secret files about my origin. I remember staring with fascination at the screen in a forbidden zone of the admin block, reading the short account of my real origin. For of course, once I had learned to penetrate secret areas on the outside, why shouldn't I try it within Binaries? Most of us wouldn't do that. But I'd always had dreams of a sister, just as Cass experienced on the outside. The supervisors hadn't reckoned on the effect of all their training on natural telepaths with our range of talents.

It was a terrible shock, to realise that all the stuff about us being lucky orphans was a big lie. The nannies had repeatedly told me that I had no sister, certainly not one who was alive. Funny coincidence, really, that this is what Cass had been told too. Perhaps it was our mother's way of protecting her, as the nannies protected us Binaries from any disturbing thoughts. Our mother – I could never call her Mum – had known I would be taken away at birth. No wonder she went mad with the guilt, when what she had done sank in. I only saw her the once, on that cruise boat. I was burning with anger, especially when I sensed her complicity in my 'rescue', even taking money for it. Too late, I sensed her physical ill health and my mind darts might have hastened her death. Oh well, just one of my many crimes. Gaston will forever suspect that I can't be trusted outside, no matter how much I do for Cass and their community.

Growing up in the Binaries, I eventually learned to say nothing, fearing the disciplinary techniques of nannies, house mothers and the teachers. Isolation, hypnosis, constant visits to the re-education block: they didn't have to hit us to make us conform. After I discovered that I had a sister alive out there, it became an obsession. I made the mistake of admitting it to one of the counsellors, although I couldn't have kept my discovery from the likes of Gaston, so I thought it best to at least try to discuss it. They acted promptly, switching my duties to surveillance and computer work within Binaries, with no outside visits allowed. That's when I snapped and ran away, to see what I could uncover at the private clinic where I was born.

Well, then I started to sense that my twin and I were occasionally in contact. Truly, at first I just wanted to meet her. But she was so touchingly innocent and trusting, the idea of taking over her life started to grow. When we met, I had the syringe full of tranquilliser with me, but I only decided to use it at the last minute. It was when I realised that she simply didn't have a clue, not an iota of suspicion that I felt burning resentment at her life outside. She was looking forward to having jolly meetings, sharing our past experiences. That day in Blenheim park, I remember thinking, she's so easy to dupe, I might as well risk it. Especially as I was strictly confined to quarters, so to speak. If they found out, I'd never get a second chance. Dr. Foucoe and the psychiatric counsellors said I had a mental illness. I can see now that this was true, up to a point. Cass and I, we're both very odd, compared with the other telepaths. Rebellious, prone to outbursts of anger and far too fond of adventures.

So, my obsession could have got her killed. I'll always feel guilty about that. When I heard how well she had adapted to Binary life, I was also very jealous. I'd given up so much. The conditioning included a fear of the outside and a deep belief that it would be a dreadful sin to try to leave. It was always warned that leaving, even if achievable, would be a permanent decision. Yet I didn't really believe that, until I did the swap. Later, when I got to know Cass through our mind construct with mirrors, I felt a great debt to her. I'll always do anything I can to help her. Visiting her in France was wonderful. It makes me wonder if I could have been like her, if we'd grown up together. She is becoming more like a Binary, as the years pass. She hasn't told me much about it, but when we created a storm together at Binaires, I knew that she had my range of abilities, including the unpleasant ones.

Now, waiting for her to make contact via the mirror, I wondered what further trouble she was thinking of causing. Alexander was out, so I had no fear of us being disturbed. At last, I saw her reflection in my mind's eye, which then transformed into her image within the mirror. I stepped in impatiently, for waiting around quietly and tolerantly is not one of my characteristics.

"Sorry, held up by work," Cass said, when we were standing in our narrow space within the mirror.

"Lucky you," I said. "Alexander wants me to be a stay-at-home wife with charity duties. That's what many of the wives do around here, at least the ones who stay married. The new house is enormous. I have an office to look after the staff and so on."

"Does Alexander want Grace to join you?"

I rolled my eyes. "Yes, he's written to that nice couple at Villa Dufour, a.k.a, you and Kastor, saying we can now take her back and thanking them for their care. He'd quite like the twins too, I've had to invent a whole saga about arranging adoption before we got married."

"The villa's up for sale," said Cass. "It's been emptied and everything's in storage. But I assume the post is being intercepted, so someone must have seen that letter. It hasn't been mentioned to me."

"No surprise there," I said. "Gaston and his crew will make sure that he gets a reply, but they're probably deciding the best solution. Perhaps I should take Grace back, what do you think?"

"Are you going to stay with Alexander, then?"

All these questions. I was increasingly impatient to know what Cass wanted of me. But I had tried to learn not to rush things. So I sighed and replied to this awkward enquiry about Alexander. "For the moment. Hell, Cass, I've only got myself to blame. He's OK, but I have to work on him – lots of ladies to distract him here. Obviously I can deal with that, but if we don't get Grace back, he'll be wanting another child. We'd get a nanny, obviously."

"She's a lovely baby – and talented too. You'd have a telepathic child to deal with."

"And she'd have to go to an ordinary school… I don't like to think about the problems she'd face. Even with my help, well, you know how it is. You went through all that, Cass – and you've told me about getting into trouble for seeming to know too much, detecting things you shouldn't know about."

"Well, it would be the same if you had another child."

"With Alexander? He's a lot older than me – nearly fifty. But even if he can still father a child, I suppose that one might turn out like a real outsider."

Cass gave me one of her smug smiles. She knew I wouldn't want that and I had sensed that she knew Grégoire was Grace's father.

"Well," I continued, uncomfortably aware that talking about this made me think it was time to move on from Alexander, "I'm pleased the twins I had with Faisal are telepathic. But he was a bit that way, although undeveloped and it suited our relationship to not push that. Alexander is just slightly intuitive. Not sure if I want to spawn one of them, the ordinary sort."

"If we ever get away from here, you could live with us," said Cass, ever the optimist.

I snorted. "That wouldn't work. Kastor has understandably only limited tolerance of me. But maybe I could live nearby. Why, do you have plans?"

"Just dreams," she said, sharing an image of an arrangement, similar to the Villa Dufour, where they could stay connected with Binaries but live separately. I shrugged, closing the subject. I sensed she wanted to discuss this lost boy, who she'd mentioned on our last brief contact.

"Meanwhile, about this boy. I suppose Kastor's warned you off?"

"Yes, but he says he'll help if I insist on searching."

"Great," I said, surprised. "So do you have an address for the mother?"

Cass told me about the Washington apartment and what she had gleaned from remote viewing.

"So she's still into the psychic stuff," I commented. "I could pose as a medium, easy."

"But Helen, you look too much like me," she said, alarmed.

I was affronted. Surely she knew that if I could pose as a nun, I could do a medium? "Please, have more faith in me," I said. "I guarantee she wouldn't link me with you. I'm thinking of a great disguise, foreign accent – and very subdued lighting."

"Where – in your home?"

"Of course not. Actually there is somewhere, a friend's house – they're both away and I'm just popping in to water plants occasionally."

"But that could easily be linked to you. Jeannette is no fool – and she'd probably run checks if she considered going to a strange house to see a psychic."

"I'll think of something," I said, warming to the idea of an excellent diversion from being a dutiful Washington wife. "Hang on, there's a museum renovation that I'm helping with. Lots of empty display rooms at the moment. Folk culture stuff – including gypsies. Could be ideal. I'll work on it."

"And what do you propose to tell Jeannette, if you pulled this off?"

"It's what she'd tell me. I can easily give her a few amazing facts about her life, just from her thoughts. But we want to know who the father is, don't we?"

"Yes – Kastor suggested it could have been an affair with a telepath," Cass agreed. "But Jeannette wouldn't have known that, most likely. Let's say the father was a telepath. Could he be one of us, who later abducted the boy, took him to a Binary centre?"

"A five year old coming in – I'd have heard about it if he came to the Woodstock centre. You say he's 13 or so now – I was still in the Binaries when all this happened."

"It could be any of the centres, most likely an American one," said Cass.

"Good point. So all we have to do is find out which of the children came from an American centre. But it means that the father has been very devious. Perhaps it was that rat Ryden Asgard?"

"I hope not," she said. "He'd be a bit young for Jeannette. She looked about 45 when I met her, so she'd be late forties by now."

"Attractive older woman, no problem for an affair with a Binary, a bit of dalliance on the outside. But Ryden didn't strike me as the fatherly type, who would take such a risk to be with his son. And it's not as if he could be with him, in Binary world."

"Unless he was a teacher," Cass said and I saw what she meant, although an unlikely possibility. "He could have then transferred to the school, to see his son grow up," she added. "Possibly with the boy having no idea."

"Definitely with the boy not knowing. The teachers there are very sharp," I advised, shivering slightly at the thought of how hard it was to deceive them in my school years. "If you're right, this guy is superb at shutting down his thoughts. Beats me, Cass. Our conditioning is thorough and highly effective. To rescue a boy and bring him up in secret, it's unthinkable!" Even more unthinkable than what I'd done to my twin, I reflected in a closed thought.

"Perhaps I'm wrong about where he is. I can see how unlikely this all sounds," said Cass.

"No, you've had two sightings of him – and you sussed that they were communicating telepathically. You don't make that kind of mistake, clever Cass." I felt pride, instead of all that past jealousy.

"OK, but Helen, be ultra careful. We don't know what this man might do if he detected that we were after him."

"Yes – but ruthless telepaths are right up my street. I promise I'll just take a quick dip into this and report back. I won't give real clues, anything like that."

"We should go – I need to get back to work. Talk again soon? Meanwhile, try just signalling me long distance to let me know what you're getting up to."

"Thought signalling could be dangerous. This guy must be constantly afraid of detection – but I think this mirror method is safe. We'll stick to that. Say in about five days, same time, same place."

"Friday," Cass said. "OK, and please, please, don't do anything risky."

I grinned. "The twins on the trail again. And there was me thinking I should join the quilt-making group. Stand by, Sis."

With that, I stepped back from the space and could see only myself in the mirror.

39

CASSANDRA

Kastor frowned when I related Helen's plan to impersonate a psychic.

"So long as it isn't linked to us in any way," he said. "But I think she's right that she won't be recognised. Jeannette would hardly be expecting you to turn up in a gypsy outfit in Washington."

He produced a folder, labelled Lochinstoun. "I told Manes you were worrying about Leo, wanted to know about the pupils and teachers. As it was me – and you – he let me see this. It's a list of them all. Apparently there are at least half a dozen who transferred from the States, because Lochinstoun is our best school. Manes wanted to know if you'd had any intuitions about the place. After Cadiz, he'd never take one of your concerns lightly again."

"I don't have any particular fears or ideas," I said. "Except normal parent ones, hoping that Leo will be happy there. But the fact that I've seen this boy at the school makes me wonder, perhaps it will be connected with Leo in some way."

"And you haven't had any dreams?"

"None that seem at all relevant. I saw the boy again, fleetingly, just walking down a corridor. I'm not trying to visualise him within the school. Helen suggested that if a teacher is involved, he might be very wary of attempts to discover how the boy got there."

"Perhaps you shouldn't look at this list, yet," said Kastor, glancing at the folder. "It's just a list of names, but with your abilities you might start to connect and focus on a name. Let's minimise the danger and wait for Helen to report."

I saw the sense in this. I felt a chill of unease at possibly putting Leo at risk. "Kastor, supposing this man just likes five year old boys. Perhaps he spotted the boy's telepathic ability, got him in. But now the boy is growing up, maybe he wants another one to focus on?"

"Child abusers at Lochinstoun? That's a problem that doesn't occur in Binary world. It would be detected so fast you wouldn't even see Gaston dashing up there to deal with it, just a rush of howling wind. Anyway, if this teacher likes five year olds, he gets lots of those at the school. No, I don't think that's the thing we should be worrying about. We need to focus on why he'd want to rescue a child, even if it was his, in secret. Why not just monitor him, then bring him in with full approval, later?"

"It wouldn't get approval, would it? Taking a child, or even a young adult, away from his doting mother? On security rationale alone."

Kastor nodded. "We don't like bringing in adults, unless they have very few people to chase after them outside. It means complicated death scenarios, as you are sadly aware."

"Or twin replacements," I murmured, "and this child wasn't a twin."

"Try not to think about it," warned Kastor. "Let's hope whoever it is doesn't know much about your powers, or your interest."

I did my best to focus on work and other Binary activities while waiting to hear about Helen's progress. I was surprised to be approached by Dominique, followed by Edouard, in the labyrinth restaurant on the

Wednesday of that week. Dominique asked politely if they could join me for a moment and I nodded apprehensively. They had no trays of food, so presumably it was not a request to eat lunch together. "Monsieur Parfait has something to say," announced Dominique, quietly. She glanced around, checking there were no eavesdroppers. Edouard was looking down, dressed more formally than when I had last seen him, wearing a business-like shirt, jacket and trousers.

"Miss Mason," he said falteringly, not looking at me. "I wish to wholeheartedly apologise for my appalling behaviour and impertinence." He paused, looking wretched, while I sat silently, not knowing what to say. Dominique was prompting him to continue. "And I can assure you," he said, in an even lower tone, "that it will never happen again."

At the end of this speech, Dominique nodded approvingly. "Good. You can go back to the training centre now." He stood up, hesitated as though he should make a small bow but instead turned and said "Thank you," in a low voice and walked out of the restaurant. Dominique stayed at my table, watching her protégé exit from the room.

"So much easier," she murmured, "if good behaviour is instilled in childhood, but he's doing quite well."

"Will he be working here, when his training is completed?"

"Heavens no. I've been offered a post in the Virginia Centre and he'll be taking an assessment to see if he can join me there. I think we can guarantee they'd agree to him going there for further training."

"And Lamella?" I asked.

Dominique rolled her eyes. "She's still quite besotted with him, unfortunately. He's attending parenting classes with her but I don't think that bonding would be appropriate. He'd make her very unhappy. We'll be dealing with that. The main thing is that both parents will follow up on their child's progress. That's the kind of thing you had in mind, isn't it?"

"It's a start," I said.

Dominique looked at the luncheon buffet and said she had only time for a sandwich, then gazed sympathetically at me, the erstwhile object of Edouard's affections. "I do hope all is well with you and Kastor, despite Edouard's unwanted attentions?"

I nodded, feeling that the question was mainly rhetorical. "Meanwhile," said Dominique with a sly smile, "you may be pleased to know that he no longer requires such strict discipline, at least in …a confined environment. I've been continuing his extra-curricular education in my small apartment here."

"I didn't mean to pick up those images, when we were at the party," I said, embarrassed under the penetrating stare of 'Dom the Dom'.

"I'm delighted you did," said Dominique, although I sensed less than sincerity in this pronouncement. "It was good for you to know that he's been disciplined. Our ways must often seem very strange to you, even after being with us so long. Edouard has proved a very eager pupil. He now knows how to behave in public – and how to sometimes misbehave when the situation is appropriate."

I smiled broadly, sharing a quick image of Edouard looking satisfied, or rather, sated, gazing at Dominique with adoration.

"I suppose you knew my twin while she was in the Binaries," I said. "She was better at discipline than I am."

"Hélène," said Dominique, with a trace of affection. "Yes indeed, she came over to us to hone her language skills. Some of us have more talent – and taste - for that than others. Such a naughty girl, but very good at French too, so I'd hoped she'd join us one day at Binaires. What's she doing now?"

"I think she's trying to be a good wife," I murmured and Dominique threw her head back and laughed as though it was the best joke she'd heard in weeks.

40

HELEN

Meanwhile, in Washington, Jeannette Summers examined a card that I had sent her in the post, anonymously. It was an invitation to see the newest psychic in town.

> *'You are invited to a complementary consultation with the renowned Madame Irina Bravitska, in Washington for just seven days. Madame Bravitska works only with a few clients, particularly specializing in bringing hope to those who have lost someone. She will look into your past, present and future and guide you with any unresolved problems, with the help of loved ones on the other side. Please call the number below to take up this unrepeatable opportunity, which is available on Thursday 3 October only. Confidentiality is assured.'*

A mobile telephone number followed, but no address. I waited patiently for her to make contact. From what Cass had said, I expected her to be cautious. As she had visited so many mediums, she would now be on a list for agencies who worked for psychics, or those who pretended to have these talents. So she would hesitate, but I reckoned she would take the bait. When my specially purchased mobile eventually rang, I knew it was her. How could she resist a complementary session with the famous Madame Bravitska, even if she suspected that this was just a lure to get her to pay a high fee for future sessions?

I adopted a cultured American accent as I answered the telephone. "Madame Bravitska's suite," I said. "How may I help you?" Jeannette assumed this was some kind of receptionist and explained she had received the invitation.

"Ah, yes," I said. "That was a very limited offer. We've had several calls already. Are you interested in seeing Madame?"

"Well, possibly," said Jeannette. "I'd like to know more about her first. It says 'renowned' but I've not heard of her – and there's no website or trace on the Internet."

My pleasant voice became confiding. "She works mainly in secret. She would be overwhelmed if she advertised and some of her more famous clients wouldn't like it. But she insisted on making this offer on her first trip to the States. She had a message, that she was needed by someone here in Washington."

"Oh yeah?" said Jeannette, cynically but I felt a wave of emotional pain from the woman at the end of the phone, as well as curiosity.

"Perhaps the invitation was misdelivered," I said. "Her secretary told me that Madame had selected the names myself. May I enquire your name?" Jeannette gave it and I feigned puzzlement, saying after a few moments, "Well, your name is on the list. Madame does not make mistakes, but perhaps this is not a good time for you to see her?"

"Complementary, the invitation said, what does that mean exactly?"

"It means that Madame wants to give an opportunity to those who are not her clients, to see her without any obligation or payment. It's most unusual. It happens to coincide with her wish to help charity work at the new Museum of Folk Culture. She's making this rare appearance because as you may know, it features the culture of gypsies, amongst others. She is the seventh child of a seventh child of an old

Romany tribe. The consultation would be just as it says, completely free."

"Well, I might be interested."

"I see," I said, with a slightly cooler tone. "As you can imagine, it's been a very popular event. I'm not sure if there are any times left, but I could check for you?"

"Please do," said Jeannette, now anxious not to miss out on seeing the medium.

I was silent, sensing that Jeannette had gripped the phone, thinking of her son. His name, I gleaned was Jason. I sent my most persuasive thoughts, making her feel that she must see this psychic gypsy and wishing she had telephoned as soon as the card had arrived. I spoke again after apparently leafing through a diary. I made sure that Jeannette heard pages turning.

"I'm afraid all the daytime consultations have been taken. Her last appointment is at 7 o'clock, but although it's free, frankly we were hoping she'd have finished by then. It'll be an exhausting day for her, with all the other slots fully booked."

"I could make 7 p.m.," said Jeannette eagerly. "I'd be most grateful. Perhaps some of the others won't turn up and she'll get some rest before seeing me."

"Unlikely," I murmured. "If you could wait just a second, I'll see if I can speak to her myself."

Jeannette hung on the line, hoping for the medium to agree to see her.

"Mrs. Summers – Madame says that she will see you. Her secretary had no idea that her invitation would be taken up by so many recipients. Less than a dozen were mailed, assuming that the short notice would mean only a handful turning up. But Madame insists she must not disappoint those who were invited."

"Oh, thank you – and please thank Madame Bravitska," gushed Jeannette. I courteously gave her the museum address, but added that she must keep the consultation private, completely confidential.

"You'll be admitted by the side door, on Klaxon Street, as the museum is not open yet and the usual staff will have left. You must be careful not to tell others about this. Madame hates publicity and certainly couldn't see anyone not booked on that day."

"Of course," said Jeannette.

"She'll know if you do tell anyone, she's amazing like that," I said.

"I won't. 7 o'clock then, I'll be there."

Finishing the call, I was pleased to note that Jeannette felt a thrill of anticipation. It was all rather too mysterious and possibly complete bunkum, she was thinking. But I had managed to convince her with my persuasive thoughts, that Madame Bravitska would be able to help her.

I sat back and took a few breaths when Jeannette rang off. Projecting that amount of convincing persuasion was tiring. I tucked away the mobile phone, which would be used exclusively for this escapade, into my handbag. I still couldn't bring myself to call it a 'purse', in the American way. My next task was to drive out of town to a fancy dress retailer and get some suitable clothes. I collected some other items at different shops, all to complete the illusion that I intended to give to Jeannette at the museum.

41

HELEN

Alexander approvingly noted my enthusiasm for the charity project at the museum, which had reached the stage of trying out displays and signage, with valuable objects still in store.

"It's good that you have something to take your mind off missing Grace. I've had a reply from your friends at that French villa," he said over breakfast and I looked up, suitably alarmed.

"She's OK, isn't she?" My manner of a concerned mother was hopefully convincing. Alexander had presumed that my rare mentions of our baby daughter was because I missed her so much and didn't want to break down in tears at the thought of being separated. It had taken much longer than he had planned to find us a permanent home.

"Well, she's been in hospital, apparently. They should have told us sooner. They're back in England now, the letter was forwarded. Really, Helen, when were they going to tell us that they were going to visit London?"

I composed a suitably disapproving expression.

"They say it may not be serious," continued Alexander, "but Grace is having some tests. We should go over and see her."

I knew Alexander had written, but hoped that he would just receive a non-committal reply and the usual enclosure of photos. He hadn't shown it to me, but he had raised the idea of bringing Grace to the States. I should have realised that while this could be arranged, the Binaries would not want to put themselves out much for me. Also, I had entrusted Grace to their care. Alexander had written to the Villa post restante address, which would have been collected by a Binary agent. News of an illness, which I knew must be untrue, meant that the Binaries were preparing for Grace to go into sudden decline, if I didn't contact them. If I wanted Grace back, it would have to be before it would be too late for her release from the Binary nursery.

Alexander looked up questioningly, wondering why I wasn't more worried about Grace.

"Oh Alexander, how dreadful!" I exclaimed, to reassure him that of course I was anxious. "Yes, we must go, but did they give you a phone number? I'll make enquiries today."

Alexander handed me the letter, which had a London address. A photograph was attached, showing Grace sleeping peacefully in a cot, looking very sweet, but rather pale. An attached sticky note informed us that this had been taken just before she fell ill. We looked at the photo, Alexander murmuring how much he was looking forward to seeing her again. He hadn't seemed interested in children when we met, quite relieved that my twins wouldn't live with us, but I'd recently sensed him longing for us to be a 'proper family'. I sighed, recalling my conversation with Cass. Whatever happened to Grace, Alexander would be hoping for more children. Meanwhile, I knew that a call to the London phone number would be transferred to somewhere in the Binaries.

"Try not to worry, she's been a healthy baby until now," he said.

I gave him a soulful look. Inside, I felt a churning at having to make this decision about Grace and the possibility of having to return to England for a fake funeral. A fleeting thought that we could have the baby's body sent to the States had to be dismissed. Even the Binaries would find it hard to produce a dead baby looking just like Grace as a substitute – and supposing Alexander wanted tests or a post-mortem that would reveal the lack of a genetic link? Most of all, I didn't want Grace to be eliminated just to make things simple.

"I'll cancel the museum work," I murmured, while sending the idea to Alexander that I should not let them down. He promptly repeated this, saying there was no need for panic. He had a busy day with several meetings and a working dinner, seeming relieved when I said he should go on his own to that. I said that I wanted to try to reach the Dufours if the news from the hospital was worrying. He nodded solicitously, saying he'd try to be back by around nine.

When he left, I went to the cupboard where I'd stored my costume and equipment for the evening with Jeannette Summers. I was irritated that the Binaries had acted so soon about Grace, but understood they'd had to respond to Alexander's letter. I waited until noon before ringing the number, since it would be 9 a.m. back in Woodstock. My call was answered by a convincing hospital receptionist, who gave me another number to ring once I had signalled telepathically who I was. My heart sunk when Gaston's cool voice answered.

"Helen, how lovely to hear from you. But of course you're worried about Grace. Romain and Sylvie Dufour are at the hospital, so asked me to speak with you."

"How serious is it?" I asked, realising that the conversation was being conducted with care, on the remote chance of it being monitored. Alexander's work involved government matters and it was possible that US agencies had him on low level surveillance.

"They didn't want to worry you. She seemed to just have a chill, but it now it's clear that it's more than that. They're treating it as possible childhood leukaemia."

"Oh no!" I gasped. Gaston transmitted a thought, *don't overdo it Helen. We all know how much you really care.*

"But they can treat that these days," I said, wondering if he could detect from my thoughts that I cared a surprising amount. But he would always think of me as shallow and ruthless. So I just said, in a plaintive tone, "Perhaps she should be transferred over here."

"Would you like me to suggest that?" asked Gaston. "She has some kind of infection, it may not be possible to move her until they've got that under control." I knew this was the crunch time. Gaston was transmitting the thought, if you want her back, you have to say so now.

"I must do what's best for Grace. Of course they shouldn't move her until it's safe to do so." *Keep her at Binaries*, I transmitted silently, with an unexpected pang of regret. I added, with a warning signal, "Alexander thinks we should come over right away."

"The Dufours will let you know if that's necessary. They're very upset, naturally, but she's receiving excellent care. I'll get Romain to ring you when he contacts me – or if you're worried in the meantime, speak to him directly. Do you have Romain and Sylvie's current number, as they are currently staying in London?"

"If you could let me have a cell phone number, that would be great."

Gaston gave me another mobile phone number and I knew this would be connected through to Kastor.

"Well, goodbye Helen, for now, and do take care." Gaston's smooth voice belied the thought transmitted with this. He was signalling that I had made my choice and would soon be called to attend a tragic funeral. Ending the call, I stared bleakly around my luxurious home. I wished I had Cass's gift of precognition, wondering if there was any chance of returning to live at least near a Binary community, so that I could feel the support of mingling thoughts and images with fellow telepaths.

Meanwhile, it seemed all the more important to make this search for information about Jeannette's son a success. I set off for the museum with a large carry bag containing an ornate dress, shawl, head dress and make up. First I would need to work with other volunteers on various displays. The unfinished Romany room had a charming gypsy caravan as its centrepiece. This had a main door accessed up a narrow wooden stairway and a small door at the back, which would have allowed rear access and disposal of slops. My plan was to have Jeannette approach the caravan by the front, to find the psychic sitting within in suitably dark surroundings. I chatted with the other volunteers as we went through the rooms with the curator, admiring the work so far. My bag of tricks was safely secured within the caravan and I was impatient for the afternoon to end. I was pleased to sense Jeannette's eagerness, also waiting for the evening appointment to draw near.

When the other volunteers left, I stayed on, saying I would just check plans for the Inuit section, with its authentically designed igloo. Admiring my diligence, they urged me not to stay too late. I had confided worries about my baby daughter to one of the women, who sympathetically judged that I was trying to keep myself busy while I waited for news.

"Oh, Helen, you must be longing just to dash over to London," she said solicitously and I nodded, as though forcing back tears. When the other women finally left, I chatted with the security officer, a friendly middle aged man who could scarcely conceal his attraction to the sweet woman who was working so hard for the museum.

"We should close up," he said when the time was approaching 5.30 p.m. "But if you want to do some more work here, I'd be happy to stay on a little."

"You're so kind, Robbie," I said, giving him one of my most alluring smiles. "But I couldn't make you do that. Look, I know how to close up and you could show me how to fix the alarm. Why don't you let me see to that? I'll just be half an hour or so, and promise to lock up carefully." He looked doubtful, but my thoughts were very persuasive.

"I don't know, Mrs. Buchanan…"

"Oh, call me Helen," I murmured. "No one will know. Just show me the alarm system – if I can't manage it, I could always call you for advice. You look tired – and the museum doesn't go in for overtime, does it?"

"Well," said Robbie, unable to see anything but my beautiful soulful eyes. "OK – it's quite a simple system, just alarms on the main and side door and these switches for the display rooms."

I bent over the control board and he smelt my expensive scent. What a woman, he thought, disloyally comparing me with his wife. Fortunately, I realised also that he knew better than to make a pass at a classy dame like me, but began to wonder if this shared breach of the rules would lead to closer encounters in the future.

"You'll need to exit by the security door here, when you've put on all the alarms." He indicated the door at the side of his security office, leading to a back path. The door had self-locking bolts that would close behind me, openable only by a code kept by the security staff and curator. I nodded efficiently, radiating calm and gratitude.

"You'll ring me when you leave?" he asked anxiously, now committed to letting me do the locking up. "Of course," I purred. "You get off home, it'll be fine."

At 5.45 p.m., alone in the museum, I went to the ladies rest room to start to transform into the mysterious psychic, olive skinned and much older in appearance. I donned an ornate gown and arranged a shawl around my shoulders. It was satisfyingly hard to recognise myself, with the dark, heavy eyebrows and black wig peeping out from a gold headdress. In the gypsy display room I placed candles on horizontal surfaces of empty cabinets around the caravan. Within the caravan, I arranged a table with two facing chairs and draped the table with a heavy velvet cloth. I placed candles within the interior, carefully shielded in glass storm protectors. I did not want to start a fire in this old wooden structure.

Finally I put a crystal ball in a heavy stand in the centre of the table. This had battery-operated illumination that would throw up an eerie light. I took a pack of tarot cards and placed them to one side of the table. The museum was located in an old house, adding to its old world atmosphere and the gypsy display room had a wide entry door, conveniently near to the corridor leading to the side entrance. There were two other doors in the room, one connecting with the next part of the museum, the other to a storeroom that had a door directly next to the side entrance. This was one reason why I had thought it so suitable for my plan. At 6.45 p.m. I turned off the alarms throughout the building and practised opening the side door, seeing if I could hide behind it and then slip into the store room. I made a quick call to Robbie, assuring him that I was leaving and had locked up. I did not want him conscientiously returning to the museum to check. I sensed that Jeannette had already arrived, waiting nervously in Klaxon Street and wondering if she should knock.

At a few minutes before 7 p.m., Jeannette was waiting outside the door. Waiting just within, I opened it before Jeannette could press the bell. Jeannette saw the door opening as if by magic, with no one standing there.

"Mrs. Summers," I pronounced, in a deep, Eastern voice, convincingly male. "You are expected. Madame Irina is preparing for you, in the room directly to your right."

She looked in the direction of the voice, hearing only the soft close of a door to one side. She turned and pushed this door, but it seemed to be locked. He had said the room on the right, but obviously not this close to the side entrance, she reflected. She walked cautiously down the corridor, with its dim lighting. Then she saw the open door of the gypsy display room, illuminated by candlelight. She stood uncertainly, looking at the caravan and hoping none of her friends would ever know she had consulted this strange psychic. I detected her thoughts easily.

"She's probably an absolute charlatan," she was saying to herself, "Just look at all this paraphernalia, it's like a circus attraction." I rustled my skirts in the rear of the caravan and called to her from the dark, shadowy inside.

"Jeannette, please enter. Take care on the steps, they're very old." My musical, hypnotic, strongly accented voice chimed with the idea of my being the seventh child of a seventh child for Jeannette. She was wondering if this could possibly be true, but the voice had the timbre she had always imagined a real Romany gypsy to have. She stepped into the caravan, glowing in candlelight.

"Please be seated," I said. I had checked that all she would see at first was a shadowy figure behind the table. At closer encounter, the low lighting showed a heavily made up woman, with eyes glinting in the flickering flames of the candles around the interior of the caravan. "I am Irina Bravitska," I intoned.

"Well, you know who I am," said Jeannette, sitting cautiously in the opposite chair. She was frightened but excited. This was at least an adventure.

"I know you are very troubled. Tell me, did you sort out the problem with your air ticket?" I was pleased to have picked up from Jeannette's thoughts outside the museum that she had delayed her return to New York, associated with difficulty in securing a flight for the following day. Jeannette looked suitably startled, but despite longing to believe in this psychic, she was considering that checking up on such details could be part of the way these people achieved impressive knowledge of their clients.

"But there is much more on your mind. How can I help you, Jeannette?"

Jeannette thought, just find Jason for me, but said nothing for a few moments. I smiled kindly.

"Yes, you are deeply worried about Jason, your dear son. He is lost to you, but…"

Jeannette stared in amazement, checking herself with the thought that this information too would be easily found, since she had toured mediums up and down the country asking about him.

"…wait a moment, he is lost but not on the other side," I said dreamily, my heavily ringed hands indicating the glowing crystal ball.

"Look into the crystal, Jeannette, and tell me what you see."

She gazed, trying to ignore the way the eerie light threw my face into ghostly shadows, making me seem a ghostly presence. I projected an image of Jason into the crystal ball. At first this was just based on sharing his likeness telepathically with Cass, but he was so near the surface of Jeannette's mind that I could soon generate it from her. Looking into the glinting glass, Jeannette saw a clear image of her son, as she had last seen him eight years before. She thought about their last day, before he disappeared in that park.

"This is a trick – I don't know how you're doing it, but you could easily obtain a picture of my son."

"I do not need tricks," I said softly. The image mutated into a little boy, running in the park. Jeannette gasped as she saw the playground equipment and the summer colours of the planting. The image was a little blurred, but clearly recognisable. Then the image changed, showing just the boy, but older, perhaps as he would now appear. I was working on an image shared with Cass, taking care not to show the schoolroom.

"Jason!" Jeannette looked up in awe. "So he is alive. Please, can you show me where he is?"

The image faded and I looked at her sadly. "It's never so simple as that. If he were on the other side, I could sense him more easily. In this world, there are too many distractions and interference in the ether. But possibly through your memories and the help of my spirit guides, we may find some clearer direction." I closed my eyes as though communing and Jeannette sat tensely, her mind in confusion, which was little help to me. I opened my eyes and gazed at Jeannette earnestly.

"The guides are telling me, we must go back in time, perhaps even to before he was born." This allowed me to detect some facts from her eager thoughts. After a few moments, I said slowly, "Ah, he was born in New York, yes? Your only child. Quite late in your marriage."

"We tried for years," admitted Jeannette. My eyes gleamed as I picked up that Jeannette and her husband had endured gruelling infertility investigations. I obtained a clear picture of Mr. Summers, an overweight businessman. Then I saw a fleeting image of another man.

"You had an affair," I murmured and Jeannette sat bolt upright, very alarmed. This was a closely kept secret. Even her friends had not known about it, still less her husband, although he had suspected as much later, when DNA testing of the lost boy's hair showed that he was unlikely to be the father. It had destroyed their marriage, but neither had publicised the reason. I could now clearly pick up an image of this man from Jeannette's thoughts, as well as their furtive meetings.

"You met him in Central Park, on a sunny day. At first you were just friends."

"How did you find this out?" gasped Jeannette. I now appeared to be in a trance, my voice seeming to come from far away. "Have no fear Jeannette, I keep many secrets for my clients. He was so attractive, you could not resist. Ah, so appealing, so kind. Blonde hair, like yours in your youth... he was younger than you. His name, that is difficult." Jeannette shivered, knowing that only she was aware of these details. I continued, drowsily. "Luke. His name was Luke Furman. And when you made love, it was magical. But the affair was very short. He went away."

Jeannette had started to sob. "Yes, he told me had to go abroad. He was always secretive about his work. I wondered if he was a spy, something like that. Maybe working for the CIA."

I was not a little alarmed, as these memories from Jeannette's thoughts became clearer. Luke was certainly a Binary. But I gazed into Jeannette's eyes, shutting down any chance of transmitting this encounter outside the mystical shadows of the caravan.

"The spirit guides tell me he knew of this pregnancy."

"Yes," said Jeannette, tears streaming down her face. "I told him, just before he had to leave. We knew we couldn't be together, he with his job, me with my marriage and work. He was very upset, promised to keep in touch."

"But he didn't."

Jeannette shook her head, desperately. "I never heard from him again."

"Yes," I said sadly. "Perhaps he was lost on a mission, it isn't clear. The guides are keeping something from me. It may be dangerous to think about him, Jeannette. Try to clear your mind so we can focus on your son."

Jeannette nodded eagerly. But I was becoming fearful that this passionate woman's thoughts would alert 'Luke'. Furman, I thought, with an inner smile: the Latin for thief was 'fur'. Naughty Luke, who decided to steal a child. I reflected that this telepath would have sensed Jeannette's thoughts straying to him from time to time, possibly giving it little attention as it was only to be expected.

"Jason disappeared before he started elementary school, but he attended a private kindergarten," I said. Partly guess work, but someone as rich as Jeannette would have opted for private kindergarten education. As I related this, I watched Jeannette's reaction, pleased to sense more information about this establishment, an expensive pre-school in New York.

"Yes, he was such a bright child. He was already reading, picking up things even before we taught him."

"And the day you lost him, you were just playing in the park."

"I was tired, closed my eyes for a moment while he was on a slide, but I must have dozed off. When I looked up, he was gone."

I sighed, muttering as though communicating with an invisible spirit guide. "No, please," I murmured. "Please tell us more." After a few moments, I gazed with deep sorrow at Jeannette. "The boy, your son, he is well, they say. But they will not tell me where. I sense that it is not in this country." This was a safe bet, since a nationwide search had been conducted. The Binaries would have tried to get him to a centre outside America, in case he slipped outside and was seen.

"Ask again!" cried Jeannette, but I had slumped back in the chair, my eyes shut in apparent exhaustion. I opened them narrowly, speaking with great regret.

"I am sorry – they will not tell us more this evening. I only sensed great danger, if you try to pursue your son. He is happy, well cared for… they at least told me that."

"But, Madame Bravitska, I must know more," wept Jeannette. "It's good to hear he is safe, but never to see him again, I can't bear it."

I sighed. "The spirits say you must think of him as dead to you, just remember him how he was. I wish I could give you better news."

"Can I see you again, another consultation? I don't care how much it costs. I feel certain you could locate him."

I stood up slowly. "Perhaps. I am now very tired, these communications across the boundaries have drained my powers. Please, you must leave now, my assistant will open the side door. Say nothing of this consultation, you must promise me that."

"I promise," whispered Jeannette, standing regretfully. She turned and climbed carefully down the flimsy ladder to the caravan. Emerging once more into the museum corridor, she saw the outer door open mysteriously. As before, this seemed to have opened without human hands. She paused at the door, intending to see if someone stood behind it but found it rigidly in position, impossible to budge. In my low male voice I murmured, "Good night, Mrs. Summers." Reluctantly, she stepped out into the street and the door closed firmly behind her.

Within the museum, I dashed back to the gypsy display room and extinguished all the candles, carefully stowing them in the large holdall bag. I stashed away the other items, looking wistfully at the tarot cards. I would have enjoyed doing a reading for Jeannette, but never mind, I had gleaned enough from the consultation. I had considered telling her that Jason was dead, but that could have made her make enquiries of the police, looking for his body. Binaries are never keen on involving the police, even in a case like this with the only information coming from an untraceable psychic medium.

When I was certain I had removed all trace of the strange event in that room, I quickly removed the make up, false eyebrows and wig. Then I switched on the alarms in the security office and quietly departed. When I returned home, I dialled the number that Gaston had given me. As expected, I was transferred to Kastor.

"Romain, how is she?" I said breathlessly, keeping up the agreed scenario of the distressed mother, although annoyed that I was genuinely quite upset.

"I'm so sorry, Helen, the news is as bad as we could have feared. They could treat the leukaemia, but she has a very serious resistant infection and she's been moved to the intensive paediatric unit."

"I need to speak to Sylvie," I said, in a desperate, low voice.

"Perhaps tomorrow," said 'Romain' soothingly. "She's too upset today."

"Of course, Alexander and I will come over, as soon as we can get a flight," I stuttered. Kastor would know that I could stall Alexander on this, but also that we would receive a call very soon to say it was too late, except for the funeral. I started to transmit a thought image of the cheval mirror, but received a warning message from 'Romain' to avoid telepathy via this unusual means of communication. Kastor had sensed that I had news, also that I was surprisingly disturbed about the fate of my baby. He was musing, in an open thought, as to whether I had picked up some of my twin's mothering instincts, when we ended the call.

42

CASSANDRA

At noon on the next day, Friday, I was punctual for the mirror connection. Helen practically pulled me into our space, obviously wanting to speak urgently.

"I'm sorry you had to decide so quickly about Grace," I said. News of her succumbing to illness had already been related to Alexander and Helen.

"Getting soft in my old age," said Helen, with false brightness. "But on the other matter Sis, you were right. Jason – his name outside - was nabbed by a Binary, but it's not clear whether the father was responsible. Obviously, Jeannette has no idea. She's grief stricken, it's the only thing she cares or thinks about, when not occupied with work." Helen relayed Luke Furman's name.

"He wouldn't be using that name now," I said. "I'm thinking, he must have found out where the boy was at kindergarten, possibly visited the place and saw how telepathic he was."

"The snatch took place in a park. And you think this Luke may be now teaching at Lochinstoun?"

"Not necessarily. He could have just wanted to bring the boy in, but it would make sense for him to stay near him, maybe transferring to any of the foreign centres with him. Why else would he bother, take such risk?"

"An emotional bond with a child," mused Helen. "We don't go in for that, as a rule, but with the way I'm feeling about Grace, I can understand it. Outside influences, Cass - I'm getting as sentimental as them. I have to keep pretending to being sorrowful about missing her, perhaps that's why."

"I've bonded with my children," I said. "We're not so unalike, Helen. I think you care about losing Grace more than you admit."

Helen sighed. "I'm guessing it will be a very small funeral. You and 'Romain' won't be there, it'd be too risky."

"I think you'll see Grace again," I said. I had a sudden vision of Helen holding a child, gazing into the older Grace's eyes.

"You'll make me cry!" said Helen. But she was pleased at this prediction. "Meanwhile," she continued, "it's over to you and Kastor now. Be very careful. You know that Jason can never go back and pick up his old life with his mother."

"Could Jeannette come in? Is she telepathic?"

"Very intuitive, but if she is telepathic it's completely dormant. It would have been a disaster if she'd suspected what I was up to or who I was, and I'm sure she didn't have a clue. Right now, she's probably desperately trying to contact that medium again. Sadly, she won't find a trace."

"Maybe there should be a few mentions of the mysterious Madame Bravitska on the Internet, you know, a few veiled hints and how clients mustn't mention they've seen her."

"Good idea, Sis, but I'll be careful not to over egg it. Less is more with this kind of deception. I'm more worried she'll be thinking about Luke again, although I tried to warn her off that."

I gazed at my twin. "You're thinking, you'll be leaving Alexander after the funeral."

"Overcome with grief, yes," said Helen. "It seems the best option. It's time I was moving on, anyway. Maybe the Binaries could help me with a disappearance, this time."

I nodded sadly and with a little wave, Helen stepped out of our space.

Kastor came back to the apartment later that day to find me surrounded by our twins and Helen's, playing with a mind tent. Grace looked the picture of health, being rocked gently in the hands of a nanny. He looked questioningly at the mind tent, which the twins were leaping in and out of as a pretend space ship.

"Hagen lent it to me, just for this afternoon," I said, "Makes a great toy."

The mind tent was designed to block telepathed thoughts to allow complete rest but this one was not switched on. Seeing Kastor's disapproval of medical equipment being used to amuse children, I smiled persuasively. "It's OK, they don't have any patient who needs it right now. But I think it's time you went back for tea, children."

Megan immediately started to round them up, while the other nanny popped Grace into her pushchair. Megan started to fold up the mind tent but I stopped her.

"You've got enough to carry back," I said. "I'll have it sent over in the morning." Megan nodded gratefully.

Before Kastor had time to consider some quality contact with them, the children were saying polite goodbyes and being ushered out of the door. As soon as the door shut, I adjusted the tent back into position and attached its cord to a power socket. The filaments in the hexagonal panes started to glow with a slowly moving sequence of lights, part of the blocking system. I lifted the flap and beckoned Kastor to join me on the pile of cushions that the children had dragged in.

"This seemed a good way of having a safe discussion," I said, when Kastor was sitting rather uncomfortably within the tent. I told him

Helen's news about Jeannette's son and he frowned.

"Not so much further, as we don't have their names within the organization," he pointed out.

"No, but that shouldn't be too difficult – bring that list of names from your study."

He fetched it obediently, but when I started to study it, looking increasingly perplexed, he smiled. "We're in a blocking tent. That includes remote viewing."

I started to take it outside the tent and he took my arm to prevent me. "This is getting increasingly dangerous. We've no idea if the man who took Jason has long distance telepathy, but it's possible, especially if he really he is a teacher at the school. They select teachers for their exceptional skills. So there's a faint chance he could be picking up Jeannette's thoughts about visiting the amazing Madame Bravitska. At the very least he might begin to guess that Jeannette has been given great hope that her son is alive – and possibly thinking of him, much more than in recent years."

"I've been having this feeling that it could concern Leo," I said. "We have to find this teacher."

"I think we should involve Gaston," said Kastor. I rolled my eyes, knowing that the security chief would disapprove of the whole escapade.

"Supposing it's Gaston who's the father!" I said suddenly, remembering that Gaston had once mentioned that he had fathered a child in the US.

"Don't be ridiculous," Kastor retorted. "He's been here at Woodstock for twenty years at least. If he had a child over there, it was many years ago. And Gaston would be so unlikely to have a relationship with an outsider, especially one where the outsider could fall pregnant. Also he's loyal to a fault, he'd never put the organization under threat by secretly bringing in a child."

"I must admit I've had no inkling it could be him – but this is all so strange, Kastor, it makes one wonder about everybody."

"I'm going to call him," said Kastor, stepping out of the tent and signalling towards the security centre. He came back into the tent and said Gaston would be with us shortly. I went to make some tea while Kastor idly examined the list, spotting names of teachers that he remembered at the school. Surely, none of them could kidnap a child, he thought and wished once again that I had left it well alone.

43

When Gaston arrived he marched straight into the apartment. Kastor must have told him that we'd be in the blocking tent.

"Well, this is cosy," said Gaston, perching awkwardly on the cushions. I thoughtfully went out to fetch chairs. The tent was large enough to drape over a hospital bed, so there was space enough. His humour disappeared when he heard the story of Jeannette's son.

"You should have both come to me earlier," he admonished. "As it happens, I do know of a child who reached the organization in a strange way. And yes, it was around eight years ago. There's a small Binary branch not far from New York and one night the security guards found a boy at the bottom of one of the manholes. He'd been drugged and was wrapped in a blanket. The alarm had gone off when the manhole was opened, but whoever left him there had planned it well, making sure the manhole was not locked on the inside for when he took the boy down there. The guards searched the area, but found no one. The five year old boy was found to be highly telepathic. They transferred him to the Virginia centre where there was a proper children's wing. They should have done more checks, of course. By the time they realised there was a search going on outside for the boy, he knew too much about the organization, and his own telepathy, to be returned."

"Why was this not better known?" asked Kastor. "I've never

heard about it."

"A decision was made to ensure great secrecy – even I don't know the name he was given."

"Surely they would have run checks to see if the father was one of us?"

"If they did, I didn't hear of them. Or if this was planned, the father could have got at the records and deleted or changed his DNA data. The whole thing was a mess. Some thought the mother had brought him there, possibly knowing she'd mated with a telepath and wanting the child to be brought up with us. I understand there was a concern about a shortage of rescued children at the time."

He paused and smiled thinly at me. "As you're aware, Cassandra, the pregnancy rate within our communities was generally low until you came along."

"So it was all hushed up," I said.

"It was felt that the least known about the episode, the better. This was hardly a rescue – taking the only child from a mother, with the police launching a nationwide search. Scandalous neglect of the basic security that we all grow up with. I'm not aware that the father's identity was ever pursued in any detail. The Americans are keener than us at recruiting telepaths into their secret services and they don't welcome investigation that might expose those agents."

"But now, it may be possible that the father is within our organization," I reasoned. "And that he was the one who left the child to be discovered, taking care to minimise the chance of the boy being linked to him."

Gaston was shrugging, contemplating this seemingly unlikely possibility, when I got up to go to the loo. I was making some more tea in the kitchen when I suddenly screamed and the two men leapt out of the tent. I was leaning on the kitchen worktop, shivering.

"It's Leo! He's been trying to contact me. I had a strange image when I left the tent, then another one just now – and I can sense him calling. It's indistinct, very unclear. He's trapped somewhere."

Kastor put his arm round me, trying to project calm. "Focus, try to see where he is."

Gaston turned to urgently signal to his officers. He also picked up the phone to contact the school.

"It must have happened while we were in that tent, so Leo couldn't reach me. He's very frightened. It's a dark place, no light at all."

"We should go over to the surveillance centre," said Kastor. "Gaston, we need a plan of the school."

Gaston nodded, remembering how I was able to locate Ryden Asgard in Casablanca, just from studying a map of the city. We all rushed out of the apartment and down to the underground station by the staircase.

44

Sitting in the train on the way to the surveillance block, I was pale and shaking.

"He's panicking, afraid he can't breathe. I can't make much sense of his thoughts otherwise."

"Try to calm him. We need to know what happened," said Kastor, also very pale.

I breathed deeply, trying to send soothing thoughts to Leo and at the same time asking who did this to him. Eventually I turned to the men and said grimly, "A teacher put him there. Oh, I think he's been buried alive!"

"Try not to put that in his mind,," said Kastor.

I had a stronger connection with Leo, powerful even at the great distance from the Scottish school. But Kastor's telepathy was up to the challenge, as he nodded to indicate he could sense him too. He was sending messages that we were coming to rescue him when the train reached the surveillance centre. Gaston travelled on to the security centre stop to fetch the school plans.

Manes had arrived at the surveillance centre, having received the alarm call. "A teacher is missing, and a boy. They're searching the school tunnels but haven't found Leo yet."

"His signalling is getting very faint," I said. "How long can someone survive without air?"

"At least a couple of hours, more if the hole is larger," said someone who had just rushed in, and I turned to see Dr. Hagen Philips. "We must focus on stopping him panicking, using up the oxygen."

Kastor and I sat down together, eyes gazing in the direction of the school as we tried to calm our son.

Manes picked up a folder. "The teacher is one of their best, Saul Pantheras. The boy is Linus Nyvern. No known connection. How could this be missed?"

"Linus, son of the god Apollo," I said, proud of the mythological knowledge I had acquired at Binaries. "Who was accidentally killed by his father…"

Kastor and Manes looked up, with slight irritation, at this interruption.

"Time for mythology later," said Manes. "There's no reason to suspect that the teacher wanted to harm him."

"When did Saul Pantheras start working there?" asked Kastor.

"About seven years ago, according to this file," replied Manes. "Exemplary record. He came from the Virginia Centre where he trained as a teacher. But it looks as though he also had considerable experience in the field as an assessor."

"For example, visiting schools and liaising with our field teacher operatives?" asked Kastor, piecing together how Saul Pantheras would have found out where the boy was being educated. "He must have followed the boy into the park where he was abducted."

Manes shrugged. "That would be consistent with the background data in this file."

Gaston entered the room with the plans of the school. Kastor nudged me, saying he'd continue to keep in contact with Leo.

"Surely they should have found him by now," I said desperately. "He must be sending out a general alarm signal."

"There are several underground tunnels – but he may be somewhere in the grounds," said Manes. "There's a general search in progress. They've detected his signal but if he's contained in a hole, or box, it could be acting as a block, preventing exact location."

I went over to the table where the plans were laid out. I took a deep breath and concentrated my gaze on the plans. After a couple of minutes, I looked up, pointing to a location on a plan of the grounds.

"I think he's here," I said.

Gaston grimaced, seeing where my finger was resting. "The old mausoleum." The others looked at each other in horror.

"Mausoleum, what, in a tomb?" I gasped. Gaston signalled to the school to focus the search there. Kastor spoke quietly to me, the only one who did not know this building.

"It's been there from before the mansion was converted into a school. It has the tombs of previous owners. It was always out of bounds, kids used to dare each other to try to get in."

A tense few minutes passed, waiting for news from the school. Finally Gaston nodded, indicating that the search party had found Leo.

"He's barely conscious, but alive."

I focused on him, trying to get a response but having to be content with sending soothing messages. Gaston turned to the others, as he received more information.

"He was in a tomb, with the lid closed. As soon as they were in the mausoleum, it was obvious which one had been recently disturbed. I'll get more details by phone. Meanwhile, the search is being directed towards tracking down Mr. Pantheras and the boy."

Hagen Philips was already on the phone to the sick bay at the school. He spoke reassuringly. "Don't worry, Cassandra. He's being taken straight to the school doctor. It seems he may have exhausted himself trying to push that lid open."

"But why did he take Leo?" I asked.

Gaston gave me an unusually sympathetic glance. "As a natural telepath, with frequent contact with Leander, your connection with him is probably much more intense than it would be for the rest of us. Also, your channel with him might be more open."

"I've been so careful, not sending thoughts, trying to block."

"The way our thought channels develop is much more rigid," said Kastor. "We train to be able to focus on an individual and our minds develop with these channels. You've probably been thinking about this mystery, particularly today when you heard his name and that of his likely father. It seems that Saul Pantheras is highly adept at picking up such thoughts and he'd have been even more alert to it, if he knew that Jeannette was also thinking strongly about her son again."

"He's probably been living with this possibility every day," murmured Manes, "training his thoughts to pick up any risk of detection."

"So he really did all this, just to be with his son," I said, feeling a slight tinge of compassion, which I rapidly suppressed, with my growing anger at the teacher. "But I'd like to kill him for doing this to Leo, to tear him limb from limb."

"Congratulations," said Gaston, "you're most definitely a fully fledged Binary, in case you ever had any doubts. That's exactly the fate I'd like Pantheras to end up with."

Kastor squeezed my hand. "Leo must have picked up your thoughts too - and he's too young to know how to conceal them. Saul

Pantheras would easily have detected that Leo was thinking about why you were so interested in those names and a boy at the school."

Manes smiled at Kastor's obvious pride in his son, murmuring, "Incredibly advanced for his age, if Leo picked up all that."

"I've been such an idiot, to pursue this," I said. Kastor knew that this was not the time to remind me that I had been warned. But he silently transmitted that the teacher would have recognised Leo's ability and would have acted quickly if Leo let slip any idea of a connection with Linus. Without my interest and investigation, the first they would have heard about it was when Pantheras's disappearance was noticed, with much less time or warning to save Leo.

"Sooner or later, it would have come out," said Manes, picking up the gist of Kastor's thought message. "But today, sensing his tracks were being discovered, he obviously panicked. Saul Pantheras must have been terrified that Leo would speak to his friends, or to other teachers. Perhaps he even innocently asked Pantheras whether he knew a child named Jason."

Kastor had picked up the school file. "Pantheras teaches the junior classes – mathematics, early orienteering skills, field biology, geography. Apparently he's very popular with the pupils."

"I'll give him popular," I said angrily. "Can I help with the search for him? Can we go up there?"

"Certainly not tonight," said Gaston. "Possibly we could arrange a helicopter in the morning. I'm not sure it would be advisable for you to go, Cassandra. If he's channelled you, he'll be extremely alert to your movements. Hagen, is there a chance that Leo could be brought down here, if he's fit enough for transport in the morning?"

Hagen looked up, a phone in his hand. "They're making him comfortable now, giving him a sedative. There were old bones in the tomb. Leander must have been scared out of his wits. His hands were tied and he was gagged. It seems Pantheras used a crow bar to lift off the stone lid."

"Leo doesn't scare easily," said Kastor, with an anxious glance at me, for I was picturing this grim scene all too clearly. "But I agree he needs some expert care, medical and psychological."

"St. Anthony's would be the more obvious choice…" began Hagen, but stopped on receiving chilling looks from Leo's parents. Our thought message of a firm 'no' resounded through the group.

"He needs to be with his mother and father," said Gaston, unexpectedly. "And Cassandra is after all an expert mind healer. Clea is here at the moment too, so she may be able to help with any subconscious factors."

Manes had sent for sandwiches and coffee, since most of the group had missed an evening meal. We sat around a meeting room table, recovering our appetites now that the threat to Leo had been removed, while Gaston consulted with colleagues about how to track down the fugitive teacher and Linus. Saul Pantheras had presumably prepared for having to leave the school at any time, possibly having identified a good hiding place. Or, they discussed ominously, he could even have involved an outsider. As Gaston said drily, he seemed to be rather persuasive with females. They thought it unlikely that Pantheras would have told the boy that he was his father before leaving Lochinstoun. This would be shocking news to an unprepared Binary and his less disciplined thoughts would be readily detected.

"So Linus may just think it's a great adventure – or an unusual orienteering exercise," I mused.

"But he'll know by now that it isn't an exercise," said Kastor. "That's always a group activity, heavily supervised."

"Do you have an up to date photograph of Linus?" I asked and Manes got up, fetching another folder. It was no surprise that the surveillance centre had regular monitoring information on all the pupils at the school, as well as the teachers. I looked at Linus's latest school portrait, a fair haired boy with a large grin, resembling the images I had captured of Janus. Staring at the picture, I tried to visualise the boy, to see if I could see him in his present surroundings. Kastor watched me warily. He felt that the least Pantheras sensed of my abilities, the better. At present the teacher might just be worried about Leo's thoughts.

"Don't try to contact Linus. We'll find them, I don't want this deranged teacher to come after you while he's out there, desperate."

"I'm safe here, surely?" I said. "I can see how going up there might be a problem, until he's caught."

"Pantheras won't harm his son and he won't come anyway near here," said Manes.

I closed my eyes, strengthening my image of Linus-Janus, using remote viewing rather than any attempt to reach his thoughts. When I opened my eyes again, I said, "He's in a kind of cottage, a small room with wooden beams. I can see Pantheras with him, speaking to him. Linus doesn't look happy – do you think he's heard the news, understands why Pantheras has taken him from the school?"

"That's enough, close down, he'll detect you," said Kastor.

"OK," I said reluctantly. "But if you have an ordnance survey map of the area, I could have a go at trying to locate that cottage."

"They could be miles away," said Kastor. "It's been a few hours since they left."

"Linus was noted to be missing at supper time, 7 p.m." said Manes. "Leo had his tea at 6 p.m. – I'm guessing Pantheras dealt with him first, then went back for Linus."

"The map idea is worth a try," said Gaston. Manes told a junior officer to go to the map store and fetch all he could find on northeast Scotland.

45

After trying my previously successful ability to dowse with a map, I was disappointed that I felt no strong location for the fugitives. "Perhaps it's because I've never met either of them face to face," I murmured. "I don't know how this dowsing works."

"The search party will go on all night and until they're found," said Kastor. "We should go back to Askeys and get some rest."

"Yes," said Gaston. "You can leave it to the surveillance and security teams now. We'll also look into the deviant teacher's background in more detail, to see what skills he's picked up along the way."

In the train back to Askeys, I tried to sense Leo's thoughts, despite Kastor saying he would be deeply asleep, sedated. "I want him to know we're here to look after him, as soon as he wakes," I said stubbornly. I agreed to drinking some malt chocolate and retiring to bed, knowing I'd probably wake up if Leo started transmitting to me.

"When shall I learn, not to interfere?" I murmured, as Kastor came into the bedroom.

"Never, I'm afraid."

"I'm sorry Kastor," I said, sipping the malt drink.

He smiled. "Life's never dull with your strange and undisciplined range of abilities. Dangerous quests are part of the package."

I shook my head. "I never imagined it would risk harm to Leo"

"You told me you couldn't ignore that kind of message, the image of the boy in the schoolroom," said Kastor. "You knew you'd be involved somehow. It was a prediction, probably unavoidable. It may also have saved Leander's life." Kastor still preferred to use Leo's full name.

"I wonder how Linus is taking it, the discovery that this teacher has been his father all along."

"We all occasionally wondered about our parents, even believing them to be dead. Jason's name would have been changed as soon as he entered the organization. But he must have a few memories of his life before he came in. The counsellors and trainers will have done their best to minimise them, but they'll surface now. Perhaps too, he'll be remembering that he was called Jason on the outside. They'll have done their best to erase that memory."

"Anyway, he'll be asking about his mother," I suggested. "Pantheras will tell him she's dead, as the boy will have been told."

Kastor nodded slowly, murmuring, "Yes, that is what he'd most likely say, along with how he 'rescued' the boy from life in an orphanage outside."

When I finally fell asleep, it was inevitable that I would have dreams. I was in a fairground, at first enjoying the sounds and bright lights of the rides and stalls. It was evening. Passing the fortuneteller's tent, I saw a gaudily dressed woman with a gold headscarf wrapped tightly round her head, gazing at me over a glowing crystal ball. I paused but the woman said nothing, narrowing her eyes as though seeing something unfortunate that was better left untold. Then I went into a ghost ride, rattling along in a train like the ones in the Binary underground system. Cobwebs brushed my face and luminous skeletons leered at me. I looked up and saw Leo dangling from a torture apparatus, about to fall into the hands of a skeleton and screamed. I woke up, as did Kastor, hearing me cry out in my sleep. But I could not sense Leo, still asleep in the sick bay. I drowsily told Kastor about the scary images and he agreed it was my mind sorting out the fears of the day.

I dropped back to sleep and into the dream. Now I was walking through the fairground in daylight, but it had become a children's play park. A woman with a small boy – in the dream, I knew they were Jeannette and Jason. A fair haired man watched them from trees around the park. Then I was in a cottage, with rain falling outside. The same fair haired man was sitting disconsolately, his head in his hands. The teenager opposite him was speaking angrily. There was a woman in the kitchen of the croft, staring at the pair, her face in shadows.

"We must go back," said the teenager, "We've had such a long journey. Now I'm tired and hungry and I want to be with the others."

"We can never return," muttered the fair-haired man, who I guessed to be Saul Pantheras. I found myself outside the cottage, looking at the landscape. I saw a small road sign at the end of the lane. The names of the places were unfamiliar and hard to see clearly. Incongruously, the fortuneteller appeared beside me.

"Hellpool, Crossed and Scaring," she murmured. "Barricades and Sandbags."

"Those aren't real places," I said irritably and the fortuneteller replied, "Near enough, my dear," then started to sing but seemed to have forgotten the words. At first it sounded like "Tum-ti-tum," then "Terra, terree." The fortuneteller smiled enigmatically and disappeared.

The scene changed again. I was sitting on a verandah, overlooking the sea. Helen was beside me at a table, holding Grace with uncharacteristic tenderness. A cream tea was spread out on the cloth and Helen said happily, "This is so great. It all turned out well, who'd have thought?"

Then I saw Leo running towards us, wearing a Halloween

skeleton outfit and I screamed again, jolting awake.

Kastor eyed me wearily. "Hellpool, Crossed and Scaring," I muttered. "I'm sure they're clues to the fugitives. I think they're in a Scottish croft, somewhere remote."

Kastor sat up, becoming alert. "Even the Scots don't have place names like that. But I'll call the surveillance centre anyway, they've got a team working through the night on this."

"Barricades and sandbags," I added. "I think that was it. Those aren't the proper names, but like them in some way. Oh, and I don't know if there's a place called 'Tum-ti-tum', 'Tara' or 'Teree' but that might be worth checking."

Kastor smiled, picking up my thought image of a gypsy woman singing. "You must have got that wrong, but I'll mention it."

It was 4 a.m. but a surveillance officer dutifully noted down the names, saying he would do a map and computer search. After a few minutes, he rang back.

"How about, Heylipol, Crossapol and Scarinish?" he asked. "And there are places called Barrapol and Sandaig near them. But they're in the Hebrides – on an island called Tiree. How on earth could they have got there?"

"Worth a try," said Kastor. "If you focus on that area, you could catch them before they move on in the morning."

"Hellpool," I murmured, "How appropriate. How dare that man do this to Leo? He deserves to be crossed and very, very scared."

"I expect he is, already," said Kastor.

"There's a woman involved," I said. "I couldn't see her clearly though." Kastor picked up the phone again. All information could be useful.

We tried unsuccessfully to sleep, waiting for more news. Eventually we got up at 6 a.m. and went over to the Binary labyrinth to take an early breakfast in the restaurant. Manes came to join us. He was excited, although looking bleary eyed and unshaven.

"We've got them," he announced. "We sent a helicopter to Tiree. Pantheras was guarding his thoughts to avoid detection, but the boy was signalling. They were with an outsider woman who's helped them. We've had to bring her in too."

"How did they get there?" asked Kastor.

"Not much information yet, but they must have driven all evening with one or more accomplices, then reached Tiree by boat. The helicopter had air rescue markings. With any luck any locals who spotted it will accept the story that they were air lifting the woman for treatment on the mainland."

I was looking dreamily towards the north. "Leo's awake," I said, smiling. "His thoughts are very confused but he seems to be OK."

"You'll see him soon," said Manes. He helped himself to a coffee. A good night's work, but there were some difficult interrogations and decisions ahead.

46

A couple of hours later, Kastor and I went to the helicopter pad to meet the group coming down from Scotland. The fugitives were taken off first, bundled quickly away by security officers. An exhausted fair haired man that I knew to be Saul Pantheras gave me a nasty, fixed stare and I flinched. It was a look of hatred. He was handcuffed but Linus was not. He too glanced at me, without recognition, following the direction of his father's gaze. A dark haired woman, restrained by a security officer, shuffled out. She was plainly terrified, looking around at the landing strip and wondering what kind of place this was. Then Leo emerged, accompanied by a young nurse. He ran towards us, grinning. He looked pale but otherwise unscathed.

The nurse stood uncertainly as hugs were exchanged and I sensed her unease at this display of affection, so I said "Leo, you must go with nurse and see the doctor."

I silently told him that we would see him later but also quickly asked, "Leo, did you tell Mr. Pantheras you'd sensed my thoughts, about the boy who was in the helicopter with you?"

Leo looked affronted. "Of course not, mummy. But he said he'd picked up something from me. I didn't really understand – he was so friendly, then so horrible."

Kastor and I looked at each other with concern, before smiling at him reassuringly as he too was led away.

Later, Gaston signalled that we might wish to watch some of the interrogation of Pantheras. Kastor was judged too involved to be one of the interrogators himself. He advised me not to come, knowing it could be upsetting, but I announced that I wouldn't miss it for the world. We entered the adjoining room with a two-way mirror. As we took our seats, next to Antoine who was already in the observation chamber, Gaston and Manes were grilling Saul Pantheras. Despite obvious tiredness, he sat insolently, glaring at his interrogators.

"Let Moira go," he said, his accent convincingly Scottish. "She knows very little, nothing about the telepathy. She just thinks Lochinstoun is a special type of private school."

"Too late for that, I'm afraid," said Gaston. "You'll be telling us next that you care what happens to her, having involved her in your treacherous plans. So it was her croft on Tiree?"

"It used to belong to her parents. She's an innocent outsider. I told her Linus's mother wanted to take him away and that I'd never see him again."

"Another outsider relationship?" asked Gaston, with distaste.

Pantheras sighed. "I couldn't have a relationship with one of us, they'd have detected my secret. Oh, come on, we all do it from time to time, they're so easy."

"Speak for yourself," said Gaston. "We're not brought up to exploit them, other than commercially. You knew that what you were doing was a threat to our whole community."

Pantheras shrugged. Manes asked him, "But why try to kill Leo?"

"Oh, that little pest," he replied wearily. In the observation chamber, I bristled.

"Guard your thoughts," murmured Kastor. "He'll soon sense we're here." As if in response, Pantheras glanced at the black-mirrored wall. But he gave no other sign as he turned to Manes.

"I think he was on to me soon after he arrived. He saw me once with Linus, just talking, and gave me that gaze he has. Bright little chap, isn't he? I could detect he was asking himself whether I was Linus's 'daddy'. I didn't expect a child arriving with such strong thoughts about parents."

"But what made you act so suddenly yesterday?"

"In the morning, I was taking one of the introductory classes, assessing how good they were at images. We were just playing with pictures of their experiences, when I detected a clear image of Linus, when he was Jason. It was a nasty surprise, then I focused on Leo and he was picturing me in a park, looking at Jason. He didn't seem worried about it, just interested. I might have known that witch's son would have unusual abilities. I asked him to produce a picture of the nursery back at Binary and he did it instantly, with an air of innocence. He knew I was trying to read his thoughts, though, trying to block."

In the observation room, I bit my lip and whispered, "Does everyone call me a witch, behind my back?"

"No!" said Kastor and Antoine simultaneously, sharing anger at this forbidden word and the casual way Pantheras used it, with a faint sneer. He did not appear to care what the interrogators thought of him, knowing he was unlikely to survive for long. Gaston shot him a bolt of telepathic pain and he flinched, but still managed an audacious smile.

"But why kill him, why not just tie him up or sedate him, so he could be easily found once you'd got away?" asked Manes.

"If he could pick that much up at long distance, he'd be able to help find where I was. Anyway, I didn't kill him – I just wanted him scared and far too worried about being in a tomb to be tracking us."

"He would have run out of air within a few hours. And the lead lining of the tomb – you knew that would make his signals extremely hard to detect. Luckily it was fragmented with age, but you didn't know that."

"Yes, well, I still thought he'd be found in time, and if not, just collateral damage. I could have simply strangled him – give me some credit for not wanting to do that. I love those children."

I was breathing fast, controlling my wish to project a terrifying image, something to wipe the cool smile off Pantheras. "Let me go in there," I blurted. "He knew Leo would probably die in that tomb, he wanted him to suffer first."

I sprang up, but Kastor took my arm, making me sit again. "He's just taunting us, Cassandra. He's almost certainly sensed you're here. He could simply stay silent, knowing his likely fate. They have to get him to tell the whole story while he's in this confiding mood."

Glancing again at the mirror wall, Pantheras said he needed a pee and was taken out for a comfort break. Gaston came into the observation chamber, giving me an unexpectedly kind look.

"Smooth, isn't he? Would you like us to bury him alive, Cassandra? That can be arranged."

"I don't understand how his obvious love for his son could be combined with such callousness," I murmured in response.

Gaston produced an ironic smile. "He didn't have the benefit of parenting classes. We've now got his full file from the Virginia centre. His performance was always excellent, but he was also a loner. There were queries that he might be gay, but no record of relationships within the community with men or women. It seems his abiding obsession was his need to be near that boy. Before you came in, he was telling us how he followed his progress, sometimes watching the mother with him in Central Park. He took the teaching training with the possible idea of becoming a field teacher, so that he could have closer contact at the boy's school, but his telepathy was far too good for that. We don't like high range telepaths to be working in those outside roles. It's a difficult life for them and there's too much risk of taking an over obvious interest in the children, if they detect potential talent."

"Did he meet with Jason, before the abduction?"

"I don't think so," Gaston replied. "But he's coming back in – we'll be asking him about the abduction now."

Coffee was brought into the observation chamber and the interrogation room. Gaston paused before returning, and placed a hand on my shoulder. This was most uncharacteristic behaviour and I looked up, startled. "No one calls you a witch, Cassandra," he said softly. "All those who know you are in awe of your talents and love you for them. We're so fortunate you're with us. You're still learning the risks and scope of your abilities - as well as the pleasures."

He glanced at Kastor, but with no trace of the lascivious images that he had created during the early days of Kastor's relationship with me. Antoine's mouth dropped open at this kind side of Gaston's nature. He knew nothing of the friendship with Aunt V and very little of the shared adventures of the past six years. Regaining his normal sardonic expression, Gaston abruptly left the chamber.

"Do you want to hear more of the interrogation?" asked Kastor, also bemused at this avuncular side to Gaston. "I can tell you all about it later if you like – meanwhile, you could go and see how Leo is getting on."

"And interrupt Clyppie? I think I'd rather stay – she wouldn't like me to interfere with the counselling, or whatever she's doing. If she agrees, we could perhaps have Leo over in the apartment this afternoon."

Kastor nodded, smiling. Our attention refocused on the interrogation room, where Pantheras was now sitting again, playing with a glass of water in front of him.

"Let's go back to the abduction," said Gaston. Pantheras shrugged, as if completely disinterested.

"You're going to kill me anyway," he said with a shrug. "Why not just get it over with?

"Kill you?" asked Gaston, his eyebrows raised. "Well it depends. Perhaps you'd rather undergo extensive treatment at St. Anthony's. There are some most interesting experiments in progress that you could help with." Pantheras paled and I thought of Ryden Asgard, reduced to the mental age of a toddler in Casablanca, now 'helping' Clea with her painful research into mind repair and the mysterious mechanisms of telepathic talent.

"In the mean time," continued Gaston, transmitting the idea that his cooperation could alter the type of fate awaiting him, "explain how you decided on abducting Jason."

"I wasn't planning it at first. It was enough just to see him occasionally in the park. Then a field teacher contacted me, asking for help in assessing a child in his kindergarten class. I didn't even realise it would be Jason, with other work on at the time and trying not to think about him too much. I remember walking into the class, posing as an inspector and I sensed his high range ability straight away. It was like a thunderbolt - I'd never been that close. In the park, I had to keep well away from them, in case Jeannette saw me. Jason was wonderful, full of thoughts and images. He also sensed me, gazing at me in wonderment. He'd never be in contact with someone he could share thoughts with so easily. I felt this bond, a wish to take him in my arms and be with him - it was astonishing, unanticipated. We're not exactly prepared for that in our careful conditioning, are we?"

"The field teacher – did he know what you were planning? What happened to him?"

"I told him the child had very little potential. I didn't want a report being sent back to one of the centres, with a request for a more assessment. I said something about low level monitoring. The teacher was surprised. Not a good telepath, but perceptive enough to know that Jason was special."

Manes looked at a file of information just received from the

Virginia Centre. "The teacher died – an accident. Not long before the abduction."

"A most unfortunate accident, yes," said Pantheras, with a sly smile. He looked with irritation at his interrogators, who were eyeing him with cold distain. "Oh, come on. Of course he had to have an accident. Just a bit more… incidental damage. Then I had to wait until interest in his case died down."

"Why didn't you eliminate Jeannette, for good measure?" demanded Gaston.

"I'm not stupid. Anyone in that park could see she doted on him, shame about that, but her death would have been an accident too far, don't you think?"

I watched with horrified fascination. This man had acted out of love for his son, an unexpected and driving passion. Would I kill to be with my children, if they were taken from me, I wondered, or was it the ruthless Binary upbringing that had caused this tragedy?

Meanwhile Manes asked, "Did you think for a moment what this would do to his mother?"

"Yes, but she's only an outsider, for heaven's sake, with no idea what it's like to be a telepath out there, living with them. Leaving the boy with those other ordinary preschool children - I knew he'd suffer, be a misfit. That's why we rescue babies, isn't it, to give them a proper chance of a fulfilling life?"

"You could have waited until he was old enough to decide for himself."

"Oh yes, that's what I'd have been told. But I didn't want to wait, what, 15 years maybe. As it is, I've seen him daily, watch him grow up, talk with him."

"Without him knowing you were his father."

"He knew we had a connection. But many of us feel that with

our teachers, some of them. I told him the truth last night in Tiree."

"And how did he react?" asked Manes.

"Confused, upset. He doesn't remember much of his past life, a lot of that had been conditioned out of him. He asked about his mother."

"And you said she was dead," said Gaston, glowering.

"Yeah, Moira didn't take that too well either. I told him by thought transfer, urging him to keep quiet when Moira was with us, but he's only 13 and he was angry, naturally. I'd have brought him round, eventually. I told him his mother wanted rid of him, that she'd been planning to ship him off to a boarding school, but when she died I had a chance to rescue him. I had to be very persuasive, his memories of his mother were surfacing, so he didn't accept my story easily. He wasn't ready to understand why I had to bring him in with us, but he'd have understood, in time."

"Do you have any idea of the damage you've done, to your son and to us?" Gaston was containing his fury, already contemplating the problems of damage limitation in this case.

"Yes – and I don't care. It was good while it lasted. I was able to be with him and help him to develop."

"Let's talk about what happened after the boy was found, in the tunnel at the New York centre," said Manes, as weary and angry as Gaston, but knowing they had to complete their investigation.

In the observation chamber, I turned to Kastor and said, "I've heard enough. I'll go back to the apartment. This Moira, what will happen to her?"

"I don't know," said Kastor. "We'll talk, later. Get some rest, I'll join you soon."

47

I was overwhelmed with tiredness, dropping on the bed fully clothed. I slept soundly, waking only when I sensed Kastor sitting on the bed.

"What time is it?" I said, sitting up, and he said wearily, "Around three. I'm glad you got some rest."

"You look awful, so tired," I said, watching his drawn features and drooping eyes.

"They're going to let Leander come over later, maybe even stay the night here."

I opened my eyes with delight. "Oh good, I was worrying he might have nightmares - he needs to be with us."

Kastor said he'd go and sleep in the bedroom by his study but I said quietly, "And I need to be with you, so I'll join you."

He nodded, pausing only to say, "You were wondering about Moira. It seems she's pregnant, which is very lucky for her. Artemis has done a quick assessment. It would appear that Pantheras is good at producing telepaths. They'll probably consider getting Moira to join us, but meanwhile she'll be cared for here. She already knows too much to return to her life easily."

"I know how that feels," I said, but relieved that the 'collateral damage' was not going to extend even further. I thought briefly of Jeannette, but knew this was no time to be worrying about the world of outsiders.

As for Pantheras, I learned the next day that his life would be spared in return for participating in Clea's experiments at St. Anthony's. I didn't want to know the details.

I was more interested in how Linus/ Jason would adapt to knowing that his mother was alive, if they decided to tell him. Under the evolving programme for more contact with parents, some kind of reunion might be considered. Perhaps the Binaries would cautiously approach his distraught mother, for example by letting her know they had tracked her appointment with the psychic gypsy and then 'found' the missing boy. But this would not be seriously considered until Linus was a few years older. I wondered what it must be like to lose a child and then meet him grown up and with an alien culture. I could understand some of that at least, from having discovered my very differently raised twin.

I had one interview with Moira, at my request. I had heard that she would receive basic training for a non-telepathic post within the community, after the baby was born. A week or so after her arrival, I was facing her in a small interview room within the detention centre. She was wearing a Binary tracksuit, her black curly hair bunched up on her head. She had a wiry, athletic build, with no sign as yet of her pregnancy. I introduced myself as the mother of the child that Saul Pantheras had hidden in the school grounds and her expression became wary. No doubt she had been told of Saul's various crimes, a troubled look flashing across her eyes as she anticipated my fury.

I smiled kindly, radiating good will. I told her that I did not blame her for Leo's kidnap.

"I came in from the outside too," I then confided to Moira. "It's an amazing life, although it takes some getting used to."

"I thought we were so in love," she said weepily. "I believed everything he said."

"That's, um, Binary training," I muttered. "The good news is that you'll be looked after very well. I suppose you don't feel at all telepathic?"

I had sensed her intuition and imagination. She looked up, forcing a little smile.

"Well, no more than anybody else. Occasionally making good guesses. I felt that Saul and I were closely in tune, you know, knowing what each other was thinking. He grinned when I told him that. Now I realise he was laughing at me, so ignorant about what he was planning."

"I didn't know I was telepathic, outside," I said. "I mean, with so many people saying it doesn't exist, it's just very confusing when you get ideas or images in your head."

"They've told me I only have very limited potential of developing it," she replied sourly.

"They're angry at the moment. We have to live so secretly and Saul Pantheras could have put us all at risk. Give it time."

"It seems I'll have plenty of that," said Moira.

"Did you know about Saul hiding my son in a tomb?" I asked.

"Of course not, the poor wee child!" she exclaimed. "I'd never have been party to that. He'd been saying for ages that he wanted us to live together, I was just excited when he rang and asked me to bring my car round to a lane just outside the school grounds. He didn't tell me that Linus would be with him. They popped up, seemingly out of nowhere. Certainly not from one of the gates to the grounds."

I had no wish to explain about the tunnels and manholes that guarded Binary establishments. "I'm so sorry this has happened to you," I said, oozing sympathetic thoughts.

"How long will I be imprisoned here?" she asked.

I realised that she hadn't been told that her stay would be

permanent. "It's early days," I said diplomatically. "You could be arrested for kidnapping out the outside, but you'll be safe here… for a while."

A warder came in to announce that our time was up. As Moira was led out of the interview room, I thought sadly that she would never fully adapt to the Binaries. She would be encouraged to try, for the alternative was bleaker than she could presently imagine. Moira also had yet to learn of how her child would be brought up, away from her care.

48

HELEN

When Cass told me how my information had helped to track down the teacher – and save Leo – I knew I'd have earned a few brownie points at Binaries. Not enough to be allowed back in, but Gaston crisply informed me that I'd shown sufficient loyalty to be allowed to live near one of the centres. It was a short call on a secure line, with no chance for me to plead that I'd like to live in England, but then I heard from Kastor. He rang on our safe number to confirm the fake funeral arrangements for Grace.

"The 'Dufours' will send a wreath, but be unavoidably detained abroad," he said. "But a couple of their friends will attend, field officers of course. They'll say all the right things. The funeral will be at Kensal Green Cemetery, do you know that one?"

"*Before we go to paradise, by way of Kensal Green*," I quoted, remembering learning this Chesterton poem at school and picturing the Victorian avenues and grand tombs of that famous London cemetery, which I'd only seen on screen images.

Kastor went over the logistics for the trip, but I was impatient to get his support for my other plan.

"I'm going to leave Alexander. He's really upset about Grace. He feels I should have pressed sooner for her to join us. But I don't want to settle down and start a proper family with him. I thought he was mainly interested in making money, but he's now mentioned it several times."

"Cassandra told me," said Kastor. "So, what's your scheme?"

"I'm going to have a nervous breakdown," I said, picturing the amused smile on Kastor's face about this unlikely event. "It seems a good cover. Grief, guilt over leaving Grace in France. I'll be inconsolable on the trip over and at the funeral."

"Naturally," said Kastor, coolly. I wish I had been speaking with Cass, who would have picked up my genuine sadness.

"The breakdown will be so bad that I'll have to go into a private clinic. Alexander will reluctantly return to the States without me."

"And then, your condition will worsen. Severe mental illness."

"Yes. I think the Binaries can arrange the clinic cover, don't you?"

Kastor was silent. I quickly added, "I mean, making sure Alexander accepts the story will be good for you and Cass as well. He's not very deep, you know. He'll sadly file for divorce, especially when I seem to want that - and then replace me fairly quickly."

"I was only thinking about the arrangements," said Kastor. "Of course Binaries will sort that. If Alexander wants to transfer you to a clinic in the US, you'll refuse, of course."

"Yes, to be near where Grace died..."

"OK," said Kastor, sounding ready to ring off. "Anything else? Lot's to do at this end to get this running."

"I was just wondering," I faltered, annoyed at not seeming my confident self, "whether you and Cassandra will be staying at

Woodstock. She mentioned that you may transfer to the newly established Devon branch?"

"We're considering it," said Kastor. "It's quite a complicated conversion of an old mine. A small part of it will be a museum, open to occasional visitors, with the main Binary labyrinth well concealed behind and below it."

"I know Cass is keen to set up similar living arrangements to the Villa at Binaires," I said eagerly.

"And you were thinking, you'd like to live nearby?" asked Kastor.

"Yes, it makes sense, doesn't it, for me to be in England. In case I have to pose as the patient in the private asylum, if Alexander visits?"

"Yes," said Kastor, "It's a possibility. I'll talk to Gaston, who'll probably wish to refer it to the Council."

The Council served only the UK Binaries. Still sounding annoyingly desperate, I ploughed on. "It wouldn't need referral to the Board, would it?" The international board might take a less generous view of the twin who had done an authorised swap with her sister. I could tell that Kastor was grinning, enjoying my discomfort.

"Anything that helps to preserve identities, after the chaos of the evacuation of Binaires, will probably be welcome to the Board," he advised. "And we could argue that having you close by means we can keep a constant watch on you."

"Exactly!" Now I sounded pathetically pleased. "And despite everything, I think Cass would like to talk to me now and then, face to face. And perhaps I could see the children…"

"One step at a time Helen," said Kastor. "But sorry, I really have to go."

When the call ended, I felt happier than in ages. So I had to take some deep breaths and look suitably bereft when I next saw Alexander. I was wearing black, with evidence of recent tears. On the flight over, I became hysterical, insisting on leaving my seat at one point because I claimed to have seen Grace's face in the plane window. Alexander was embarrassed, quickly explaining my grief to the air crew. They were sympathetic, fetching me an extra pillow and urging me to rest. But then, we were in first class. I calmed down but sobbed incessantly, muffling it out of consideration to the other passengers, by turning my face to the pillow.

The funeral was convincingly grim. I tried to follow the tiny coffin on its journey into the crematorium furnace, with three men having to hold me back. I cried out that I could hear her crying, although of course no one else heard this. One of the funeral group was the doctor from the private hospital where Grace had supposedly been treated. In a quiet aside to Alexander, he handed over his card and said that he could be contacted, day or night, if Alexander had concerns about me. The hospital included a private clinic at another site for acute psychiatric cases, he murmured. I gave no sign that I heard.

In the hotel, I fondled the little matinée jacket, her last clothing before the hospital admission, refusing any refreshment. I paced the room all night, saying I could hear voices. Early in the morning, while I was slumped on the bed, exhausted but still weeping, I heard Alexander calling the helpful doctor. I was whisked away to the private asylum, with Alexander holding my hand and saying it would only be a for a few days, to help me through this painful time.

"I'll stay of course," he said.

"No, you mustn't," I muttered, "You have your work. I need to be here in case Grace comes back. She'll need me, I should have been there for her. The voices are telling me to stay…" More tears. The kind staff gave me an injection to help me sleep and before I dropped off, I sensed Alexander's relief at being able to get away.

Alexander flew back to Washington, but rang every day. I refused to speak to him and eventually the kind psychiatrist broke the news to him that I had developed an acute form of schizophrenia. I might recover, the doctor said, but I was currently having violent episodes, needing restraint. The Binaries knew all about that kind of mental disturbance of course. Meanwhile I was kept at a safe house, with no outdoor excursions permitted. The security staff were very vigilant, given my history, but they needn't have worried. I caught up with films and reading, biding my time until the Binaries advised I should make a call about wanting a divorce.

I sensed that Alexander had already found consolation with one of those smart Washington women, slightly piqued that he could get over me so easily. It was the best for him though. He didn't ask for me to be transferred to the States, but offered a generous settlement that would ensure my care indefinitely. He sent occasional letters and I sent mad ones back. I signed all the necessary documents for the divorce in a rare lucid interlude, sending a sad, final note to him, saying I was in contact with Grace and that I was often quite happy.

49

HELEN

At last I received a call from Cass, telling me that the Devon move was on and that she'd persuaded the organization to acquire a cottage for me, just half a mile away from the outside house being converted for them. I was relieved that the authorities had not decided that it would be easier to stage a death for me as well as Grace, thus ending my story, but that would have meant risking Alexander coming over again. His communications had tailed off, now that he was engaged and busy trying to get his fiancée pregnant.

The cottage was great. It was a come down to live without staff, although I still had some of those secret Swiss funds to help with the little luxuries and after all, the settlement from Alexander would more than pay for living expenses. A field officer rather sourly told me that sufficient monies would be transferred. I guess they were envious of my freedom. I set myself up as an artist, selling occasional paintings to tourists in the village. The French refugees from Binaires had mostly relocated abroad, but a few had opted for Devon and the gardener from Villa Dufour, my sweet Force Musculaire, came to help me with the garden. Via a local art class, I met Ross, a hunky man who appreciated a lively woman like me as a diversion from his dull wife. I nicknamed him privately and to Cass as 'The Bearded Wonder', saying he was like the actor who played Ross Polldark, with a beard. Cass never met him, naturally. I was the only 'outside' visitor to their house, apart from deliveries. An additional perk was that Aunt V was allowed to make occasional visits. I reckoned Gaston had authorised that. On at least one of her visits, he happened to be at the Devon centre, checking the security at the museum. When Aunt V coyly suggested that she wanted to take a trip to the nearby beach, I didn't spoil it for her by letting her know I sensed that Gaston would be on that beach.

I kept my visits to Cass to a minimum, trying not to be there at the same time as Kastor. She and Kastor had a lovely house overlooking the sea. They lived quietly and Gaston had prepared the subterfuge well: no one would have guessed this was a home for Binaries.

Nearly a year after the dramas with Binaires and kidnap by that teacher, I was sitting on a verandah with Cass, enjoying the view with a glimpse of the Atlantic Ocean beyond. Leo was away at school, but the rest of the children were over for the afternoon, playing noisily within the house, supervised by a Binary nanny.

"Grace is thriving in the Binary nursery here," said Cass. She is so much the kinder sister. She was wondering whether it would be permitted for Grace to be brought over one day when I was visiting.

"It's OK, Cass," I assured her. "I'll maybe get to know her a little when she's old enough to come and play here."

I had prepared the tea and sandwiches myself. Cass raised her eyebrows as I proudly sat the tray down. "Well, I've had to improve my culinary skills," I said. "I've made some scones, too. Aunt V gave me intensive tuition when she was staying last week."

"Cream tea?" asked Cass. She shared her dream image of us having such a spread.

I snorted. "Some of us have men that are mainly interested in our bodies, you know. I seem to eat all the time down here and have to watch the calories."

"Well, you keep busy with the garden and everything," murmured Cass, her thought images clearly picturing 'Force Musculaire' and the Bearded Wonder. "And if you can stay, Grégoire may be coming over for a drink tonight."

"Really?" I said, keeping a casual tone. In fact Grégoire had managed a few trips to my cottage. I had blocked that from Cass, since she didn't need to know everything. Although with her telepathic abilities and our close chanelling connection, she was likely to have picked up on it. She suddenly grinned, letting me know that of course she knew that I was seeing Grégoire.

"Oh Sis, it's going well," I blurted out. For I had been longing to discuss this. "But he keeps talking about another baby. You and your parenting programme! I've told him there's no guarantee of a son, or twins."

"I suppose you no longer hear from Alexander?"

I shook my head. "Well, he's made occasional contact with the supposed private nursing home where I'm languishing with incurable mental illness. He's found someone else, he'll be quite OK," I added, as if this meant nothing at all to me.

The scones were good. Clever me, Aunt V had said I had a gift for baking. "It's turned out well, overall, hasn't it?" I said, leaning back in the whicker chair.

"Yes, this is almost as good as living outside, but with the Binary connections too," she said, nodding. The Binaries had bought an adjoining farm, making a secret tunnel to the Devon Binary branch possible: a similar arrangement to the one they had at Villa Dufour. Another tunnel connected the house to the farmhouse. The children could attend nursery school with other Binaries, while visitors could travel via the tunnel. They could occasionally come overland, but wanted to minimise the chance of being seen or having to talk to outsiders.

"What about that wicked teacher, Pantheras?" I asked. I was out of the loop for hearing much news about Binary life, and would not have dared to ask if we were with Kastor.

"He's still in St. Anthony's," said Cass. "But I don't think he's being subjected to too much experimentation. And Clyppie is over the moon, now that she's the star of the medical conferences again. Her latest paper, on '*Subconscious drives concerning repressed parenthood*,' was very popular, apparently."

"I bet," I said, thinking about repressed parenthood. I had more than a little understanding, now, of how that felt. "And the boy he took – Jason-Linus, how's he getting on?"

"Kastor said the school reports are good, he's adjusted. Pantheras will never be released and can never see Linus again."

"Well, only a Binary could recover from finding out his father was a murderer, kidnapper and liar," I said coolly.

"But I do hope that one day Linus can see his mother again," said Cass. "It would be difficult to ensure secrecy, and of course confusing for him, having to be called Jason again…"

I laughed. "It's never going to happen, Cass! Far too risky."

"Well, maybe," said Cass. "But I've heard that the Council have considered that there is a faint chance of a meeting when Linus is older, if he wants to see her. Kastor mentioned that they're already planning something of the sort for Phoebe Star, you know, the twin who had to come in here at 15. She's expressed a wish. It'll just be her mother, not her dad. Mrs. Cavendish has been visited in confidence and sworn to secrecy. Plus I'm sure they've made her understand what might happen if she told anyone. Her husband didn't know about the other twin, so they'll set it up without him being involved."

"Amazing," I muttered, genuinely impressed. "I mean, astounding that they'd consider it. What with the end to the baby 'rescue' programme, a review of punishments, prohibition of sex therapy in most circumstances - well, you've achieved a Binary reformation!"

"It's the closest we can come to actually 'coming out' and living alongside them. I understand that now."

"And you forgive me, for forcing you in here?" I asked, watching my twin's face carefully.

"Of course. It was the right destiny for me, the one I really needed. I believe that we all have several possible destinies laid out for us, with apparent free will to decide between them – but only one is the correct choice. I sometimes think of the gods laughing as we clumsily make our way through life, missing opportunities, choosing the wrong person or direction. They could make it easier…"

"So you're getting into mythology too, in your old age?" I chuckled. "Is that why there's a mermaid in your bathroom? I was wondering."

"I bought that for Kastor. He was a bit bemused, but it's so hard to buy something for Binaries, especially the men. They have everything they need already. While we can always use a new piece of jewellery."

Cass smiled, sharing thoughts of Kastor's reaction when she had produced it on his birthday in early November. "My very own mermaid," he'd said, when he got over the surprise and how cleverly she had concealed the gift from his telepathy, "I suppose this is to stop me being lured in by those mischievous mermaids within your mind."

A corner shelf in the bathroom, well out of the children's reach had been constructed specially for the china figure. Watching me catch these mental images and snatches of conversation, Cass added shyly, "Kastor said that the mermaid looked quite like the one who so nearly trapped him in my sea of thoughts."

"Whereas my mind is more like a large prison, full of cells and warders wielding whips," I said bitterly.

"You're so hard on yourself," said the ever sympathetic Cass. "You're brave, resourceful and a brilliant telepath. And you survived that awful abduction at birth – and all that conditioning - pretty well, even if…"

She was remembering my treacherous swap with her. I said

quickly, "Yeah, a survivor, that's me. But with us, well, it's now OK isn't it?" I gazed uncertainly, always needing reassurance from her.

"Well, I worked hard on the Council – and via them to persuade the Board to let you come here. I wouldn't have done that if I didn't want you around."

I smiled. Cass did look contented and she was able to indulge in those peculiar mothering instincts of hers. Also, she had Kastor.

Peels of laugher sounded from within the house. In a careless way, that didn't fool Cass for a moment, I said, "I might as well go and see the children."

I got up and went in the direction of the voices. The children were running around upstairs, with the nanny making feeble attempts at control. She knew that discipline could be relaxed in this house.

From the landing window, I looked down at Cass, sitting on the verandah and cradelling her cup of tea. I thought of all we'd been through in the seven years since her innocent quest to find me. Our existence and security would always be precarious, given the suspicion and distrust of our kind by ordinary humans. Cass seemed very happy to be in Binary world, despite its risks and problems. I knew, perhaps better than she, that she would lie and fight to protect the organization and its members. Perhaps she would also kill for them. She had reformed them a little, but they'd done a binary conversion on her at the same time. Cassandra the catalyst and convert, I thought, before leaping in front of the children and setting them off in a conga around the house, singing at the tops of our voices. Below, I sensed Cass gazing at the peaceful view and knew that she was thinking about Kastor, working away on his projects, deep in the Devon Binary labyrinth.

THE END

Printed in Great Britain
by Amazon